THOU ART THE MAN

Also Available from Valancourt Books

THE ROSE AND THE KEY
J. Sheridan Le Fanu
Edited by Frances Chiu

THE KING'S ASSEGAI
Bertram Mitford
Edited by Gerald Monsman

THE MAGIC GOBLET
Emilie Flygare-Carlén
Edited by Amy H. Sturgis

THE SEEN AND THE UNSEEN
Richard Marsh
Reprint of the 1900 edition

THE JOSS: A REVERSION
Richard Marsh
Reprint of the 1901 edition

ROUND THE RED LAMP
A. Conan Doyle
Edited by Robert Darby

THE SORROWS OF SATAN
Marie Corelli
Edited by Julia Kuehn

MARIUS THE EPICUREAN
Walter Pater
Edited by Gerald Monsman

IN MAREMMA
Ouida
Edited by Natalie Schroeder

VALANCOURT CLASSICS

THOU ART THE MAN

BY

Mary Elizabeth Braddon

Edited with a new introduction and notes by
Laurence Talairach-Vielmas

𝔎𝔞𝔫𝔰𝔞𝔰 ℭ𝔦𝔱𝔶:
VALANCOURT BOOKS
2008

Thou Art the Man by Mary Elizabeth Braddon
Originally published in 1894
This edition © 2008 by Valancourt Books

The cover of this edition reproduces the cover illustration from the
yellowback edition of *Thou Art the Man* (London, 1895). The image
is courtesy of the Spencer Research Library, University of Kansas,
whose assistance is gratefully acknowledged by the publisher.

Library of Congress Cataloging-in-Publication Data

Braddon, M. E. (Mary Elizabeth), 1835-1915.
Thou art the man / by Mary Elizabeth Braddon ; edited with a
new introduction and notes by Laurence Talairach-Vielmas.
p. cm. – (Valancourt classics)
ISBN 1-934555-37-1 (alk. paper)
1. Family secrets – Fiction. 2. Epileptics – Fiction.
I. Talairach-Vielmas, Laurence. II. Title.
PR4989.M4T47 2008
823'.8–dc22

2008001355

Design and typography by James D. Jenkins
Published by Valancourt Books
Kansas City, Missouri
http://www.valancourtbooks.com

CONTENTS

INTRODUCTION

OVER the last three decades, the sensation novels and golden-haired demons of "the author of *Lady Audley's Secret*" have been resurrected by feminist criticism and have appeared on university syllabuses. However, few of the late novels of the prolific Victorian authoress Mary Elizabeth Braddon are still in print today. And yet, many of them are worthy of attention, highlighting Braddon's ability to adapt her fiction to changes in the social scene. Constantly looking for new plot devices to thrill her readership, Braddon adapted the "sensational" scenario which had made her famous, remorphing over and over again the literary genre launched by herself, Wilkie Collins, and Ellen Wood in the 1860s. In over fifty years, Mary Elizabeth Braddon published eighty-five novels, writing up to two or three novels a year, not counting the fiction she wrote anonymously or under a pseudonym for penny and halfpenny journals. Braddon was not just a novelist. She also edited two magazines, *Belgravia* and the *Mistletoe Bough*, a Christmas annual; she wrote poems, plays, short stories, and even fiction for children. Often deemed immoral, Braddon's works elicited much criticism among those who defended "high literature" and feared the corruptive power of popular literature. It is difficult to determine, however, whether the hostile attacks of the literary establishment stemmed from the immorality of her fiction or her life, which was as sensational as her fiction—if not more so.

Her parents separated when Mary Elizabeth Braddon was still a child, so her mother, Fanny Braddon—daughter of Patrick White, an Irish Catholic and Anne Babington, a Protestant—brought up her three children, Maggie, Edward and Mary Elizabeth, alone.[1] When Edward left for India and Maggie married an Italian and settled in Naples in 1847, Mary Elizabeth Braddon remained with her mother, who provided a reasonably good education for her daughter. In 1857 the twenty-two-year-old Mary Elizabeth Braddon, wishing to support the household, went on the stage, under the stage-name of "Mary Seyton." In 1860 she swapped her costumes for a pen and published her first novel, *Three Times Dead, or, The*

Secret of the Heath, later reprinted as *The Trail of the Serpent*. In the same year, she met the publisher John Maxwell with whom she started to live in 1861. Though Maxwell was already married to a woman incarcerated in a lunatic asylum in Dublin, Mary Elizabeth Braddon took care of his five children and bore him six illegitimate children, five of whom survived childhood. Her fame was sealed with the success of *Lady Audley's Secret*, serialized between 1861-62 in *Robin Goodfellow* and the *Sixpenny Magazine*, and *Aurora Floyd*, the first instalment of which was published in *Temple Bar* before the last instalment of *Lady Audley's Secret*. The former was published as a three-volume novel the following year. By 1866 Braddon had already published nine three-volume novels. She was also editing and contributing to *Belgravia*, which Maxwell had just launched, while continuing to serialize novels elsewhere. In 1867 the deaths of her mother and sister, together with the hostility of the critics, precipitated her nervous collapse, complicated by an attack of puerperal fever. Her production stopped for a year.

Braddon was not only denounced for the impropriety of her fiction; she was also accused of plagiarism, especially after the publication of *Circe*, a reworking of the French writer Octave Feuillet's play, *Dalila* (1857). Braddon was well read and travelled extensively throughout her life, fuelling her fiction with manifold influences. She could read and write in French, had a subscription to the French circulating library Rolandi in London, read French journals, such as the *Revue des Deux Mondes*, and loved French literature from Balzac and Zola to Flaubert, Maupassant or Dumas— although their names often figure in her fiction as tell-tale devices, giving her characters a fragrance of licentiousness, immorality or flightiness. Balzac particularly marked several of her novels, such as *Birds of Prey* (1867) and its sequel, *Charlotte's Inheritance* (1868), in which a poisoner reads Balzac. Her 1891 novel *Gerard* was also based upon Balzac's *La Peau de chagrin*. Her novels of the 1880s were more significantly branded by the influence of French naturalism. The recurrent theme of alcohol and the figures of drunkards, as in *The Cloven Foot* (1879), in which a French ballet-dancer takes to drink, or *The Golden Calf* (1883), in which the drinking and smoking male protagonist becomes paranoid and deluded, typify Braddon's reliance on naturalistic themes and motifs. Shifting from Balzac and Flaubert (as exemplified by *The Doctor's Wife*, a reworking of Flaubert's *Madame Bovary*), to Zolaesque characters, Braddon followed the literary trends of the era, adapting French characters to English society and often featuring degenerate English gentlemen. Her growing interest in the theory of heredity to explain her characters' behavioural instincts differed radically from her earlier use of heredity as a means of escaping a murder sentence, as in her first sensation novel *Lady Audley's Secret*.[2] By the 1880s, her Zolaesque characters had gained in psychological depth. The use of the heredity motif, moreover, illustrated in *The Golden Calf*, *Phantom Fortune* (1883), and *Ishmael* (1884), also gave Braddon a chance to display her talent for realistic delineations of medical cases. This is most evident in *The Golden Calf*, in which Braddon describes the male protagonist's degeneration and his gradual descent into *delirium tremens*, in *Thou Art the Man*, in which the male protagonist eventually becomes mad, and in her 1907 novel, *Dead Love Has Chains*, in which the hero is found mad after a nervous breakdown and has to go into a nursing home.

Published over thirty years after *Lady Audley's Secret*, *Thou Art the Man* is, in fact, a good illustration of the evolution of Braddon's fiction. Although the novel remains faithful to Braddon's plot recipe, it brings the most Gothic ingredients up to date by turning to evolutionist theories. But Braddon's female characters move away from the Radcliffean stereotype of the persecuted Gothic heroine: they are active and wilful, gradually becoming genuine female sleuths and digging out the secrets of the past by probing the mind of the suspected murderer and researching the history of epilepsy.

Braddon's Buried Manuscripts

The plot of *Thou Art the Man* is very close to Braddon's 1888 novel, *The Fatal Three*, in which a man, suspected of having murdered his first wife, suffers from a memory lapse and is haunted by nightmares. But far more than *The Fatal Three*, *Thou Art the Man* clearly shows how Braddon's reworking of earlier sensation novel motifs was designed to match late-Victorian anxieties. The obsession with degeneration and the figure of the female sleuth as a version of the New Woman give the novel a *fin-de-siècle* flavour. Throughout her career, Braddon was very much aware of "the popular taste," as a reviewer of *Lady Audley's Secret* acknowledged in 1862,[3] constructing "wild" stories and characters and constantly readapting their "wildness" to the concerns of modern Victorian England. Her sensational heroines of the 1860s, as Henry James suggested, were no longer "picturesque Italian[s] of the fourteenth century, but . . . English gentlewom[en] of the current year, familiar with the use of the railway and the telegraph."[4] Secularizing and domesticating "the apparently higher (or at any rate, more romantic) mysteries of the Gothic romance,"[5] as Patrick Brantlinger has argued, Braddon, just like other sensation novelists, revamped Gothic motifs and plot patterns in order to disrupt the conventional perception of everyday reality. This is certainly the case in *Thou Art the Man*, a novel whose title overtly acknowledges its debt to Poe's Gothic tales. Indeed, this novel, which also echoes Sophocles's *Oedipus Rex* or the Old Testament narrative of David and Bathsheba wherein David is compelled to acknowledge his own guilt when Nathan says "Thou art the man," may also be read as a rewriting of Edgar Allan Poe's 1844 short story, "Thou Art the Man," in which the murderer of Barnabas Shuttleworthy, Charles Goodfellow, directs the investigation so as to lead the detectives away from himself and onto Shuttleworthy's nephew.[6]

The opening of *Thou Art the Man*, published over thirty years after *Lady Audley's Secret*, gives the impression that Braddon's heroine, Sibyl, Countess of Penrith, is another Lady Audley, dissimulating her dark secrets beneath fashionable furs and expensive sables. But Lady Penrith's fashionable appearance at the beginning is deceptive, for this late-Victorian novel portrays women detecting male secrets, thus completely rewriting Braddon's older plots dealing with female criminality. In the very first scene, the female character receives a "letter from the dead." Whilst readers may wonder whether the ghostly message is meant to indicate the crimes of the past coming to haunt Lady Penrith, this image of buried writing issuing from the grave instantly constructs the female character as a reader and an interpreter. Braddon's heroine becomes a female sleuth, not only deciphering linguistic signs but also trying to decode the intertextual layers of the quotation from the Gospel embedded in the note: "Out of the grave, the living grave, a long-forgotten voice calls to you. Where their worm dieth not, and their fire is not quenched." Indeed, Braddon updates the prototypical Gothic heroine—who generally strives to read and interpret the unknown and mysterious world around her—into a Victorian female investigator, the Gothic atmosphere and the prevailing wilderness of the opening merely providing a Radcliffean backdrop. In Braddon's Gothic, moreover, the female detective does not discover the stories of domestic entrapment and live burial of her foremothers: the mysteries are male, and so are the criminals. Because the beginning of the novel features an active female protagonist who decides to "hunt out" the writer of the letter she has received, Braddon reverses gender expectations and clearly sets her novel apart from her sensation novels of the beginning of her literary career and their improper female characters. This time, men are incriminated and the novel features female characters who fear they might have inherited their fathers' sinful nature as well as male characters who literally degenerate. The theme of heredity thus becomes a pivotal motif. The question whether Coralie may have inherited her father's features—the "Urquhart hardness," which is visible in many of the family portraits hung on the walls of Killander Castle—sets the tone of a narrative which is punctuated by anxieties related to the inheritance of morbid traits. The theme of epilepsy structures the novel in a similar way. The biblical quotation, in fact, refers to the ninth chapter of the Gospel of Mark in the New Testament, recording the story of a man who shows his possessed son to Jesus. In fact, the boy suffers from epilepsy, and is healed by Jesus. The intertext encapsulates and foreshadows most of the tensions of the novel: oscillating between demonic possession and clinical discourse, constructions of epilepsy—and of evil—hesitating between the supernatural and the physiological.

The Late-Victorian Gothic Villain

Braddon's biblical reference revamps the manuscript of traditional Gothic narratives into a modern text. Not content with rewriting the heroine, Braddon also revises the cursed Gothic hero and turns him into a character doomed by his unruly physiology. The fear related to the reproduction of the past permeates the beginning of the story. Before marrying Sibyl's father, Sir Joseph Higginson, Sibyl's mother falls in love with her cousin, Brandon Mountford, only to learn that he is married to a lunatic. When Sibyl follows in her mother's footsteps and falls in love with her cousin, who bears the same name as his father, Brandon Mountford, the reader may believe here that the sins of the mother will be visited upon her daughter—hence that the present is but a repetition of the past. However, it is not the women who are cursed in Braddon's late-Victorian novel, but the men. Though proud of their lineage, the male aristocratic characters are tainted with criminality, and their "race" is doomed to become extinct. Braddon is here influenced by the theories of the Frenchman Morel, who believed that the degenerate was likely to become infertile and disappear. Ironically, though Sibyl's mother, the penniless but aristocratic Lucy, agrees to marry the "newly rich" pit-owner Joseph Higginson, the latter, with his broad sinewy hands marked by early toil, is no Beast that Beauty has to marry to save her sisters from poverty. Beasts are more likely to be of aristocratic descent than to belong to the rising middle-classes. Just as Sibyl's mother could not marry her cousin who was already married to a woman locked up in a lunatic asylum, Sibyl cannot marry her cousin who fears he is tainted with the hereditary epilepsy he has inherited from his mother.

Historically speaking, diseases have frequently been seen as demonic invasions and associated with supernatural powers. Epilepsy is no exception. As Owsei Temkin argues, epilepsy, "more than any other disease, was open to interpretation both as a physiological process and as the effect of spiritual influences."[7] As suggested above, constructions of epilepsy have often been poised between supernatural interpretations and medical explanations. The late-Victorian fascination with epilepsy may perhaps account for its popularity as a literary motif during this period. Seen through the prism of heredity, moreover, the hero's epilepsy efficiently rewrites the Gothic stereotype of the cursed male protagonist. In the case of *Thou Art the Man* heredity is presented as a modern and fashionable issue. At the end of the novel, Coralie fears her nature "could not escape the hereditary taint—if the

modern craze about heredity has any foundation." By hinging her
narrative upon such modern issues, Braddon anchors her story in
the midst of contemporary debates, particularly those concerning the criminal type. The novel is indeed steeped in criminology,
a science which emerged at the beginning of the 1870s and was
destined to thrive in the last decades of the century. Throughout
the nineteenth century, British scientists and pseudo-scientists
were reflecting on the causes of criminal behaviour and on the
responsibility of criminals, as typified by the rise of physiognomy
and phrenology in the 1820s and 1830s, for instance. Research
was often—if not always—carried out among subjects found in
jails and lunatic asylums. Gradually, the conception of the criminal changed throughout the nineteenth century, and reformers
constantly sought to find suitable regimes for the prisoners, and
experts started to make a distinction between "habitual" and "acci-
dental" offenders and attempted to set up typologies of criminals
which might help find them adequate punishments for each cat-
egory.[8] Braddon alludes to such issues through her male protagonist, as when Urquhart tells Mountford that the lack of motive for
the murder will suggest his insanity and prove his irresponsibil-
ity—hence incurring a lifelong imprisonment instead of the death
penalty. Originally, acquittal was generally granted when the man
was totally deprived of his understanding and memory and did not
know what he was doing, "no more than an infant, than a brute or
a wild beast."[9] Later, the "'wild beast' form of knowledge"[10] was
abandoned to favour other criteria, such as the existence of delusion and the absence of knowledge of right and wrong. Gradually,
as mental physiology developed, such theories gave way to psychi-
atric interpretations and alienists competed—and not infrequently
conflicted—with judges in legal courts. By the end of the nineteenth century, epilepsy had become central in debates on criminal
responsibility. As the famous alienist Henry Maudsley argues,

> When a murder has been committed without apparent motive,
> and the reason of it seems inexplicable, it may chance that the
> perpetrator is found on inquiry to be afflicted with epilepsy. It
> is an important question, then, how far the existence of this
> disease affects his responsibility.[11]

Medical officers attempted to establish objective criteria of criminality and analyzed the nature of the offenders' physical and mental disabilities. The criminal type was read through the theories of heredity and increasingly associated with degeneration. The *fin-de-siècle* criminal was aligned with the weakest and was considered very close to the feeble-minded and the insane. Cesare Lombroso's theory of the born criminal, expounded in his *Criminal Man*,[12] was grounded upon the premise that 70% of criminals were biologically programmed to commit crimes. According to this theory, physical and psychological "anomalies"—abnormalities—typified the criminal's closeness to primitive people and animals and proved the link between criminality and atavism. As these anomalies could be identified, measured, and therefore classified, Lombroso turned criminology into anthropology to explore the characteristics of the criminal. Lombroso saw atavism as the primary biological cause of criminal behaviour and paid little attention to socio-economic factors in the first editions of his *Criminal Man*. He gradually included congenital illnesses and forms of *dégénérescence* in his criminal type, increasingly merging criminality, insanity, and epilepsy. Because Lombroso believed that crime did not result from the criminal's free will but was determined by biological, psychological (and to a certain extent, as he suggested in the later editions, social factors), it could and must be clinically examined and treated, thereby transforming criminals into medical patients.

For Lombroso, crime resulted from physical and psychological inferiority—hence his perception of women, non-whites, the poor, and children as potentially criminal. Relying heavily on Darwinian theory for his portrait of the born criminal, especially when he equated savages and children, he posited that "individuals replicate the evolution of the species in their development from fetus to adulthood."[13] Yet, as suggested above, Lombroso was to use disease as an explanation for crime more and more. In the fourth edition of *Criminal Man* (1889) he develops his views on epilepsy for the first time, defining epilepsy as a cause of born criminality alongside atavism and moral insanity. The idea that epileptic patients might commit crimes during their fits was common; but Lombroso turned epilepsy into "a universal substructure of all

criminal behavior."[14] Examining the epileptic anatomically, physi-
ologically, psychologically, using physiognomy and pointing out
"degenerative anomalies,"[15] he tried to demonstrate the closeness
of the epileptic to the born criminal, constantly strengthening
degeneration theory. His aim was to show that epilepsy was "an
obvious and important point of contact between criminality and
moral insanity."[16] He furthered his parallels by claiming that, just
like born criminals, epileptics displayed tactile insensitivity, were
left-handed, highly religious, and had a tendency to "vagabond-
age,"[17] wandering far from home like sleepwalkers, most often as
an effect of loss of consciousness.

The medicalization of human behaviour in the late nineteenth
century, as illustrated by Lombroso's theory of the born criminal,
which constructed atavism as pathological and saw epilepsy as "a
brief caricature of crime,"[18] typically marked *fin-de-siècle* popular
fiction, from Robert Louis Stevenson's *The Strange Case of Dr. Jekyll
and Mr. Hyde* (1886) to Arthur Machen's "The Novel of the Black
Seal" in *The Three Imposters* (1895), both of which link criminality
to epilepsy. It stands to reason that the portrait of Braddon's criminal, involved in a motiveless murder, suffering from hereditary
epilepsy and wishing to live and wander aimlessly in South Africa
is very much influenced by criminal anthropology. Unlike Stevenson, who uses London as a criminal locale, Braddon's *fin-de-siècle*
Gothic uses exotic Africa to map out the civilized man's struggle
against his own primitivism as developed by contemporary psy-
chiatric discourse. In the 1880s and 1890s, however, if the popular
Havelock Ellis and his successful *The Criminal* (1890) or Darwin's
cousin, Francis Galton, seemed to subscribe to the Italian positivist
school, the English medico-psychiatric Establishment was generally opposed to Lombrosian criminology and rejected the idea of
the criminal constitution. Revealingly, even Henry Maudsley, who
drew on Morel's theories and firmly believed that crime was hereditary and particularly focused on epilepsy as a form of degeneration,
revised some of his arguments concerning criminal constitution
in the late 1880s, using Lamarckian theory of evolutionary heredity to show how inimical social conditions could create biological anomalies and be passed on to succeeding generations, as the
French *Milieu Social* school contended. Thus, if issues of biological

and psychological determinism continued to fuel European criminology, climaxing with the eugenics movement in the twentieth
century, the combined weight of hereditary and environmental
factors were increasingly considered as acting simultaneously.[19]

It is in the midst of such heated debate that *Thou Art the Man*
unravels its plot, with a cursed hero less doomed by fatality than
by his physiology and a parson who resolves the enigma thanks to
his experience of the East End. Braddon proposes a modern revision of Gothic stereotypes, hinting at the current criminalization
of the poor, merging poverty, the "degenerative" effects of modern
urban life and hereditary epilepsy and recalling how inimical social
conditions were seen as responsible for the creation of biological
anomalies which could in turn be passed on to succeeding generations. The Gothic vocabulary she uses to portray her male character—the "shadow of a dark fate," the "omen of impending evil,"
the "ghastly heritage"—personifying epilepsy as a "foul fiend"
who first seizes upon the male character in the school chapel, as
a "devil," "hideous spectre" or "shadow"—reworks Gothic termi-
nology to describe the mysteries of mental physiology. When in a
trance, the epileptic character becomes one of the living dead, as
if he had "been dead and in his grave." Braddon's Gothic terminol-
ogy, mingled with late nineteenth-century scientific and pseudo-
scientific discourses, from psychological and biological debates
to sociomedical theories as found in evolutionism and criminal
anthropology, highlights the way in which such discourses gener-
ated fears concerning the human subject. Increasingly, man was
seen as half-human, half-beast.[20] Epilepsy, construed through both
demonology and criminology, thus proved highly significant. It
could stage physical transformation and turn—in a shake—a beau-
tiful-looking man into a monstrous creature: "transformed from
man to devil, yet knowing himself man, fighting against his evil
genius, conscious of his criminal instincts, yet unable to conquer
them." The motif of the metamorphosis of the gentleman into
"a bloodthirsty murderer" or a "human wild beast" becomes, in
fact, a powerful literary tool to figure the two faces of man, the
respectable Dr. Jekyll and the murderous Mr. Hyde, driven by evil
impulses and "blind violence."

Braddon's portrait of her hero's mental degeneration is heavily influenced, moreover, by contemporary theories of racial degeneration. Brandon Mountford is not just an English gentleman: his African past aligns him with the superstitious and bedevilled Dark Continent. His mind thus becomes a territory to be explored, a terrain where geography and psychology merge. As a matter of fact, the modernity of Braddon's late-Victorian novel also filters through to the reader in her multiple references to Victorian missionaries and explorers. Mountford's family boasts three generations of British colonizers: Mountford's grandfather, General Mountford, who fought in Arthur Wellesley's Indian Campaign, and his father, Major Mountford, a captain of engineers under Sir Robert Napier who died in India of jungle fever. As already suggested, the "practised hunter" has, in addition, spent five years on the "Dark Continent" where "bulk, beads, and blackness are the chief characteristics of female beauty." The three generations of military men trace British imperialist history, from the Indian Mutiny of 1857 to the Transvaal rebellion of 1880, and, significantly, Braddon has Brandon Mountford living in South Africa just before the annexation of the Transvaal in 1877, a historical landmark of British imperial power.

Braddon's "Imperial Gothic"[21]

Just as criminal anthropologists attempted to read the criminal's features in order to demonstrate his closeness to primitive people and to prove the link between criminality and atavism, Braddon foregrounds reading as a detective activity likely to lead to the truth about the fictional suspected criminal's identity. Part of the investigation consists in reading the explorer's nonfictional writings on Africa, which Sibyl has kept. As a matter of fact, Brandon Mountford's book has both a historical and a metatextual function in the narrative. *Thou Art the Man*, though published in 1894, is set in 1886, thus recalling public interest in African life and the political unrest in South Africa following the Cape Frontier or Kaffir Wars (1779-1879), the Anglo-Zulu War (1879) and the First Boer War (1880-1881). Moreover, it also pivots around the issues of "barbarism" and "civilization," the fear of degeneration, which fuelled the literature of the period, particularly marked by the publication of Rider Haggard's imperialist fiction: *King's Solomon's Mines* (1885), *She: A History of Adventure* (1887), and *Allan Quatermain* (1887). In the vein of Captain Richard Burton's and other contemporary explorers' narratives, Haggard—who had, interestingly, spent five years in South Africa, like Braddon's male character—featured the unknown Dark Continent as a territory to be "explored and conquered," in Rebecca Stott's words.[22] In his novels, the male characters go on a quest, penetrating and investigating the mysterious Dark Continent to discover the dangerous female criminal at the heart of the story and the dangers of female sexuality. The conflation of woman and Africa underlay much imperialist fiction of the late nineteenth-century. The male quest is in fact an anthropological hunt, and the explorers seek the stigmata of atavism on the unmapped body of Africa/woman.[23] Just as anthropological science focused on the criminal's cranium and used women's stunted brain-size as evidence of their atavistic features, the anthropological romances of the 1880s featured male explorers searching for the very signs by which to read the dark woman as an evolutionary throwback.

Braddon had undoubtedly read Haggard's novels, as Haggard had a publishing contract with John (known as Jack) and Robert Maxwell. The link between Haggard's imperialist novels—especially *She: A History of Adventure*—and Braddon's novel, is mostly evident in the construction of the narrative. Braddon's play on texts is reminiscent of Haggard's novel, structured around a series of embedded texts, and where writing, reading, decoding and even translating texts are prominent activities: the narrator receives a manuscript from Horace Holly, the guardian of Leo Vincey, who himself receives a series of manuscripts when he comes of age, telling about the history of his ancient family. The male heroes' exploration of Africa is thus both textual and spatial, as they map out the mysterious dark continent, gradually penetrating the land ruled by Ayesha, *She-Who-Must-Be-Obeyed*, who murdered Leo's ancestor. In *Thou Art the Man*, Braddon not only seems to revisit Haggard's imperialist romances of the 1880s, but also to rework the figure of the male explorer investigating the secrets of primitive female sexuality. Reversing gender stereotypes and featuring a male character as an evolutionary throwback, Braddon relies heavily, as has already been suggested, on contemporary criminal anthropology, as illustrated by the works of Havelock Ellis (*The Criminal* [1890]), Francis Galton (*Inquiries into Human Faculty and its Development* [1883] and *Finger Prints* [1892]) or Max Nordau (*Degeneration* [1895])—all of which often associate criminal suspects with "foreign territory in general and colonial subjects in particular."[24] Furthermore, Braddon's *Thou Art the Man* interestingly appears to rewrite what Lawrence Millman terms the "male novel," "written by men, for men or boys, and about the activities of men."[25] Though "adamant to the charms of the Hottentot Venus," Mountford seems nevertheless to have been contaminated by his contact with Southern women. Subjected to untamed drives, the character of Mountford turns the male plot of imperialist romance into a female quest in which female characters investigate a dark continent which is, ironically, male. In fact, the secrets which lie at the heart of Braddon's novel are all male. So, Sibyl discovers that her father has an illegitimate daughter and that Hubert Urquhart has kept Mountford prisoner for ten years, and Coralie finds out that her father is a murderer. Most significantly, Mountford's secret disease opens the narrative onto the mysteries of man, the ape beneath the skin of the civilized gentleman. Like Stevenson's Jekyll and Hyde, Mountford is two-faced—"the same but not the same." He is the "wild beast," "the tiger [that] seizes its prey, and killed [Marie Arnold] more swiftly than the tiger kills." The Dark Continent thus lurks in the background of Braddon's novel, whether the female detectives read about Mountford's exploration of Africa or whether the exploration is turned into a "fabled journey into the unconscious or the heart of darkness of the explorer."[26]

Revealingly, Mountford's victim is associated with exoticism and wilderness too. When Marie Arnold appears, she is described through the "warm and quick impulse of her southern nature," and the "man of the world," Hubert Urquhart, might well become "the slave of the unsophisticated girl." Marie Arnold is the dangerous female Other who threatens to unsettle gender and political spheres. Though merely *dressed* in black and of French origin, Marie Arnold resembles the colonial "native": with her uncertain origins, she is mysterious, might be "any age," and is hard to identify. Moreover, the female character bears signs of degeneracy.

The sound of the sea, like "the great voice of Nature mourning the degeneracy of man," can be heard as Sir Joseph explains to Mountford that she is in fact his illegitimate daughter. Close to Sibyl, Marie Arnold does not learn to become ladylike. Like Haggard's Ayesha, her femininity resonates with hints of retrogressive evolution.[27] Her irritability, her impressionability, and her "hawk-like gaze" intimate her latent violence as she becomes more and more jealous of Brandon and Sibyl's growing intimacy. More significantly still, her ability to turn men into slaves and thus rewrite colonial history is potentially dangerous.

Hence, Braddon imports numerous *fin-de-siècle* motifs associated with "uncivilized" peoples and territories, and adapts them to late-Victorian Britain. If Marie Arnold is killed and vanishes from the narrative, the hero's secret—his hereditary epilepsy—must be sought in the wilderness, as he tells Sibyl: "I had made up my mind to leave this place with my story untold; to carry my secret—if it should be a secret—away with me into the wilderness, to bury it there in the explorer's shifting camp." As his mind is aligned with the African wilderness, Brandon Mountford exemplifies how his contact with Africa has released his own savage instincts. The male brain thus becomes the mysterious unknown territory that needs to be explored by the female anthropological investigators. Indeed, though they do not travel overseas, Braddon's imperialist explorers are the heroines of the narrative, reading medical and anthropological essays. Yet, what these female sleuths discover are not the dangers of uninhibited female sexuality but the dangers of men's uncontrolled murderous instincts. As Braddon's female characters increasingly uncover the links between men and animals, the novel subverts the evolutionary theory which defined woman as the "missing link" between man and the animal kingdom. Braddon's female characters are no criminals, and Mountford is very quickly seen as one of the very specimens British explorers would have classified as savage. Revealingly, though Mountford has inherited his mental disease from his mother, he believes his heritage comes from his father: "My poor father's fate was a sad one—and he left a gloomy heritage to me." Whether they are plagued by mental disease or "grovel like a hound," Braddon points to men as guilty of all the crimes and full of bestiality, like Hubert Urquhart. It is her female characters who are gradually and shamelessly led to expose them.[28]

From the Persecuted Heroine to the "New Woman"

Braddon's female sleuths are thus decidedly modern. Unlike in Gothic novels, where the criminal ancestor leaves his bloody manuscript to the following generation, in Braddon's narrative female writing takes the lead. In order to keep an eye on Lady Penrith's discoveries, Hubert Urquhart asks his daughter to keep a diary and to send it to him so that he may check his daughter's ladylike qualities. Of course, Urquhart only seeks to survey Sibyl's whereabouts. Ironically enough, Coralie soon turns the normative activity that her father tries to impose on her back on itself. She devises a system of "double entry," writing what she means her father to read in one volume ("Cora's diary: for paternal perusal") and her own "little reveries" in another. As she plays with the very tools her father intended to control her aunt and herself with, Coralie challenges masculine authority and, in Heidi Johnson's words, liberates herself "from the prescribed role assigned to her in serving her father's expectations and fantasies."[29]

Interestingly, Coralie is a foil to Braddon's golden-haired demon in *Lady Audley's Secret*. She is physically at the antipodes of the fair-haired angel Victorian society idolized, with "such blue eyes, such long lashes, such dear little mouths, such lily and rose complexions, and lovely golden hair." Coralie is ugly and masculine; she cannot keep house, she loves smoking, "horsey talk," stables, kennels, and billiard rooms. Motherless but not naive, she is well aware of the mercenary aspects of marriage, and she hunts the best party, playing the dumb woman and reading magazines instead of high literature because men, she argues, like silly women. Although it was her father who first encouraged her to write, Coralie soon imagines herself as a professional writer living alone after his death. Leaving her father to live with Sibyl, the woman writer blots out the male parent from her life, and liberates the feminist forces of Braddon's narrative. For Braddon's novel may well contain an ultimate textual secret. As feminist criticism has argued, the imperialist romances of the 1880s—just like the new genres which appeared in the late nineteenth century, such as naturalism, or New Realism—were often seen as a way to counteract the threat of feminism and to "masculinise the novel."[30] Indeed, the obsessional construction of the female Other as evidence of woman's retrogressive evolution could be read as a male response to the horror of the enfranchisement of women. In addition, the rise of the "New Woman" and the fear that the New Woman's excessive sensitivity might "invade and infect the whole of society with a degenerative femininity"[31] increased *fin-de-siècle* anxieties all the more. With her intelligent and autonomous female sleuths, who can read, write and unmask the apes beneath civilized men, Braddon may therefore also be offering us her critique of the genre even as she exploits it, debunking the stereotypes of her time and denouncing the fictions which branded women by reading and writing them as dangerous and degenerate. By turning the armoury of Killander Castle into a library and foregrounding learned female protagonists, Braddon gives her heroines the weapons to fight back against male dominion. It is true that both Sibyl and Coralie turn out to be inefficient detectives, and Braddon eventually chooses to let a man complete the inquiry. Yet, nearly all her male characters die, Mountford's mind "wandering in . . . an endless labyrinth" and Urquhart lying in "a state of semi delirium," whilst Braddon teasingly closes her novel on her ugly heroine giving hunting breakfasts and lashing out with her sharp tongue.

LAURENCE TALAIRACH-VIELMAS
Toulouse

January 2, 2008

LAURENCE TALAIRACH-VIELMAS is Senior Lecturer in English at the University of Toulouse—Le Mirail (France). She is the author of *Moulding the Female Body in Victorian Fairy Tales and Sensation Novels* (Ashgate, 2007) and is currently working on a book-length project on Wilkie Collins, *Medicine and the Gothic*, to be published by University of Wales Press.

NOTES

1 The materials in this biographical section were taken from Robert
   Lee Wolff, *Sensational Victorian: The Life and Fiction of Mary Eliza-*
   beth Braddon (New York: Garland Publishing, 1979). See also Jennifer
   Carnell, *The Literary Lives of Mary Elizabeth Braddon: A Study of Her*
   Life and Work (Hastings: The Sensation Press, 2000).

2 In the 1860s, Braddon also resorted to mad male characters, as exemplified by her rewriting of Charlotte Brontë's *Jane Eyre* in the short
   story "The Mystery at Fernwood" published in *Temple Bar* 3 (Nov.
   1861): 552-563; 4 (March 1862): 63-74.

3 *Spectator* 1791 (October 25, 1862), 1196.

4 Henry James, "Miss Braddon," *The Nation* (9 Nov. 1865), 593-595.
   Republished in *Notes and Reviews* (Cambridge, Mass.: Dunster House,
   1921), 108-116, 112-113.

5 Patrick Brantlinger, "What is 'Sensational' about the Sensation
   Novel?" *Nineteenth Century Fiction* 37 (1982), 1-28, 4.

6 See Heidi H. Johnson, "Electra-fying the Female Sleuth: Detecting the
   Father in *Eleanor's Victory* and *Thou Art the Man*," in Marlene Tromp,
   Pamela K. Gilbert, and Aeron Haynie (eds.), *Beyond Sensation: Mary*
   Elizabeth Braddon in Context (Albany: State University of New York
   Press, 2000), 255-275, 264.

7 Owsei Temkin, *The Falling Sickness: A History of Epilepsy from the*
   Greeks to the Beginnings of Modern Neurology (Baltimore and London:
   Johns Hopkins University Press, [1945] 1994), 3.

8 See Neil Davie, *Tracing the Criminal: The Rise of Scientific Criminology*
   in Britain, 1860-1918 (Oxford: Bardwell Press, 2005).

9 Henry Maudsley, *Responsibility in Mental Disease* (5th ed., London:
   Kegan Paul, Trench, Trübner & Co., 1892), 90.

10 Maudsley, *Responsibility in Mental Disease*, 92.

11 Maudsley, *Responsibility in Mental Disease*, 227.

12 Cesare Lombroso, *Criminal Man*. Edited and translated by Mary
   Gibson and Nicole Hahn Rafter, Durham and London: Duke University Press, 2006.

13 Gibson and Rafter, 161 in Cesare Lombroso, *Criminal Man*. Edited
   and translated by Mary Gibson and Nicole Hahn Rafter. Durham
   and London: Duke University Press, 2006.

14 Gibson and Rafter, in Cesare Lombroso, *Criminal Man*, 11.

15 Lombroso, *Criminal Man*, 248.

16 Lombroso, *Criminal Man*, 247.

17 Lombroso, *Criminal Man*, 253. Lombroso manifestly relied on the records of Philippe Tissié (*Les Aliénés voyageurs* [1887]), which gave examples of epileptics moving involuntarily for miles and months.

18 Lombroso, *Criminal Man*, 257.

19 See Neil Davie, *Tracing the Criminal: The Rise of Scientific Criminology in Britain, 1860-1918* (Oxford: Bardwell Press, 2005).

20 See Kelly Hurley, *The Gothic Body: Sexuality, Materialism and Degeneration at the Fin de Siècle* (Cambridge: Cambridge University Press, [1996] 2004).

21 The formulation is that of Patrick Brantlinger. See his *Rule of Darkness: British Literature and Imperialism, 1830-1914* (Ithaca and London: Cornell University Press, [1988] 1990).

22 Rebecca Stott, *The Fabrication of the Late-Victorian Femme Fatale: The Kiss of Death* (Basingstoke: Macmillan, 1992), 93.

23 See Stott, *The Fabrication of the Late-Victorian Femme Fatale*, 88-125.

24 Ronald R. Thomas, *Detective Fiction and the Rise of Forensic Science* (Cambridge: Cambridge University Press, 1999), 212. Ellis systematically compared criminal anatomy with some foreign place, an "historically exotic territory with certain recognizable landmarks" (Thomas, 209). Ellis argued that the criminal's features were close to those of the "lower races" from Africa, India, Australia, or China, the latter bearing in turn a resemblance with the apes. Following Ellis, Galton's vocabulary for describing fingerprints ranged from "islands" to "deltas." He compared fingerprints with "the crests of mountain ridges," reading "boundaries" between "little worlds," thus viewing the criminal body as a territory to be conquered and controlled by forensic scientists (see Thomas, *Detective Fiction and the Rise of Forensic Science*, 201-219).

25 Lawrence Millman, *Rider Haggard and the Male Novel. What Is Pericles? Beckett Gags* (Unpublished Doctoral Dissertation, Rutgers University, 1974), cited in Stott, *The Fabrication of the Late-Victorian Femme Fatale*, 90.

26 Brantlinger, *Rule of Darkness*, 246.

27 For a study of retrogression, see Gillian Beer, *Darwin's Plots: Evolutionary Narrative in Darwin, George Eliot, and Nineteenth-Century Fiction* (Cambridge: Cambridge University Press, [1983] 2000), 114-135.

28 Even Gertrude, Mr. Carpew's daughter, does not hesitate to betray

her father: "I suppose it's awfully wicked for a girl to hate her father, but I can't help hating mine for the cruel trick he has played upon you."

29 Johnson, "Electra-fying the Female Sleuth: Detecting the Father in *Eleanor's Victory* and *Thou Art the Man*," 262.

30 Lyn Pykett, *The "Improper" Feminine: The Women's Sensation Novel and the New Woman Writing* (London: Routledge, 1992), 36.

31 Pykett, *The "Improper" Feminine*, 141.

A CHRONOLOGY OF MARY ELIZABETH BRADDON

1835: Born 4 October, 2 Frith Street, Soho Square.

1847: Her brother Edward goes to India. Her sister Maggie marries an Italian and goes to Naples to live. M. E. Braddon stays alone with her mother.

1857-60: Goes on the stage as "Mary Seyton."

1860: Publishes her first novel, *Three Times Dead, or, The Secret of the Heath*, reissued in 1861 as *The Trail of the Serpent*.

1861: Starts her liaison with the publisher John Maxwell, whose wife was incarcerated in a lunatic asylum in Dublin. Maxwell launches *The Halfpenny Journal*, a weekly periodical to which she contributes several novels anonymously (*The Black Band; or, The Mysteries of Midnight; The Octoroon; or, The Lily of Louisiana; Captain of the Vulture; A Romance of Real Life*).

1861: *The Lady Lisle.*

1862: *Lady Audley's Secret.*

1863: *Aurora Floyd; Eleanor's Victory; John Marchmont's Legacy.* Writes *The White Phantom; The Factory Girl; or, All Is Not Gold that Glitters;* and *Oscar Bertrand; or, The Idiot of the Mountain* for *The Halfpenny Journal.*

1864: *Henry Dunbar; The Doctor's Wife.*

1865: *Only a Clod; Sir Jasper's Tenant.* Writes *The Banker's Secret* for *The Halfpenny Journal.*

1866: *The Lady's Mile.* Maxwell sells *Temple Bar* and founds the monthly *Belgravia.* M. E. Braddon becomes the editor and publishes under the pseudonym of "Babington White." Braddon purchases Lichfield House in Richmont where she would live with Maxwell and her children for the rest of their lives.

1867: Publishes *Circe* in *Belgravia* under the pseudonym of "Babington White." Accused of plagiarism. *Rupert Godwin*, a rewriting of *The Banker's Secret* as a three-volume novel.

1867-68: *Birds of Prey* and its sequel *Charlotte's Inheritance*; *Dead Sea Fruit*.

1868: Death of mother and sister. Nervous collapse and attack of puerperal fever.

1870: *Milly Darrell*.

1871: *Fenton's Quest*; *The Lovels of Arden*.

1872: *To the Bitter End*.

1873: *Lucius Davoren*; *Strangers and Pilgrims*.

1874: Death of John Maxwell's wife. Marries Maxwell on 2 October. *Taken at the Flood*; *Lost For Love*.

1875: *A Strange World*; *Hostages to Fortune*; *Dead Men's Shoes*.

1876: *Belgravia* sold to Chatto and Windus. Braddon ceases to be its editor. *Joshua Haggard's Daughter*.

1877: *Weavers and Weft*.

1878: *An Open Verdict*. Founds *The Mistletoe Bough*, a new Christmas annual to which she will contribute several novels and novelettes, such as *Flower and Weed* (1882) and *Under the Red Flag* (1883).

1879: *Vixen*; *The Cloven Foot*.

1880: *The Story of Barbara*; *Just As I Am*.

1881: *Asphodel*.

1882: *Mount Royal*. Writes plays (*Married Beneath Him*; *Dross*; *Margery Daw*).

1883: *The Golden Calf*; *Phantom Fortune*.

1884: *Ishmael*.

1885: *Wyllard's Weird*.

1886: *Mohawks*; *One Thing Needful*.

1887: *Like and Unlike*.

1888: *The Fatal Three*.

1889: *The Day Will Come*.

1890: *One Life One Love*.

1891: *Gerard*.

1892: *The Venetians*.

1892-93: *The Christmas Hirelings*, a Christmas novelette.

1893: *All Along the River*.

1894: *Thou Art the Man* published in three volumes (London: Simpkin, Marshall) after having run serially in Leng's *Sheffield Weekly Telegraph*.

1895: Death of John Maxwell. *Sons of Fire* (last three-volume novel).

1896: *London Pride*.

1897: *Under Love's Rule*.

1898: *Rough Justice; In High Places*.

1899 Daughter Rosie (Lachlan) dies. *His Darling Sin*.

1900: *The Infidel*.

1903: *The Conflict*.

1904: Death of brother. *A Lost Eden*.

1905: *The Rose of Life*.

1906: *The White House*.

1907: *Her Convict; Dead Love Has Chains*.

1907-8: Stroke which deprives her temporarily of the use of her limbs.

1908: *During Her Majesty's Pleasure*.

1909: *Our Adversary*.

1910: *Beyond These Voices*.

1911: *The Green Curtain*.

1913: *Miranda*.

1915: Dies 4 February.

1916: *Mary*, her eighty-fifth and final book.

SELECT BIBLIOGRAPHY

Boyle, Thomas. *Black Swine in the Sewers of Hampstead: Beneath the Surface of Victorian Sensationalism.* 1989. London: Hodder & Stoughton, 1990.

Brantlinger, Patrick. "What is 'Sensational' about the Sensation Novel?" *Nineteenth Century Fiction* 37 (1982): 1-28.

Casey, Ellen Miller. "Other People's Prudery: Mary Elizabeth Braddon," in Don Richard Cox (ed.), *Sexuality and Victorian Literature.* Knoxville: University of Tennessee Press, 1984, 72-82.

Carnell, Jennifer. *The Literary Lives of Mary Elizabeth Braddon: A Study of Her Life and Work.* Hastings: The Sensation Press, 2000.

Cvetkovich, Ann. *Mixed Feelings: Feminism, Mass Culture, and Victorian Sensationalism.* New Brunswick: Rutgers University Press, 1992.

Dallas, E. S. "*Lady Audley's Secret,*" *The Times* (18 November 1862): 8.

Gilbert, Pamela K. *Disease, Desire, and the Body in Victorian Women's Popular Novels.* Cambridge: Cambridge University Press, 1997.

Harrison, Kimberly and Richard Fantina (eds.), *Victorian Sensations: Essays on a Scandalous Genre.* Athens, OH: Ohio University Press, 2006.

Hughes, Winifred. *The Maniac in the Cellar: Sensation Novels of the 1860s.* Princeton: Princeton University Press, 1980.

James, Henry. "Miss Braddon," *The Nation* (9 Nov. 1865): 593-595. Republished in *Notes and Reviews.* Cambridge, Mass.: Dunster House, 1921, 108-116.

Mansel, Henry. "Sensation Novels," *Quarterly Review* 113 (1863): 481-514.

Oliphant, Margaret. "Novels," *Blackwood's* 94 (Aug. 1863): 168-183.

_____, "Novels," *Blackwood's* 102 (Sept. 1867): 257-280.

"Our Female Sensation Novelists," *Christian Remembrancer* 46 (July 1863): 209-236.

Pykett, Lyn. *The "Improper" Feminine: The Women's Sensation Novel and the New Woman Writing.* London: Routledge, 1992.

Rae, W. F. "Sensation Novelists: Miss Braddon," *North British Review* 43 (Sept. 1865), 180-204.

"Sensation Novels," *Spectator* 41 (8 Aug. 1868), 931-932.

Tromp, Marlene, Pamela K. Gilbert, and Aeron Haynie (eds.) *Beyond Sensation: Mary Elizabeth Braddon in Context.* Albany: State University of New York Press, 2000.

Trodd, Anthea. *Domestic Crime in the Victorian Novel.* Basingstoke: Macmillan, 1989.

Wolff, Robert Lee. "Devoted Disciple: The Letters of Mary Elizabeth Braddon to Sir Edward Bulwer-Lytton, 1862-1873," *Harvard Library Bulletin* 22 (1974), 5-35, 129-161.

_____. *Sensational Victorian: The Life and Fiction of Mary Elizabeth Braddon.* New York: Garland Publishing, 1979.

NOTE ON THE TEXT

The Valancourt Books edition of *Thou Art the Man* is based on the yellowback edition of 1895. *Thou Art the Man* was first published in three volumes (London: Simpkin, Marshall) in 1894, after having run serially in *Sheffield Weekly Telegraph*.

Thou Art the Man

CHAPTER I

A LETTER FROM THE DEAD

There were masses of black cloud in the grey evening sky, and a misty darkness brooded over the shoulder of the moor, as the barouche,[1] with its fine, up-standing greys, came swinging round the curve of the road leading to Killander Castle—a more luxurious carriage than is generally to be met with on a Cumbrian Moor—but this carriage belonged to a lady whose importance filled the land to the farthest limit of moor and valley, and away to the edge of yonder distant sea whose leaden waves were edged with livid spray at this sunset hour of a stormy October afternoon.

The lady—Sibyl, Countess of Penrith—was sitting alone in her carriage, wrapped in dark fur, with a proud, clearly cut face showing pale between the sable of her close-fitting toque and the sable collar of her long velvet mantle. Her eyes had a dreamy look as they surveyed the desolate landscape, the undulating sweep of moorland, the distant grey of the sea. The droop of the sensitive lips suggested mournful thoughts, or it might be only a pensive reverie in harmony with the sullen atmosphere, and the dark monotony of the landscape.

Suddenly, out of the very ground, as it seemed to Lady Penrith, a rough-looking man came running after the carriage. The footman looked round at him, as if he had been a dog, and took no further heed than he would have taken of a dog. The coachman drove steadily on, touching the muscular shoulders of his sleek greys daintily with the point of his whip, quickening the pace as the sky darkened.

The man came running on, giving chase to the carriage, and waving an arm in a ragged fustian sleeve.

"Stop," cried Lady Penrith, and the coachman pulled up his horses, in the midst of the bleak, bare moor, and the footman alighted from the box and came to the carriage door, touching his hat with gloved fingers, mute image of obedience and subserviency.

"That man wants to speak to me," said her ladyship. "Wait."

3

The vagabond's footsteps drew near. He was at the carriage door in less than three minutes, breathless and hoarsely panting, with a sound like the grating of rusty iron. He looked like a shepherd out of employment, ragged, gaunt, hungry-eyed.

"Are you Lady Penrith?" he asked.

"Yes," answered her ladyship, with her purse open in her hand, having only one idea as to the man's motive in following her carriage.

Beggars were rare on that moorland road, but this man was evidently a beggar, she thought; and not being a political economist, her first impulse was to relieve him.

He said never a word, but fumbled under the ragged shirt which hardly hid his lean breast, and produced a folded scrap of paper, which he flung into the lady's lap, then turned and ran away—across the moor this time, as fast as he had run after the carriage three minutes before.

"Follow him," said Lady Penrith to the footman, and the footman went tripping and stumbling over the stony moor, nearly falling down at every second step.

The hungry vagabond vanished into the dim grey of evening before the over-fed lackey in his buckled shoes had gone fifty yards across that uneven ground.

He came back, breathlessly apologetic, and explained the impossibility of catching a man who ran like a rabbit.

"Do you know who he is, or where he comes from?"

"No, my lady. Never saw him before, to my knowledge."

"There is no village in that direction nearer than Cargill, and that is three miles off. He must have come from Cargill, I suppose. A beggar, no doubt. That will do, James. Home."

Home! The word, how often soever she might pronounce it, had always a sound of irony in her ear. What likeness was there between the English ideal of home and Killander Castle, on the Cumbrian moorland; or Penrith House, Berkeley Square; or the Mimosas at Cannes; or the Den, near Braemar; or any habitation owned by Archibald, Earl of Penrith? There are men and women who can create an atmosphere of domestic peace in a log-hut in the Australian bush, or in a lodging-house at the East End of London. There are others who, among a dozen palaces, cannot make one home.

A pale streak of yellow light on the western edge of the moor showed where the sun had dipped below the horizon. A colder wind blew from the far-off sea, and Lady Penrith shivered as she took up the scrap of soiled paper from her lap, and held it gingerly with the tips of her gloved fingers.

It was less than half a sheet of notepaper. There was only a few pencilled words in four straggling lines along the paper; and those few words were so difficult to decipher that Lady Penrith had to pore over them for a long time in the waning light before she made them into the following sentences:—

"Out of the grave, the living grave, a long-forgotten voice calls to you. Where their worm dieth not, and their fire is not quenched."[2]

No signature; no indication of from whom or whence the message came. A madman's scrawl, no doubt, inspired by some half-cloudy purpose in the troubled brain of lunacy. The ragged wretch whom she had taken for a beggar was doubtless some wandering lunatic, harmless, and therefore permitted to ramble about the countryside. A religious enthusiast, perhaps! The scrap of Scripture pointed that way.

Lady Penrith resolved to drive to Cargill next day and search out the history of the writer, if indeed he lived there, as seemed likely; unless he were to be found in one of those lonely cottages scattered here and there over the face of the moor, between Penrith and Ardliston, the little seaport whence coal and iron were shipped for the south. A great tract of wild country, broken only by small and solitary hamlets, lay between these two points. The coal-mines and smelting works and miners' villages all lay northward of Ardliston. The landscape on this southward side of the harbour was wild and gloomy, but had a certain stern beauty of its own, and was not disfigured by mining operations of any kind.

Lady Penrith was interested in the troubled mind which had prompted that pencil scrawl. A call to repentance, no doubt; such a summons as the pauper Puritan, seeing rank and beauty roll by in a three-hundred-guinea barouche, not unseldom feels himself called upon to deliver. There was really nothing to wonder at. There was hardly anything exceptional in the incident, unless perhaps it were that the man should have been there in the nick of time, as her ladyship's carriage went by. Yet even that circumstance was easy enough to understand if he were an inhabitant of the district. She drove in that direction often, and as a person of mark in the neighbourhood her habits were doubtless noted and known.

No, there was nothing curious in the incident, nothing worthy of much thought; and yet she thought of nothing else during her homeward drive. She carried the thought with her under the great grey gateway with its iron portcullis; and into the hall, where the atmosphere of smouldering logs and hothouse flowers had a feeling as of the warm, sweet South she knew so well; and up to her own sitting-room, where the slip of soiled paper lay on her lap as she sipped her solitary cup of tea. His lordship and his lordship's friends had been out shooting all day; her niece—a niece by courtesy—had gone with the luncheon cart, and the lady of Killander Castle had the great mediæval fortress all to herself in the October gloaming.

Presently she drew the lamp nearer, and scrutinised that pencilled scrawl even more closely than before in the bright white light.

"It is not the writing of an uneducated man," she said to herself, and then her head sank lower, as her elbow rested on the cushioned arm of her chair, until her forehead almost touched the slip of paper on the table in front of her. She sat there some minutes, lost in dreamy thought.

"How strange that the hand should be like his!" she murmured. And then after a pause, "Is it really like, or do I fancy a resemblance because he is so often in my thoughts?"

Then, after another lapse into reverie,

"He was not in my mind to-day. I had other things to think of. I was brooding on the hard realities of life; not upon its losses and regrets."

She took up the paper, and studied it again, noting every stroke of the pencil.

"It is like the writing of the dead," she said at last, with conviction. "The hand which wrote was the hand of a gentleman. I must hunt out the writer. I shall not rest until I find out who and what he is; a madman, no doubt; but should he be in poverty and distress I should like to help him—if it were only because he writes like the dead."

She rose, and went across the room to the large old-fashioned escritoire,[3] where most of her letters were written, and where, among numerous pigeon-holes and quaint recesses, there were two deep drawers, provided with Bramah locks.[4] She unlocked one of these, and dropped the scrap of paper on the top of the neatly-arranged packets of letters, tied with different-coloured ribbons—letters which were in some wise the record of a woman's life. There was one of these packets—the thinnest of them—tied with a broad black ribbon.

Lady Penrith stood for a minute or so with the drawer open, looking down at those letters bound with the black band; then she slowly closed the drawer and locked it, and as she turned away from the escritoire her eyes were dim with tears.

That fancied resemblance in a handwriting had been like the lifting of a coffin lid for one last look at the dead face underneath. All the passion and the despair of a long buried past had come back to Sibyl Penrith at the bidding of an unknown lunatic who happened to write like the man to whom she had given her girlish heart ten years ago.

She was sitting in her low chair by the fire, in the shadow of a tall Indian screen, when the door opened suddenly and an exuberant young woman came noisily into the room, and brought the dreamer back in an instant from the past with its fond regrets to the present with its manifold obligations.

"Oh, such a day!" cried the new-comer. "You were better off even in your dreary afternoon drive. I had to wait, and wait, and wait for those men, till I was absolutely ravenous, and the hot dishes were utterly spoilt. I shall never go out with the luncheon cart again, unless I have three or four pretty girls to back me up. Those selfish wretches would be punctual enough then; but they don't mind reducing poor plain me to the verge of starvation."

"Poor plain Cora," said her ladyship, as the girl seated herself at the tea-table and began a spirited attack upon the cakes and buns which Lady Penrith had left untasted. "Girls who really think themselves plain don't talk about it. They live in the hope that it is a secret between themselves and their looking-glasses."

"Oh, but I am an exception to your rule," protested Miss Urquhart, with her large serviceable mouth full of Scotch bun. "When I was twelve years old I found out the difference between beauty and ugliness. I heard all the pretty little girls admired—'such blue eyes, such long lashes, such dear little mouths, such lily and rose complexions, and lovely golden hair,' while I observed that people called me good, or clever, or sensible! So I looked steadily at my image in the glass, and I faced the unpleasant fact.

"'You are plain, Coralie,' I said to myself; 'unmistakably plain. You have tolerable eyes, and good teeth; but your nose is a failure, your complexion is pallid, and your mouth is just twice too large for prettiness. Never forget that you are plain, my dear Coralie, and then perhaps other people won't remember the fact quite so often. Shake hands with Fate; accept your thick nose and your pallid complexion as the stern necessities of your existence, and make the most of your eyes and teeth, and your average head of hair.' That is the gist of what I said to myself, in less sophisticated language, perhaps, before I was fifteen, and from that line of conduct I have never departed. So if I have come to nineteen years of age without being admired, I have at least escaped being laughed at!"

"You are a bright, clever girl, Cora, and have quite enough good looks to float your cleverness, and to win you plenty of attention."

"Do you really mean that?" asked Miss Urquhart, turning a pair of keen brown eyes upon Lady Penrith. "Well, you who are among the handsomest of your sex can afford to be generous. The men are civil enough to me, certainly; and I believe some of them like me, in a way, as a jolly good fellow, don't you know."

"I think you ought to leave off being a jolly good fellow, Cora, and remember that you are a young lady, now your twentieth birthday is drawing near," said her ladyship, with kindly seriousness.

"What, leave off cigarettes, and horsey talk, forego my morning fun in the stables and kennels—give the billiard-room a holiday—and take to embroidering window curtains and reading the last book of the Honourable Somebody's travels in Timbuctoo. So I would, Auntie, if I could only make up my mind which line is likely to pay best in such a case as mine—the well brought up, stand-offish young lady, or the free and easy young person whom her male acquaintances talk of as 'good fun,' or 'not a bad sort.'"

"Perhaps you will explain what you mean by paying best?"

"Oh, I'm sure you catch my meaning. Which line will bring

the most eligible offer of marriage? That is the question. Of course there is a sprinkling of proper-minded young men, the cream of the Peerage and the landed gentry, who could only be won by a proper-minded young woman; but I doubt if among these chosen ones there is a chance for such as I, and I have observed that the ruck of young men prefer the society of a girl who is distinctly on their own level, a little below them rather than a little above. That is why chorus girls and barmaids often get on so well in the world."

"Ah, Cora, what a pity you should have learnt so much about the seamy side of life!"

"Yes, that comes of being brought up by a father instead of a mother. Had my mother lived she would have reared me in a state of guileless innocence. I should have thought burlesque boys and pantomime fairies a kind of semi-angelic creatures, and I should never have heard of a barmaid; whereas the governor used to entertain me with the gossip of the clubs every morning at breakfast, the only meal he took at home."

"My poor Coralie! And your father—pray don't call him governor—taught you that your mission in life is to marry?"

"Well, if I can; badly, if I can't; at any rate to get myself some kind of a husband, so as to take myself off the paternal hands. At least, that was his idea a year or two ago. Now that you are so good to me and let me be here and in Berkeley Square, he is no longer so keen on my marrying. So long as I don't worry or burden him he is satisfied. But when you grow tired of me——"

"I am not going to tire of you, Cora. I mean to grow fonder of you, if you will let me."

"Let you! Why, I worship you. You are my ideal of all that is perfect in woman. If the leopard could change his spots I would prove my sincerity by trying to be like you—in grace and dignity and high and pure thoughts——"

Lady Penrith acknowledged these compliments with a sigh.

"Ah, I know you have only a poor opinion of yourself, you don't half know how good you are."

"Good! I am nothing, Cora; a passive nonentity; a piece of human furniture that fills an allotted space in Lord Penrith's establishment, and which is of no importance in the world either for good or evil."

"That is hard, ain't it," sighed Coralie. "With your beauty you ought to have done as much harm as Cleopatra. You ought to have seen fleets destroyed and armies slaughtered for your beaux yeux,[5] or kept two kingdoms in commotion, like Mary Stuart. Or even in these degenerate modern times you might have set the town in a blaze, been the cause of separations and divorces, Belgian duels, and Mayfair suicides.[6] With beauty, and such wealth as yours—to be only Lady Penrith. No, it is not much after all. And yet how many people envy you—I, myself, for instance!"

"I hope you are above so paltry a feeling, Cora."

"Don't hope anything exalted or noble of my father's daughter," said Coralie, renewing her attack upon a pile of crisp biscuits, and munching as she talked.

"I don't like to hear a daughter speak of her father as you speak of yours, Cora," Lady Penrith said gravely, "and I would much rather you left his name out of our conversation. You ought to remember that he and I have long ceased to be friends."

"I ought! I ought!" cried Cora. "I am a wretch to forget," and then she put down her biscuit and sighed remorsefully. "It was so good of you to rescue me from my shabby, lonely life; it was so good of you to forget that I am Hubert Urquhart's daughter."

"You are my husband's niece. That gives you a claim upon me, Cora."

"There are hundreds of women who would laugh such a claim to scorn; and you have plenty of girls of your own blood to care for; those nice Hammond girls, who are devoted to you."

"They are very good girls, but they have a mother to look after them."

"And I was motherless and alone, educated in a second-rate school, kept by a needy French woman in a shabby suburb beyond the Bois de Boulogne, and eating my heart out in a dingy lodging-house, which had but one virtue, that it was near my father's favourite clubs. Oh, how I hated that dark, narrow street under the shadow of St. James's Church, and the joy-bells and death-bells, and the clock that struck all the weary hours; and the smart weddings, which served only to remind me how little chance I had of ever being married in a respectable manner; and the landlady, who would come in and squat down uninvited upon the wretched sofa—until I felt tempted to ask whether the law between landlord and tenant made it her sofa or ours—and who condoled with me because I must be so lonely with my books and piano! As if books and piano were not better than her cockney company. Oh, it was a bottomless pit of squalid misery from which you rescued me. I ought to be grateful."

"Don't talk about gratitude, Cora. Be happy. That is all I want of you."

"I'll do my best," answered the girl briskly. "I don't know whether it is the chef or Mrs. Ricketts who makes these too delicious biscuits, but whatsoever hand mixes the paste it is the hand of genius. And now I must go and give myself a warm bath, after all the mud and mire of the day's diversion, and spend an hour or so in making myself just endurable."

"Put on one of your prettiest frocks," said Lady Penrith. "Mr. Coverdale is a good enough match for any young woman."

"The Honourable and Reverend John Coverdale! It looks rather nice upon the address of a letter. But do you suppose for one moment, Aunt, that a serious and cultured Anglican parson would ever look with the eye of favour upon me?" asked Cora, pausing with her hand upon the door.

"Love delights in incongruities. Mr. Coverdale is highly intellectual, and I believe both kind and conscientious. He is just the husband to——"

"To reform me! Ah, Aunt, if it were any use trying for him."

She opened the door quickly, and was gone. Lady Penrith heard her whistling a music-hall melody, learnt in the smoking-room, as she went along the corridor.

"That is the warmest affection I get in this house," thought Sibyl Penrith, as the notes died away in the distance. "I wonder whether she is false or true? An Urquhart, and true! That would indeed be an anomaly. But then there is the other side. Her mother may have been a good woman."

She wanted to think well of this motherless girl if she could, for pure pity, although the girl was the daughter of that man whom she regarded as her worst enemy, the man who had turned the sweetest gift of life to bitterness and despair. She believed the worst of Hubert Urquhart, her husband's half-brother; and yet, hearing from Lord Penrith that Hubert Urquhart's daughter was living alone and neglected in a bachelor lodging-house, all her kindly instincts rose in the girl's favour, and she lay awake a whole night thinking how she could serve this unhappy waif, whose misfortune it was to belong to such a father.

There was one thing Lady Penrith could not do. She could not cross the threshold of any house inhabited by Hubert Urquhart.

She spoke to her husband on the morning after that night of troubled thought.

"I have been thinking of what you told me yesterday about your brother's girl," she began. "I don't like the idea of your niece being in such a miserable position, and if you don't object I would like to take her to live with me. There is plenty of room for her, both here and in the country."

"Yes, there is room enough, undoubtedly. We are not a large family," said Penrith, who had fretted himself with an angry wonder at the absence of an heir.

Two children had been born to him, and had died in infancy. It seemed to him that there was a curse upon his union with a woman who had never flattered him so far as to pretend she loved him. She had given him herself and her wealth, the plaything of Fate, the slave of adverse circumstances; and it seemed to him, and perhaps to the wife also, that a blight had fallen upon their offspring, the withering blight of a home where love had never entered.

"You have no objection, then?" asked Sibyl, after a pause. They were in the hall, in the great stately house near Berkeley Square, one of those few houses in West End London, where rank may live within high garden walls, hidden from the outside world. The garden was gloomy, after the manner of London gardens, despite all that horticulture could do in the way of carpet beds and showy creepers. The house was grandly ugly without and splendidly luxurious within. The wife's wealth had been spent lavishly upon that long-neglected pile, and could the last Earl of Penrith have revisited his own mansion his astonished ghost would hardly have recognised the rooms which, in his own day, had been conspicuous for the shabbiness of their curtains and carpets, and the ugliness of their furniture, of the later Georgian period. Under her present ladyship's regime the house had been furnished and decorated throughout after the fashion of Louis Seize;[7] and it might have been the mansion *entre cour et jardin*[8] of a Legitimist nobleman in the Faubourg St. Germain. Space and light, grace of line, and delicacy of colouring distinguished those large and lofty reception-rooms, that airy hall, with its double sweep of shallow marble stairs, its groups of palms, and gracious marble forms of Fawn and Nymph, Cupid and Psyche.

Penrith paced up and down the hall with an inscrutable countenance. He was a man in whom speech seemed in some wise an effort.

"You won't mind my having your niece as a kind of companion, will you, Penrith?" urged his wife.

"Mind? No, of course not. It is very good of you to suggest the thing. All I fear is that the girl may prove a bore to you."

And so the matter was settled, and Coralie Urquhart was transferred with her meagre belongings from the shabby second-floor in Jermyn Street to Penrith House, where there was room and verge enough to allow this young lady her own sitting-room, as well as a spacious bed and dressing-room. She declared that she felt like a princess amidst her new surroundings, and so much the more so after Madame Lolotte, her ladyship's dressmaker, had taken her measure for a complete set of frocks and outdoor garments to suit all the requirements of her new life.

Sibyl was far too delicate to suggest any overhauling of the girl's existing wardrobe, but a few judicious questions elicited the fact that Miss Urquhart possessed exactly five frocks, three tailor-made and threadbare, while the remaining two were evening gowns, a year and a half old, and too small to be worn without torture.

"The Pater's tailor gave me a start with those nice little tweed frocks, when I came from Paris, but he has turned disagreeable since then, and won't give any more tick."

Coralie was mildly reproved for that last word, and Madame Lolotte was sent for and told that she must produce a season's dresses for Miss Urquhart before the end of the week. She shrugged her shoulders and elevated her eyebrows, and then exhibited all her neat little teeth in a caressing smile.

"Pour Milady on fait l'impossible," she said. *"Mais, mon Dieu, quatre jours pour faire faire un trousseau!"*[9]

In the result the impossible was done, so far as the production of two delicious little walking-gowns and three party-frocks, of a most exquisite simplicity, yet with a certain boldness of style and colouring which set off Miss Urquhart's plainness.

"Elle est franchement laide, la p'tite,"[10] the dressmaker told Lady Penrith's maid at a later interview. "But it is an original style of ugliness, and I like it better than your milky-skinned English, with their faces in papier-maché."

Henceforward, Coralie's life was a bed of roses—or would have been had she been without conscience and without heart. Unluckily for her, she had not yet attained that hardness which rises superior to all moral feelings, all vain compunctions; but she was her father's daughter, and she was in a fair way of becoming like him.

He had a serious conversation with her the night before she left him to become a member of his brother's family.

"Cora," he said, thoughtfully, lying back in the one comfortable armchair which his landlady provided for her victims, and smoking his favourite briar wood, "you and I are not likely to see much of each other while you are under Lady Penrith's protection."

"Why not?" she asked, wonderingly.

"Because her ladyship hates me like poison. Never mind why she hates me. It is an old story, and a long one. I don't reciprocate the feeling, and I am profoundly interested in the lady and all that concerns her. By the way, you keep a diary, of course? Most girls do."

"Do they? Then they must have more to write about than I have had since I left Madame Michon's. What should I put down? 'Tuesday: Poured out father's coffee. Went for a walk in the Green Park with the landlady's daughter. Began another novel, rather stupider than the last. Why does Mudie[11] send one the books one doesn't ask for, instead of the book one has been wanting for the last three weeks? Went to bed at half-past eleven. Father had not come home.' Do you think that sort of record would be worth keeping?"

"Happy the woman who has no history," answered her father sententiously. "Well, you will keep a diary in future, if you please,

Cora; and you will keep it in such a manner as will admit of your allowing me to read it. You will have plenty to record at Penrith House and Killander Castle. You will have her ladyship—a most interesting study, a poem and a history incarnate. I want you to observe her closely, and to write down everything that concerns her—her actions, sentiments, opinions, the people with whom she associates, and the esteem in which she holds them."

"Father," said Cora, looking at him with wide-open eyes and hardening lips, more earnestly than she had ever looked at him in her life before, "you want me to be a spy!"

"No, my dear; I only want you to be an observer. My interest in Lady Penrith is founded on the purest motives. I want to put an end to the feud between us, which is perilous for her and unpleasant for me. I know her miserably mated to my brother, who is—well, about as bad as they make 'em," continued Urquhart, taking refuge in slang. "I have no doubt I can be of use to her in the future—financially, in the protection of her fortune, and otherwise—and I can only serve her by watchfulness, personal or vicarious. It is just possible that this kindness to you means a change of feeling towards me—a holding out of the olive branch. So much the better if it does; but in any case you must watch for me, since I can't watch for myself. You will find out her friends and her enemies, and on which side the peril lies——"

"Will you assure me that you are her friend, and that no harm to her can come of anything I may tell you?"

"I do assure you that I am her friend. I will go further, and tell you that ten years ago I was her adoring lover. She refused me—her heart was buried in another man's grave—and a few months afterwards she married my elder brother. The match was of old Sir Joseph Higginson's making, I have no doubt. She accepted a coronet—with a wry face, perhaps, but accepted it, all the same, as women do. The old romantic feeling of mine died out of me long ago; but Sibyl Penrith is still a great deal nearer and dearer to me than any other woman, and I should like to help her if ever she have need of help. She is too rich not to be robbed; she is too handsome not to be tempted. You will be with her in a confidential capacity; you are keen enough to scent either danger, and to pass the warning on to me. You can send me your diary weekly."

"I can't understand how you can be of any use to her."

"I don't ask you to understand," replied Mr. Urquhart, with admirable nonchalance, puffing quietly at his briarwood.

CHAPTER II

CORA'S DIARY

I HARDLY know how I should dispose of my evening hours at Killander Castle, if father had not imposed this task of diary-keeping upon me. My aunt leaves the drawing-room as the clock strikes ten. I don't believe she goes to bed before midnight, but as she has never invited me to a "causerie"[1] in her room, and as she always wishes me a distinct good night in the gallery where we light our candles, I feel that solitude is my portion, and that I am left to my own resources till the next morning.

I have always been a wretched sleeper; and one of my worst miseries at Mme. Michon's was to hear the church clock chime the quarters all through the long dreary night, perhaps until five o'clock in the morning, when I dropped into the slumber of sheer exhaustion, and dreamt dreams that were darkened with the consciousness that the dressing bell would ring at six, and that I must be dressed and in the class-room at a quarter to seven. Oh, weary servitude! oh, joyless days and restless nights! When I find the wheels of life dragging somewhat heavily at Killander Castle, let me remember the dreary round of school work, the scanty fare of the school table, the burden of too frequent church services, and the ever-present consciousness that I was the worst-dressed girl in the school, and that my bills were always in arrear. I must, however, admit that Mme. Michon treated me fairly and kindly, after her lights, considering that she stood in danger of losing by me. It was Mme. Michon's pupils, on whom my poverty inflicted no inconvenience, who made me feel the agony of being poor. If I had not been the niece of an Earl, I think they would have trampled upon me. My blue blood went for something, and I took an aggressive attitude against every girl who represented the wealth made in commerce. Well, that is "an auld sang," thank heaven, and Lady Penrith; and I am here in this Cumbrian Castle, lapped in luxury, with fine raiment in my wardrobe, and plenty of pocket-money; and if the life is rather dull now I am not the less grateful to Providence and my uncle's wife. As for my uncle himself, of whose race I am, and on whom alone I have any claim, he throws me a word now and then as he might throw a biscuit to one of his spaniels, and cares less, I fancy, what may become of me than what may become of the dog. He is a curious man—handsome, in a certain faded style, like a portrait by an old master that has been spoilt in the cleaning. He is straight as a dart, tall, well set up. He is said to have the grand manner, which I take to be a manner of caring for nobody in the world but one's self.

At ten o'clock my aunt bids me good night in the long gallery leading to her rooms, and I cross the head of the great staircase, and retire to my own den, to yawn over a novel or to write my diary, till midnight.

Inclination would take me to the smoke-room, where I believe I should be not altogether unwelcome; for the men must have exhausted their stock of improper anecdotes by ten o'clock, and must have begun to grow tired of their own society. They have told me severally, and on different occasions, that I am good fun. How much I should prefer being "good fun" downstairs in that comfortable billiard-room, to moping up here over a dull novel, or my still duller diary!

The proprieties forbid me masculine society after ten o'clock; so to thee, O Diary, I turn, and try to interest myself in a study of character. Lady Penrith's character in particular.

There is a certain fascination, I find, even in the dullest diary, when it is about one's self—one's own feelings, likes and dislikes, odd fancies, rebellious promptings against Fate and Mrs. Grundy;[2] but it is not so interesting when one writes about other people. My father honoured me by expressing a desire to read my jottings about her ladyship; I have therefore commenced a system of diary-keeping by double entry. What I mean him to read I write in one volume; my own little reveries I keep to myself in another volume. I suppose he really was in love with Lady Penrith, years ago, when I was a child, moping my little life away in the depths of Yorkshire, with my middle-class maiden aunts. Yes, I suppose

he was really and honestly in love with her, and not attached to
her only on account of her wealth; and yet I can hardly imagine
my father a romantic lover, caring for anything above and beyond
his own interest. There is a hardness about him, just as there is
about his lordship, and which I should call the Urquhart hardness,
for I can see the same character indicated in many of the family
portraits on these walls—a cold, calm concentration of purpose
which I take to mean absolute selfishness. Yet it may be that even
a man of that hard nature might be moved to forget himself by
such a woman as Sibyl Penrith in the flush of her girlish beauty.
She is absolutely beautiful now at nine and twenty. She took me
to three very big parties before we left London, and she was the
handsomest woman amidst a crowd where I felt that to be plain
was to be conspicuous. Yes, any man might have loved and suffered
for such a woman; only I think Sir Joseph Higginson's coal-pits
would have more attraction for my father than the loveliest face
that ever shone upon mankind. In any case I can understand what
a bitter blow it must have been to him when she married his elder
brother.

I wonder who the man was who died—the man she loved—the
man in whose grave her heart is buried? Who was he, and where
is that grave where her heart lies dead and cold? Yes, I believe her
heart is with the dead. She goes through life like an animated
statue, coldly beautiful, benevolent, charitable, religious; polite
and amiable to a most unsympathetic husband; fulfilling all the
duties of that station to which it has pleased God to call her, and,
if I read her right, caring for nothing in the world except her books
and piano.

So much for my private opinions and speculations in volume
two; and now for my observations upon life in general and Lady
Penrith in particular in volume one, which, if my father insist, I
shall allow him to peruse.

CHAPTER III

CORA'S DIARY: FOR PATERNAL PERUSAL

WE have been at Killander Castle for more than two months, and there has not been an event worth recording, or, indeed, any circumstance that can be honoured with the name of an event, till this afternoon. The life here since the beginning of August has been as luxuriously monotonous as life on Tennyson's Lotos Island,[1] only we have not enjoyed such a climate as tempted Ulysses and his companions to a perpetual repose. The weather has been—distinctly British.

His lordship spent the latter half of August and a great part of September in Scotland—shooting. He arrived here towards the end of last month, bringing a few friends with him, for more shooting. My aunt declined Scotland for this autumn. She wanted nothing but rest, after a busy season. Killander is her most established home. Here she has her largest collection of books and music, her favourite Broadwood,[2] her finest garden and hothouses; here, in short, she has all the things in which a great lady with an empty heart can take delight. Here, too, she is within a drive or even a long walk of the house in which she was born, and the village where she knows every cottage and most of the inhabitants, from the bent old grandfather to the year-old baby. I have done a good deal of cottage-visiting with her since we came here; and I must confess that I find cottagers, with their everlasting woes and incurable ailments, utterly insupportable, and I am puzzled to understand the order of intellect which can take pleasure in personal contact with them.

To relieve their wants is a duty and an inclination which I can understand in a person as rich as Lady Penrith, who can never feel any the poorer for her beneficence; but surely there are clergymen's wives, and sisterhoods, and people that one could employ for all this dismal, uninteresting work, instead of bothering about every detail of every old woman's miserable existence, as my aunt does. However, all this twaddle seems to interest her, and I have to sit or stand by while she listens to long rigmaroles about rheumatics, or sick children, or drinking husbands, or sons out of work, or daughters that have gone wrong. It is one treadmill-round of human misery, to be mitigated by doles of such miserable amount—taken in relation to her ladyship's wealth—that they really might just as well be distributed by a bailiff, or homely drudge of a curate's wife. Why Lady Penrith should amuse herself by sympathising—or pretending to sympathise, for it can't be real—with all those squalid miseries I can no more understand than I can fathom the minds of those women who get up at half-past six every morning to attend matins, when they might enjoy the best hour of the day, the hour between waking and getting up, with a cup of strong tea and a volume of Guy de Maupassant's stories.[3]

I have never allowed my ennui or my sentiments to escape during the frequent martyrdom of this cottage-visiting. Far from it. I shake the dirtiest paws, sip the vilest tea, and win all hearts with my jolly-good-fellow manner, which has given the cottagers the idea that however sternly Conservative "The Castle" may be, Miss Urquhart is at heart a Radical.

Sometimes I have been tempted into wondering whether all this active benevolence, this sympathy with the sick and sorrowing poor, may not be a self-imposed penance on the part of Lady Penrith; the expiation of her maturer years for some sin of her girlhood. Yet, I cannot think that this passionless nature ever deviated from the straight path. Her character must have always been spotless; superior to every temptation. And, again, for a woman born rich there are so few temptations. Satan must offer so choice a bait when he fishes for the rich man's soul.

What other idiosyncrasies besides this regard for the poor have I observed in my aunt's character? First, her love of music, which amounts to a passion; secondly, her love of books, which astonishes me, books not being at all in my way. I never read a book when I can get a newspaper; and I infinitely prefer *Truth* and the *World* to any of the authors who are called classics. Nor do I see that book-learning is of the slightest use to any young woman who does not want to write school-books or go out as a governess. The little I have seen of masculine society has shown me that men detest "culture" in a woman. The men who go in for learning themselves hate a rival in their own field. Scholars don't want sympathy from women. They want blind admiration. And the average man—a monster of ignorance about everything that is not in the news-papers—shrinks from a well-informed woman as from a drawing-room pestilence. To please the sterner sex a woman should know just enough of politics to be able to listen intelligently to the old fogies and middle-aged bores, and enough about sport and society scandals to be able to carry on a touch-and-go conversation with a young man of average intellect. She may say a smart thing now and then, but she must never pretend to be a wit. She must accept her position as man's inferior, and honour and revere her sultan.

If my father favours me by reading the last remarks he will perceive that I have taken his lessons in worldly wisdom to heart, and that I am studying how to please a potential husband. There is one here, Mr. Coverdale, Lord Workington's only son, who would be well worth pleasing—but, alas, alas, penniless and plain must shoot at lesser game.

To return to Lady Penrith. She is a reading woman, and her morning room is lined with books, all of her own collection, and entirely distinct from the orthodox library of standard authors on the ground floor. I amused myself a few days ago, while I was waiting to go out driving with her, by a careful study of these books. I have been told to study the lady's character, and some part of her character must reveal itself in the books she chooses.

I found poetry strongly represented by poets old and new. Byron, Shelley, Keats, Browning, and Tennyson are lavishly spread along the shelves, in various editions, with a richness of binding and variety of style that mark the lady's appreciation. Milton and Shakespeare are equally honoured. The poets fill a large section of the bookcases near the fireplace; and on this side of the room my aunt has her favourite armchair, tea-table, and Japanese screen. If anything could make me fond of reading, it would be such a room as this. The novelists are here also,—Scott, Dickens, Thackeray, Lytton, George Eliot, and here and there a volume by a lesser light. Then come biography, history, criticism, metaphysics. My aunt seems to have taken all learning for her province, as somebody says of himself. One block of books especially interested me—for they suggested a warm interest in a subject which I should consider very remote from Lady Penrith's line of thought. On the shelves below the poets, and within reach of her hand as she sits in her low *bergère*,[4] I found a collection of books upon African travel and African sport, from Livingstone[5] downwards. I never saw so many books upon one subject in any library I ever looked at.

I ask myself, with natural wonder, how and why a woman who is utterly indifferent to sport in England and Scotland should be keenly interested in sport in Africa; why a woman who has travelled very little in Europe should be interested in books of travel in that uncivilized quarter of the globe. The only answer to the riddle which offers itself to my mind is that the lady's interest in Africa is vicarious, and that the man to whom she gave her heart in youth was in some manner associated with the dark continent. I have found her poring over Burton or Cameron, Stanley or Baker,[6] in the lazy hour between afternoon tea and the dressing bell. I once ventured to ask her how she could find enjoyment in books which to me appeared essentially dull and dry, and she looked up with her sweet smile, and answered—

"There is not a single page in these books without interest for me, Cora."

"And would you like to travel in Africa?"

"Dearly."

"Why don't you, then?"

She gave a faint sigh before she answered.

"Hardly any woman could run the risks and endure the hardships to which these men exposed themselves; and if any woman could, the world would not let her do it. My duties are at home."

"Were I you, I would hold every duty subordinate to my own whim," said I. "If I wanted to roam about African deserts, and ride across African swamps, and see the Falls of the Zambesi[7] or the Mountains of the Moon,[8] nothing should prevent me. I would defy opinion, as Lady Hester Stanhope[9] did."

I like to tease her about her wealth and its omnipotence sometimes. I think it is the sting of conscious poverty which goads me to remind her what a power she possesses, and how poor a use she makes of it.

How deeply sad her face was while she spoke of Africa! Yes, that is the charm. Her lover must have been a wanderer in those wild pathways. The next time I found myself alone in her morning room I made a further examination of her African collection. I looked for any volumes by less familiar names, thinking that among these I might find some book written by the man she loved. Very few men travel much in strange lands without delivering themselves of a book. Sooner or later the thirst for paper and print takes possession of them. They hunt up their old journals and random records of sport, and eke out their own scanty materials with plagiarism from Burton or Stanley.

I found one volume—a thinnish octavo—which attracted me for two reasons. Firstly, it was more delicately bound than any of the other books. Secondly, it showed signs of having been more read.

The title was unpretentious—"My African Apprenticeship." The name of the author was Brandon Mountford; the year of publication 1874—just twelve years ago.

On the fly-leaf I found a brief inscription—"From B. M. to S. H. May 6, 1876."

B. M., of course, stands for the author; S. H., for Sibyl Higginson. It was not till the following year that Sir Joseph Higginson's daughter became Lady Penrith. Dear little book, to give me such precise information about yourself. "B. M. to S. H." Only a lover would write thus. Anyone upon ceremonious terms would have written, "From the author."

I looked into the pages. The usual thing! Descriptions of scenery, descriptions of storms, sunsets, sunrises, aurora borealis, wonderful effects of sky. Perils of being eaten by savages or wild beasts. Perils of having nothing to eat. Lion-shooting, fever, friendly natives. Nothing of personal history to tell me what manner of man Brandon Mountford was. But that vellum-bound book, with its delicately tooled edges and gold lettering, and with leaves that opened so easily, with here and there a rose-petal or a withered violet, told me one fact for certain. Whatever "B. M." may have been—saint or sinner—Sibyl Higginson loved him, and Sibyl Penrith cherishes his memory.

Oh, irony of Fate, that one woman should own over a million, and sit in her lonely room brooding over a dead man's book, while thousands of women in the world are striving and wrestling to get themselves decently married for the sake of food and raiment, a shelter, and a fireside! Had I a tenth part of Lady Penrith's money, what a variety of pleasures, excitements, and enjoyments I would wring out of this too brief existence of ours!

I peeped into the billiard-room after lunch to-day, and saw Mr. Coverdale knocking about the balls by himself in a low-spirited way, so I lingered in the room for a few minutes, looking for last week's *Punch*, and presently he invited me to play a fifty with him. He is a poor player, and I am a poor player, though I have done my possible to make up for the deficiencies of my education by playing whenever anybody condescends to ask me, and by practising whenever I can get the table to myself. The fifty took a longish time, for besides our slow scoring, the honourable and reverend John was in an expansive humour, and talked a good deal of his views, which are ritualistic to a degree that verges upon Romanism. I humoured him to the utmost—indeed, in religious matters I am ritualistic if I am anything—and we had a really interesting conversation, in which I seemed to get more in sympathy with this cold pattern of propriety than I have ever been before. Indeed, as we put our cues into the rack he made me a little reproachful speech which was to my mind a compliment.

"You are like St. Paul at least in one attribute, Miss Urquhart," he said. "You can be all things to all men. No one who heard you talking slang with the shooters yesterday would anticipate your delightful conversation to-day."

Now observe, O author of my being, that your daughter's delightful conversation had chiefly consisted in holding her tongue. I had let him talk, and only said just so much as was necessary to lead him on to descant at large upon the theme he loves. Intelligent listening means sympathy, comprehension, everything, to a talking man.

The clock struck three. My aunt generally drives out at three o'clock, and as a rule I go with her. It is one of my duties, or privileges, whichever I like to call it. I rushed up to my room, put on jacket and hat, snatched a pair of gloves, and flew downstairs to the hall and out to the great flight of steps which approaches this stately castle.

The barouche was at the door, and my aunt was already

seated in it. At sight of my flying figure on the steps, the footman descended from his perch, and opened the carriage door. In another minute I was seated at her ladyship's side.

"I did not know you were coming with me, Cora," she said, and I detected a shade of annoyance in her tone.

Offended at my unpunctuality, no doubt, thought I; but it struck me afterwards that upon this particular afternoon she wanted to be alone.

I apologised for my late appearance, and she affected an interest in my account of Mr. Coverdale's conversation: but I could see that her mind was otherwhere, and that she spoke at random.

We drove to Cargill, a village on the seaward side of the great dreary moor which separates Killander Castle from all the civilised world northward of its walls. Her ladyship stopped the carriage at the first house in the village.

"I am going to some of the cottages, Cora," she said, "but I shan't stay long in any of them. Would you like to sit in the carriage till I have done? There is the *Nineteenth Century*[10] to amuse you."

She pointed to a half-cut magazine on the empty seat. I hate those learned periodicals which presuppose a corresponding erudition on the part of the reader: and the notion that Lady Penrith did not want my company gave a stimulus to my curiosity. I jumped out of the carriage with alacrity.

"I had much rather see your cottagers than read the *Nineteenth Century*," said I.

We went into several cottages, with the usual result. Ailments, rheumatic and internal, sore legs, swollen faces, all the disagreeables of life—sons out of work, husbands given to drink—the old, old story. My aunt was sympathetic, took note of all necessities, and promised relief. In all this I could see nothing out of the beaten track; but I observed that in every cottage she asked the same questions about a man she had seen upon the moor on the previous afternoon, a man who looked like a shepherd, very ragged and poor, and, as she thought, not altogether right in his mind. No one was able to identify the person she described, though many suggestions, more or less wide of the mark, were offered. She exhibited wonderful pertinacity in this inquiry, and we went from hovel to hovel till I was heartily sick of the subject. What did I care for a ragged man who was or was not of weak intellect?

"I should like to help this poor creature," said my aunt; and she charged every one of whom she inquired to make it his or her business to find the ragged personage, in order that he might be clothed, and put in the way of being restored to his right mind.

"Is there any asylum for lunatics in the neighbourhood from which the man could have escaped?" she asked of an elderly woman, who had given more signs of intelligence than the other aboriginals she had questioned.

"None nearer than Durrock, and that's a good forty mile from here."

The search was evidently hopeless, and my aunt's benevolent intentions were to bear no fruit. The afternoon was cold and windy, with that parching east wind which is harmful alike to complexion and temper. I felt that my nose was blue, and I knew that I was in a very acrimonious state of mind.

The change from stuffy cottages to the bleak outer air was too trying to have been patiently endured by a saint; yet Lady Penrith seemed alike unconscious of the nipping cold outside and of the frowsy warmth within.

Not contented with this wearisome house to house inquiry, she drove a long round on our way home in order to repeat her questions at half a dozen isolated cottages; and it was nearly dark before the towering bulk of the Penriths' stronghold appeared across the grey distance. I never look at that mediæval castle without a faint pang of envy, which no amount of recently acquired wealth, much as I adore money, could inspire. That legacy of past ages stirs the small modicum of romance in my nature. I envy Lady Penrith the possession of that fine old fortress; and I am proud to think I am one of the race whose forbears held it in the days when every great nobleman was a warrior chieftain; proud to think that I am descended from ancestors who fought for king and country, when England was young and bold and warlike, rather than from some plodding lawyer who won his peerage in the dust and din of the law courts, and by subserviency to the powers that be.

So you see, father, you who are of the world worldly, there is a thin thread of romance still running through the warp and weft of your daughter's character. All your lessons in the craft that rules mankind have not extinguished my reverence for the past, and my belief in the value of ancient lineage—a value in one's own secret estimate of one's self, the feeling that, come what may, one is better than the ruck of mankind, better inherently, by a superiority which dates from the Crusades, and which no achievement of newly made wealth can cancel.

I contrived to suppress all demonstrations of vexation during that long, cold drive, with its circuitous extensions, but I could not quite restrain my curiosity.

"You must have some special reason for being interested in this ragged man, I should think, aunt, by your earnestness in searching for him," I said, when we had turned our backs upon a wretched stone hovel, half hidden in a dip of the moor.

"You are right, Cora; I have a reason," she answered quietly, and in a tone that forbade further questioning.

I hugged myself in my sealskin jacket and muff—her gifts—and told myself that I must wait for time and chance to show me the nature of her reason. It must be a very strong one—if I have any power to read her face.

All the resources of my intelligence are henceforth pledged to the solution of this social mystery. I have very little to think about, now that the all-absorbing question of ways and means has been made easy for me; and for want of interest in my own insignificant existence I am naturally thrown upon speculations about my aunt.

If John Coverdale would only condescend to fall in love with me life would take different colours—would change from dull, uniform grey to the brilliant variety of the rainbow. Not that I am in love with that handsome pattern of propriety, mark you; but every girl wants a lover. The conquest of man is woman's mission—the only mission worth a woman's thought; and not to be admired and loved is to be outside the pale.

I am plain, let me not forget that—plain, but not repulsive. I have good eyes and teeth, and you have told me that my face lights up when I talk, that my complexion improves by candlelight, and that I have a quality which you call "chien,"[11] and which is not without its charm for the opposite sex, especially the duller

members of that sex, who are apt to be caught by smartness and
gumption in a woman. This much of praise have you given me, O
my father, in the course of our conversations across the morning
coffee and rasher.

Am I smart, have I gumption, I wonder? I recall the stories I
have heard of plain women and their conquests; and it appears to
me that the unbeautiful have been very often winners in the race.
One hears of men who forsake lovely wives to go to perdition for
plain and even elderly mistresses. One hears of men who line their
bachelor rooms with pictures of beautiful women—who go about
declaring that only perfect loveliness can charm them—and who
unite themselves in lifelong union with sallow complexions and
snub noses.

I will remember all these anomalies when I am inclined to
despair of my own fortunes. And in the meantime I will devote
my leisure to the study of my aunt's character.

She has been very good to me, and I ought to love her dearly.
There are times when I tell myself that I do so love her; and then,
perhaps, a cold wave of doubt comes over me. She is so handsome,
so calm and self-possessed; she has been so favoured by Fortune
and Nature in all those respects where I have been hardly used. Is
it human in me to love her? More especially when I much doubt
if she has any affection for me? She is a woman whose life is ruled
by fixed principles and ideas. I believe she endures me and protects
me, just as she goes to church on bleak, uncomfortable mornings,
because the thing is a duty and has to be done.

CHAPTER IV

A MARIAGE DE CONVENANCE

Two and thirty years before that bleak October afternoon on which
Coralie Urquhart descanted in her journal, Sir Joseph Higginson,
of Arlington Street and Ellerslie Park, startled his friends and neighbours by an aristocratic alliance, and the bringing home of a lovely
girl-wife to reign over his country house near Ardliston. Sir Joseph
was forty-nine years of age at the time of his marriage, plain of face

and clumsy of figure; but he was one of the wealthiest pit-owners
in the North of England, and, if his immediate surroundings were
surprised at this union, society in London regarded the marriage
as the most natural thing in life. Here was the Earl of Allandale,
on the one part, with a large family, the offspring of two poorly
dowered wives; and here was a millionaire of mature years, against
whose position nothing could be said except that he had made it
for himself; and against whose moral character no slander had ever
reached the ear of the great world. Decidedly, pronounced society,
Lord Allandale had done wisely in uniting his youngest daughter—
youngest of a family of eleven—to Sir Joseph Higginson.

The young lady herself was never heard to complain. Whatever dream she had cherished of a different union was a dream
that had found its own tearful ending before she saw the lord
of those Cumbrian pits. She was told that her acceptance of Sir
Joseph would be advantageous to her family, as well as an assurance of high fortune to herself. He could help her brothers, some
of whom were public officials, while the more enterprising of the
band dabbled in trade and exhibited their patrician name upon the
prospectuses of newly launched companies. She, as his wife, could
be useful to her sisters, since his spacious mansion in Arlington
Street would offer a better stage for matrimonial efforts than the
somewhat shabby old house in Mayfair, which the Mountfords
maintained with a struggle, and whose chief merit was to be found
in certain unsavoury traditions of old-world scandals, duels, elope-
ments, family quarrels, forced marriages, which clung to the panelled walls of those low-ceiled rooms in which Lord Allandale's
ancestors had lived, and loved, and hated, and suffered for more
than two centuries. Lord Allandale professed an affectionate pride
in the house because his family had held it so long; but he was fain
to confess that it was inconvenient and insanitary, and that it cost
him a "plaguy lot of money" to keep the roof from tumbling in
and the windows from falling out.

"If I were to sell the old gazabo[1] to a pork-butcher from
Chicago he would pull it down and build a little palace on the site,
or scoop out the inside and restore it in the style of the seventeenth
century," said his lordship; "but I shan't part with it while I have a
shot in the locker, and we must pig in it as best we can."

Pigging was not an elegant expression, but it seemed hardly inappropriate, for the upper floors were divided into bed-chambers not much larger than a modern pigsty, and of inconvenient shapes for the most part, in which the Ladies Mountford and their honourable brothers were almost as crowded as an Irish peasant's household amid the fertile fields of Kerry. For compensation they had Basingstoke House, a great barrack in Hampshire, on a windy hill westward of Basingstoke, where there were five and thirty inconvenient bedrooms.

Lady Lucy Mountford submitted to fate, in the person of Sir Joseph Higginson, and became at once mistress of the house in Arlington Street, palatial, splendid, rich in all things that make the outward grace and glory of life, and of Ellerslie Park, in Cumberland, a colossal Tudor mansion, designed by an architect of the highest fashion, who would not suffer the smallest alteration of his plans. It had been discovered, or at any rate alleged, later that the fashionable architect was a fraud, that his Tudor houses were none of them genuinely Tudor, but only Tudoresque, and that he had stolen his flashiest ideas from the sober Flemings of Antwerp and Ghent. Notwithstanding which condemnation from the ever-advancing critic, who is always getting beyond the perfection of yesterday, Ellerslie was a remarkable house in a very fine situation, with turrets and broad embayed windows that looked wide over land and sea.

Sir Joseph owned most of the land to be seen from those windows, and he owned a whole district of collieries and colliers' cottages, which were happily unseen by the inmates of Ellerslie, and which lay in the furthermost dip of the long, low hill. He was the wealthiest man and the largest landowner in that part of the county, and he was not without his enemies—no prosperous man ever escapes the hatred of the unsuccessful. "It is the bright day that brings forth the adder." Sir Joseph was as popular as most county magistrates and employers of labour; but it was said of him that he was a hard man, and that he never accepted less than twelve pence for his shilling. He had begun life as a toiler in those pits of which he was now owner. It was said of him that everything he touched turned to gold; that he had Satan's luck as well as his own; but this is an assertion commonly made about every

man who from small beginnings attains to gigantic wealth. The
world sees only the speculator's success, but does not see, or at
least readily forgets, the failures and disappointments that made
the game of speculation difficult. It keeps no count of the hours
of heart-sinking when the fortune already won trembled in the
balance, and when it was only by hazarding all that the game could
be saved. Joseph Higginson was talked of as a modern Midas;[2] and
very few people knew or remembered what arduous stages there
had been on that long uphill road to the pinnacle of success. He
knew and remembered that he had been more than once on the
verge of bankruptcy, and that he had more than once risked the
game of life upon a single throw. He had shown himself a man of
infinite resources, keen observation, and he was said to have had
the gift of prophecy in a degree granted to but few financiers.

He had reached the age of forty-nine, ostensibly a bachelor,
and had gratified his nephews and nieces, most of whom he had
helped to rise considerably from their original status, by the assertion, often repeated, that he never would marry, when a chance
meeting in the board-room of an insurance company, where he
was chairman, brought about an acquaintance with Lord Allandale, who was one of the directors. Your impecunious nobleman
is apt to incline towards the low-born millionaire, and Allandale
flattered Sir Joseph by telling him how much he had heard about
his work in the North, and how interested he was in seeing the
man who had done such good work. An invitation to a little dinner
at his lordship's house in Hertford Street followed a few days later.
It was a man's dinner, and Sir Joseph hardly hoped to see the ladies
of the family; but four out of the party of six left soon after ten
o'clock—three to go to the House, where there was an important
division coming on, and the fourth to look in at three or four smart
dances—whereupon Lord Allandale proposed an adjournment to
the drawing-room.

"I don't know whether you know my wife," he said. "She goes
out a good deal more than I do?"

"I have met her ladyship at parties, but I have never had the
honour of an introduction," answered Sir Joseph, meekly.

"Come up and be introduced now," said the Earl, cheerily. Sir
Joseph laid down his half-smoked cigar in the old Derby dessert-

plate. He had observed that in noble families, however impecunious, one always found old china and Queen Anne silver, to excite the
envy of the newly rich. He laid down his cigar, and pulled himself
together, smoothing down the wrinkles in his white waistcoat.

He was a stout man, short-necked, broad-shouldered, and
always wore a white waistcoat, whether the thing were in or out
of fashion, excellent or intolerable. He followed his host up the
narrow Mayfair staircase, which was decorated with those shabby
family pictures and engravings of country houses which indicate
widespread connexions and a long history. How different, he
thought, to his staircase in Arlington Street, where all was newly
splendid, created at a blow, by one sweep of the upholsterer's hand!
Here, portraits, miniatures, battle-pieces in which Mountfords had
figured, views of country seats, were stuck about anyhow upon
casual nails.

The drawing-room, low and roomy, occupying the whole of
the first floor, seemed full of women; and yet there was no one
but Lady Allandale and her daughters, a flock of young women
in gauzy white gowns, with a general impression of white azalias
and ostrich feathers, standing about before the looking-glasses,
pluming themselves ready for conquest, while they waited for the
big family carriage that was to take them to a ball. They reminded
Sir Joseph of a group of beautiful swans, pruning their plumage
on the bosom of a summer lake. He was lost in admiration of the
general effect, rather than of individual beauty; he could scarcely
command his attention while he was being introduced to a large
lady in peach-coloured brocade and diamonds, who was putting
on a glove which seemed decidedly too small for the fat and jew-
elled hand it was required to cover. The hand came out of the
glove, and offered itself in the friendliest way to Sir Joseph.

"I think Sir Joseph and I knew each other very well before to-
night, though we had not been introduced," said Lady Allandale.
"You were sitting next me at luncheon the day they launched the
Harmonia, I remember. And we were near neighbours at Lady
Downton's big dinner-party the other day."

Sir Joseph assented smilingly. He adored a peeress, wherever
he met one.

"I had the honour of taking in Lady Hetherington."

"What, Amanda, my step-daughter? She is always charming. Let me introduce you to my daughters, Sir Joseph. Lady Selina, Lady Laura, Lady Jane, Lady Rosina."

The four white swans smilingly accepted the introduction, with gracious bendings of slender throats. Lady Selina was the eldest of the brood, a very mature swan. The room was too dimly lighted to allow Sir Joseph to note the difference in their ages. The Mountfords were a race renowned for good looks, and to the millionaire's eye the four sisters appeared equally beautiful. And then he suddenly perceived a girl sitting at the piano, in a pale blue cashmere flock— pale blue was a favourite colour thirty years ago—a girl with her hair swept back from her fair sweet face in a careless bunch of long loose curls, tied with a blue ribbon; a girl in whose young face and candid eyes, looking up at him across the piano, he saw a loveliness infinitely beyond the grandiose beauty of the four swans.

"That is my youngest daughter, Sir Joseph," said Lady Allandale, following his eyes. "She has not yet left the schoolroom."

Lady Lucy rose shyly, embarrassed by the gaze of Sir Joseph's great brown eyes, eyes that reminded her of a friendly ox in Basingstoke Park. She and Sir Joseph stood looking at each other for a few moments, equally embarrassed, almost as if some instinct of mind or heart foreshadowed the union of their lives.

She gave him her hand, tremulously, under the spell of his earnest gaze, or the presage of her fate. The youngest of many daughters is doomed to flower late, and Lady Lucy, despite her cashmere frock and schoolroom status, was nineteen; and had her own little history, not altogether of the schoolroom; a history which gave a touch of pathos to the lily-face.

"A lovely young creature, but I'm afraid she's rather sickly," was Sir Joseph's unspoken commentary.

He was only allowed ten minutes in this elysium of fashionable houris.[3] Her ladyship's carriage was announced, and the white daughters crowded down the staircase, followed by the ampler mother, on whose footsteps Sir Joseph and Lord Allandale attended.

Sir Joseph paused on the landing, while her ladyship's bulky form was slowly descending, and addressed himself in parting speech to the damsel from the schoolroom—

"I'm afraid you must feel very envious of your sisters at such a moment as this, Lady Lucy," he said.

"I don't see why all girls should be supposed to be fond of dancing," she answered rather pettishly. "I don't care about it."

"And you are not longing for next season, when you will be presented, I suppose?"

"No."

"Lucy has seen too much of it all, from the outside," said Lord Allandale, patting the graceful shoulder in the blue frock. "She is disillusioned before her time. Come, Sir Joseph, if you really mean to vote with your party to-night, you'd better be off. Your carriage has been at the door for the last half-hour."

This was the beginning of Sir Joseph's acquaintance with Lady Lucy Mountford. They were married early in the ensuing season, at the church in Piccadilly, while daffodils were still blooming in the Basingstoke meadows. It was a very grand wedding, and all London talked of the marriage; some people descanting on the cruelty and wickedness of so ill-assorted a union; others expatiating upon the wonderful match Lord Allandale had secured for his portionless youngest; and a third section declaring that he ought to have done better for her.

"A girl of such remarkable beauty ought to have looked higher than a man who began life in a coal-pit," said one of Lady Allandale's dearest friends.

"But if the man has got out of the pit and made a big fortune in coals, I don't think a woman with five daughters need complain of her luck," said another.

"A woman with five daughters ought to consider herself lucky when she gets off one of the five," remarked a third matron, with some asperity, being herself the mother of an only daughter and reputed beauty, who had been hawked all through England and over half the Continent of Europe without satisfactory result.

The Allandales were content with their bargain, and so was Sir Joseph. He had taken pains to make himself agreeable to the young lady in every manner that came within the limits of his capacity. He had consulted her tastes and feelings, deferred to her wishes, and had let her understand that the life she was to lead with him would be a life of perfect independence and wide liberty. She was

to be, not his slave, but his queen. She laughed at first at the idea
of Sir Joseph as her adorer, and in her girlish talk with her sisters
treated the whole affair as a joke; but his earnestness and honesty
were not without their influence upon her mind, and after a long
and serious conversation with her mother, in which Lady Allandale
lifted the decent veil which had been spread over the financial position of the family, and showed her youngest daughter the bleak
and barren prospect which lay before her and her sisters, unless
some of them married well and were able to help the others, Lady
Lucy gave a resigned sigh, and promised that she would try to like
Sir Joseph well enough to marry him.

Lucy adored her mother, and was fond of her sisters, though
they were of the world worldly. She had dreamed her dream,
and had done with all such dreams for ever, she told herself. Sir
Joseph's rugged honesty of purpose had won her esteem; and if
it were indeed her destiny to marry for the welfare of her family,
and to lessen the burden upon her father's dwindling income, it
would be well for her that she should marry an honest man, whom
she could at least respect; love being for evermore impossible. She
had seen the young men of her mother's circle, seen them from
her privileged position as a young person still in the schoolroom,
who was free to sit in the background, and look on as at a play;
and she had been impressed by their shallowness and self-assur-
ance. She preferred the conversation of Sir Joseph, who sometimes
misplaced an aspirate, but who always talked sensibly, and never
pretended to more knowledge than he possessed, to the vacuous
slang of youth that had graduated on suburban racecourses, learnt
dancing at after midnight clubs, and received its final polish in
London music halls.

When Sir Joseph, after wooing her in his own fashion with
supreme delicacy, asked her in simplest language to be his wife, she
answered with a gentle candour which completed his subjugation.
She told him that she had given her whole heart away a year ago in
a happy summertide at Basingstoke House—given it unasked, and
almost unaware of her own feelings, till she awoke to the bitterness and despair of having loved a man who never wooed her, and
who was not free to be her lover.

She told her little story of a girl's romance falteringly, and towards the end with tears, which she struggled heroically to suppress.

"I am afraid he guessed my wretched secret," she said, burning blushes suffusing cheek and brow, as she sat by Sir Joseph's side with lowered eyelids, one cold and trembling hand clasped in those broad, sinewy hands of his, which had never lost the markings of early toil. "I am afraid he read my heart only too well. We are distant cousins, Sir Joseph, and he was almost as familiar as a brother would have been. One day he said very seriously that he had a secret to tell me. I had seen for ever so long that he was unhappy, that the shadow of some hidden grief would creep over him in the midst of our gaiety, when everything in life seemed made for happiness. I was hardly surprised when he told me that he was a miserable man. Early in life, before he left the university, he had married foolishly. That one word was all he ever said to me about his marriage. He had never owned that marriage to his people; but he had done his duty, or, at least, he hoped he had done his duty to his wife. A son was born, and soon after his birth the poor mother went out of her mind, and then her husband found that there had been madness in her family. He had done what was right, he assured me. He had placed her in the best and kindest care, and he had hoped for her recovery, although the doctors gave him little ground for hope. Years had gone by, and the case was now pronounced hopeless. Her mind was gone, but her physical health promised long life. There was no such thing as divorce in such a case as this. He was her husband to the end of his life."

"Did he tell you that he loved you?" asked Sir Joseph, under his breath.

"No, no, no," protested the girl eagerly. "Not by one word, not by one look."

"Then he is a good man, and deserves a better fate. God reward you, my dear, for having opened your heart to me. I am not afraid to try and guard that pure heart from every temptation that can assail an old man's wife—if you only like me well enough to trust yourself to my loving care, Lucy."

"If I am to marry at all I would rather be your wife than anyone else's," she answered gravely; and thus ended Sir Joseph's courtship.

From that hour till the last hour of her life Lady Lucy never complained of her portion in this world. Sir Joseph kept his promise in the spirit as well as to the letter. He was a devoted husband, and his wife reigned as a queen in that northern settlement where the name of Higginson was a charm to conjure with. She had her model village, where even the men and boys who worked in the pits were able to live with some degree of comfort. She had her schools, and a church of her own creation, built and endowed at Sir Joseph's cost; her cottage hospital; her almshouses for the aged and helpless. Within that small kingdom she was worshipped as a saint; and in Arlington Street she was able to hold her own with her contemporaries and equals in the social maelström, while she had the proud privilege of helping three of her sisters to marry creditably and comfortably, and thereby to reflect honour upon the house of Mountford. If, having married rank rather than money, those ladies were inclined to look down upon their worthy brother-in-law, Sir Joseph never allowed resentment to harden his heart or tighten his purse-strings against them or their belongings. He let the husbands fish in his salmon river and shoot his pheasants, and he let the wives ride his horses, and recuperate their exhausted energies in the comfort of his country house. He never refused to become sponsor for any of the numerous babies, nor ever withheld the expected goblet or porringer of solid gold. In a word, he used his wealth in a large-minded fashion, and succeeded in being talked of by his four sisters-in-law throughout the length and breadth of society as "a dear old thing."

Sir Joseph had been married nearly three years when a son and heir was born in the great grey Tudor house at Ellerslie, a son whose advent brought joy unspeakable to the father's great, honest heart; but this flower in the garden of domestic life was a pale and fragile blossom, and drooped and withered before the end of a year. In the following year there came a daughter, but the father, who had seen his hopes blasted, was slow to let his love go out to this new-comer. He was afraid of loving her too well, lest he should be called upon to suffer the anguish of a second bereavement.

The girl-baby throve, however, and was the delight of her mother's life, the all-absorbing occupation and amusement of Lady Lucy's happiest years. Millais'[4] picture of mother and daughter hangs in the hall of Killander Castle, to which mansion it was transferred after Sir Joseph's death—the portrait of a woman in the full flush of mature beauty, with a tall, willowy girl, in a pinafore, leaning against her mother's shoulder, with sunny tresses ruffled as after some childish sport, and solemn, dreaming eyes—the eyes which, shining starlike in the baby face, had won for her the name of Sibyl.

Sibyl was eleven when that picture was painted, and before her twelfth birthday the picture was all that remained to Sir Joseph of his loved and lovely wife. She died in the pride of her strength and beauty, being thrown out of the light phaeton which she had driven for years in perfect safety. A nervous horse, a narrow road, a great coal-waggon in the way, and swift, sudden death for the woman whom Sir Joseph Higginson had worshipped with unwavering devotion from the hour she laid her hand in his and accepted him as her husband. If she had not given him the love that youth gives to youth, she had at least been true and steadfast through all their years of wedded life. She had shown no sign of weariness or disgust, she had never depreciated her husband or hinted at her own superiority, by right of early training and patrician birth. She had carried with meekness, and yet with dignity, the power which great wealth gives to the mistress of a household. Her husband's life had been rounded into perfect harmony by this woman; and in losing her it seemed to Joseph Higginson as if there were nothing left for his grey hairs but to go down in sorrow to the grave.

He was of too tough a fibre for grief to kill. He went on living somehow, though the light was quenched in the lamp, and the music was dead in the lute. He tried to comfort himself with the love of his daughter, his only child and heiress, Sibyl, who grew in beauty as the years ripened and waned. She was very tender and devoted to him, but she could not fill the empty place in his heart. One only had he loved with the whole strength of his rugged nature, and she was gone. He took to money-making as the one pursuit that brought distraction, occupation, fatigue of brain, and soothing sleep as the sequence of labour. He had long ago made his fortune and ruled off the total of a life's industry, eminently satisfied with the result; but now he entered himself afresh in the race for gold, and, stung by the grief that gnawed his heartstrings

he who had been hitherto cautious in all his investments speculated wildly, and by a curious irony of fate was successful in every
enterprise. During those years of his widowhood his name was a
power on the Stock Exchange, and men flung their money eagerly
into any scheme in which he was interested. He was said to have
trebled his fortune in that headlong race. To him the business of
money-getting had superseded every other interest, personal or
general. The Stock Exchange was his card-table, and he played the
game of speculation with all the passionate concentration of the
habitual gambler—the man who is a gambler, and nothing else.

During this period of financial activity Sir Joseph lived for
two-thirds of each year in Arlington Street, preferring to be near
the scene of action, within a half-hour drive of the actual money
market; but his mines were still something to him, and he spent
the last of the summer months and the whole of the autumn at
Ellerslie Park, where Sibyl lived with her two governesses, Miss
Minchin, a homely English person who had been with her pupil
from the nursery days of reading lessons in words of one syllable, and Fräulein Stahlherz, an accomplished Hanoverian, who
was familiar with almost every phrase of Wagner's orchestration,
played all Beethoven's sonatas that are playable on the pianoforte,
knew Goethe and Schiller by heart, and was mistress of French
and Italian, to say nothing of English, which she spoke more cor-
rectly than anyone else at Ellerslie. Under this lady's conscientious
tuition, and with the faithful Minchin to minister to her comforts,
look after her health, see that she never sat in damp boots or suffered
from chilblains, that the dentist was consulted at regular intervals,
and that tonics were exhibited at the least indication of languor,
Sibyl had grown to eighteen years of age before it occurred to her
father that she was a young woman, and that she had a right to
take her place in the world as his daughter. She would have to be
presented at Court, and introduced to society, that society upon
which Sir Joseph had persistently turned his back ever since his
wife's death.

The idea of this necessity worried and embarrassed him. His
wife's mother, Lady Allandale, was dead, and her son's wife, Lady
Braemar, was a person whose house was eminently fashionable,
but by no means the most fitting house for girlish innocence.

Sir Joseph felt that the time was at hand when he must provide a chaperon for his daughter. There was one ready to his hand in the person of her spinster aunt, Lady Selina Mountford, a lady of small means, very well received in the very best circles, and familiar with all the works and ways of the great world.

He felt the difficulty of the position all the more because there was somebody else to be thought of at Ellerslie: a young woman who, without Sir Joseph having ever intended as much, had become in somewise an adopted elder sister of Sibyl's, who had shared all the privileges of Fräulein Stahlherz's erudition, and some slender portion of Miss Minchin's assiduity, and who, albeit seven years older than Sibyl, was still young enough to feel the contrast between the social importance of the great heiress and her own insignificance.

A year after Lady Lucy's death the two governesses and their pupil were startled one dull wintry afternoon by the appearance of a mouldy leathern vehicle, drawn by a knock-kneed bay horse, and popularly known in the district as the station fly. On the box of the station fly, and almost obscuring the driver, was a large grey trunk, metal bound, and of foreign aspect.

Governesses and pupil stared at this phenomenon from the bay window of the spacious schoolroom, and as they stared the elderly coachman descended painfully from his box and opened the door of the vehicle, whereupon there came out of the leathern darkness a young fresh face, with rose-red cheeks and sloe-black eyes, and a bush of black hair brushed upward from a broad, square forehead.

This bright and vivid countenance was set upon the well-shaped figure of a young woman who might be any age between eighteen and twenty-five. She was tall, broad-chested, with finely rounded arms that showed under her close-fitting black stuff gown. She was clad wholly in black, a dense black which looked like deep mourning, although she wore no crape. Her dress was plain to Puritanism.

"She must be a new housemaid," said Miss Minchin; "but Ball ought to know better than to bring her to the hall door."

Ball had dragged the stranger's trunk up the steps into the

porch by this time, while the footman looked on. The newcomer disappeared within the great stone porch; Ball, the flyman, clambered on to the box; the fly drove off, and Sibyl and her governesses went back to their various occupations—Fräulein to the perusal of the last number of the *Rundschau*, Miss Minchin to an elaborate task of needlework on her own account, being the reconstruction of her last summer's Sunday silk gown, and Sibyl to her practice of one of Chopin's mazurkas.

No more was seen of the dark-eyed young woman for a week, when Sibyl met her one afternoon in a passage near the housekeeper's room. They looked at each other with mutual interest, open on the part of Sibyl, furtive on the part of the stranger.

Could she be a servant? Sibyl wondered. Assuredly not a housemaid, for the housemaids at Ellerslie Park all wore a livery of lavender cotton in the morning, and were white-capped and aproned all day. This young woman was capless and apronless. The bloom on her cheeks had faded somewhat since the day she alighted from the station fly. Her dark eyes had a troubled look.

Sibyl was on her way to the housekeeper's room, to ask for something for a sick child in one of those cottages which had been her mother's kingdom, and over which she now reigned, a youthful queen.

"Will you send little Jane Barber soup once a day, and jelly and custard pudding on alternate days, Mrs. Morison?" she asked of the comfortable-looking housekeeper, whose ordinarily placid countenance was furrowed by her strenuous study of the butcher's book.

"Yes, ma'am, soup and jelly shall be sent. Poor little mite, I'm afraid she's not long for this world. Is there anything else I can do, Miss Sibyl?"

Mrs. Morison's address fluctuated between the formal "ma'am" and the affectionate "Miss Sibyl." She had kept Sir Joseph's house when the heiress was born, and worshipped her accordingly.

"Yes, Mrs. Morison, there is something I very much want you to do for me," replied Sibyl, quickly. "Tell me all about that pretty young woman in black who came here in a fly just a week ago."

Mrs. Morison's brow grew even more troubled than it had been over the butcher's book.

"Indeed, Miss Sibyl, I can't tell you much, not if I was to tell you all I know. The young person dropped from the clouds, as one may say. I hadn't had one word of notice of her coming, from Sir Joseph or any body else; and if she hadn't brought me a letter from him I might have taken her for an impostor, and turned her out-of-doors."

"A letter from father? Do let me see it. Is he coming soon? I am so longing for him."

"He doesn't say a word about coming home, ma'am. The letter is all about the young woman."

"Let me see, let me see," Sibyl cried eagerly, holding out her hand for the letter.

Mrs. Morison had to unlock a desk, and to select the said letter from among various other documents, a slow business, and seeming slower to Sibyl's impatience. At last, however, the letter was produced, taken out of the envelope, carefully unfolded, and re-perused by Mrs. Morison before she handed it to her master's daughter.

Sibyl read as follows:—

"The Carlton, Thursday evening.

"My good Morison,

"Marie Arnold, the bearer of this letter, has been lately left an orphan, and I have taken upon myself to provide her with a home. She is of humble birth, and has no grand expectations. It is my wish, therefore, that while giving her a comfortable home at Ellerslie, and taking her as much as possible under your own wing, you should not allow her to acquire any fine notions, or to fancy herself a young lady. You will be kind enough to find her some light employment in the household. If she is clever with her needle, as I am told she is, you might allow her to be useful to Miss Higginson, and in the schoolroom generally. I am told that she has been well educated in a convent school, in the South of France, where she was born. She is a Roman Catholic. I hope this fact will not be used to her prejudice, and that she will be encouraged to attend the services of her own church, so long as she herself desires to remain a member of that church.

"You will please provide her wardrobe, and give her a reasonable amount of pocket-money. She will, of course, have a bedroom of her own, and not be placed on a footing with servants.

"Yours sincerely,
"J.H."

"Not on a footing with the servants," repeated Mrs. Morison, as Sibyl handed her the letter. "There's my difficulty, you see, Miss. Find her light occupation—keep her ideas humble—and yet not make a servant of her. It isn't easy."

"Yes, it is, you dear old Morison. Let her be in the schoolroom, and have her bedroom near the schoolroom, and let her come and sit with me in my own room very often, in my recreation hours. I like her looks. And if she is French, she will help me to improve in my French conversation. And she can tell me all about the South; and she can go for long rambles with me. Miss Minchin and the Fräulein are wretched creatures to go out with. Neither of them knows the meaning of the word ramble. They can only walk. Tell Marie to come to my room this afternoon at half-past two. I am free from then till four, and she and I can have a good talk."

"Not allow her to acquire fine notions, or to fancy herself a lady," repeated the housekeeper, reading a passage from Sir Joseph's letter, with a puzzled brow. "I don't know how that will hold with letting her be your companion—to go out walking with you—or to be with you in your own sitting-room. I don't know if that will quite answer to Sir Joseph's instructions, Miss Sibyl."

"But I do. Father means that Marie and I are to be friendly, or he would never have suggested her being useful in the school-room. The schoolroom means me. She shall be useful. She shall help me to support the burden of two governesses. That will be a work of real utility," cried Sibyl, with a happy laugh.

Mrs. Morison had heard that joyous laughter very seldom since Lady Lucy's death, and her heart warmed at the sound. The girl had been the sunshine of the house before that bitter parting between devoted mother and adoring child; but that great grief had clouded the joyous nature, and for the greater part of the year of mourning it may be said that Sibyl endured life rather than that she lived.

The sound of her own laughter shocked her even to-day. She looked down at her black frock with a stifled sob.

"Oh, how can I feel happy, even for an instant," she murmured, in self-reproach, "when she is gone?"

"I'll send the young person to your room at half-past two precisely," said Mrs. Morison, with a cheery air. "And I shall be very grateful to her, my pretty one, if she helps you to forget your loss," mused Mrs. Morison, when Sibyl had gone; and then the worthy woman polished her spectacles, which had suddenly grown dim.

CHAPTER V

FROM THE FAR OFF LAND

SIBYL'S own particular retreat was in a tower at the southern angle of Ellerslie House, and it was one of the prettiest rooms in a house where beauty and harmony of furniture and decoration had been achieved regardless of cost, and with the aid of all the new lights which high art has cast upon our domestic surroundings. The room was octagonal, and the eight panels accommodated frescoes of the four seasons, alternated with four allegorical figures representing Dawn, Noon, Evening, and Night, these executed in a decidedly French manner, at which sturdy English art might lift the nose and shrug the shoulder of contempt, but which for decorative purposes was admirable. Madras curtains of pale amber, chairs and sofa covered with sea-green silk, piano, tables, book-shelves, and mantelpiece all in white enamelled wood, gave delicate brightness to the room, which was lighted by four tall casement windows overlooking sea and moor, and the village of Ardliston straggling along the edge of the cliff, with its snug little harbour sunk deep in the hollow of the hills. Sibyl could see all the outer world for which she cared from those four windows. She had spent an occasional summer at Scarborough, and she had seen the glory of the English lakes; but the world she loved was this world of far-reaching moorland and far-reaching ocean.

At half-past two on that summer afternoon Marie Arnold stood in the golden light, while her wondering eyes slowly made the circuit of the room, and then concentrated their gaze upon the owner of these luxurious surroundings, who stood smiling at her, a gracious figure, and pale sweet face, a tall slip of a girl, slenderly formed, and with only the promise of beauty, a figure and face which were both curiously contrastive with the strongly built and well rounded form, brilliant black eyes, and vivid colouring of the young woman from the sunny south.

Sibyl asked her if she could speak English.

She replied modestly, "Ver leet'l," but her father was an Englishman, all the same, she informed Sibyl, and she hoped to learn English very quickly.

"Oh, mais non, non, non," cried Sibyl, "learn very slowly; do not learn at all," she went on in her pretty girlish English-French. "I am going to talk French with you always. I shall get on so much faster with you than Fräulein, because you will never correct me. You will not, will you, Marie? You won't take the faintest notice of my faults in grammar, and you will only stop me when I am so bad that you can't tell what I mean. Is that a bargain?"

"But, Mademoiselle speaks like an angel," protested Marie with her pretty southern flattery.

"No, no, I am wretched as to grammar. Fräulein stops me every minute: first a wrong tense, and then a wrong gender, and then the form of the sentence is all wrong, and then I have said devant[1] when it ought to have been avant;[2] or sauf[3] when I should have said excepte.[4] As if it mattered! That is not the way to teach a girl to speak a foreign language. The way is to let her talk and talk and talk, as the birds sing, until her instinct teaches her what is right and what is wrong. Come and sit on my sofa, Marie—isn't it a darling sofa?—and tell me all about yourself, and the country where you were born."

Marie sighed, and obeyed, and presently they were sitting on the sofa, the fair head close beside the dark shining hair that had grown in the sun, and which had sunny gleams, even in its darkness. The large dark eyes had golden lights in them, as if they too had taken beauty from the southern sun.

"Tell me, tell me all," urged Sibyl, always in French, delighted to be able to talk without apprehension of the Fräulein's nice criticism, "unless it grieves you to talk of your home."

"No, no, mam'selle, it does not grieve me. I have wept all my tears. I have wept my fill since my mother died—just a fortnight ago."

"Only a fortnight! And my mother died only a year ago. Ah, I can feel for you," and the white, slim hand stole into the French girl's coarser hand, and tears rained from Sibyl's violet eyes.

The very name Mother was a charm to make her weep.

"She was not always kind, mam'selle, but I was sorry all the same when she died. She was only ill for a few days, and she was unconscious towards the last, so that we could never say good-bye. She drifted out of life in a long sleep, and I was left alone there in our little villa at Mougins, alone with the poor dead mother, and not knowing what was to become of me any more than the great white cat she had been fond of knew what was to become of him."

"Had you no uncles and aunts, and people?" inquired Sibyl wonderingly.

She was so richly provided with relatives upon the Allandale side of her house—to say nothing of numerous humbler Higginsons—that she could not imagine an existence unsurrounded by kith and kin.

"No, mam'selle, I have no one, and I never heard that my mother had any friend in this world, except Sir Higginson."

"You mean my father, Sir Joseph."

"Yes, Sir Joseph Higginson."

"But how did your mother, so far away, happen to win my father's friendship?" inquired Sibyl.

"Her husband was an engineer, who worked under Sir Higginson when he was establishing great ironworks at Fontaine-le-roi, near the Belgian frontier," explained Marie Arnold. "That was many years ago, before I was born. My father was killed one night on the railway six months before I was born, and Sir Higginson was very good to my mother. She was not a peasant, mam'selle, and yet she was not quite a lady. She had no dot⁵ when my father married her, and she had never learnt to work for her bread. When she was left a widow with an infant she was quite helpless. She would have starved perhaps if your father had not taken pity upon her. 'Your husband was killed while he was in my service,' he told her, 'and I shall provide for you for the rest of your days,' and he kept his word nobly. My mother went back to her own country before I was born, and we lived in a little white house at Mougins, looking over the hills, and the pine woods and the sea."

"Where is Mougins?"

"It is a little town on a hill near Cannes. Mam'selle knows Cannes, perhaps?"

"No; but I have heard my aunts and cousins talk of it. Some of them go there every winter. And so you were reared near Cannes, on the shores of the Mediterranean? I suppose you think that sea over there ugly, in comparison?" said Sibyl, pointing to the ocean she loved.

"It is greyer than our sea, mam'selle, and it looks always like our sea in bad weather."

"And what do you think of our hills and moors?" asked Sibyl, with a somewhat peremptory air.

"Very ugly, mam'selle. I miss the rolling olive woods, the cypresses, the valleys where the roses grow. I miss the perfumed air, and the sunshine most of all."

"Don't you call that sunshine?" asked Sibyl, pointing to the southward windows.

"Very fair for a sunny afternoon in February, mam'selle, not for June."

"Ah, in June, no doubt, your Mougins would be simply intolerable, like a sandy desert in Africa."[6]

"No, mam'selle, there is always a cool breeze across the hills, a breath from the unseen snow mountains, and there is always shade in the pine woods, always freshness from the sea. It is only foreigners who fancy they cannot live in our country in the summer."

"Did my father ever come to see you at Mougins?"

"Yes, mam'selle, years and years ago; before I went to the convent."

"What convent? You are not a nun, are you?"

Marie laughed, for the first time in Sibyl's hearing.

"No, mam'selle, but I was educated at a convent at Grasse."

"Is that far from Mougins?"

"Only a few miles. You can see one place from the other, across the valley. I used to look from the convent windows, and I could almost distinguish the green shutters and the red roof of my mother's house, and the pink blossom of the almond trees in the garden."

"And so you were educated at a convent? How odd!"

"I am a Roman Catholic, mam'selle, and most Roman Catholic children are educated in convents."

"Well, you are to be in the schoolroom, my father says."

"I am to make myself useful in some way, mam'selle, Sir Joseph said, when I saw him in London."

"Did you see him—quite lately?" Sibyl asked, eagerly.

"Yes, mam'selle. He sent a person—his private secretary, I believe—to take me to England directly after my mother's funeral."

"Yes, yes, old Mr. Orlebar. I know him very well. He lives here when father is at home. A funny old man, isn't he?"

"He was very kind to me, mam'selle, all through the long journey, and then he took me to a beautiful house—like a palace, almost—in London, where I saw Sir Joseph, and he was very kind, and he told me that he would always be my friend, as long as I conducted myself properly, and he wrote a letter to his housekeeper. And then I stayed one night in that splendid house, and saw the picture gallery, and all the beautiful things in the great saloon, and early next morning Mr. Orlebar took me to the station, and put me into the train, and told me what I was to do when I came to the end of my railway journey. And that is all my history, mam'selle."

"Poor Marie," sighed Sibyl, ever so compassionately, "I am so sorry for you. And if your mother was not always kind to you—still she must have loved you—her only child—and you must have loved her."

Sibyl had been wondering at Marie's dry eyes, since she herself could hardly speak of her dead mother without a rush of tears.

Marie hung her head, and paused before she replied.

"I loved some of the nuns better than I loved my mother," she faltered. "Mother Anastasie, for instance. Ah, she was so good to me. It almost broke my heart to leave the convent, because of parting with her. I used to walk over to Grasse to the convent chapel every Saint's Day; but it was to see Mother Anastasie that I went so far, for I could have heard mass in our church at Mougins. She was always pale and delicate, and they said that there was something wrong with her heart; but she taught more and worked harder than any of the nuns. She taught music and drawing. All the children loved her, but I don't think one of them loved her better

than I. And just a year ago on Corpus Christi I went to the convent,
and missed her in her place at the organ; and after the service one
of the lay sisters came to me, with her eyes streaming, and took
me by the hand and led me to the burial ground where there was
a new-made grave heaped with roses. She could scarcely speak for
sobbing, but at last she told me how Mother Anastasie had been
found only two days before sitting at the chapel organ in the afternoon sunshine, her hands still upon the keys, but her head fallen
back against the edge of the high oak chair. She had died like that,
mam'selle, alone, no one near her. They had heard the sound of
the organ cease after she had played one of Mozart's finest glorias,
as they walked in the garden in their recreation hour, and they
thought that Mother Anastasie was staying in the chapel for prayer
and meditation. They watched the chapel door, hoping she would
come out in time to take a little walk with them; but the bell rang
for the class, and they all left the garden. It was an hour later before
anyone took the alarm and went to look for her."

Marie's eyes were no longer tearless, and her last words were
made almost inaudible by her emotion.

"You must have loved her very dearly," said Sibyl, full of
sympathy.

"Yes, mam'selle—she was my spiritual mother, the mother
of my mind and soul. If I were to live to be ever so old I think I
could never commit a sin without her image rising up before me
to stop me from wickedness. My own mother was fond of me, in
her way; but she was, oh, so different from Mother Anastasie. She
loved gossip, and cards, and pleasure of all kinds. She did not care
for books, or flowers, or pictures. She went to High Mass every
Sunday morning, but that was all. She sat about on the walls, or
in the olive woods, with her neighbours, all the rest of the week,
except when she could get anyone to drive her to Cannes, to see
the fine shops and fine people."

"She was not often unkind to you?" questioned Sibyl.

"No, she was not often unkind; and she never beat me."

Sibyl shuddered at the idea of a mother beating her child,
she whose only image of motherhood was an image of supreme
gentleness.

"But her pleasures were not my pleasures," pursued the French girl. "There was no link between us; and the two years that I spent at Mougins after I left the convent were the dullest years of my life. I missed my old companions, and the music, and games, and the studies even—though I used once to think them a burden—and my soul sickened at the gossip, and the cards, and the quarrels— quarrels about nothing, a cracked oil jar, a handful of vegetables, loud talking from one door to another, quarrels that seemed to begin and go on for the sake of quarrelling."

"Poor Marie! There are no quarrels here. Fräulein is rather worrying, but Miss Minchin is as good as gold; in spite of her fidgety little ways. I call her Mousie, because she is brownish-grey, and quick, and quiet, like a mouse. She doesn't mind. But you must not call her Mousie—not just at first."

"No, no, mam'selle, that is understood," replied Marie, discreetly.

This was the beginning of a lasting friendship, which grew with the passage of time. Marie was accepted in the schoolroom as a useful companion alike by governesses and pupil. She had been taught to use her needle with exquisite art, and the Fräulein was not above getting her handkerchiefs marked by those skilful fingers, in return for which service she helped Marie to acquire a little German, without taking the trouble to give her formal lessons. Marie was quick, and learnt any new thing with wondrous ease. She had a fine ear for music, and delighted in Sibyl's piano.

As a companion in Sibyl's walks she was incomparable, for she knew not weariness, and her light, springy step carried her over the moorland as easily as if she had been some wild creature reared upon those breezy downs. She was Sibyl's friend and play-fellow for five years, with Sir Joseph Higginson's approval, and it was only now, when Sibyl had attained her eighteenth birthday and all the Mountford aunts were beginning to pester Sir Joseph about her appearance in society, that he began to wonder how he was to dispose of the humble companion when the heiress came to take her proper position in the great world.

"It is all very well to keep Sibyl back for a year or so," said the only unmarried aunt, Lady Selina Mountford, who took upon herself to advise all her married sisters, their husbands, and belong-ings, and used to lie awake o' nights in her pretty little house in

May Fair, worrying herself about the family troubles. "It is all very well for you to keep her buried alive at Ellerslie for another year. As your heiress she will have a choice of eligible partis[7] whenever she may appear; but she ought to come out before she is twenty. She looks rather thin and delicate at present. I think another year may improve her," said Lady Selina, as if she were talking of a turkey that was being fattened for Christmas, or a young horse that was "furnishing."

Sir Joseph promised to bring out his daughter before she was twenty, and thus, upon one subject at least, freed Lady Selina's nights from care.

"There is always something to keep me awake," sighed the spinster. "Braemar's boys are too terrible. How he is ever to pay their Oxford debts passes my comprehension. And now I am told they play baccarat at some dreadful club in London, where young men who have no money lose twenty thousand pounds at a sitting; and Felix threatened his father he would marry a girl he met at the Stephanotis, another dreadful club where they dance."

There was thus a year of respite for Sir Joseph, during which he might be able to find a comfortable settlement in the matrimonial line for the humble companion, so that she might not too keenly feel the difference in her position and that of Sibyl as sovereign mistress of the house in Arlington Street, and with all the town eager to pay her homage.

"I don't want her to feel the difference," mused Sir Joseph with a profound sigh, as he paced the terrace in front of his Tudor mansion. "It wouldn't be fair that she should. It wouldn't be fair."

He sighed again deeply, for as yet no eligible pretendent[8] to the hand of Marie Arnold had appeared in that remote northern region; and he began to fear that none might be found in the district.

The girl was a Papist, objection number one—but an objection which had been disregarded by a needy evangelical curate, who, on ascertaining that Sir Joseph meant to give his dependent a handsome dowry—amount not specified—had urged his desire to make her his wife, and possibly to snatch a brand from the burning by winning her over to the Evangelical Church.

The alliance would have been respectable, as the young

Levite, though needy, was of a good Northumberland family, and of unimpeachable morals; but Marie did not like the curate, and would not hear of marrying him.

"I shall never marry," she told Sir Joseph. "I want to be Sibyl's slave and companion always."

"My dear girl, that is all very well while Sibyl is here," replied Sir Joseph; "but when she goes to London and is swallowed up in the gaieties of the London season, with hardly an hour of leisure for home life—you can't be her companion then."

"Let me be her maid, then, and wait upon her, and sit up for her at night, and help her to undress, and hear all about her pleasures and gaieties."

"No, Marie, not a servant. You must never be her servant—you must never think of yourself as a servant. I want to see you happily married before Sibyl marries. You are six years older than Sibyl—four and twenty. You must have been in love half a dozen times, I should think."

"Never," said Marie, with an emphatic shrug. "I have even tried to fall in love—with a curate; not this one, but the tall, good-looking young man who was here before him, and whose sympathies were all with my church—with that young doctor, Dr. Dewsnap's son and assistant. But there is no such thing as love in my nature, I think. I adore Sibyl, and I love you; and that is all the love I am capable of feeling."

"Ah, we shall see, Marie. Trees that are long in flowering bear very fine blossoms. The aloe, for instance, and the magnolia," said Sir Joseph, patting her shoulder, as he trudged along by her side, a sturdy, active man, although his seventieth birthday had been kept by the pitmen with beef and beer, and noisy rural sports, and dancing and fireworks, nearly a year before.

He was very fond of Marie Arnold. He liked to have her to sit with him and his daughter of an evening. He liked to hear her sing her pretty French chansons, full of coquetry and dainty love, blue skies and sunlit valleys, fountains, orange trees, eglantine and honeysuckle, bees and butterflies, songs that touched none of life's serious phases, nor ever hinted at old age or death.

In this springtide of Sir Joseph's seventy-first year, he happened to be at Ellerslie for a short time, with Marie as his only companion, and this companionship drew them nearer together than they had ever been before.

Never until now had Sir Joseph been at Ellerslie without his young daughter to hang upon his footsteps, and ride and drive with him, and play billiards with him, or sing and play to him of an evening. Marie had been a secondary figure while Sibyl was present, but when April began Sibyl was at Hastings, whither she had been despatched suddenly at Dr. Dewsnap's instigation, to cure a cough which had hung upon her all the winter. There were great things being done in the pits, alterations and extensions which required Sir Joseph's supervision, so he had been unable to go with his daughter—who had been confided to the care of Miss Minchin, Fräulein Stahlherz having gone back to her native Hanover—and for the first time in his widowhood he found himself pacing the long drawing-room at Ellerslie, or taking his morning constitutional on the terrace, without that graceful figure near at hand.

She was to come home as soon as the cough was actually cured, by warrant of the Hastings doctor, and in the meantime she wrote to her father daily, telling him of all her walks and rides, her excursions to Battle or to Pevensey, her readings of the Norman Conquest in Thierry,[9] Green,[10] and Freeman,[11] and her longing to return to her father and Ellerslie.

His life in that great house would have been very dreary—for he had no visitors at this time, and his secretary, Mr. Orlebar, was not a lively person—if he had not found Marie an attentive and vivacious companion, pleased to do all that Sibyl was accustomed to do for him.

Mrs. Morison shrugged her shoulders when she saw the foreign waif filling the absent daughter's place. She liked Marie, but she disapproved of that young person's exaltation.

"He told me not to give her any fine notions when first she came here," mused the housekeeper, "and now he is giving her fine notions himself. A young woman who spends all her evenings in the long drawing-room will never be contented to take a humble position in after-life."

It was not more than three or four days after Sibyl left Ellerslie, when a stranger appeared upon the scene; a gentleman who called upon Sir Joseph one afternoon, and sent in his card, upon which appeared the name of

Brandon Mountford,
Travellers' Club.

Any Mountford was secure of a welcome from Sir Joseph, who was never tired of showing kindness to his wife's kindred; but the name of Brandon touched him with a curious thrill which was closely akin to pain.

Brandon was the name of the distant cousin to whom Lucy Mountford had given the innocent love of her young heart. That Brandon Mountford had died in India, two years after Lady Lucy's death; but he had left a son, and in all probability this was the son.

These thoughts went swiftly through Sir Joseph's brain as he looked at the card, which had been brought to him in his study— the room in which he interviewed agents and tenants, and trans-acted business of all kinds connected with his estate.

"Mr. Mountford is in the drawing-room, I suppose?" he said. "I'll go to him."

He found the stranger standing in front of a wide window, looking landwards over the valley, and the river winding through it. A man of about eight and twenty, Sir Joseph thought, tall, well set up, with a fine, frank countenance, well cut features, the Mount-ford nose, which inclined to the aquiline, bright blue eyes, light brown hair, curling close to the well shaped head, and a complex-ion tanned by a hotter sun than ever shone upon Cumbrian cliffs.

"I am very glad to see you at Ellerslie, Mr. Mountford," said the old man cordially, holding out a broad hand in friendly welcome. "Come to have a look at our North Countree, I suppose. You must come and put up here for a week or two, and let me show you a coal pit, if you have never seen one."

"You are too good, Sir Joseph; but I haven't come here with any intention of quartering myself upon you, though I have come to ask you a favour. Here's Braemar's letter, to vouch for me as an insignificant but not disreputable member of the house of Mount-ford. I happened to hear from him of your splendid salmon river, and was seized with a longing to cast a fly in the waters he praised so warmly."

Brandon Mountford here produced an unsealed letter, over which Sir Joseph ran his eye carelessly.

"You want to have a go at our salmon. Well, my dear fellow, fish away to your heart's content. There are plenty of scaly gentlemen, but they are deuced shy, and you may be up at five o'clock every morning for a week and yet not early enough to catch them. Then after a few blank days, perhaps you may get a run of luck. I used to enjoy the sport myself thirty years ago, when I was still young enough to wade breast high in the river in a Scotch mist from seven in the morning to seven at night, and relish my dinner and my whisky toddy all the better for the day's work. Where are you staying, Mr. Mountford?"

"At the Higginson Arms at Ardliston."

"A cosy old inn and a capital landlady, but I think we can make you rather more comfortable at Ellerslie. You'd better go and fetch your portmanteau."

"Indeed, Sir Joseph, I had no idea——" protested Mountford.

"You will be nearer the salmon," pursued his host, "and I can give you a keeper who knows every yard of the water. You'll find this house uncommonly quiet, for I am here on business, and have invited no one since Christmas. My daughter is away, and I have only a—sort of—adopted niece, who cuts my newspapers for me and reads me to sleep after dinner—a nice, bright girl, who sings charmingly."

Sir Joseph grew suddenly thoughtful. What if this Brandon Mountford, who had dropped from the clouds, were the very man he wanted—an honest man, and a husband for Marie Arnold? He liked the look of the young man—a gentleman to the tips of his fingers—good blood showed itself in every line of face and figure—penniless, no doubt. The Mountfords were all poor—property in Ireland for the most part—family numerous—chieftain weighed down by innumerable portions and allowances to daughters and younger sons.

"Braemar tells me you have travelled in Africa," said Sir Joseph, glancing at the letter in his hand, "and that you have won some renown already as a hunter of big game."

"My gun is my only road to fame, Sir Joseph. Yes, I have spent five years on the Dark Continent."

"You must have gone there very young."

"I sailed for the Cape soon after my twenty-first birthday, and within a year of my father's death. Africa has been my country from that time to this. I am only in England as a visitor."

"You mean to go back?"

"Yes, I mean to go home."

"A strange fancy for a young man with all the world before him."

"I know no grander world than the shores of Zambesi, no happier life than the freedom of the wilderness."

"You can tell me your adventures over a glass of Mouton[12] to-night. Go and get your portmanteau."

"You are too kind, Sir Joseph; but are you sure I shan't be in the way? If you have come to the north on business you may find yourself bored by a visitor."

"I never put myself in the way of being bored," answered the old man, bluntly. "You may be sure I shouldn't ask you if I didn't want you here."

"Then I shall be delighted to come," said Mountford. "I only regret that I shall not see my young cousin. Braemar was full of her praises."

"She is a good little girl," said Sir Joseph. "I don't think my life would be worth sixpence a day without her."

And then his thoughts went back to the girl's mother, and to those far-away days when he sat by Lady Lucy's side in the Hertford Street drawing-room, and she told him her little story of a misplaced love. Was this Brandon Mountford the son of that Brandon Mountford? he wondered, nervously anxious to be enlightened.

"Your father was in the army, I think," he said, tentatively.

"Yes, in the Engineers. He died in India, as brave a soldier as ever fought there."

"And your mother—is she no longer living?"

The young man's face flushed at the question, and a troubled look came into his eyes.

"My mother died many years ago, while I was at Wellington.

She had been—a great invalid—ever since my birth," he answered, with painful pauses in the final sentence.

Sir Joseph felt that he had been cruel to push the question, but he had wanted to be sure of his facts; and now he was sure. This man was the son of that distant cousin to whom Lucy's young heart had gone out, and who doubtless had given her love for love; the man so unhappily mated, so faithful to that tragic bond.

"If I can do him a good turn I will," thought Sir Joseph. "He shan't go back to Africa if I can hinder it. He would make a capital husband for Marie. They would be a splendid couple."

Brandon brought his portmanteau and fishing tackle to Ellerslie in the course of the afternoon, and dined alone with Sir Joseph in a snug tapestried parlour which the millionaire preferred to the great dining-room, with its lofty carved oak buffet and decoration of gold plate. The two men sat a long time over their wine, though Brandon did but small justice to Sir Joseph's famous Mouton. He was a tremendous smoker, however, and consumed nearly a dozen cigarettes while Sir Joseph entertained him with reminiscences of his juvenile struggles, and the hazards and successes of his manhood. It was late when they went to the long drawing-room, and Brandon, who had forgotten his host's mention of an adopted niece, was startled at seeing a young woman, neatly dressed in black silk, with a bunch of tea roses at her waistband, seated reading near a lamp-lit table. She had not dined with them, yet she had the air of being one of the family.

Sir Joseph introduced Mr. Mountford to this young lady, who was called Miss Arnold, yet who spoke with a French accent, and whose dark eyes and warm olive complexion were decidedly un-English.

"And now, Marie, you can sing us one of your little songs," said Sir Joseph, settling himself in a luxurious chair, with evident resignation to impending slumber.

He was asleep before Marie had finished her first song, and Brandon and the young lady were practically alone, a fact which seemed less embarrassing to her than to the man not long returned from Mashonaland,[13] and from a society in which bulk, beads, and blackness are the chief characteristics of female beauty. It was a new thing for Brandon to find himself in a solitude of two with a handsome young woman, whose history, associations, and character were utterly unknown to him.

She sang the inevitable "Si tu savais" with a good deal of feeling, and in a rich contralto voice; and then De Musset's "Ninon,"[14] and then a little Provencal ballad, and then another, at Brandon's urgent request. When he could not with decency ask her to sing any more, he entreated her to play something—Chopin, Thalberg, Strauss, Sebastian Bach, Porpora, Lulli—anything she chose. He would have kept her at the piano all the evening if he could, rather than face the ordeal of conversation with a strange young person; but she rose and shook her head at the question of playing.

"I am no pianist," she said. "I have never played anything but my own accompaniments. Miss Higginson plays magnificently. I should never dare to attempt the piano where she is. I only learnt to play after I was grown up."

"What kind of music does Miss Higginson prefer?" asked Brandon.

"Oh, all the great masters—Beethoven, Mozart, Mendelssohn, Chopin—and she extemporises exquisitely. The piano to her is a living creature, her most intimate friend. She and her piano talk to each other for hours together. I can only sit in a corner, at my needlework, and wonder at her. She is far away from me—in another world."

"Yes; my little girl has a genius for music," said Sir Joseph, awakened at once by the cessation of song. "And Marie has a fine voice and a pretty taste, hasn't she, Mountford?"

Brandon said all that was proper and complimentary about Miss Arnold's singing, and felt infinitely relieved by the worthy Baronet's return to consciousness and conversation.

"I hope I may have the pleasure of hearing Miss Higginson play before I leave Ellerslie," he said, presently. "Does she return soon?"

"That depends upon her doctor. She is not to leave Hastings without his permission."

"You must miss her sadly."

"I should be lost without her if it wasn't for Marie. She takes care of me. She is like a second daughter to me. By the way, Marie, Mr. Urquhart is coming in a day or two. Don't forget to tell Morison to have his room ready."

Marie's cheek and brow crimsoned, and the dark, strongly arched brows contracted in a frown.

"What brings Mr. Urquhart here again so soon?"

"The same attraction that brings Mr. Mountford—my salmon-river. He will be company for you, Mountford," added Sir Joseph to his guest. "Urquhart's brother, Lord Penrith, is a neighbour of mine. Urquhart lost his wife only a year ago—married badly, a poor parson's daughter—and he contrives to spend a good deal of his life at Killander Castle. It suits him uncommonly well, you understand; for he has my shooting and fishing as well as his brother's."

Brandon watched Marie Arnold's face while Sir Joseph was talking, and wondered at the angry and troubled look which clouded a countenance that had been gay and smiling a few minutes before. There must be some strong reason for her dislike of Mr. Urquhart, he told himself; and he became more interested in the girl's character and history from this moment.

CHAPTER VI

IF IT COULD HAVE BEEN

HUBERT URQUHART arrived three days after Mountford's establishment at Ellerslie, by which time the stranger had made himself at home in his new surroundings, had explored gardens and park under Marie's guidance, had seen a coal mine and an iron mine, had become very good friends with Sir Joseph, and had won the approval of Sir Joseph's head keeper. Urquhart's arrival was no more welcome to Brandon than it was to Marie Arnold. The old acquaintance was civil to the new-comer, but was evidently displeased at finding a stranger domesticated at Ellerslie; the more so perhaps when he heard that the stranger was a connection of Sir Joseph's, and had a legitimate claim upon his hospitality.

Mr. Urquhart was thirty-four years of age, had been in a cavalry regiment, and had sold out just before the abolition of purchase[1] in the army. He had married badly, as Sir Joseph told Brandon; had married in haste and repented with equal celerity. He had not been unkind to his wife, but he had been neglectful, and even his battered conscience had felt some remorseful twinges when the poor faded prettiness, which had once been so purely pink and white, faded out of life altogether, suddenly, after the birth of a second baby, which only survived the mother by a fortnight. She died at the Yorkshire parsonage in which the greater part of her life had been spent, and where her orphan daughter, Coralie, was now being cared for by a widowed grandfather and two spinster aunts.

Those remorseful pangs of conscience, for a wife from whose death-bed he had been absent, did not long discompose the gentle-manlike equanimity which was a mark of race in Hubert Urquhart. He went back to his patrimonial home a free man, and took his ease in the house of his elder brother, Lord Penrith, still a bachelor, and burdened with an estate richer in acreage and historical interest than in revenue. The Penriths had been poor for three generations, and were getting poorer as land declined in value. Lord Penrith had just missed three great heiresses, having tried his hardest for all three, and having been near acceptance with each. There was a something wanting in his nature where women are concerned. That cold hardness of the Urquhart character might have sub-jugated some meek, sentimental girl, whose dream of love is of upward-looking, worshipping affection—the love of the brooks for the moon—but heiresses have got beyond that kind of sentimen-talism. They require to be worshipped themselves; and the more exacting among them require sincerity in the worshipper.

Lord Penrith had never been able even to seem sincere; and in each case he found finally that he had but made the running for some hot-headed, impetuous lover who was able to put a little heart into his courtship.

Crushed by his third disappointment, Penrith had retired to his Cumbrian castle, and into himself, and already bore the reputa-tion of a misanthrope and a woman-hater. He had almost aban-doned the hope of restoring the fortunes of his race by a wealthy alliance. The Anglo-American marriage, the strictly modern blend of the feudal castle and the Trans-atlantic oil-well had hardly come into fashion at that time, and Lord Penrith, having failed to attach himself to English coin in the possession of English beauty, retired to his tent, like Achilles, and sulked there, content to shoot and fish and hunt and farm, remote from society and woman's wiles.

He was Hubert Urquhart's senior by five years, a man of graver character, but of the same hardness of fibre. Hubert had a kind of surface pleasantness which served his turn in society, and which made him more popular than his elder brother.

The Urquharts were a handsome race,—always allowing for that hardness of expression which was a family characteristic. Penrith and his brother were both tall, strongly built yet slender, with commanding carriage, and a thoroughbred delicacy of hand and foot. Both had the Scottish type of features and complexion, long, thin noses, thin lips, cold grey eyes, and auburn hair, and they were men who looked their best in Highland clothes, which made up by the picturesque for what was wanting to the wearers in personal charm.

Hubert Urquhart's keen grey eye scanned Brandon from head to foot, weighed him in the balance, and found him wanting—as a man of the world.

"I am told you have spent half your life in Africa, Mountford," he said in a pause of their sport, as they sat on the river-bank discussing a snack of bread and cheese and a bottle of Bass.

"Not quite. My life has lasted twenty-six years, of which five have been spent in Africa."

"Why did you go?"

Brandon's brow clouded at the question.

"I had been ill, and my doctor told me to live in the open air."

"You could have done that in Argyleshire or Connemara."

"No doubt, but I preferred Mashonaland."

"A curious fancy," said Urquhart, with a slightly contemptuous air. "I have never yet been able to realise the motives of a man who runs away from civilisation, unless he is running away from debts and difficulties at the same time, which, of course, was not your case. And you really found the Crocodile and the Zambesi Rivers more attractive than the Rhine or the Arno?"

"Infinitely more attractive. I grant that the European rivers have all the charm of association; that there are some names— Tiber, for instance—which act like a spell. But that untrodden world yonder has what the civilised world has not—freshness and mystery."

"Ah, you hanker after the unexplored and the unknown. My

ideal is a place like Monte Carlo, where there are good hotels, pretty women, and a trente et quarante table,—to say nothing of pigeon-shooting. I have never been further afield for pleasure than southern Italy, and I hope never to go. What do you think of old Higginson?"

"A splendid old man—plenty of grit, and plenty of heart."

"A sturdy old Briton, ain't he? A distinctly native production. The kind of man we all pretend to be proud of, and whom we all laugh at."

"I have not yet discovered the ridiculous side of his character."

"Ah, you are a connection, and you think it a point of honour to take the good old bloke seriously. I am indebted to him for infinite hospitality. I like his house, his shooting, and his river and I like him; but for all that I can't help seeing that he is a capital joke. His frank boastfulness, for instance—his missing aspirates—his prosy recapitulation of the various steps by which he mounted Fortune's ladder. The worst of such men is that they can take nothing for granted. Everything in their lives must be expatiated upon."

"I like his frankness, and I don't mind his bragging, which is a part of his frankness."

"Oh, come now, Mountford, hang frankness—call it frank egotism. Candour is only a synonym for want of manners. Your candid man goes about the world plaguing everybody with his own feelings and his own affairs. The first lesson a well-bred man learns is the art of self-suppression, and that the outside world doesn't care twopence whether he's alive or dead. What is your opinion of Sir Joseph's handsome niece—ward—whatever you like to call her?"

"You have just told me that reticence is a sovereign merit in civilised man, and yet you question me about my opinions."

"Opinions are always interesting. Marie Arnold is a handsome woman. We are both men, and we are both mortal. We can hardly help admiring her."

"You have expressed an opinion that serves for both of us. There is nothing left for me to say."

"You think her handsome, then?" questioned Urquhart, with keen eyes bent upon his companion.

"Of her type, most assuredly."

"But you don't care for the type, evidently?"

"I confess that there is a little too much prodigality in form and colouring for my ideal. That southern splendour dazzles me more than it attracts. The type I most admire is of a paler beauty. There is an ethereal Raffaellesque fairness which is to my mind the perfection of loveliness."

"You are thinking of your cousin, I fancy," said Urquhart, still keenly watchful of his companion's face.

"Of my cousin. You mean Miss Higginson, perhaps? I have never seen her, but her portrait as a child does certainly realise my ideal—allowing for the disadvantages of that nondescript age, when face and form have lost the charm of infancy without acquiring the grace of girlhood."

"How is it that you have never been here before?"

"There is no 'how' about the matter—no reason why I should have been here sooner, or why I should have come at all—except the stream yonder. My connection with Ellerslie is of the slightest. My father and Lady Lucy were a kind of distant cousins, and Miss Higginson and I are just one stage further apart on the family tree. If you look at the Mountford pedigree you will find my name in an obscure bracket near the edge of the document, while Miss Higginson, as granddaughter of the present Lord Allandale, occupies a central position."

"Miss Higginson is a personage anywhere and everywhere—a great heiress and a great beauty—after your Raffaellesque type."

The beer-bottles were empty by this time, and the soothing digestive pipe was finished, so the two men went back to the river, and for the rest of the day were better occupied than in idle conversation. Perhaps Urquhart had asked all the questions he wanted to ask, yet he tramped back to Ellerslie House in a somewhat discontented mood, for being himself innately insincere, he found it difficult to credit anybody else with sincerity.

"Pretends not to admire her," he mused, as he and Brandon walked up the hill between four and five o'clock, after a disappointing day. "I never knew a man who did not depreciate the woman he was in love with. They like to throw another man off the scent, even when there is no particular reason for concealment."

It was one of those halcyon days which April steals from
May or June, and they found Sir Joseph taking tea on the terrace,
with Marie ministering to his comforts, buttering his thin dry
toast, and measuring out the precise amount of cream he liked
in his cup. The old man was basking in the afternoon sunshine,
basking also in the sense of well-being, of a life profitably spent, of
a great fortune honourably acquired, of the power which wealth
gives when that wealth is realised out of the thews and sinews of
working men, and when a whole population depends for its bread
upon one man. At a nod of Sir Joseph's head, those villages yonder,
scattered on the bleak moorland, might be reduced to idleness and
penury. He had been, upon the whole, a beneficent employer. He
had never forgotten that he had once worked for his bread, or that
his mother had risen at five o'clock on winter mornings to go out
washing; and his sympathy with working men and women had
never been lessened by his own luxurious surroundings. He knew
as well what they wanted now as he knew what he wanted fifty
years ago when he was one of them. The link between him and his
people had never been broken. When there were strikes and lock-
outs over half England, Sir Joseph's peace was unthreatened. His
men laughed Trade Unionists to scorn. They wanted no Socialist
friends from Newcastle or Shields. They had the best friend they
could have in Old Joe; and so long as Old Joe was above-ground
they would work for him and trust him. He had made it the study
of his life to be in advance of his men's necessities, and to concede
advantages unasked that were soon afterwards being fought for
with murderous rancour in other districts. Little wonder, then,
that Sir Joseph Higginson's influence was rooted deep in the hearts
of his people. His young wife's brief residence at Ellerslie had been
a reign of beneficence, and it had been Sibyl's delight to continue
the good work her mother had begun; so the voice of the Socialist
charmer, charm he never so wisely, was powerless to arouse evil-
feeling among the men of Ellerslie.

The salmon-fishers were received with cordiality by Sir Joseph,
and with a certain mute emotion by Marie Arnold, who blushed at
their coming, blushed as she had never done when Urquhart came
alone, he himself noted with sullen jealousy. There was evidently
a flirtation on foot already between Brandon and her, and Bran-

don's indifference was only an assumption, Urquhart told himself, as he drew his chair to the tea-table and watched Marie while she poured out tea for the new arrivals. He marked her lowered eyelids, those full, firm eyelids which had a look of marble above their dark lashes; he noticed the tremulous uncertainty of her hands as they moved among the cups and saucers. Yes, this new-comer had made a deeper impression upon her foolish little mind in three days than he, Urquhart, had made in all his lengthy visits, and with all his subtlest flatteries and most delicate attentions. He had hated Mountford from the outset as a dangerous interloper; and now he was assured that he had not hated him without cause.

Hubert Urquhart had fallen in love with Marie Arnold on his first visit to Ellerslie, a three months' widower; but he had been careful to give no indication of his feelings. He had been studiously courteous, and he had ventured on an occasional compliment; but he had gone no further, waiting to be sure of his ground before he declared himself.

From the beginning he had made up his mind that Marie Arnold was nearer and dearer to Sir Joseph than the old man had told the world. His casual way of talking of her, sometimes as the daughter of a man who had been killed in his service, sometimes as a kind of adopted niece, did not deceive Mr. Urquhart. He saw that Sir Joseph was as proud of Marie's beauty and accomplishments as he was of Sibyl's more refined attractions, that his eyes turned as fondly upon the alien when the two girls stood beside his chair bidding him good night, as ever they turned upon his acknowledged daughter. Urquhart had no doubt that Marie too was his daughter—the issue of some intrigue which had lightened the cares of his work in the Belgian mining country, and it occurred to him that even an unacknowledged daughter of Sir Joseph Higginson would be no bad match for the impecunious scion of a noble house. He was cautious, however, and went to work deliberately, although he was deeper in love with Marie Arnold than he had ever been with any woman in his life. It may be that there was something in the warmth and quick impulse of her southern nature which charmed him by contrast with his own cold and sluggish temperament. Ice and fire could not have been more different; but the ice trembled and melted at the touch of that fire, and the hard, battered man of the world owned himself the slave of this unsophisticated girl.

"Festina lente," he said to himself. "I can't afford to marry her unless there's money in it."

He had heard a good deal about a certain Andrew Orlebar, Sir Joseph's factotum, secretary, and alter ego; and he fancied that this Orlebar would be the right man to put him on the right tack. Orlebar must know all about Marie's origin, and Marie's expectations. The only question was how much of that information Mr. Orlebar might be disposed to impart in answer to judicious pumping.

Heretofore Mr. Urquhart had been unlucky in finding Orlebar absent from Ellerslie, either watching his chief's business in London, or on some Continental mission. He was a man who needed no more warning or preparation for a journey to Egypt or India than commoner men require for a trip to Brighton or Paris. He lived, moved, and breathed only for his employer, had neither kith nor kin, tastes nor pleasures of his own—a colourless, faithful, stolid, unenjoying machine, fashioned in the likeness of man.

This time Urquhart had taken care to be sure of Orlebar's presence at Ellerslie before he offered himself as a visitor; and here in the glow of the afternoon sunlight came this very Orlebar, shuffling along the terrace, faded, dusky, grey amidst all the wealth of colour in a garden unfolding its beauty to the spring. He made a discordant note in that harmony of brilliant hues, a patch of dirty grey which offended the eye. He brought his chief a packet of letters—the afternoon mail—and they two were soon sitting apart, with heads close together and brows bent, over the open letters, by the marble balustrade, and at the base of a marble Pan, which seemed to look down at them in grim derision of their money-grubbing instincts. What did money matter to the great god Pan, the forest wildling, who had all the wealth of nature for his own?

Marie questioned the men about their day's sport, and Urquhart noticed how her glances turned shyly to Mountford, and dwelt on his face while he talked, and even lingered there when he was silent. Towards him, Urquhart, she had shown only avoidance; had made all pursuit of her difficult; had been openly scornful when he praised her beauty or seemed to hang entranced upon her singing—seemed only, since music was a missing sense with most of the Urquharts, and for him a barrel-organ in a London street playing the latest music-hall melody, or a brass band in the park braying the last flashy waltz, realised all that music should be.

Marie sang her little French songs at Sir Joseph's bidding upon this evening just as she had sung on previous evenings, and Sir Joseph slept through the music as before; but Mountford perceived a change in her manner. She was less at her ease than she had been when he and she had been practically alone. She was silent in the intervals of her singing, and she retired early.

When she was gone Sir Joseph challenged Mountford to a game of cribbage, in which the old man excelled; and Urquhart strolled off to the billiard-room in quest of Andrew Orlebar, who had dined with them, and had disappeared immediately after dinner, neither sharing the after-dinner claret nor the after-dinner cigars.

"Curious fellow, Orlebar," explained the master of the house; "he neither smokes nor drinks. He has no vices; and I sometimes think he has no virtues. He is the nearest approach to a calculating-machine that a warm-blooded animal could attain to."

"And remarkably useful to you, no doubt, Sir Joseph," said Mountford.

"Invaluable. The human calculating-machine is the rarest product of nature. Your average accountant is distracted by the burden of his own egotism, his passions, domestic anxieties, temptations, proclivities. My friend Orlebar is arithmetic incarnate."

Mr. Orlebar had a den of his own adjoining the billiard-room—by courtesy, "Mr. Orlebar's study;" in actual appearance, an accountant's office, a place of pigeon-holes, and ledgers, and dockets, and files, its most interesting literature a long row of Whitaker's Almanacks, sole record of the passing years.[2] The room was conveniently situated for Sir Joseph, who was fond of billiards, and liked to run in and out of his secretary's den as occasion prompted.

Urquhart took down a cue, and amused himself with a few experimental shots, with his eye upon the half-open door of Orlebar's room. Yes, the grey old man was there. Urquhart heard the

scratching of his pen. He went to the door and looked in at the bent
shoulders and iron-grey head, leaning over a page of foolscap.

"Can I tempt you to put down your pen and take up a cue, Mr.
Orlebar?" he asked.

Orlebar looked at him quietly, neither surprise nor gratifica-
tion expressed upon his blunt physiognomy.

"I don't play billiards," he said; "I sometimes mark."

He drew a sheet of blotting-paper over a page of closely-
ruled columns, filled with figures, and left his desk, as if ready for
conversation.

"Don't let me disturb you, if you don't care to play."

"I have finished my evening's work," answered Orlebar, "and I
am going out for my evening constitutional."

"What, you walk after dinner, do you?"

"Always, Mr. Urquhart, wet or fine. No machine will go on
smoothly without oil—and locomotion is the only oil I know of
that will keep the human machine in good working order. I walk
six miles per diem."

"Let me walk with you," said Urquhart, with a friendly air. "Sir
Joseph and Mr. Mountford are at cards. I should like a walk."

"Won't it bore you, though, such a walk as I take, up and down
the terrace, so many turns for a mile? It is not the kind of walk a
young man like you would care for."

Urquhart looked at the dull, grey face before he answered.
There was a lurking shrewdness under the surface stolidity of Mr.
Orlebar's countenance which told him that any attempt to conceal
his own motives would be worse than useless. It would damage his
chances of getting any help in this quarter.

"I don't care where I walk as long as I keep moving," he said,
"and I particularly want a little chat with you."

"Come along, then," said Orlebar, opening a glass door which
gave on to the terrace; and in the next minute he and Urquhart
were walking side by side in the misty stillness of a mild April
night. "You want to talk to me, you say. You want a tip for the
Stock Exchange, no doubt. You've a fancy for some new venture,
and you think Andrew Orlebar is up to the dead."[3]

"My dear Mr. Orlebar, I am not a speculator, for the best of all
reasons. I have never had any capital to invest."

"There are men who speculate without capital; but I am glad you are not one of those," said Orlebar. "They don't often last."

"The subject upon which I want to talk to you is one that touches me much nearer than any money question could."

"Then it must touch you very near."

"It does, for it is an affair of the heart."

"And you come to me for advice in a love-affair!" exclaimed Orlebar, with a dry laugh. "That's the oddest idea I've heard of for a long time. Do I look like a man to advise a lover how to win his mistress?"

"Frankly, you don't," said Urquhart, echoing his laugh, "but in my case you can give very valuable advice, since the lady I am in love with is a kind of ward of your chief's."

"Marie Arnold. You are in love with Marie, are you? Well, you might make a worse choice. She is a handsome young woman, she has a fine voice, she has been well brought up, and has good principles."

"And she will not be without a dowry, I conclude."

"Ah, then, you are not so deep in love as to leave money out of the question."

"My good Mr. Orlebar, I am a man of the world. I made one foolish marriage—a sweet girl, pure as an angel, but without a rap. I am too old to make a second blunder of the same kind. If I were a rich man I should be proud to marry Miss Arnold without a penny; but I have only a younger son's portion, and I have a daughter to maintain. Sir Joseph must naturally desire to find a husband for his ward."

"Why naturally?"

"Because her position in his household is anomalous, and must lead to complications, now that Miss Higginson is grown up."

"Why anomalous?"

"Oh, my dear Orlebar, you must see the difficulty of the case quite as clearly as I do," said Urquhart, growing familiar. "Here is a beautiful girl who is and yet is not a member of Sir Joseph's family. There is no avowed relationship, yet Sir Joseph is evidently as fond of her as of his daughter and heiress. Think of the difference between the positions of those two girls; and consider the bad feeling which that difference must awaken in poor Marie's mind, a year or so hence, unless she marries and takes her place in society on the strength of that marriage. Who, with a grain of worldly knowledge, can doubt that her claim upon Sir Joseph is just as strong as Miss Higginson's?"

"You mean that she is neither more nor less than Sir Joseph's unacknowledged daughter," said Orlebar.

"That is my meaning—and my fixed conviction."

"So let it be, my dear sir," was the bland reply. "You know very nearly as much about Miss Arnold as I do. I was sent to a little mountain town in Provence to fetch the young lady, at Sir Joseph's bidding. Her mother had died rather suddenly, and she, poor child, was alone, and friendless, except for a few good-natured gossips, her dead mother's neighbours, too poor and too insignificant to be of much use to her. I brought her to London, and from London despatched her to Ellerslie, where she has lived ever since. Sir Joseph told me that her father was a clever engineer, who was of great assistance to him in the working of an iron mine, and who was killed while in his service. For my own part I see nothing remarkable in the fact that a man in Sir Joseph's position should show kindness to the widow and orphan of so valuable a servant."

"That he should show kindness, no; but that he should introduce the engineer's daughter into his home and take her to his heart,—there I think you will own he oversteps the mark, and strains credulity. By the way, how old was Marie at the time of her father's death?"

"She was not born."

"A posthumous child! Was she born soon after her father's death?"

"I cannot gratify you with such minute details."

"I have no curiosity upon the point,—only as a man of the world, you must forgive me if I doubt your chief's account of the transaction. I am so fond of Marie that I should like to know all I can about her parentage; in her interest rather than my own. I could love her no less had she been a beggar's brat. I don't want to entrap her into a marriage that would mean poverty,—but if Sir Joseph would make a respectable settlement—a settlement in accordance with his own large means——"

"You have not beaten about the bush with me, and I'll be frank with you, Mr. Urquhart," said Orlebar, gravely. "You are right in supposing that Sir Joseph considers his ward's position somewhat anomalous—or rather that it may appear so when his daughter comes down to the full blaze of the society footlights, while Marie Arnold is left at the back of the stage. I believe I am justified in saying that he would like to see this young person married to a husband whom she could love, and he could approve. With such a husband he would be disposed to treat liberally upon the question of settlements; and I should say that Miss Arnold's dowry might be anything between twenty and fifty thousand pounds. You know, of course, that the larger sum would be as easy a matter to Sir Joseph as the smaller. It would be a question of his own inclination and judgment what amount he should give."

"Undoubtedly! And do you think he would favour my suit? Apart from the money question, I am not a bad match for a young lady in Miss Arnold's position. I belong to one of the oldest families in Cumberland, and I am heir presumptive to an earldom."

"Lord Penrith is still a young man, Mr. Urquhart."

"True; but he is a young man with an old man's habits and ideas; and I don't believe he will ever marry."

"That is a point in your favour. But to be frank with you, I doubt if Sir Joseph would quite approve of your antecedents. His ward would have to be very much in love with you in order to win her guardian's consent to the match."

Urquhart's brow contracted at the suggestion. He knew in his heart that Marie Arnold's present feeling for him was nearer dislike than love; and he knew that he would have a hard battle to fight before he could get her to be his advocate with Sir Joseph. His hope had been that Sir Joseph would adopt him as a suitor, and force his suit with Marie. He did not despair, however, having seen many cases in which love began with aversion.

"As for my antecedents," he replied, after a longish pause, "I don't fancy I have been worse than most young men of family; and having sown a few wild oats I am all the more likely to settle down as a respectable family man. If I could win such a wife as Miss Arnold I should have a spur to ambition, and might make my way in the political world. With Penrith's interest and Sir Joseph's I might be able to achieve a distinguished public position."

"The aspiration is at least creditable. The best advice I can give you is to win the lady. With her on your side there may be a chance of victory. Sir Joseph would do much to secure her happiness," concluded Orlebar in the friendliest tone, and then within himself he said, "But unless I am vastly deceived in my estimate of his knowledge of character, he will never entrust her happiness to a foxy-haired gentleman of your particular type."

While this conversation was being carried on in a perambulatory fashion on the terrace, where the sound of the sea came in with an undertone of monotonous melancholy, as if it were the great voice of Nature mourning the degeneracy of man, another conversation, of which Marie Arnold was the subject, was going on in the drawing-room.

Sir Joseph played his first two games with spirit, but the third game had hardly begun when his attention flagged and his play became careless.

"What do you think of my adopted daughter?" he asked abruptly.

"I think her a very handsome young woman," Mountford answered easily. "There could be hardly two opinions upon that point, and she seems as amiable as she is good-looking."

"She *is*," replied Sir Joseph, quickly. "There is no seeming in her case. She has lived a good many years under this roof, and no one has ever had occasion to find fault with her. She is a dear, good girl, the daughter of a man who was killed in my service. I deemed it my duty to look after her and her widowed mother, and I have never had cause to repent that I undertook the responsibility. She has lived in this house as Sibyl's friend and companion, and she has never shown the slightest jealousy of my little girl's advantages. I don't want her to find out how great a difference the outside world can make between a great heiress and a young woman who is practically a nobody. I should like to see Marie comfortably married before the end of this year; married to a man she can love, a man who shall be worthy of her love."

"There should be no difficulty in finding such a man in the wide circle of your acquaintance, Sir Joseph," said Brandon, gravely, without looking up from his cards.

He had an uncomfortable feeling that there was some serious

intention in his host's discourse, an intention that involved himself.

"No, indeed. I know plenty of young men on their promotion, decent fellows enough, to whom a wife with twenty thousand or so for her dowry would be like a gift dropped from heaven. But I should like to find a husband of whose antecedents I know more than I can know about a casual acquaintance of the West End or City, a man who comes of a good stock, and in whom honour and generous feeling are hereditary qualities. I believe in heredity, Mr. Mountford. My father was a peasant, but he was an honest man, and he could trace his descent from many generations of honest, God-fearing men. We plebeians have our old races as well as you patricians."

"I have never doubted that. On the Allandale estate there are peasant families that were settled on the soil before the signing of the great Charter freed them from their heaviest burdens."

The game continued languidly, till Sir Joseph laid down his cards with a thoughtful sigh, took off his spectacles, and leant back in his chair.

"That girl doesn't like Urquhart," he said, abruptly. "I wonder whether you noticed the change in her manner to-night."

"Yes, Sir Joseph, I saw that Miss Arnold seemed hardly in her usual good spirits this evening. Has Mr. Urquhart made himself obnoxious to her in any way?"

"Not to my knowledge. It is only a womanish prejudice for which she can give no reason. I sounded her about him the last time he was here. She doesn't like him; doesn't know why; objects to the colour of his hair or the shape of his nose, perhaps. I didn't argue the matter with her, and I shouldn't have had him here again if he hadn't offered himself. It wouldn't have been neighbourly to say no—and here he is. However, if she had liked him ever so well I should have felt very doubtful about letting her marry him. I have heard some disagreeable stories about his conduct in relation to women."

Brandon was silent. He had not been favourably impressed by Lord Penrith's younger brother; but he did not want to injure that gentleman's chances with Marie Arnold, having made up his mind that Urquhart was honestly in love with her.

Sir Joseph had questioned him before to-night about his own plans for the future—the scheme of life which he had made for himself—and Brandon had told his host that he meant to go back to Africa. His future lay there, in a wandering life. He had no other ambition—no other desire. The old world of civilisation could offer him nothing in exchange for the limitless horizons of the desert, and the victories of the practised hunter.

Sir Joseph had argued against the foolishness of this idea, and now to-night he took up the thread of a former conversation.

"I can conceive no greater waste of life than to tramp about a sandy wilderness and shoot lions, with occasional intervals of malarial fever," he said.

"The life suits me as no other life could," replied Brandon.

"But have you no tie to bind you to your own country? Have you never been in love; or have you given your English heart to a blackamoor?"

"Since my boyish passion for my tutor's daughter, a buxom young woman of nine-and-twenty, whom I adored when I wore Eton collars, and to whom I wrote six-page love-letters every week while I was at the University, I have been heart-whole," replied Brandon, with perfect frankness. "Nor does my passion for the land of the Zambesi extend to her living products in the shape of black beauty. I have hitherto been adamant to the charms of the Hottentot Venus."[4]

"And you are free—free to fall in love with a handsome woman and to marry her?"

"No, Sir Joseph, I am not free to marry, and I shall never marry."

"You are not free! Do you mean to tell me that you entangled yourself by a foolish marriage while you were a lad—married the young woman of nine-and-twenty, your tutor's daughter?"

"My tutor's daughter was far too wise to reciprocate my boyish flame. She married one of the senior masters, and is on the high road to become wife of a bishop."

"Yet you say you are not free to marry?"

"There are reasons in my family history which should forbid marriage in my case, Sir Joseph," Brandon answered, gravely.

And then, as in a vision of the night, there came back upon

the old man a fair young face turned to him in a sunlit room, a sad pale face, streaming with tears, and a gentle voice telling him a cruel story of marriage and motherhood ending in lunacy. Yes; this young man's mother went out of her mind soon after his birth, and there was a strain of madness in his blood. It was only right that he should live and die unmarried; and yet—but for this cruel bar—what an excellent husband he would have made for Marie.

Sir Joseph believed in himself as a judge of character, and he had formed a high opinion of Brandon Mountford's rectitude and good-feeling. And then he would have liked to have shown kindness to the son of that man whom Lucy Mountford had loved, with a girl's innocent fancy, before she had seen the face of her low-born husband.

CHAPTER VII

URQUHART CONSIDERS HIMSELF ILL-USED

That suggestion of a possible marriage had stirred the waters of Marah[1] in Brandon Mountford's memory. In every man's mind there is some Marah-pool which needs but a breath to disturb its bitter waters. With him the pool lay still and deep; yet he had an ever-present consciousness that it was there, a silent sorrow, which made his life different from the lives of other young men.

The fear of hereditary madness was the shadow that wrapped him round, and set him apart from men of his own age and circumstances, and hemmed him in with considerations which but rarely block a young man's pathway.

He looked back to-night in the solitude of his bedroom at Ellerslie, with the casements flung open to the soft spring night, and with all the waste of dark waters stretching far away to the distant silvery line that marked the horizon, touched with starlight. He looked back, as he often looked, and remembered his solitary childhood with his father's mother, old Mrs. Mountford, widow of General Mountford, who had fought in Arthur Wellesley's Indian campaign.[2] He remembered that sad childhood, his father away in India, a captain of engineers under Sir Robert Napier,[3] his grand-

mother a gloomy woman, evangelical, with pinched means, and a
bitter sense of disappointment in her only son, despondent alike
of the here and the hereafter. He remembered how when he was
between fourteen and fifteen he had been sent from Wellington
College to a house at Highgate to see his dying mother, the mother
whose face he had never looked upon within his memory. A lucid,
or semi-lucid interval, had marked the ebbing away of life, and she
had entreated to see her son, her baby, as she called him piteously.

The tall lad stood beside her bed, holding her wasted hand in
his, looking down at her with tearful eyes; and her first impulse
had been to repudiate him.

"Who is this great boy?" she asked. "Mine was a little baby."

The nurse tried to explain to her, but she did not listen to the
explanation. She was looking at the boy's face, and that told her
more than anything the nurse could say about the years that had
gone, and the changes made by time.

"Yes, yes, you are my boy," she cried. "You have your father's
eyes. Where is he—where is my husband? Why doesn't he come to
me? He is very—everybody is unkind."

The lad stayed at the doctor's house until all was over, and saw
much of his mother in those last few days—those weary closing
hours of life, during which her mind was clearer than it had been
in all the melancholy years since her son's birth. From doctor and
nurses the son heard the history of those years of seclusion: her
delusions, her fancies, the gleams of reason, the intervals of utter
darkness. He saw the rooms in which she had lived, brightly furnished, home-like, comfortable even to luxury; and he understood
how the absent husband had cared for his helpless wife, shirking no
outlay that could ensure her well-being. He walked in the garden
where she had walked, a spacious, old-fashioned garden, where the
trees and shrubs and holly hedges had been growing for more than
a century, and from which he could see the great city veiled in its
smoke-curtain, vague, formless, monstrous. He walked there full of
melancholy thoughts. The poor mother—all his life long a prisoner
within those narrow bounds. No, not quite a prisoner. She had been
allowed carriage-airings whenever her condition permitted her being
taken out of doors—carriage-airings in the custody of a mad-house
nurse. She had been no better off than a state prisoner, at best. Years

afterwards, when he saw the rocky island of St. Marguerite, and the fortress in which the masked prisoner endured long years of silent solitude,[4] his thoughts went back to the sitting-room at Highgate, and the sunny garden above the great smoke-bound city.

Those few days at Highgate made a crisis in Brandon Mountford's youth. He went back to Wellington an altered being, and masters and boys were alike struck with the change which his mother's death had made in him. It was odd that he should take his loss so deeply to heart, they said, since he had seen very little of his mother, a confirmed invalid. Over Brandon's life henceforth there brooded the shadow of a dark fate. He had talked to the doctor at Highgate, had pressed him closely upon the question of hereditary lunacy, had inquired into the nature of his mother's malady, and had discovered that the mental flaw had first showed itself in the form of epilepsy, from which she had suffered as a young girl, but having, as it was supposed, entirely outlived the tendency to that terrible disease, she and her parents had kept that dark experience of her girlhood a secret from her husband and his family, an offence which old Mrs. Mountford had never forgiven.

Over him, too, hung that horror of possible epilepsy. He brooded on this possibility, and magnified its terrors as only youthful imagination can. He thought of himself as a creature apart from his fellows, marked with the signs of a revolting disease. When the fifth chapter of the Second Book of Kings was read, he compared himself with Naaman the leper; but, alas! the age of miraculous cures was past; there was no river in which he could wash and be free from the tendency that was in his blood, the ghastly heritage from his dead mother.

He exaggerated all his boyish ailments, saw in every headache an omen of impending evil. It may have been by reason of these gloomy thoughts, or it may have been because his fears were rightly grounded, and that the fatal tendency was latent in his constitution, that the dreaded evil happened. He was nearly eighteen years of age when the first attack occurred. The foul fiend of epilepsy seized upon him one evening in the school chapel, rent and tore him, and left him shattered and weakened, with a dull despair in his heart. Henceforth he knew himself doomed. One after another these horrible convulsive seizures would tear at brain and body, until reason would be wrecked in the struggle, and madness would close the scene. As it had been with his mother, so it would be with him. He gave up all idea of the army. He went to Cambridge, worked hard there, and in his three years of University life had only that milder form of epileptic seizure which French physicians call le petit mal, in contradistinction to the severe and convulsive type, or le grand mal.[5] Sometimes, in his rooms, with his books open before him, or on the river, the sculls in his hands moving slowly with measured beat, there would be a sudden lapse of consciousness. He would go on rowing, perhaps, with a mechanical motion; or the sculls would cease to work, and the boat would drift with the stream for a little way, the man sitting there lost to the world around him, knowing nothing till the slow awakening as from a trance, with the knowledge that he had lost himself, that in those few minutes reason and memory had gone. The consciousness of this malady darkened those days which should have been full of pleasantness; but he managed to take a very creditable degree, to the delight of his father, who enjoyed a year's furlough in his son's society, travelling through France and Italy. At Brindisi father and son parted, on board a P. and O. steamer, parted never to meet again on earth, for within a few months of his return to India Major Mountford died of jungle fever, and Brandon was lord of himself and of his small estate.

The first use he made of his independence was to shake off the trammels of civilisation, and to set his face towards the wilderness. His Cambridge doctor had told him that his best chance of warding off future attacks, and of outgrowing his malady, would be found in a free, adventurous life—sport, travel—under God's sky. Much learning was a thing for him to avoid; nor would he be wise in going to the Bar, or in taking up medicine as a profession. He stayed at Cambridge and worked for his degree, only to gratify his father. He had no ambition of his own in association with the civilised world. If he was to go through life torn by devils, let the tormentors come upon him in the desert, where there would be none to see him in his agony, or at least no one whose scornful pity could smite him to the quick.

His life in the wilderness had been on the whole a happy life. His love of sport and adventure had grown and strengthened with the growth of his skill as a marksman and his acumen as an explorer. Not often had his hereditary malady overtaken him in the midst of his wanderings, but he had not been altogether free from such visitations, and he knew that the tendency was still uncon- quered, an enemy kept at bay, for the most part, but not beaten.

What assurance had he that epilepsy might not sooner or later develop into dementia, as in the case of his mother?

Sir Joseph had not even hinted at his idea of Mountford as a husband for Marie; so there had been no harm done, the old man told himself, as he reflected upon last night's conversation with his guest, while he took his morning walk on the terrace, before the nine o'clock breakfast. Brandon had started for the river some hours before, having risen at dawn; but he and the keeper had gone down to the stream alone, Urquhart pleading a headache as a reason for staying indoors.

Marie Arnold appeared on the terrace, looking bright and fresh in her pink cotton frock and black silk apron, soon after eight, and joined Sir Joseph in his walk.

"A long letter from Sibyl," said the old man. "She is coming back early next week. Her cough has quite gone, and she is pining for home. You'll be glad to have her back again, won't you, Marie?"

"Very glad. Ellerslie is not Ellerslie without her."

"And about this time next year she will be getting herself ready for the first May Drawing-room, and then good-bye Ellerslie, and good-bye girlhood," said Sir Joseph with a sigh. "She will be swal- lowed up alive in the fashionable whirlpool, and you and I will lose our hold upon her."

"I'm not afraid of that, Sir Joseph. I don't think anything the world can do will ever change her."

"Well, perhaps you are right. Her mother passed through the ordeal unchanged. She was in the world, but never of it. She was like that young woman old John Evelyn was so fond of, who went dancing through the fiery furnace of Court life, play-acting and singing, and waiting upon the Queen, and talking to the King, in a society where half the women were—unmentionable, and yet remained a saint to the last.[6] Ah me! Sweet Mrs. Godolphin died in the bloom of her youth and beauty, like my dear wife. Well, Marie, we must reconcile ourselves to the inevitable. Sibyl's schoolroom days are over, and you are no longer a young girl. You must marry, my dear; we must find a good husband for you."

"Please don't anticipate Fate, Sir Joseph," said Marie, with a little nervous laugh, and a vivid blush. "If Providence means me to marry, the husband will appear in due time—and in the meanwhile I shall be quite content to live my own quiet life here, with old Mrs. Morison, while you and Sibyl are in London."

"And you will not think yourself hardly used—you won't think it hard that Sibyl should have all the pleasures the great world can give while you are buried in this dull country home?"

"What right have I to envy Sibyl her life? I ought to feel nothing but gratitude for your goodness to my mother and me. If you had made me a servant I ought to have been contented."

"Don't, Marie, don't! You pain me when you talk like that. I want you to be happy, independent, assured of a bright future. I want you to feel that you have a claim upon me, a strong claim—that you are as much to me as an orphan niece could be—more than a niece—almost as much as a daughter," added Sir Joseph, his eyes dim with tears.

"You are all goodness to me. I have had more affection from you than I ever had from my mother, and Sibyl has been all a sister could be. Do you think I am going to complain because her lot is cast in the great world and mine out of it?"

"You are a good girl, and your lot may be happier than hers, perhaps. Who can tell?"

Life went on quietly at Ellerslie after this conversation between Sir Joseph and his adopted daughter; but that idea of finding a husband for Marie Arnold was still uppermost in his mind, and he was startled when Hubert Urquhart came to him in his study two days later and avowed his affection for Miss Arnold, an affection which he only waited Sir Joseph's consent to declare to the young lady.

"What! Have you said nothing to Marie about your feelings?" asked Sir Joseph.

"Nothing definite. I may have hinted at the state of the case. It has been hardly possible for me to be in her society, and not let her see that I adore her."

"And how has she taken your hints, or your adoration?"

"She is an enigma to me, Sir Joseph. Yet I can but think if I had your approval—if you showed yourself really in favour of our marriage—she would not look unkindly upon me."

"Oh, you think she would not object if I urged your suit. Well, Mr. Urquhart, I'll be frank with you, and confess that you are about the last man I would choose as a husband for my adopted daughter. I may as well call her my adopted daughter, for I have all a father's affection for her."

"I am assured of that, Sir Joseph," said Urquhart, "but I am at a loss to understand your objection to me as a match for a young lady who, I am informed, is the daughter of a mechanic, and who therefore would make some advance in the social scale if she became the wife of an earl's younger son."

"'Kind hearts are more than coronets,' Mr. Urquhart. Your lineage is unobjectionable; but I cannot say as much for your character or antecedents."

"I may have gone the pace a little," admitted Urquhart; "but I have sown my wild oats."

"It is not your wild oats I am thinking about, so much as the character of the sower," answered Sir Joseph, gravely. "I have heard stories of your unkindness and neglect as a husband, Mr. Urquhart. Forgive me if I say that you have not a good character from your last place. I have been told that your wife died of a broken heart."

"Then you have been told lies, Sir Joseph. Society seldom forgives a man who marries out of its ranks. I married a country parson's penniless daughter; and any unhappiness there may have been in her life was the result of circumstances over which I had no control. Were I to marry your adopted daughter I conclude you would make a settlement which would secure her from the pinch of poverty, and which might help me to carve out a career for myself, either in politics or at the Bar."

"I would do much for a man she could love, and whom I could trust," replied Sir Joseph, gravely. "No question of money should stand between her and happiness. But, to be frank with you once more, you are by no means the man I would choose."

"I understand," said Urquhart, pale with anger, yet trying to be courteous. "You have made your choice already, perhaps? Mr. Mountford is the man you would prefer."

"Mr. Mountford is out of the question. He is a bachelor by inclination and is bent upon a roving life in South Africa."

"Perhaps, Sir Joseph, after your frank depreciation of my character—I had better pack my portmanteau and leave the salmon to more favoured anglers. I have no right to inflict an unwelcome guest upon your family circle."

"Don't talk nonsense, man. I may object to you as a husband for an impulsive, inexperienced girl—but that's no reason why I should turn you out of doors. Stop as long as you like; only give Marie no more hints of your adoration. I have an idea that she is tolerably heart-whole, so far as you are concerned."

Urquhart did not order the packing of his portmanteau. The salmon river was very attractive at this season, and it would not have suited his plans to leave Ellerslie, above all to leave Brandon Mountford master of the situation; for let Sir Joseph say what he would, Urquhart thought that Mountford's pretensions would be favoured. Mountford's family was as good as his, Urquhart's; and Mountford's antecedents offered no ugly blots to the inquiring eye. He had done well at the University. He had never made himself notorious by riotous living or debt. He had won renown as a fine shot and a sagacious explorer, and had published a record of his travels which had been praised by the critics and appreciated by the public. In such a man as this Urquhart saw a dangerous rival. He saw, too, that Marie was interested in Mountford, and that it needed but some show of sympathy on his part to win her heart. Here, however, he was puzzled. Mountford seemed careless of charms which kindled Urquhart's warmest feelings. Was this coldness simulated, the mask of some deep design; or was the man really indifferent? Urquhart watched him closely, and could surprise no touch of tenderness amidst his unvarying courtesy; yet his own natural bent towards dissimulation inclined him to believe that Mountford was masking his batteries. There are some women who care only for the unattainable; and it might be that Marie thought all the more of Mountford because she had been unable to subjugate him. Urquhart had tried the other plan and had failed ignominiously.

Mountford had been nearly three weeks at Ellerslie, and seemed to have interwoven himself into the family life. Sir Joseph had taken a cordial liking for him, and it was the old man's hearty kindness which induced him to protract his visit much beyond his original intention.

"I don't know what we shall do without you when you leave us," said Sir Joseph. "We shall miss him sadly when he goes, shan't we, Marie?"

He did not see Marie Arnold's blush, as she bent over the newspaper she had been reading, and he thought her answer was cold and careless. And then he remembered Brandon's determination to remain unmarried—a resolve that was perhaps over scrupulous, since his mother's malady might have bequeathed no fatal taint to him,—and he thought it a merciful dispensation that Marie Arnold should be careless and indifferent.

It was after seven o'clock when Mountford came home that evening. He had been for a lonely ramble over the moor, glad to escape from Urquhart's society, even at the sacrifice of sport. Urquhart's conversation was the essence of worldly wisdom, of the streets streety; and a man who has spent his happiest years in the solitary places of the earth, and has communed with God and Nature under tropical stars, does not find much salt or savour in the gossip of clubs, or the intrigues and money troubles of men about town.

"I never knew such a fellow for not being interested in things that interest other men," said Urquhart discontentedly, when one of his choicest anecdotes had fallen flat. "I don't believe you care even for the turf."

"Not a jot," answered Brandon. "I admire a race-horse because he is the perfection of blood and speed, not because he can win a cup."

"Your indifference makes you very bad company," grumbled Urquhart. "We can't all shoot lions."

To-day Brandon had bathed his brain and senses in solitude, and he felt all the better for the long ramble in the wild bleak country. He had seen Killander Castle afar off, tall and grey above the ridge of the moor, and he had wondered idly whether he would ever see it nearer, and what kind of a man its owner, Urquhart's eldest brother, might be. And now in the fading light he walked up the hill, and by the winding shrubberied road that led to Ellerslie

House. A carriage was driving a little way in front of him as he passed the lodge-gate. It disappeared at the first turn of the road, and he thought no more of it, until he saw it standing before the porch while a footman busied himself in carrying various articles of luggage, handbags, books, umbrellas, and such small deer, into the hall.

From the hall came a sound of voices, Sir Joseph's strong baritone, and a girlish voice which was like music, so low and sweetly toned. Could it be the daughter of the house? Brandon went into the hall feeling shyer than he had ever been in his life before. In those last days of confidential intercourse in Italy, when the father and son had talked together as man and man, Major Mountford had told his son that pathetic story of a hopeless love, struggled against valiantly, and never revealed. The thought that he was going to see the daughter of the woman his father had loved thrilled him strangely. He had been told that Sibyl was like her mother, and it was with a feeling almost of awe that he approached the girl of eighteen.

He remembered an old photograph, grey and faded, a poor little photograph taken on the beach at Bognor by an itinerant photographer—the portrait of a girl in a broad-brimmed hat and an old-fashioned frock, but with oh, so sweet and delicate a countenance—features so refined in their chiselling, such lovely lines of chin and throat, and such a slender, graceful figure! His father had taken that poor little photograph from his despatch-box. It was on glass, and it had accompanied him all over India without coming to grief; and from the shadow-land of death and vanished years the young face had looked at Brandon dimly, like a ghost.

Yes, there were the same features, the same gracious lines, the same soft depth in the dark grey eyes that were looking at him now.

"Hullo, Mountford," cried Sir Joseph, gaily; "the master of the house has come home. No more lax behaviour now! We shall have to mind our manners. Come and be introduced to my tyrant."

Sibyl held out her hand to him in the frankest, friendliest way.

"I am ever so much obliged to you for helping to keep father in good spirits," she said.

CHAPTER VIII

DREAMING AND WAKING

LIFE at Ellerslie took a new colour for Brandon Mountford after that day. It had been pleasant, easy, unconventional from the beginning. He had felt the cordiality of Sir Joseph's welcome, the assurance that his presence gave pleasure to his host—but these things made an every-day happiness, and there was nothing wonderful or dream-like in a well-found country house, a fine salmon river and a cheery old man who had begun his ascent to Fortune's Temple on the lowest rung of the ladder.

Sibyl's coming had changed the country house into an enchanted palace, the wind-blown terrace and lawns and shrubberies overlooking the bleak Irish Sea into an earthly paradise. Her coming had changed life into a lovely dream. Her light figure moving to and fro on the rough banks of the river transformed that stream into a magical watercourse leading to an unexplored Eden. When a boating expedition was proposed one day he almost expected to find the boat drifting into the azure light of caverns as blue as the vast blue vault at Capri. He expected anything wonderful and abnormal rather than the rude, grey hills and the barren moorland.

In the beginning he surrendered himself blindly to the enchantment of this girl's society. He knew that he could never think of himself, or be thought of by Sir Joseph, as a possible husband for this heiress of mines and millions. Sir Joseph had frankly stated his ambitious hopes for his daughter.

"She must marry a peer, my dear Mountford," he said. "I want her to rise to the sphere which her mother left when she stooped to marry me. I want to see her a Countess, before I die. She is pretty enough, and she will be rich enough to be a Duchess—if there were an eligible Duke. I won't marry her to a fortune-seeker or a profligate, Mountford. I may be ambitious, but I won't sacrifice my girl's happiness, even to make her a peeress."

All this had been said more than once before Sibyl's return, and all this Mountford had accepted as inevitable—a decree of destiny, since Sir Joseph was the kind of man to carry out his own ideas to the letter, and it would be hard if among the bachelor Peers of Great Britain a worthy as well as a titled husband could not be found for his heiress. Mountford knew himself out of the running.

"Were I a Duke, and the inheritor of a couple of shires, I should be just as ineligible as I am now," he thought. "Nothing would ever induce me to link my life with a dearer life, and blight the heart that loved me."

Having thus made up his mind about himself—having set himself resolutely on the side of the celibates—Brandon Mountford made the mistake which men are apt to make in such circumstances. He was too secure of himself. He thought that he might reckon in advance of the Greybeard, Time, and think of himself as a middle-aged unimpressionable misogynist, while he was still in the very morning of life, much fresher in heart and brain than the majority of young men, since he had never blunted his feelings in the mill-round of youthful dissipations—had not wasted the first fervent love of boyhood upon the syrens and sylphs of the music-halls or the dancing-club—had not been spoiled or wearied by the vacuity and parrot-speech of the modish young lady, who is by way of being sporting or fast.

To Brandon Mountford an English girl in the morning of her youth was almost a new creation. Had Aphrodite herself met him in some cavern of that bleak shore, in the half light of daybreak, she could not have seemed more enchanting than Sibyl in the grace and purity of her unspoiled girlhood. He yielded unresistingly to the charm of her presence, accepted her friendly advances, telling her lightly that she was to think of him as a newly discovered poor relation, something of the nature of an uncle.

"You might as well call me uncle, Miss Higginson," he said one day, when he was assisting Sibyl and Marie not to catch salmon.

They had taken a good many lessons in the art of throwing a fly, but had not yet achieved the distinction of a bite.

"Oh, I couldn't possibly do that," Sibyl answered, decisively; "you are much too young for an uncle. I'll call you cousin, if you like, though perhaps even that would sound foolish. But we are a kind of cousins, aren't we?"

"Yes, we are cousins—in the third degree."

"I'm glad of that. I like to know that I am related to you. Father likes you so much, quite as well as if you were his nephew. Please call me Sibyl in future. Miss Higginson is dreadfully formal, and it is such an ugly name."

It was agreed therefore that they were to call each other Brandon and Sibyl.

"We are actually cousins," Sibyl explained, the first time she uttered the visitor's Christian name in her father's hearing, "so it would be absurd to go on mistering and missing each other."

The speech was so frankly spoken that Sir Joseph took no alarm at the idea. He, too, had accepted Brandon Mountford as a harmless bachelor cousin. He had met dozens of such young men in society; young men as harmless, and often as necessary, by reason of their helpfulness in all the minor details of domestic life, as the often-quoted cat. He had no idea that such an existence could menace his dearest hopes.

The time came, too soon for Brandon's peace, after ten or twelve days of unalloyed bliss, when the young man knew his own peril. He knew that he loved Sibyl with the love that means the happiness or misery of a lifetime—or, at least, of all life's best years. There may be healing for such a wound, but it is a cure so gradual and so tardy that the convalescent hardly knows whether the passing years have conquered his passion or worn out his heart.

He knew that he loved her—knew that his delight in her society was something stronger and deeper than a man's pleasure in the company of a lovely and fascinating girl—knew that the lightest touch of her hand thrilled him, that the sound of her voice, heard casually from the garden while he was writing a letter by the open window of his own room, would set his heart beating and make him write nonsense.

They had been rarely alone together; they had only talked to each other in the lightest strains upon the most casual subjects. Marie was always with them, walking by sea or moor, lounging on the terrace, lingering over the friendly tea table, visiting the stables, driving, riding, Marie was as inevitable as Sibyl's shadow. Brandon might have thought that this perpetual companionship on Miss Arnold's part was in obedience to orders from Sir Joseph; but Sir Joseph's whole way of life was too unsophisticated to allow of such an idea. No, Sir Joseph trusted his guest, and it was for his guest to prove worthy of the confidence that had been so freely given. Brandon knew that he had been received on the strength of his race; warranted trustworthy, as it were, because of the good blood that flowed in his veins, the gentleman's heritage of honour and self-respect. Not for all that this earth can give of happiness would he have proved himself unworthy of the good man's confidence.

Thinking over that "shadowing" of Sibyl by Marie Arnold, he accounted for it to his own satisfaction as a sign of the elder girl's jealous attachment to her adopted sister. It must be jealousy, and only jealousy, which made Marie dog their footsteps, and intrude her own personality upon every conversation, every small scheme of amusement. There were times when he could see that even Sibyl was annoyed by the elder girl's obtrusiveness. They could talk of no subject in which Marie would not take her part, sometimes talking sheer nonsense, in her eagerness to join in their conversation.

Whatever the feeling was which influenced this strong and passionate nature, it was a feeling that totally changed the girl's manner—and the change, in Brandon's opinion, was greatly for the worse. He could but compare the Marie Arnold of the present— vehement, excitable, dictatorial even—with the Marie Arnold of those quiet days before Sibyl's return. Then the dependant had been all gentleness, modest, retiring, given to thoughtful silence rather than overmuch speech. Now she was loquacious, irritable, capricious, changing without apparent reason from exaggerated gaiety to sullen gloom—resenting unintended slights, exacting, pettish.

To Brandon the change became hourly more mysterious, and more worrying.

"You know Miss Arnold better than I do," he said to Urquhart one evening in the billiard-room, "and perhaps you can tell me if she is often as disagreeable as she was to-day during our river excursion?"

"In my sight Marie Arnold can never be disagreeable. She is simply the loveliest woman I know, and the most fascinating."

"I did not know you were so ardent an admirer. She is handsome, unquestionably—in a certain style—and I can understand your admiring her. But I think you will admit that she has changed for the worse since Miss Higginson's return."

"Possibly. I dare say she feels her false position a little more keenly when Sibyl is at home."

"You are pleased to talk of a false position—but really I don't see where the falsehood comes in. Sir Joseph treats her with unwavering kindness."

"Sir Joseph treats his collie dog with unwavering kindness; but do you suppose such a girl as Marie—conscious of the highest gifts a woman can possess—does not feel the difference between the acknowledged and the unacknowledged daughter—the heiress and the dependent?"

"I don't think Miss Arnold—or any friend of Miss Arnold's—has the right to jump at conclusions upon such a subject as that," returned Brandon, with grave displeasure.

He liked, and even respected, Sir Joseph Higginson, and on that account alone was inclined to resent the insinuation that this girl, whose presence was an ostensible fact in the family circle, could be the offspring of some low intrigue. Much more did he dislike the idea that Sibyl's companion and friend should be a base-born sister, the inheritor of a mother's shame.

"Perhaps, as Sir Joseph is a very good fellow, and a millionaire, the wisest course for all of us is to imagine his moral character stainless," Urquhart retorted, with an open sneer. "For my part I am inclined to think him human, and that his affection for Marie Arnold has its root in an unforgotten love of his youth. I don't believe in abstract benevolence—or adopted nieces."

Suddenly, swiftly it was borne in upon Brandon Mountford that this Paradise along whose sunlit paths he had been wandering, lost in a dream of unquestioning bliss—was a Paradise from which he must flee; and that, once having left Eden, those good angels, Self-respect and Honour, standing with flaming swords on either side of the gate, would forbid his return. He had been trusted in that household—he had been warned by implication against any attempt to win Sibyl's heart: and now he shrank appalled, bewildered, yet overjoyed, at the thought that her heart was almost won.

Yes, albeit they were so rarely together and alone, even for a few minutes, he had seen the signs of a growing interest in him and his life. He had seen the fair young face steeped in those sudden overwhelming blushes which tell of nascent love. He had seen Sibyl start at his footstep—beam with gladness at his approach. He had seen her intense interest in those stories of his travels which he had told casually at first, and with a diffident apprehension of becoming a bore, but which both Sibyl and Marie had urged him to enlarge upon, and to repeat not once but several times—stories of lions— stories of savage foes—stories of fever—stories of tricksters and card-sharpers at Port Natal—stories of buffaloes lost or dead—of extinguished camp fires—there was no detail of his adventurous wanderings in which those two listeners were not interested.

"I feel like a modern Othello with a pair of Desdemonas," he said lightly, one afternoon as he was sculling lazily with the current, while Sibyl and Marie sat in the stern of the skiff, Sibyl holding the rudder-lines and then he quoted, almost automatically—

> "She loved me for the dangers I had pass'd:
> And I loved her, that she did pity them."[1]

"Oh, Sibyl," he cried, as the nose of the boat swung suddenly round, "what a jerk! Is that your idea of steering?"

"I beg your pardon, Brandon. I thought that barge was coming towards us."

"That barge" was hugging the furthermost shore, about a quarter of a mile away. Brandon glanced at Marie, and was surprised at the angry light in the large, dark eyes; surprised at the searching gaze which the elder girl fixed upon Sibyl's drooping eyelids and blushing cheeks.

CHAPTER IX

IN THE PINE WOOD

BRANDON MOUNTFORD had talked of leaving Ellerslie several times before his final resolution to fly from danger; but on each occasion Sir Joseph had pressed him to stay.

"You don't want to be in London, Mountford," he said. "You are not a man about town like Urquhart. London can get on without you, even though the season has begun. Urquhart tells me he must be in town before the twentieth. You may as well stop till then. You two fellows are company for each other; and I like to see young people about my house."

And on each occasion Brandon had weakly yielded, believing that if sadness should be the bitter after-fruit of joy the sadness would be for himself alone, and the girl he loved in secret would go on her way, happy and heart-whole, to gladden some luckier life than his.

But now it had been made clear to him, by casual looks and tones, and innocent girlish emotions, that his love was returned—and there was no choice for him as a man of honour. He must go. It was not a question of ways and means. Had there been no barrier but his poverty between the heiress and himself, he would have hazarded being thought a fortune-hunter, and would have risked a rough refusal from Sir Joseph. He would at least have pleaded his own cause, offered the devotion of an honourable man, and taken his chance with the father. But between him and the woman he loved, there stood a hideous spectre,—the shadow that walketh at noon-day—the terror of a disease whose lightest aspect would chill that tender womanly heart, and whose fiercer phases might bring disgust as well as fear to the mind which now associated him with only noble and gracious things.

Horrible, thrice horrible, that the girl he loved should ever look upon him in the clutch of those devils whose grip he had once felt, rending and tearing him. A year of cloudless wedded life could not obliterate one moment of that grisly horror, when the face she loved would be convulsed and changed, and the lips she had kissed would be disfigured with foam and blood.

No, love and marriage, the natural lot of other men, from the peer to the ploughman, were not for Brandon Mountford. Fate had given him good looks, a keen intelligence, a fine frame,—but Fate had laid upon him the burden of hereditary disease, and he must bear his burden with manly fortitude. He must not let an innocent and loving girl wither under the blight that lay upon him.

Once during those happy days at Ellerslie, just when he was beginning to realise the fact that his love was returned, and was beginning to foreshadow the sorrow of parting, he was reminded of his misery by an attack of "le petit mal." Sitting in the sunlit garden watching Marie and Sibyl playing tennis—two supple flying forms, in gowns whose whiteness flashed in the sunshine—the cloud¹ came over him. He sat with fixed unseeing eyes, knowing nothing, till he heard a clock striking the hour, and awakening as from a dull and heavy sleep, he saw that the two girls had left the tennis court, that the net had been taken down, and he was sitting alone. That attack, slight and harmless though it was, roused Mountford to immediate action. Finding it very difficult to resist Sir Joseph's hospitable urgency, strengthened as it was by his own unwillingness to depart, Mountford made all his preparations for departure quietly one morning, packed portmanteau and fishing tackle without asking help from anybody, with all the handiness of a traveller accustomed to roughing it in an uncivilised country. He had made up his mind irrevocably. He would leave Ellerslie next morning for London, spend the summer among his friends in or near London, and go back to Africa in the autumn. He meant to say nothing more about departure till he met Sir Joseph at breakfast on the following morning, when he could take a swift and sudden leave on the pretence of a summons from a kinsman, which excuse would not be a very great divergence from truth, since an old bachelor uncle, his mother's elder brother, who had made a fortune as a banker in Melbourne, had for some time been urgent in his invitations.

Mountford had excused himself from accompanying Urquhart to the river, and had left Sibyl and her inseparable companion sauntering together on the terrace outside the breakfast-room, perhaps waiting for him to propose river, or sea, or moorland ramble. Whatever they might have intended, Brandon Mountford left them to their own devices, and went straight to his room, where he began the prosaic task of folding his clothes, and disposing them in two well-worn portmanteaux, which smelt of tar and sea-water; and of looking over and packing his supply of flies and tackle, thinking with a despairing mournfulness of the river which he might never fish again. Never had he been so happy—or so unhappy—as at Ellerslie. He paused in his morning's work once as he crossed the room, arrested by his own image in the cheval glass. He stopped to survey himself, deliberately, from top to toe, looking at himself with the smile of bitterness, the smile that curls the lips with an upward curve, while the eyes remain fixed and gloomy.

"Not half a bad-looking fellow," he commented scornfully, "tall, well set up, a broad forehead, a bold, well-opened eye, features fairly regular, skin without a blemish."

And then he took a book from the pocket of his portmanteau—a thin, cloth-bound octavo—and opened it at a page which had been read often enough for the volume to open of its own accord at that particular place.

This was the passage he had marked with the broad, heavy stroke of a red pencil:—

"Characteristics—turgescence of face, distortion of mouth and eyes, immobility of pupil, bloody froth issuing from mouth. This is the usual attack, or the grand mal."

"Not much room for a man to be vain of his looks who is subject to such a transformation as that," he said to himself, as he put the book back into its hiding-place.

He had bought this exhaustive treatise upon his malady, by a specialist, after his first attack, and had read and re-read the dismal details so coldly, so plainly described, not for the study of the sufferer, but for the calmer intelligence of the healer, the man of science, to whom the most revolting of maladies is only an interesting study, most interesting, when most terrible.

He had read the whole history of this strange disease. He had read of individual cases, and their abnormal developments. He had hung with a grisly fascination over the story of the unhappy victim, who, after being subject to epilepsy in its normal form

from his childhood, at seven and twenty years of age suffered a
sudden change in the nature of his malady, and became the victim
of a murderous instinct which he resisted with the greatest difficulty, wrestling with himself as the demoniacs of old wrestled,
fighting against the savage thirst for bloodshed which urged him
to slay even his nearest and dearest, the mother he loved, the father
he had honoured and obeyed all his life.

The story of horror had eaten itself, like some corroding acid,
into Brandon's brain. What if over his distorted mind that same
fierce thirst for blood should come—suddenly, like a fiery atmosphere steeping his senses—suddenly, like the branding heat of the
tropical sun leaping out of a tempestuous sky? There was no reason
why he should not suffer a change as terrible as that which had made
this Swabian peasant's life an existence of fear and trembling.

Horror unutterable, to have won the woman he loved, to have
promised to care for her and cherish her, to be trusted and loved
by her; and after a year or so of bliss to wake one day a creature of
demoniac impulses, transformed from man to devil, yet knowing
himself man, fighting against his evil genius, conscious of his criminal instincts, yet unable to conquer them, unable to save himself
from his own insane longings, and seeing the wife he worshipped
fall at his feet, his idol and his victim.

Yes, in that homicidal fury he might murder her—her, the
woman he loved.

The horror of the thought was strong upon him as he sank
into a chair by the bed, and buried his face in the pillows. It was
foolish to have opened that accursed book, he told himself, a
book not intended for the lay mind. What good could it do him
to read of extreme cases? His was not an abnormal case—might
never become severe or exceptional, although his mother's history
had been of the saddest. He bore no resemblance to his mother,
physically. She had been fragile and delicate, pale, ethereal. He was
strongly built, like his father, tall, and broad shouldered, hardy and
active. He had been living down the danger of inherited malady
ever since those first threatenings of evil. No, he would not be such
a coward as to dwell upon hideous forebodings. He would make
that one sacrifice which honour and conscience demanded of him.
He would live and die a stranger to those domestic ties which form

so large a portion of man's happiness; but he would not poison his solitary existence by brooding over darkest possibilities.

He would call Christian philosophy to his aid. He would not look beyond the evil of to-day, towards the potential misery of the coming years.

Argue with himself as he might, the opening of that book had unhinged him. He left his packing half finished, and went down to the drawing-room whence he had heard the sound of the piano, and two fresh young voices in an Italian duet, which he knew well as a favourite with the two girls. The gong sounded for luncheon as he entered the room, and Sibyl rose from the piano. They all three went together to the dining-room, and took their seats at a table that was much too large for so small a party. Sir Joseph had gone to Carlisle on railway business, and Urquhart was spending the day on the banks of the river.

"I thought you were with Mr. Urquhart," Sibyl said to Brandon, "or that you would hardly have deserted us all the morning."

"I had some work that I was obliged to do. I was a martyr to duty."

"Letter-writing, I suppose. I know what a burden that is," Sibyl answered lightly. "I could not spare one of my innumerable aunts and cousins, but it weighs rather heavily upon me when they all want long gossipy letters. There is not much material for gossip at Ellerslie."

"No, I suppose you do find a dearth of incident sometimes," Brandon answered absently, his eyes looking down at his plate.

He ate hardly anything, and might be said to lunch upon a glass of claret and a biscuit—and he who had been accustomed to sustain the leading part in all their conversation to-day hardly spoke a word.

He looked up suddenly and found Sibyl's eyes fixed upon him, the fair young face full of anxiety. She blushed as their eyes met.

"Whatever your work was, I'm afraid it was too much for you," she said hurriedly. "You are looking very white and tired. Is he not looking ill, Marie?" she asked, with an embarrassed air, as if she wanted to cover her own too anxious regard for his welfare by making it a general question.

"I daresay Mr. Mountford feels the sudden change to summer

heat as much as the rest of us," Marie Arnold answered, "but whatever his sufferings may be, he ought to be flattered at finding himself the object of such solicitude on your part."

Sibyl gazed at her in wondering distress—could this be Marie, Marie who had loved her with more than a sister's affection? Marie, her slave, her worshipper, whose sympathy had never been wanting in her life till within these last few weeks, when an inexplicable change had been coming over her?

They sat in silence till the end of the meal—an idle formula for all three. They rose in silence, and Sibyl walked listlessly to an open window on her way to the garden, while Marie went quickly out at the door, so quickly that Brandon had no time to open it for her. He followed Sibyl to the garden, overtook her on the terrace, and walked by her side, slowly and for the most part dumbly, to the sunk lawn, where the girls often played tennis.

"We shall have no tennis this afternoon, I'm afraid," said Sibyl, obliged to talk about something, since her embarrassment made silence painful. "Marie is not in the humour for tennis."

"She seems rather in an ungracious mood. Is she subject to that kind of outbreak?"

"She is a little impetuous and hot-headed at times, but she never used to be out of temper with me."

"I fancy jealousy is at the bottom of the mystery, Sibyl."

"Jealousy?"

Sibyl echoed the word with lips that trembled faintly as she looked at him.

"Yes, Miss Arnold has one of those unhappy tempers in which affection takes its most exacting form. She loves you intensely, and she is jealous of the slightest kindness you show to anyone else. She sees that you are inclined to be my friend—to accept me as a kinsman—almost as a brother——"

"Almost as a brother," Sibyl echoed, in a whisper so faint as to escape Brandon's ear.

"She saw your kind concern about my haggard looks, and she was angry that you should be anxious about anyone but herself. You must care only for her. She loves you with all her heart and mind—as we are told we must love God—and she wants all your heart and mind in return."

"She has always been warm-hearted and affectionate, but I had no idea she could be jealous. She was never so disagreeable as she was to-day."

"No? It was hard that she should grudge me your kindly feeling to-day of all days, for it is my last at Ellerslie."

He could not keep his eyes from her face as he made the announcement. He had meant to tell her nothing of his intention till next day, and then to take a hurried farewell, to give no time for the betrayal of strong feeling on either side. But seeing her tender concern for his health, so innocently indicated in her womanly speech at luncheon, his resolution had faltered, and he had abandoned the idea of getting over all difficulties by a brutal suddenness. No, he thought, it was better to tell her quietly, and, if need were, to explain his motives. He could not let her think that she was nothing to him, and that her love had been wasted on a stock or stone.

Her face whitened, and after walking at his side in silence for a few minutes she sank helplessly upon the first garden seat to which they came, sank down without a word, and sat pale and dumb.

"The work which tired me this morning was the work of packing my portmanteaux," Brandon pursued. "I travel without a servant, and like looking after my own belongings. I have had a glorious time at Ellerslie, and I never can be grateful enough for your kindness, which has made the place as dear and as homelike as if I had been born here, or for Sir Joseph's generous hospitality to a man who had no claim upon him."

"Oh, but you have a claim upon him—in his mind a very strong claim. You are my mother's kinsman, and he loves all whom she loved, or who belong to her by race or kindred."

"He is the most generous man I know. There are men in his position who might dislike me because I am the son of the man whose despairing, unspoken love was given to Lucy Mountford. You know my father's story, I daresay, Sibyl?"

"I know that he loved my mother, before she and my father ever met, with a love that could never be told, for he learnt to love her unawares—and too late. My father told me the story a year ago when he gave me some of my mother's jewels. It pleased him to talk to me about her, and her trustfulness in him."

"Yes, he loved her too late. That is the story, a common story in

Mayfair. My poor father's fate was a sad one—and he left a gloomy heritage to me."

"I don't understand—do you mean that he left you poorly provided for?" faltered Sibyl.

"Poorly provided for! Sibyl, do you think I am the kind of man to whine because I have to bear the burden of narrow means? I can cry with Othello—'Steep me in poverty to the very lips.'[2] I can laugh at poverty—could fight the battle of life with the best of the rich men I know. The inheritance which darkens my life is a heavier cross than the pinch of poverty. My heritage is a malady which sets me apart from my fellow-men, and which has determined me to go down to my grave without wife or home—a wanderer on the face of the earth."

Sibyl listened silently, but her tightly clasped hands and the tears which trembled on her eyelids were enough to indicate her feelings. She had only one idea of hereditary malady, and that was consumption. She had heard of those who were doomed in their cradles to early death; of lovely girls fading in the dawn of youth; of young men drooping and withering when life seemed fairest; victims of a fate which those who knew their family history had foretold from the beginning of the life-journey.

Faintly, timidly, she murmured words of hopefulness. "You look so strong, and you have led such an active life, Brandon. Surely, even if your father was consumptive, there is no reason that you should inherit——"

"Consumptive!" exclaimed Brandon, catching at the word. Yes, it was better for him that she should believe the hereditary taint to be that—only phthisis—a disease which has always an interesting aspect to the lay mind—the gradual decay, the fatal beauty of hectic colouring and lustrous eyes. Far better that she should think him the foredoomed victim to consumption than that he should be forced to explain the horrible truth, to trouble her imagination with hideous images. "I have accepted my fate, Sibyl," he went on. "It is only within the last few weeks that I have felt the cruelty of my destiny,—but I should be something less than a man if I were to ask the girl I love to share my burden."

"If she really loved you she would wish to share it—to be your nurse and comforter, should your fears ever be realised, or to help you to forget that you have any cause for fear—until, perhaps, you and she would be able to look back in the time to come, and smile at your past fears."

"No, no, Sibyl, that is an alluring picture. Great God, what a world of happiness you spread before me with a few little words. No, Sibyl, such happiness is not for me. I have to carve out a sterner path for myself—to be content with a life of adventure—to find my companions and pleasures in scenes so shifting and varied that the tasks and dangers of my daily existence will crowd out regretful memories, and leave no time for brooding upon that which might have been. I have made up my mind. I shall never marry."

"I have no doubt it will be easy for you to adhere to that resolution," Sibyl said, with an assumed lightness, wounded to the quick by a speech which to her own mind implied a rejection of her sympathy. "You are fond of a life of adventure; and if you do not care for anybody, and are not likely to care——"

"If I do not care! Oh, Sibyl, you know as well as I do—you must surely know—how much I care; how entirely my life has slipped out of my own keeping and has become dependent for all its sunshine upon another life. Why should we fence with facts, and make elaborate speeches to each other as if we were strangers, as if it were not in our blood to care for each other—you, the child of the woman my father adored, and who gave him her love, not knowing that he was fettered and bound? I had made up my mind to leave this place with my story untold; to carry my secret—if it should be a secret—away with me into the wilderness, to bury it there in the explorer's shifting camp. All my plans were made for a sudden departure to-morrow morning, without a word of love or sorrow; but one little look of yours just now at luncheon was enough to break down every determination. I resolved that you should at least know how dearly you are loved, and how Fate has foredoomed your lover. I am glad Miss Arnold has given me a chance of saying all this to your ear only; but even had she been as watchful of you as she usually is, I must have spoken—even her presence could not have silenced me."

"If you really mean what you have said, if it is not mere idle flattery, perhaps meant only to spare me the humiliation of having seemed to care too much for you——"

"Sibyl, I have not spoken half the truth."

"I can't help believing you," she said naively. "I hardly think you would be so cruel as to deceive me. Yes, Brandon, I do believe that you love me, as truly and faithfully as I love you; and I want you to understand that even at the worst, if you were destined to suffer long years of ill-health—to die while you are still young—in spite of all that love and care can do to save you—even if it were so," she went on, her voice broken by sobs, "I have no higher hope than to be your wife, your nurse, and your consoler, to lighten all the burdens of life for you, to crowd into those short years of yours all the happiness that this beautiful earth can give in its fairest places, under the brightest skies. Let me be your wife, Brandon. I know that you are poor, and that my father has other views—ambitious ideas which he will forget for my sake. He has only to know how much I care for you, and he will consent to anything I ask."

"Stop! for God's sake, stop!" cried Brandon, starting to his feet, snatching away the hand upon which she had laid her own with a tremulously fluttering touch. "You don't know what you are talking about. Hereditary phthisis is bad enough—a martyrdom for patient and nurse—a melancholy pilgrimage towards an untimely grave, along a path beset with stones that wound and thorns that tear—not by any means the poetical fading from life which poets have taught you to believe. But phthisis is a kindly disease compared with the doom that hangs over me. My lot is the torment you have read of in the Gospel. I am the man possessed of devils; and there is no Divine Healer upon earth now to exorcise Satan's Crew.[3] The devils have it all their own way. Science has only found palliative measures, she has found no more, for the epileptic. He must bear his burden. As yet my malady has not shown itself at its worst, but the worst will come, no doubt, in due time. I, too, shall be an interesting case—my paroxysms will be worthy of record in the text books. God knows what form those latter phases may assume. It might be murder."

"Brandon! Oh, how can you say such things? It could never be! You are giving yourself up to groundless fears. I am not afraid——"

"Not afraid, even of devils? Ah, Sibyl, I know, I know! With good women love means a vocation for martyrdom. But I am not the man to accept such a sacrifice. My dear love, my dear, dear love, you have given me a memory to cherish and take comfort from through all the days of my life. You have made me ineffably happy; but my happiness must go hand in hand with renunciation. I must never more be your friend and companion, till the years have made us grave, elderly people, and I can be the homely, unobtrusive ami de la maison[4]—a godfather, a souffre-douleur[5] for your children. Let me kiss you, just once—the kiss of a long farewell; and then I shall be able to say—'She has loved me—I have lived.'"

The words came in a torrent. The man looked radiant, exalted by the passion of self-sacrifice.

Sibyl had risen from the bench, and was standing looking at him pleadingly, with parted lips that seemed to be struggling for words in which to oppose his decision. He caught her suddenly in his arms, and silenced those tremulous lips with a kiss.

"Once, and once only," he said. "That kiss has to last me for life."

He released her from his arms, and looking up saw Marie Arnold standing a few paces behind Sibyl, as if she had suddenly stopped in her approach to them.

The look in her face chilled him—checked the rushing tide of passion. What a terrible face it was, pale to ghastliness, with livid lips. If this was what jealousy made of the girl he remembered in the bright friendliness of their earlier acquaintance, jealousy must be indeed a fiendish passion.

Her expression changed as he looked at her, but quickly as she controlled her countenance, he could see the effort it cost her to quiet those writhing lips, and summon up a pale cold smile.

"I have been looking for you everywhere, Sibyl," she said. "I wanted to know your plans for the afternoon."

"I have no plans. I think you might allow me an afternoon to myself, without roaming about in search of me like an unquiet spirit."

"An afternoon to yourself and Mr. Mountford, I suppose you mean?"

"Precisely. Mr. Mountford and I have a good deal to talk about on his last day at Ellerslie."

"His last day!"

The words came in a gasp, and Marie's large dark eyes turned to Mountford with a look of undisguised despair.

"Is that true?" she asked. "Are you really going away—to-morrow?"

"Yes, Miss Arnold; even the most delightful visit must end. My visit to Ellerslie has been unconscionably long."

"But Sir Joseph doesn't know that you are going. I heard him begging you to stay till the end of the month—only yesterday."

"Sir Joseph is the soul of hospitality. He will know all about my plans to-morrow morning."

"He will be surprised, I think, when he knows all," answered Marie, with an open sneer.

Sibyl was walking towards the house. Marie followed her, leaving Mountford alone on the tennis lawn, looking idly along an opening in the shrubbery towards a sunlit patch of sea which glittered like a jewel far away at the end of the glade.

He walked and mused for nearly an hour. He did not want to be alone with Sibyl now that the last word had been spoken; still less did he wish to be in her company under the hawk-like gaze of Marie Arnold, whose manner this afternoon had disquieted him beyond measure. There had been a passionate intensity which betrayed something more than jealousy of an adopted sister. Lightly as he esteemed his own powers of pleasing, he could hardly doubt after to-day that it was for him this strange young woman cared. Contiguity, her secluded life, which had brought her so seldom into the society of a man of her own age, had made her more impressionable than the common herd of girls, he told himself; and while all his thoughts had been absorbed by Sibyl, the elder girl had been nursing her foolish fancies, wasting her feelings upon one of those sentimental attachments which make the misery of the emotional temperament.

"She will fall in love with the next decent-looking young man who comes to Ellerslie," he thought contemptuously, setting the slightest value upon a regard which no look or word of his had ever courted.

He thought of Marie only as a foolish and impulsive young person, whose persistent presence had bored him in his too brief hours of happiness, whose ill-humour of to-day had distressed Sibyl.

He returned to the house, after an hour's idle strolling, finished his packing, and then, finding it was only six o'clock, went back to the grounds, intending to walk to the river, and perhaps return with Hubert Urquhart, who had been studiously civil to him, and whom he had of late avoided with a persistence that might look like incivility. He knew that Hubert admired Marie, and it seemed to him that the best thing that could happen for Sibyl—if not the happiest thing for the girl herself—would be Marie's marriage with Urquhart. A young woman with such a temper as this young woman had exhibited to-day would be a danger to Sibyl's peace, so long as she remained an inmate of Sir Joseph's house, and uncontrolled by the strong hand of a husband. The best thing for such a girl would be to marry, and find her master, as she would inevitably do in Hubert Urquhart.

On this last day, Brandon had scrupulously avoided the afternoon tea hour in the drawing-room or on the terrace, an hour which he had hitherto enjoyed as almost the pleasantest in the tranquil gladness of his days at Ellerslie. After those passionate words and that farewell kiss he shrank from meeting Sibyl, till the family dinner should bring them together, when Sir Joseph and Urquhart, and possibly the curate, who often dined with them, would make sentiment impossible. In the family circle he and his dear love could meet and talk and bid each other good night with the calm reserve of friends who were nothing more than friends.

A long bank of clouds piled up against the western sky had hidden the sun when Brandon went back to the shrubbery, and there was the suggestion of rain in the atmosphere. Urquhart and the gardeners had been sighing for rain, and now it seemed they were likely to have their desire. The air was colder with the approach of evening, and Brandon felt the chilling change as he entered the little fir wood that sheltered Ellerslie from the northwestern gales.

Under the dark foliage of the firs the grey of evening had already gathered, although sunset was still far off. Brandon was glad to find himself in that faded light, glad of the solitude, glad even of the gloom which hung about the long narrow alleys, cut through the monotony of the tall brown shafts. Heavier shadows crept over the irregular masses of undergrowth, rhododendron, berberis, and laurel, which made a darkness below in harmony with the darkness above.

A terrible depression of spirits had followed upon Brandon's exaltation of a few hours before. In those brief moments by the tennis lawn, when Sibyl was clasped in his arms, and their lips met in the farewell kiss, he had fancied that the mere knowledge of having loved her, and being loved again by her who was for him the most perfect among women, would suffice for the consolation of his after life—that he could not be utterly unhappy, having been so beloved. But now his spirits had sunk into a gloom deeper than the sadness of the morning when a single page of that fatal book had reminded him of his miserable inheritance. A despondency more painful than he had ever known had taken possession of him within the last few hours, a despair that weighed upon him like an actual burden, as if a leaden hand—the gigantic hand of some monstrous being—were pressing down upon his brain. It was even worse than despair. It was abject fear, fear of he knew not what, a vague, inexplicable dread which chilled his blood, and slackened every nerve. He longed to be once more within touch of his fellow-man. He tried to quicken his pace, hoping to meet Urquhart returning from the river. It was along this woodland path that the fishermen generally returned. Yes, Urquhart would come this way, soon perhaps—or it might be that it was too early for him.

Brandon tried to remember the hour, but could not. Was it late or early—early afternoon, or evening? Or was this grey dimness the mysterious grey of dawn, before the sun is above the horizon? It was not an hour since he had paused in the hall to compare his watch with the eight-day clock, supposed to be an infallible timekeeper; and yet he did not remember if it were evening or morning. Even the memory of his impassioned scene with Sibyl had grown shadowy. Was it only a dream, after all? He had dreamt that she had been kind, that she had confessed her regard for him, had offered to share the burden of his days. Yes, it must have been a dream. His whole existence seemed strange and dreamlike. He had no assurance of anything but the straight, brown shafts—like the pillars of a rude Indian temple—which rose up on every side of him—and even those looked dim and blurred as he gazed at them with eyes which slowly fixed themselves, and from which the faculty of sight slowly faded.

The leaden hand pressed harder and heavier upon his brain. He felt the dull beating, the agonising pain under that inexorable pressure. He staggered a few paces further, blindly, helplessly, struck his shoulder against a tree on the right hand, reeled to the left, and grazed his hand against a tree on the other side of the path, and then fell like a log, head foremost, in a tangle of arbutus and rhododendron, fern and brier.

Brandon Mountford's next knowledge of his own existence was a sharp, gnawing pain in his right shoulder, a pain that made him aware that he was lying in a cramped position, with the greater part of his weight bearing upon the right arm and shoulder. He was aware, too, of a chilling rain, falling steadily through the darkness, a rain that must have been falling for some time, for the rhododendron bushes, through which he thrust his hands in his struggle to raise himself, were dripping.

It was pitch dark under the fir trees, not a star to be seen in the heavy blackness of the sky, to which he looked up wonderingly, again puzzled as to the lapse of time. Was it the darkness of evening, or of midnight? he wondered.

He got upon his feet with an effort, and stumbled a few paces forward, catching at the trees as he went, stumbled on a little way, weak in limb, confused in brain, and then stumbled against something lying in the fern at his feet, stumbled and fell on one knee, his extended hand clutching at the obstacle as he fell. His hand touched another hand, his fingers closed automatically on the soft fabric of a woman's gown, the silky softness of fine cashmere, such as he had seen Sibyl and her companion wear for tennis and boating, the material which both girls wore oftener than any other. Dim and clouded as his brain was after the long interval of unconsciousness, he knew the touch of that soft fabric. How often he had thrilled at the brief contact as he drew the folds of Sibyl's skirt away from the gunwale when she was seating herself in the boat.

Yes, even in that troubled half-consciousness his sense of touch recognised something associated with the girl he loved.

"Sibyl, Sibyl!" he called, with a hoarse, half-stifled cry.

He had no thought of any other than Sibyl. His clouded

memory hardly recalled the existence of that elder girl who had been Sibyl's shadow.

In the darkness, under the cold night wind that was moaning in the fir trees, under the rhythmical dropping of the rain, pattering on rhododendron and laurel, noiseless on bramble and fern, he knelt beside that prostrate figure; he clutched that cold and stiffening hand.

There was just light enough for him to see the white gown, the white face staring upward.

Oh, God! was she dead?

He bent closer and closer, peering through the darkness, and suddenly a cry broke from his lips—a cry that was not all agony.

Surely that was dark hair that framed the whiteness of the face, not Sibyl's soft, fair hair. Or was it only the darkness of night that made the hair seem black?

Was she dead?

He tried to raise the lifeless form upon one strong arm, while he felt with the other hand for the beating of the heart. She had fainted, perhaps, and that icy rigidity of the fingers he had clasped was only the sign of a swoon.

Oh, God! this was verily death! No heart-throb beat below his trembling hand. There was nothing but the fluttering of his own quickened pulse as he waited and listened, with his ear low down against the girl's breast.

"Not Sibyl," he kept muttering to himself. "It is Marie—poor Marie—but why, how——"

He started from his knees with a shriek of horror. The hand that had been lying on her breast was wet and dabbled with blood. He knew the touch of that. For the hunter and the dweller in the wilderness there could be no uncertainty as to that thick and viscous fluid which covered his clammy fingers and trickled about his wrist.

CHAPTER X

"WHAT DO YOU KNOW ABOUT THIS?"

BRANDON MOUNTFORD's senses were still confused by the horror of his discovery when he saw a light approaching slowly and indeterminately among the tall, dark fir trunks, now appearing, now disappearing, as the man who carried it moved circuitously about.

The position of the light—near the ground—and its oscillation, indicated a stable lantern. Whoever carried it there was the promise of light—light, which in this crisis meant help.

Brandon tried to call to the man, but his lips were dry and dumb, his convulsed throat could shape no sound. He wanted to shout his loudest, but the effort produced only a hoarse whisper—and again he felt the iron hand pressing down his brain, benumbing every muscle, paralysing every nerve. His knees bent under him, and he sank at the side of the dead woman whose face he feared to see.

The dark hair, the dark hair! There lay his hope. It could not be Sibyl.

He stretched out a tremulous hand, and laid his cold fingers lightly over that colder countenance—trying to read those features as a blind man would have read them. He felt the marble skin, the parted lips, the widely-opened eyes—but the blind man's sensitive touch was wanting. His hand told him nothing—it gave him only the dismal assurance of death.

And all this time the light went wavering in and out among the dark fir trunks—receding—advancing. Again he tried to shout, but the muscles of his throat were tightened to choking, and soundless.

Thank God the light came nearer—close. Either his low moan of almost voiceless agony was heard, or the lantern had revealed that whiteness amidst the dark underwood—for the man who carried the light came running to the spot with an exclamation of horror.

"Look here, Joe—she's fainted—she must ha' been lying here ever so long."

The two men came closer—the lantern-light shone upon the dead face.

Yes, it was Marie Arnold.

A strange half-savage sound burst from Brandon's lips—an inarticulate cry, which was almost a laugh. The relief, the rapture of knowing that this dead clay was not Sibyl, made him, for that one wild moment, cruelly indifferent to the fate of any other woman upon earth.

"Lord help us! I'm afeard it's something worse than a faint," remarked the other man in a scared voice, while Tom held the lantern over the dead face and the blood-stained whiteness of the gown, and then slowly turned the light full upon the man who knelt beside the corpse.

"It's Mr. Mountford," he said, wonderingly. "Do you know anything about this piece of work, sir?"

"No," Brandon answered, like a man talking in his sleep.

"When did you find her?"

"I don't know."

"Oh, come, sir, you must know when you found her. Us two have been looking for her ever since nine o'clock. They're all in a dreadful way up at the house—and nobody knowed what had got you, neither. Miss Higginson was like mad with fright. She's been roving about the gardens for over an hour, hunting for Miss Arnold, and she only went back to the house to satisfy Sir Joseph. Come, sir, can't you throw no light upon this ghastly business? It looks terrible like murder."

The man looked from the marble face upon the ground to the living face staring down at it, and almost as much like marble in its colourless rigidity. Darkest suspicions lurked in the minds of the two stablemen as they looked from the dead to the living, and back again from the living to the dead. With true north-country caution they suppressed all further exclamations, all comments on the hideous act and the wonder of it. But, with furtive glances at Brandon as he knelt by the corpse, they began in low voices, and with a matter-of-fact air, to discuss what ought to be done.

"Don't move her," said Tom Dane, the elder of the two stable-men; "she mustn't be touched till constable has seen her."

"Who's to fetch constable?" whispered Joe, looking at Brandon.

"You'd better run to the stables, and send a lad on horse-back, and then come back to me as sharp as you can. We mustn't lose sight of him."

The last sentence was in a whisper, but their caution seemed needless, for Brandon had the look of a man who neither heard nor heeded the things around him.

"You ain't afeard to stop along of her?" asked Joe, also in a whisper.

"No, I ain't afeard. Look sharp, and send up to the house for Mr. Urquhart, same time, and bring him along here. He'll have to break it to Sir Joseph; poor old gentleman!"

"He won't get over it easy," muttered Tom Dane, standing with the lantern in his hand, looking down at the dead face, the white raiment, dyed with that dreadful stain which spread over breast and shoulders, changing the whiteness to a hideous red; loathsome to the touch, horrible to the sight.

He asked no further questions of the man he had found stooping over the corpse, and whose answers had been strange enough to alarm the least suspicious mind. His glances followed Brandon as he lifted himself slowly from his crouching position beside the corpse, and moved a pace or two backward. At the faintest sugges-tion of flight the stableman would have laid violent hands on this guest of Sir Joseph's, of whom Tom Dane knew very little, save that he had always behaved as a gentleman in his relations with the stable, acknowledging every service with a gentlemanlike tip, which was more than could be said of Mr. Urquhart.

Brandon moved no further than the nearest fir tree, and stood leaning against the rough brown trunk, inert and motionless. He remained in the same listless attitude for an interval that seemed very long to Dane, who shifted and fidgeted about among the fern and brambles, and changed the position of his lantern every now and then, looking at the dead face as if he almost hoped to see life return to those clay-cold lineaments.

"What o'clock is it?" Brandon asked, suddenly breaking the

silence which weighed upon Tom Dane's senses like a nightmare dream.

"Past ten, sir."

"Past ten! And I left the house before dinner. What have I been doing, where have I been? In this wood—this wood—all the time?"

The words were spoken dreamily, in vague self-questioning.

Brandon was struggling against a headache which made speech agony.

Tom Dane put down the whole thing as a clever bit of acting.

"Oh, come now, sir," he cried, forgetting his determination to say nothing, "you know where you've been, and what you've been doing, and how this poor young woman came by her death. You know a good deal more about it than I should like to know. I don't ask you no questions, and I don't want you to commit yourself, as the saying is, but shamming ain't no good with Tom Dane. That cock won't fight."

Brandon looked fixedly at the speaker, but made no reply. That direct—yet vacant—gaze was the look of one who hears without comprehending; but the groom having made up his mind that this man was a murderer, saw only a studied assumption of lunacy.

The time seemed interminable to Tom Dane before his quick ear caught the rustling sound of footsteps among the thick growth of primroses and daffodils that carpeted the little wood; and yet it was less than half an hour before Brennam reappeared accompanied by Hubert Urquhart. They had run most of the way from the house, and both were breathless, the gentleman the more so, doubtless as the more sensitive in frame and temperament.

Urquhart bent down to look at the corpse, gingerly, as if fearing to spoil the spotlessness of his evening clothes by contact with that dead form, stained with the dark stream in which the young life had ebbed away.

"Yes, it is Miss Arnold. Poor girl, poor girl! What does it all mean? What troubles could she have had to bring her to such a pass as this? Why should she kill herself?" he muttered.

"I don't believe she did kill herself, sir," said Dane; "it looks a precious sight more like wilful murder than sooicide, to my fancy. I didn't ought to be talking about my fancies, perhaps, but I've had an ugly time of it in this here wood, and a man can't help thinking when he's left face to face with a murdered corpse."

"Hold your tongue, Tom; you mustn't talk about murder."

"Very well, sir; I dessay you're right, but I shall think all the more."

Urquhart turned to Brandon, looking at him with keenest scrutiny.

"What do you know about this, Mountford?" he asked shortly.

"Nothing. I found her lying there. That's all I know. It was dark. I saw a figure in a white gown lying among the bracken. I thought at first," with a shudder, "that it was Sibyl. I could not see the face. It was only when they brought the lantern that I was sure it was Marie Arnold."

"But where had you been all the evening? They waited dinner for you and Marie. I was late myself, but I was in the drawing-room at a quarter past eight, and we did not go to dinner till half-past. Where were you? What were you doing?"

"Where was I? Here, in this wood. What was I doing? Lying like a log—as unconscious as that dead girl. I can just remember falling against one of those trees, and then all was darkness. If there was thought or sensation in my brain, I remember nothing that I thought or felt."

"It was a fit of some kind, then, I suppose?"

"Yes, it was a fit—not the first, but by far the longest lapse of consciousness I have ever had."

"I did not know you were subject to such things."

"They are not things a man cares to talk about. But you needn't trouble about my malady; that is a minor detail, just now. What we have to find out is how this poor girl came by her death."

The clouds were clearing from his brain, and in manner and aspect he was rapidly becoming the Mr. Mountford of everyday life, whom Tom Dane knew and respected. Was he really recovering from an interval of lunacy, the stableman wondered; or had he made up his mind that shamming was useless now that clear-headed Mr. Urquhart was here to investigate the hideous business?

"You had a lapse of consciousness, you say," said Urquhart. "Have you any idea how long it lasted?"

"I am not very clear on that point. I had been feeling ill ever since the morning; but I was worried, and my mind was too occupied to allow me to take much notice of my own sensations. Had it been otherwise, I might have suspected that the fit was coming, might have been wise enough to shut myself in my own room. But I had a good deal to think about, and I am a man who wants space and movement for thought. I may have roamed about the wood for a longish time. I know I rather expected to meet you on your way from the river. As for the time, all I know is that the sun had not gone down."

"Did you see anything of Miss Arnold while you were about in the wood?"

"No. The last I saw of Miss Arnold was when she and Miss Higginson left the tennis lawn together about an hour after luncheon. Have you finished your interrogation, Urquhart? I wonder you didn't begin by warning me that anything I might say would be used against me by-and-by."

"I wonder that you should wonder at my asking questions in the face of such a mystery as that," retorted Urquhart, pointing to the figure on the ground.

"A mystery. Yes, you are right there. It is a mystery," said Mountford, pressing his hand upon his brow.

The troubled look came back to his face. When he dropped his hand from his brow there was a dazed expression in his eyes, and a nervous movement about his lips. He walked a few paces away, and seated himself upon a felled trunk which lay across the tangle of bracken and ivy. He rested his elbows on his knees, and let his head droop forward upon his clasped hands, and thus, in dead silence, waited for the next act in the tragedy.

Urquhart lighted a cigar, and walked slowly up and down a little bit of pathway near which the dead girl lay. This narrow track between the fir trunks was not the most frequented way across the wood; but it was the nearest way from the river to the gardens, and it was the path which the salmon-fishers had generally used. The spot where Marie lay was not more than twenty yards from the footpath.

The village constable arrived, with a coastguardsman to help him in maintaining authority, should he find the situation too much for him single-handed. The groom told him that they had got the murderer, and it would be his duty to take him into custody. There was a lock-up—a very old building close to the sea, which had done duty in the past chiefly as a place of detention for smugglers, and which still smelt of cordage and tar.

The constable approached the scene with a stolid, business-like air, and knelt down to investigate the attitude and appearance of that marble figure from whose aspect the other two men shrunk with a thrill of pain. It was a ghastly thing to see the deliberate way in which the official lifted the clay-cold hand, and noted the wounds on breast and shoulder.

"It's a bad business," he said, rising slowly, and looking from Urquhart, standing erect and tall at a few paces from the corpse, to Mountford, sitting in a crouching attitude, with his knees drawn up to his chin, pale as death, with roughened hair, and soddened garments stained and plotched with moss and clay.

Urquhart had not stopped to put on an overcoat. He was in evening dress, smart and trim, shirt perfectly fitting, hair well brushed, hands showing white in the gleam of the lantern, a man evidently called away from the dinner table and all the amenities of life to look upon this mysterious horror. The constable contemplated him with respect not unmingled with admiration. How different a creature looked this other man, sitting on the fallen tree, with brooding brow and lowered eye-lids, and clenched hands in which the swollen veins showed like cordage—clenched, yes, and darkened with a stain which the constable's keen eyes noted as he drew near with lifted lantern, examining Brandon Mountford with an insolent deliberation.

"What do you know about this, sir?" he asked roughly.

"Nothing," answered Brandon, lifting his bloodshot eyes. "Nothing more than your own eyes can tell you. I found her lying there, as she lies now. An hour ago, two hours, three hours? I don't know. It seems an eternity. You are the third person who has questioned me."

"There'll have to be a good many more questions asked before this here business is done with," said the constable.

He stepped aside, and took counsel with Urquhart, keeping an eye upon Brandon all the time. He felt that this gentleman in

evening dress, with calm and easy bearing, was a person in authority, and the best adviser he could have.

"Does Sir Joseph know?" he asked.

"Sir Joseph knows nothing. I shall go straight to him when we
have settled who is to carry—her"—he could not bring himself to
utter the dreadful word which would better have described that
burden—"to the house. I shall hurry on before and tell him."

"But we mustn't let him go, sir," whispered the policeman,
with a look which indicated Brandon.

"Let him go!" Urquhart echoed, with a movement of surprise.
"Who says he wants to go?"

"Nobody, sir, but he might cut and run, you see. Things look
very black against him. It'll be my duty to lock him up."

"Do you know who he is, man? Mr. Mountford, a cousin of
Miss Higginson's!"

"I can't help that, sir, not if he was her brother. If he's done it
he'll have to answer for what he's done. There can't be no favour
in a murder case. I'm bound to arrest him."

"What, before the inquest?"

"Yes, sir. We mightn't be able to find him after the inquest.
Cool as he seems, sitting there, waiting, his hands are all over
blood. There can't be no doubt he's done it. He seems dazed like,
but if ever there was guilt in a man's face, he's the man who did it.
I shall have to arrest him, sir. It's my duty."

"Then I suppose you must do your duty—but the thing is
absurd. As for the stains on his hands—well, he found her lying
there, and touched her, no doubt, in the surprise and horror of the
discovery. You might just as well arrest me."

"He won't be locked up long if he ain't guilty, sir. The inquest
will be to-morrow, I dare say, and then the truth may come out. I
don't believe she did it herself, poor young lady."

"I am going to Sir Joseph. Do what you like—only make
arrangements for the removal—to the house."

The request was accentuated by a shrinking glance towards
the spot where Marie Arnold lay; and then Hubert Urquhart
started on his errand of dread, and walked with rapid footsteps
towards the shrubbery gate.

He had been, or had seemed, calm and unshaken throughout

the discovery of the crime; but at the thought of what he had to do, cold drops of sweat broke out upon his forehead, and his knees felt weak and tremulous as he hurried unsteadily along.

"I don't like having to tell him," he muttered to himself. "It's hard lines for that old man. He was very fond of her."

Sir Joseph and Sibyl were at the end of the terrace nearest the shrubbery, evidently waiting for news of the missing. Was it about Marie or about Brandon that she was most anxious, Urquhart wondered, as he approached father and daughter.

"Have they found her?" Sir Joseph asked, eagerly.

There was no need that Marie's name should be spoken. There could be no question as to the subject of his anxiety.

"Yes—something has happened. I must see you alone," Urquhart answered in a low voice, putting his arm through Sir Joseph's as he spoke, and drawing him gently away from Sibyl.

"What is it?" she cried, following them distractedly. "Why am I not to know? What has happened to them—to Brandon—to Marie? Speak out, Mr. Urquhart. I will know the worst."

She caught hold of his arm. He had never seen her so agitated. She stood by his side, looking at him with questioning eyes, pale, breathless, resolute.

"Sir Joseph, for God's sake—the truth is too horrible! I can't, I can't tell her——"

"Speak out, man!" cried Sir Joseph, fiercely. "Leave off torturing us. What is it? An accident—a calamity—is she hurt?"

"Yes."

"Badly hurt?"

Urquhart nodded.

"Dead?"

"Yes!"

"O God, my poor girl! My beautiful Marie, my sweet, kind loving girl! Dead! Great God in heaven, how could she come by her death?"

"That is a mystery which will have to be solved. Brandon Mountford found her in the fir wood—stabbed to death. Whether it was suicide or murder——"

"It was murder—foul murder!" cried Sir Joseph. "Why should she kill herself? She hadn't a care. She knew that she was loved, fondly loved, by an old man, who could deny her nothing. If she had not the first place she knew that she was very dear to me—she was content. Some incarnate devil has killed her. Where is she? Let me see her."

He rushed towards the path by which Urquhart had come, Urquhart following him closely. Sibyl sank upon a garden seat, faint and helpless.

Dead! Did Death always come like this, as a horrible surprise, amidst the flush and warmth of life? Dead, murdered, they said. But who could have killed her—who, in all this wide, wicked world, could have had any motive for murdering Marie Arnold?

Suicide? Yes, that was more likely. To Sibyl, who had youth's proud contempt for life—it seemed not impossible that Marie should have killed herself. She remembered that despairing look in her adopted sister's face, as she turned from Brandon to Sibyl in the garden; a look which to Sibyl, as to Brandon, had been a revelation. And if she loved him as Sibyl loved him, and knew that he was cold to her love, might not this passionate soul have revolted against the burden of life, and flung it off like a worn-out garment?

This was how youth thought of youth. Age argued that there could have been nothing wanting in a life so sheltered and cared for as Marie's had been.

The dismal procession came to a side door opening into a lobby at the bottom of the servants' staircase. A mattress and a coverlet had been fetched from the nearest lodge, and the dead girl had been carried decently by four of the stablemen, while the constable and the coastguardsman had escorted Brandon Mountford to the lock-up.

"Did he make any fuss about going?" Urquhart asked Tom Dane.

"Not he, sir—went like a lamb—didn't seem to care what they did with him. I'm afraid it's a true bill, Mr. Urquhart."

"It looks bad, Tom; but there's no knowing."

This was on the terrace, after Tom's work was finished, and the dreadful burden had been carried to Marie Arnold's bedroom, the spacious and prettily furnished bedroom of which she had been so proud, a room full of gifts from Sir Joseph and his daughter. And now Sir Joseph was sitting by the bed, while the family doctor bent over the corpse, examining the wounds that had killed her.

"She didn't kill herself, Dewsnap?" questioned the old man, in a voice that was but just audible.

"Not she, Sir Joseph. She has been murdered—savagely murdered. There are three wounds—one near the collar bone—deep but not fatal—one piercing the right lung—one in the heart—instant death. Have they found the knife?"

"I don't know."

"Ah, I hope they will find it. A deer-stalker's knife, or something in that line, I take it. Poor girl! A sad loss, Sir Joseph. My heart bleeds for you. Such a fine, handsome girl—cruelly sacrificed. I hope they'll find the fiend who did it."

The doctor laid the sheet lightly over the disfigured form, and drew near the mourner at the foot of the bed.

"You must try and bear up against this calamity, for your daughter's sake, Sir Joseph."

"For my daughter's sake!" Sir Joseph repeated huskily, as the doctor crept noiselessly from the room, leaving him alone with the dead. "Yes, for my daughter's sake. Poor Marie! She was nobody's daughter—a working man's child—a waif, whom I adopted—and loved. I was very fond of her—my God, my God!"

He let his face fall forward on the coverlet at the edge of the bed, and sobbed aloud. Even yet, though she was lying there cold and motionless—though that which had been Marie Arnold lay within touch of his hand—he could not realise the fact of her death. Barbarously murdered; and three hours ago he had been walking up and down his drawing-room grumbling because she was late for dinner. This morning at breakfast she had opened his newspapers for him—opened and cut them and folded them in the way he liked, and had laid them before him, bringing her glossy dark hair close to his face as she bent to place the evening paper in front of his breakfast cup. He had never doubted that he loved her; but he had never known till now how dear she had been.

"Great God!" he cried, springing to his feet, "bring me face to face with the man who killed her. There should be no mercy. Oh, let me see him held fast in the grip of the law—let me be sure that he shall swing for it."

He rushed out of the room, ran downstairs and out to the

terrace, like a madman. Urquhart, the doctor, and the stablemen were all clustered together, talking excitedly, but in undertones.

"Have they found the murderer?" asked Sir Joseph, going up to them.

"Nobody can know that yet awhile, sir."

"Have they found anyone—arrested anyone?"

"Yes. They have taken Brandon Mountford to the lock-up," answered Urquhart.

"Brandon Mountford!" repeated Sir Joseph, in blank amazement.

A low wailing cry sounded like an echo of Sir Joseph's ejaculation, and a slim white figure rose out of the neighbouring dusk and came towards the group of men.

It was Sibyl, who had been forgotten in the horror of Marie's mysterious death. She had been sitting in the darkness, unobserved, unthought of, while the heavy footsteps crossed the terrace and went up the stairs with their dismal burden.

She came to her father's side, and laid her hand upon his arm. "Father, you won't allow such a shameful thing to be done? You won't let them bring disgrace upon Mr. Mountford—your friend—your guest? What could he have to do with her death? You'll send—you'll go to the village, and insist upon his being set at liberty instantly? You will, won't you, father? It is a disgrace to us that such a thing should have happened—our guest—my kinsman—so shamefully insulted."

Her vehemence took her father by surprise. He had never seen his daughter strongly moved before—knew nothing of her capacity for deep feeling.

"My child, it's no business of mine. No interference of mine could have prevented it. Brandon Mountford! It's a mistake, no doubt. He could have had nothing to do with her death. But she has been murdered, Sibyl—foully murdered. She has been murdered, and the ruffian who killed her must be somewhere—close at hand, perhaps—in hiding. It was folly to arrest Brandon Mountford and give the real murderer time to get away. Why was he arrested? Who put it into Coxon's head to do such a thing?"

"Dane knows more about it than I do," answered Urquhart. "He can tell you."

Dane told his story with an air of conviction that chilled Sir Joseph's blood. It was inexplicable—a hideous mystery.

Sir Joseph and his daughter heard how Mountford had been found kneeling beside the corpse, his hands and clothes stained with blood; his manner agitated, hopelessly confused; unable to give any account of himself during the hours in which he had been missing.

"He was more like a lunatic than a man in his right senses," concluded Dane.

Sibyl heard and remembered Brandon's words of only a few hours before. He had painted in strongest phrases the horror of his hereditary malady. He had told her that there was no limit to the dark possibilities of that dread disease. He knew not what phase it might assume. It might be murder.

Yes, those were the very words which he had spoken, when he tried to cut himself off from her sympathy—a doomed wretch, worse than a leper, since with him physical malady might pass into moral delinquency—a creature beyond the pale of human love or friendship. And now she heard how he had been found with blood-stained hands beside the murdered girl, unable even to assert his innocence, allowing himself to be led off to gaol without protest or remonstrance.

"He seemed to take it all for granted," said Tom Dane.

CHAPTER XI

BEFORE THE CORONER

DAYLIGHT, which solves many mysteries, brought to light the weapon that had slain Marie Arnold. The knife that killed her was found lying among the thick tufts of primrose and foxglove a few yards from the spot where she was murdered, and it was a knife which the keeper who had attended the two men in the salmon-fishing identified as belonging to Brandon Mountford. He had seen him use it fifty times, he told the solicitor from Carlisle who was watching the case in Mountford's interest.

Convinced of Mountford's innocence, and anxious to protect his guest, even in the midst of his own trouble, Sir Joseph had telegraphed to his solicitor that morning, and he had arrived at Ellerslie at noon, and had occupied himself for more than an hour in looking about him, and questioning the servants who had been concerned in the tragedy of the previous night.

The inquest was opened at the village inn at three o'clock in the afternoon, by which time everybody in the neighbourhood had heard the details of the murder, or had evolved from his or her inner consciousness details far more elaborate than the actual facts of the case.

There was a general impression that Brandon Mountford was the murderer, and had been caught red-handed before he could withdraw the knife from his victim's heart; and there were conflicting theories as to the motive of the murder. The most popular hypothesis was that he had pursued her with dishonourable proposals, and, finding himself scorned by her, had killed her in an access of blind fury—an act which he doubtless had repented as soon as the thing was done. That this quiet gentleman, who had won everybody's good word, was a concealed lunatic, was now the general idea; and Tom Dane, the stableman, was the first and principal witness. He described the finding of the body, and how Brandon Mountford had been discovered kneeling beside the corpse—his hands stained with blood, his countenance pale and agitated, his manner wild and incoherent.

"Had he any weapon in his hand?" asked the Coroner.

"No. His hands were empty."

"Did you think it strange that there should be blood upon his hands?" asked Mr. Fangfoss, the solicitor. "Would it not seem to you natural that he should have touched the body in order to find out if there was life left in it—he being the first to find the deceased?"

"I didn't think about that, sir. I only thought that Mr. Mountford's manner was very strange."

"Stranger than the occasion warranted?"

"Well, sir, I should hardly have looked to see a gentleman like Mr. Mountford—a gentleman who has travelled and roughed it among savages, I've heard say—struck all of a heap as he was when I found him—half like a man that had gone silly. I should have expected him to recover his equerbrillium sooner than he did. But there's others who saw him, and they can speak for theirselves."

"What time was it when you found the body in the wood?"

"A little after—it might have been a quarter past. I heard the clock strike soon after I left the stables."

Hubert Urquhart was the next witness.

Asked if he had assisted in the search for the missing girl he answered in the affirmative. The search had begun immediately after dinner, when it had been ascertained that neither Miss Arnold nor Mr. Mountford was in the house. Mr. Mountford had been seen going out to the gardens at six o'clock, and had not been seen by anyone in the house after that hour.

"When was Miss Arnold last seen?"

"She was with Miss Higginson in the drawing-room at tea-time."

"That would be about five o'clock, I suppose?" suggested the Coroner.

"From half-past four to half-past five."

"Were you at tea with these young ladies yesterday?"

"No; I was by the river."

"What time did you go back to the house?"

"At half past seven, or it may have been a quarter to eight."

"Is that your usual hour for returning?"

"I have no particular hour. I have been governed by circumstances—the weather, the sport, my own inclination."

"I take it that you went back to the house later than usual last night, Mr. Urquhart?" said Mr. Fangfoss.

He was a keen-looking man, thin, fair, with smooth, sandy hair, and a countenance that was little more than a profile. He had a quick, bird-like manner of turning his head to one side with an interrogative air, and nobody had ever been able to surprise his full face.

"Yes, I was later than I generally am."

"You generally took tea with the ladies before half-past five, I think?"

"Sometimes—not generally; but I don't think you need occupy the Coroner's time with these trivial details."

"Small details sometimes lead up to large facts. You went home by the wood, I believe?"

"Yes, I went by the shortest way from the river to the house."

"Did you hear nothing, or see nothing unusual on your way?"

"Nothing."

"Did you meet Miss Arnold?"

"No."

"Nor Mr. Mountford?"

"I met no one."

"Were you alone?"

"Yes."

"How was it the keeper who usually attended upon you was not with you yesterday?" asked Mr. Fangfoss.

"Simply because I dismissed him early in the afternoon, having no further need of his services."

"You did not want him to carry your tackle?"

"No, my tackle is kept in a hut near the river. I had the keeper's boy with me at the river, ready to carry home my fish, if I caught any; but as I caught none the boy wasn't wanted."

"Oh, you had no luck with your rod yesterday, though you were fishing later than usual?"

"None."

"When did the boy go home?"

"At the same time I did, I suppose; but as his way was not my way I can't answer for the fact."

"And you met no one—you saw nothing, heard nothing in the wood?"

"I have answered that question already to his Honour."

"I'm sure you won't mind answering it over again, to oblige me," said Mr. Fangfoss, with his chirpy little air, and an insinuating slant of his sandy head.

"I do not object, but I repeat that you are wasting time. I heard nothing. I saw nothing but the trunks of the firs, and the pathway by which I walked. I met no one."

This closed Urquhart's evidence. The room was crowded and the day was warm, and the witness looked heated and weary as he sat down. He gave a little start on glancing across the crowd, for among the spectators he saw the last person he expected to see in that room. Sibyl Higginson stood in the background, wedged among the villagers, and looking over the shoulder of the short, stout mistress of the inn where the inquest was being held. She was dressed in black, and wore a hat which shaded and almost concealed her face, but he could see that she was very pale. Why had she come there? Her presence betrayed an intense interest in Mountford's fate.

The man who found the knife in the wood testified to the fact of finding it, and that he knew it to be Mountford's property.

"Mr. Mountford has no wish to dispute that fact, but he does not know how long the knife may have been out of his possession," said the lawyer. "It is some time, perhaps a week, since he used it."

"Can he say that it has been missing during that time?" asked the Coroner.

"He is not clear upon that point, but he can recall the last time of using it when he was in the boat."

The lawyer went on to argue that there was no evidence whatever against Brandon Mountford. He had been the first to discover that a murder had been committed, and he had been found, stupefied with horror at the deed, by the grooms who came to the spot with their lantern immediately after he made the discovery. To suppose that any man would be calm and collected in such a crisis would be to suppose that man wanting in natural feeling. The young lady had been known to him, and had been his companion in many pleasant hours. He had last seen her beautiful and happy, full of life and high spirits, and he found her lying alone in the darkness foully murdered.

Would any man be perfectly calm and self-possessed and able to give a very clear account of himself under such conditions? Yet because this man had shown signs of agitation and distress he had been haled off to a village lock-up, and treated like a convicted criminal. Mr. Fangfoss ventured to say that he had never heard of any more outrageous abuse of ignorant authority in the whole of his experience of the rural police.

There was much reason and much vigour in Mr. Fangfoss's harangue, but the fact of Mountford's absence from the house during the same hours in which Marie Arnold had been missing made an impression upon the jury which no arguments of the lawyer could weaken. That he had been found on the scene of the murder with blood-stained hands and blood-stained clothes was much; but that circumstance, startling as it was, could be more easily explained than the fact of his disappearance during the very time at which Marie had been missing, a disappearance which involved a complete departure from all his habits, and a marked breach of domestic etiquette. That a guest who until yesterday had been undeviating in punctuality, should keep everybody waiting dinner, and should offer no excuse for his absence implied a state of things in which passion had got the better of prudence, and had overthrown all the laws of a gentleman's existence.

The Coroner had dined at Ellerslie more than once during Mr. Mountford's visit, and he knew him as a person of courteous manners and perfect consideration for others. To the Coroner as well as to the jury his conduct on the previous evening seemed incompatible with innocence.

The verdict was wilful murder against Brandon Mountford. The inquiry before the magistrate was to begin on the following day, and in the meantime Brandon Mountford was to remain in the lock-up, with every probability of being committed for trial after the magisterial inquiry.

CHAPTER XII

ENCOMPASSED WITH DARKNESS

IT was night, and Brandon Mountford was sitting in the dismal old building by the sea, which had served as a prison-house for many generations of poachers, sheep-stealers, and smugglers; marauders and depredators, on land and water; rioters and insubordinates of every kind; had served as a prison-house in those bitter days when the criminal code was written in blood, and the full stop of every sentence was a hempen necklace. If the ghosts of all the men and women to whom those four bare walls had been the ante-chamber of the grave could have haunted the place, the air would have been thick with the spirits of wretched creatures whose doom, looked at in the milder light of to-day, appears judicial murder.

It was what the sons of the soil called an "unked" place. The crumbling plaster on the bare walls was blotched with straggling

stains and patches of damp, and all along the lower part of the walls
there had crept a dull, slimy moss, like green rust, while the brick
flooring was slippery with the same parasite growth. Cobwebs had
thickened in every corner, and the spider had her fill of vagabond
flies which came in at the grating when the place was empty, for
the window was left open day and night.

The furniture consisted of a table and two chairs, large, heavy,
and clumsily made, but which perhaps from their age might have
been precious in the estimation of the collector. There was a wide
old fireplace, with a grate half eaten away by rust, and which still
contained the ashes of a fire kindled months ago. Dust and grime
were upon everything, neglect and decay were in the very atmosphere of the place, an all-pervading odour of dirt and smoke and
mildew. Desolation and despair were in the sounds that came in at
yonder rusty grating, the moaning of the barren sea, and the shrill
wail of the rising wind.

The custodian of this dog-kennel had been civil, for after all
Mr. Mountford was a gentleman, and even if he were guilty and
had to swing for it, he must have friends who would be likely to
pay for any kindness shown him in his dark hour. With that conviction, Coxon, the village constable, had provided comfortable
meals which the prisoner hardly tasted, had offered to light a fire,
which the prisoner declined, had brought a newspaper and a pair
of candles when evening closed in, and had sent a lad to Ellerslie
for a change of linen and a supply of tobacco.

Brandon's pipe had been his only solace during those barren
spaces of time before and after the inquest. He had not read
a line of the provincial newspaper which had been brought for
his entertainment. He had sat and stared at the sky, and pondered gloomily—brooding upon the story of the past, recalling
old impressions—but, most of all, recapitulating the history of
the malady to which he was subject, as he had read it in the text
books—a dismal and a harmful study to a man in his case.

The image of the Bavarian peasant had been with him in his
solitude, the man in whom the impulse towards murder was so
strong a tendency that with each fresh crisis of his malady the
struggle to resist his own fierce longings had been harder, and
with each recovery there had been in the patient's mind a wonder-

ing thankfulness at not having succumbed—at having got over the attack without satisfying the savage thirst for blood.

Brandon Mountford pondered the story of this unhappy being; a man whose boyhood and youth had been mild and inoffensive; in whose warped nature the murderous instinct had only come with ripening manhood. He compared the Bavarian's history with his own. Till yesterday his paroxysms had been of a mild and normal character; but yesterday he had felt the gloom of an overwhelming despair, a burden too heavy to be borne, until, as he sank deeper and deeper into that dark gulf of despondency, it had seemed as if all the powers of hell were let loose in his brain. A rage, an agony, a revolt against Fate had taken possession of him. He thought of the girl who loved him and offered herself to him, and whom he dared not take to the heart that yearned for her—dared not because of the curse that was laid upon him.

He cried aloud in his anguish that the curse was devilish, not the chastisement of a just and merciful God, but the mocking torment of devils rejoicing in their power to make man's best gifts of no avail.

To-night, in the still monotony of his shabby prison-house, where the fitful candle-light played fantastic tricks with the stains and blotches on the wall, as the flame wavered with every gust from the sea, to-night he recalled the sufferings and sensations of yesterday evening, and his memory grew clearer with every hour of meditation and solitude.

All that he thought and felt before he fell headlong under the fir trees was clearly recorded by memory, but the period of unconsciousness which succeeded was a blank. He might have been dead and in his grave for all he knew of those hours between the fall and the awakening. Anything might have happened to him; anything might have been done by him; but if that interval had not been inactive, if in that lapse of consciousness a new man had arisen within him and moved him to strange actions, there was no trace in his memory of the things that he had done. Never before had he experienced such a lapse of consciousness. His former seizures had been brief. This fit, with its appalling duration, its long period of coma, or dreamless sleep, was a new development of his disease.

The murder seemed motiveless, savage, the act of a maniac

impelled by the lust of blood. Who else was there—who so likely as the wretched epileptic—to do such a deed of horror?

He remembered, shudderingly, that he had felt a growing dislike of Marie Arnold, resenting the way in which she had thrust herself between him and Sibyl, making all confidential talk impossible, and in some wise spoiling those delicious hours of innocent friendship.

Yes, he knew that he had disliked Sibyl's adopted sister, and that yesterday, on discovering the clue to her conduct, he had felt only a contemptuous wonder at her folly, only a careless scorn for a woman who could give her love unasked; when, if she had eyes or reason, she must know that the man she loved was devotedly attached to another.

He was startled from these gloomy thoughts by the sound of voices outside his door. The key turned with a scrooping sound in the rusty lock, the door opened, and a tall slim figure in black came towards him, hat and veil hiding the face in the dim light. But for Brandon Mountford there was only one face on earth, and he was quick to recognise his visitor.

"Sibyl, my Sibyl, how adorable of you. My dearest girl, how shall I thank you?"

He would have taken her in his arms, but she held herself away from him. She laid her hand lightly on his breast, holding him at a distance, looking him full in the face.

"Brandon, I have come because I want to know the truth to help you, if I can. I know that you are innocent. You never could have committed that awful crime—you of all men on earth. It is not possible."

"One would hardly think so," he answered, with a curious slow smile that frightened her. "In my right senses I have no inclination towards murder. I thought your friend a tiresome person, when she hung upon our footsteps and never allowed us five minutes' quiet talk from heart to heart. I used to think that rather hard, Sibyl; but that is scarcely a reason why I should murder her. No, my beloved, in my right senses—when I know what I am doing—I should be utterly incapable of such a crime—as incapable as your father, or you. But last night I was not in my right senses. A sullen rage against life and fate had seized me. My soul rebelled against the God who made me, and gave me a heart to love, a mind to revere all that is fairest and best in womankind, and then said to me 'Thou shalt take no woman to thy heart, thou shalt live and die alone.' My senses grew dim in that red cloud of anger, and when I came out of that blood-red stupor, murder had been done within a few yards of the spot where I found myself. Who knows, Sibyl? How dare I affirm that I was not the murderer? It was my knife that did the deed."

"But had you that knife about you yesterday?"

"I think not. It is some days since I used it, but it may have been among the things in my room. I had been packing my fishing-tackle, and I had been absent-minded and preoccupied all the morning. I did a good many stupid things in the course of my packing—put things into the portmanteau and took them out again, in a futile, muddle-brained way. My mind was full of you, Sibyl, and our parting—the parting that might be for ever. I might easily enough have put that knife in my pocket instead of putting it in the case with the tackle."

"Oh, you must not say these things—you must not say that it was possible—you must not think of yourself as a possible murderer. You cannot believe yourself capable of such a crime—you cannot, unless you are utterly different from the man I have thought you—unless there can be two natures—two separate existences in one man," argued Sibyl, despairingly.

Only now, perhaps, in this dark hour, had she realised the strength of her love—now, when she made herself one with him—when she felt and suffered as if his guilt, if he were guilty, was her guilt, a burden laid upon her as much as upon him—or as if this semblance of guilt—this cloud of horror which encircled him—encompassed her too, and she must struggle through this darkness to the light of truth.

"Why do you say such things?" she pleaded, agonised by his silence. "You must know that you are innocent, that however the knife came to be there, near that poor murdered girl, you did not use it."

"I know nothing—except that there was an interval of darkness, a blank in my existence, of which my memory tells me nothing. How can I tell that I may not have done this thing, in that interval, prompted and urged by devils? You know how the tormentor—cast out of a human sufferer—drove the herd of swine headlong to their death. That may be taken to illustrate the epileptic tendency, the driving power of evil—the irresistible impulse towards some act of blind violence—the rending and tearing of the fiend within, the devilish instinct to which murder or self-destruction becomes a necessity."

"But you have never felt this dreadful impulse—you have read of such things, and the thought of them may have haunted you—but these horrors have never come within your own experience. When you were in the wilderness, away from civilisation, almost beyond the reach of the law, were you ever wicked or cruel then, Brandon? Did you ever kill one of your fellow-creatures?"

She shuddered as she asked the question.

"No, Sibyl. I never lifted my hand against my fellow-man. I was not a hard taskmaster. I never had any inclination to be cruel. Those who knew me in Africa can tell you that our black comrades loved me as if I had been their brother and their king. No; the impulse to slay was never upon me—but once—when I had the fever, and thought in my delirium that I had two heads, and that all the throbbing agony was in one, and if I could shoot that I should be out of pain. My chum had as much as he could do to wrench the pistol from my hand before I could fire. I wanted to shoot that superfluous head which was causing me such agony. Yet I only knew this from the man who told me about it. I have no memory of my ravings, or of my attempted suicide. There sometimes are two natures in the same man—the nature in calm and well-being—the nature in storm and madness. You are an angel of compassion and mercy, Sibyl. You come into my solitude as a ray of light from Heaven—but you cannot help me, dear; and all you have to do henceforward, is to forget that there was ever such a man."

"I shall never forget, and I will never believe that you were a murderer—even in delirium. It could not be."

"There lies the mystery, Sibyl, the mystery of what can or cannot be in such a case as mine. You must leave me to my fate, my beloved—gallows or mad house—or acquittal and liberty. Whatever may happen, you have only to forget me. There is a curse upon my life which no woman shall share. The nobler, the better, the truer the woman, so much the less would I link my life with hers. It was angelic of you to come here; and you must come and go as an angel, leaving no trace of your footsteps, only peace and consolation in my heart."

He knelt down to kiss her hands, in a fond idolatry, and then becoming all at once calm and practical, he questioned her as to her coming.

"I walked here. I had my maid with me. She is waiting at the inn. Coxon was very good. They all know me about here, and would do anything for me. Not for my own sake, but because I am my father's daughter. They all love and honour him."

"He is a good man, and deserves to be loved. How does he take this trouble, Sibyl—this inexplicable horror?"

"He feels it terribly. I have hardly seen him since last night. He has been in his own room all day with the door locked. I begged him to let me in, to share his grief with me; but he would not even open his door to answer me. He told me—almost roughly—to go away and leave him to his sorrow. He was so fond of her—fonder of her even than I was, and yet God knows I loved her dearly, and that if I could for one instant believe that you killed her I could not bear to see you or be near you. I might pity you, but your presence would be a horror to me. But I know that you had nothing to do with her death."

"Help me to find her murderer, then, that is the only thing you can do for me, Sibyl. Find the motive and the murderer, if you can. You know Marie Arnold's history, her friends, and enemies."

"She had no enemy. She was a kind, warm-hearted girl, and had never offended or injured anyone."

"She may have had some rejected lover. There is not much difference between a jealous lover and a madman. She may have been murdered in a paroxysm of despairing love."

"The only offer she ever rejected was from Mr. Tweedie, the curate, and one could not suspect him of madness and despair. Poor young man. He would not hurt a worm."

"One never knows the men who are capable of a destroying passion. But how did her murderer come by my clasp knife?"

"He may have stolen it, in order to fix you with the crime."

"Not that kind of murderer. Passion is reckless and sudden in all its acts—not deliberate and designing."

The creaking door opened again, and Coxon ushered in another visitor.

"Mr. Urquhart to see you, sir."

"Sibyl!" exclaimed Urquhart. "What in Heaven's name has brought you here?"

"My anxiety for a friend falsely accused of a dreadful crime. I am glad you are here, for that shows you sympathise with Mr. Mountford in his cruel position, and perhaps you can help me to save him."

"I'm afraid it would need more than mortal power to do that," answered Urquhart. "Nothing less than supernatural intervention seems likely to be of any use here. We want the angel who liberated Peter.[1] With him, and a fast cutter in the offing below, we might do something."

His cynical air, his scornful use of an example which to her was sacred, offended Sibyl. Yet she welcomed his presence, as that of someone who might be helpful to Brandon Mountford.

"You mean that he ought to try to escape—to run away, as if he were guilty?" she asked.

"Yes, if he is not in a position to prove his innocence—and upon my word I don't see how he is to do it. Facts are uncommonly strong. The fact that you were missing at an unusual hour, for instance, Mountford—that you were found—as you were found——" he hesitated at this point, as if even for his hard nature there was agony in the thought of Marie Arnold's death—"and the fact of your knife being the weapon used—your knife—stained to the hilt with—her heart's blood."

The words choked him; he stopped suddenly—then with a frown and a shrug went on—

"It's a ghastly business, Mountford. You must see for yourself how black it looks."

"I see that as plainly as you, but I am not going to run away."

"Ain't you? Remember after to-night, unless to-morrow's inquiry should be adjourned, you mayn't have a chance of escape. From this place—with the people about here—you may get away as easily as Bazaine got away from St. Marguerite;[2] but if the inquiry ends in your committal, and you are transferred to Carlisle, it will be all over with you, and you must stand the racket."

"I mean to stand the racket. If I am guilty let me suffer. If I am innocent—well, I suppose Providence will watch my case, and the real facts of the murder will come to light, somehow."

Urquhart stared at him in blank amazement.

"You talk of yourself as if you were not sure of yourself—as if you might have murdered her," he exclaimed.

"I am not sure of myself, or of what happened during my lapse of consciousness any more than an habitual sleep-walker can be sure that no strange thing has happened during his sleep.[3] The fact that he can remember nothing is no proof that nothing has happened."

"No, no, I understand. You are right in that," said Urquhart, evidently impressed, "and this murder was so motiveless, so unnecessary; a girl whom no one could have hated—young, beautiful. Why should anyone murder her? It is a terrible case—terrible, for if you should be pardoned on the ground of lunacy, that would mean a lifelong imprisonment.[4] At Her Majesty's pleasure! Think what those words mean. A life, Mountford, a life! There are men pining in madhouses to-day who were shut up when the Queen was a young woman, when everything in this world was different from what it is to-day. Men who have never seen the world we live in; who would not recognise the cities they once knew or the places in which their boyhood was spent. Men whose lives have rotted away inside the walls of Hanwell or Colney Hatch."[5]

"But if he is innocent, as I feel and know that he is—flight would be madness; it would be to stamp himself guilty."

"My dear Sibyl, that is a girl's heroic way of looking at things. I, as poor Mountford's friend, take a more prosaic view. All the chances are against him if he stay to stand his trial. Nobody can doubt that he will be committed for trial. On that point there can be no question. Between to-night and to-morrow morning there is the possibility of getting him away. It is only a possibility, mark you, and it will require sharp action on the part of his friends—you and me, for instance—and a lavish use of money; but it may be done. After to-morrow it may be impossible; it will be impossible if the inquiry finish to-morrow."

"You hear what he says, Brandon?" said Sibyl, appealingly, the tears streaming down her pallid cheeks, her hands clasping Brandon's arm; as he stood motionless, seemingly unmoved by Urquhart's urgency.

"Yes, I hear him—but I will take my chance."

"No, no, you must escape; think what the danger is—death, or a lifelong misery. Brandon, be rational, for my sake!"

He looked down at her with a smile which transfigured him.

"My angel, for your sake! What would I not do for your sake? But, dear love, between you and me there is a great gulf fixed. What does it matter where I live, or how I die? I must live or die apart from you."

"Brandon, for my sake! Don't trouble about the future. Providence may be kinder to us than you think, if we are true to each other. We will get you away from this place—out of England—if you will only be governed by us. We can do it, Mr. Urquhart. The people here will do anything for me——"

"And for hard cash," interjected Urquhart.

"All you have to do is to let us act for you. Everything must be done in a few hours. You won't refuse to make the attempt, Brandon, for my sake, for my sake."

She urged that one argument which a woman thinks infallible when she loves and knows herself beloved.

"Is there no risk for her in the attempt?" Brandon asked, turning to Urquhart.

"Not the slightest. Sir Joseph is a king in this place, and can do no wrong; and his daughter shares his immunity. The people will be blind, deaf, dumb, if she asks them—and pays them."

"Sibyl, you shall be the ruler of my life. If you wish me to make my escape—although in the very attempt I stand self-accused——"

"No, no, it will only give you time. Who knows if some new evidence may not be found, when you are far away. The murderer may confess; some clue may be discovered, some link in the chain of circumstances which no one can foresee or imagine now. Only be guided by us, Brandon, and all will go well."

She spoke with confidence. Her look was full of hope as she clasped his hand at parting.

"Come along," said Urquhart, "there's no time to lose."

CHAPTER XIII

"GRUDGED I SO MUCH TO DIE?"

"Now," said Sibyl, when she and Urquhart were walking along
the windblown path towards the inn where she had left her maid,
"now, Mr. Urquhart, what is the first thing to be done?"

He was astonished at the firmness of her tone, the air of resolute courage in so young a girl; a girl who never before had been
brought face to face with crime or danger; a girl who, in the circumstances, might have been forgiven had she abandoned herself
to hysteria in her own room, instead of being here under the dark
night sky, ready to dare anything for the man she loved.

"You must be very fond of him," he said, grudgingly, "or you
would never have come to this place to-night."

"I am very fond of him, and I no more believe that he killed
poor Marie"—with a stifled sob—"than that I was walking in my
sleep in the wood, and that this hand of mine killed her. There
was some one else—some one who will be found and brought to
justice in God's own good time."

"Perhaps; but God's own time may be soon enough to prove
His omnipotence, yet not to save an innocent man's neck."

"I did not think you would care so much for him as to trouble
yourself what became of him. I am sorry for having been so mistaken in you, Mr. Urquhart. I thought you hard and worldly, caring
for no one but yourself; but the hour of trouble has shown the best
side of your nature."

"Oh, one can't help feeling sorry for a fellow in such a fix as
that. What you and I are going to do may be a risky thing; but if we
can get him off safely—well, it will be a life saved, most likely; for I
don't think the verdict would be anything less than wilful murder.
You and I may know that if he did the thing he did it in an interval
of aberration; but there is no evidence to show that he was ever
out of his mind, and the theory would hardly hold good with a
jury, or even with the Home Secretary afterwards."

"Nothing would ever make me believe him guilty."

"Ah, that's a woman's way of looking at the matter. You love him; ergo he can do no wrong. Even in a moment of lunacy there would be a special providence to keep him straight. Another man—as good a man—might give way to an irresistible impulse of jealousy and anger—the impulse to destroy the creature he loved best in the world, perhaps. Such things have been. But no such a thing could happen to your lover."

There was an offensive tone in that last word which passed by Sibyl like the idle wind. She was supremely indifferent about Mr. Urquhart's opinion of her conduct. She thought of him only as she might have thought of a paid servant who promised to be useful in a dire extremity.

The road along which they were walking skirted the face of the cliff, and ascended towards the village, which was a little way inland, and on higher ground than the coastguard station and lock-up—a long straggling village of pitmen's houses, with an inn at each end and a rustic shop here and there. The houses were better built than most pitmen's houses, and the village boasted a workmen's club and reading room, and an infirmary, while about half a mile off, in a rustic lane, backed by the woods which joined Ellerslie, an old grey stone manor house had been fitted up as a convalescent home, where the pitmen and their wives and children were provided with rest and care after any serious illness or any accident of their trade.

The lock-up was away from everything except the coastguard, and the constable's cottage close by. It had no doubt been found that with the coastguard on one side and the constable on the other, this village gaol was tolerably secure as a temporary place of durance.

"Tell me what we have to do?" Sibyl said, presently.

"We have to get your friend clear away before daylight. I have been thinking it out since we left him. The only thing to be done is to get him on board a fishing smack which will land him somewhere along the coast, the farther from here the better. When he is on board her he can change his clothes for a spare suit of the fisherman's which can be ready for him, and his own things can be stowed away or thrown overboard. When he sets foot on land again he must appear as a rough sea-going man whom no one will think of identifying with the missing gentleman from Ellerslie. What you have to do is to get as much ready cash as you can scrape together—not less than two hundred pounds—and bring it to me as soon as you possibly can. I shall wait for you and the money at the Fisherman's Rest—the inn at the other end of the village—not the Higginson Arms, where you left your maid. And while you are getting the money I shall be making my bargain with the men who are to find the boat, and trying to secure Coxon, the constable."

"I have my own account at the Carlisle Bank. My father opened an account for me on my last birthday. I can write any cheques you want."

"Cheques are no use. The men wouldn't look at a cheque—least of all Coxon, whose conscience will have to be bought. You must get me gold or notes."

"It will be difficult. I could only get them from father."

"Then you must appeal to your father. This is a matter of life and death, remember, and we have only three or four hours. When to-night is gone our chance will be gone."

"I know, I know. Yes, it must be done. My father must help me."

They parted on the threshold of the Higginson Arms, commonly spoken of as the Arms, a house with certain pretensions and which had been known to accommodate an occasional tourist—a low, stone house, with a parlour that was the pride of the landlady's heart, and whose chief ornament was a monstrous and stony-looking stuffed salmon, in a glass case.

Here, in contemplation of a round table, furnished with a large assortment of pious literature, sat Miss Higginson's maid, Ferriby, yawning dismally.

She started up at her mistress' entrance.

"Lor, miss, I thought you was never coming back," said Ferriby, who had been promoted from the village school to attendance on Sir Joseph's daughter. "It's past eleven o'clock."

"I can't help that, Ferriby. We must make haste home now; come along."

Not a word said Miss Higginson to her maid during the hurried walk through a lane and across a field, to a gate which opened into Ellerslie Park. It was a long and lonely walk under a threatening sky, and Ferriby, with the vivid remembrance of last night's horror, felt as if the air were thick with ghosts.

They heard the stable clock striking twelve before they came to the side door near Sibyl's rooms, the key of which door was in Ferriby's pocket.

"It will be daylight at four," thought Sibyl, "only four hours."

She was glad to see the lighted windows of her father's study, and to know that either he or Andrew Orlebar was still up.

"Shall I get you some lemonade and a biscuit before you go to bed, miss?" asked the maid. "You must be dreadfully tired after that long walk."

"Nonsense, Ferriby, you know I think nothing of such a walk. I don't want anything, and I'm not going to bed just yet. But you can go as soon as you like. I shan't want you any more to-night."

"Not to brush your hair, miss? I should like to give your hair a good brushing. It might be a relief to your poor head."

"No, no. There is nothing amiss with my head."

"Oh, miss, I don't believe there can be a head in this house as doesn't ache—after what we all went through last night," and Ferriby burst into tears.

"Go, go!" cried Sibyl, imperiously. "Do you think tears can do any good?"

"They can't bring her back," whimpered Ferriby; "but they ease an aching 'eart. Let me take your 'at and scarf, miss, at least."

"No. Haven't I told you to go to bed? Don't worry me."

Ferriby, upon being thus cruelly snubbed, went sobbing upstairs. She was a year or so older than Sibyl, who had taught her in the Sunday School, and whom she adored. This was the first time her young mistress had spoken so unkindly.

"Who can wonder at it?" whimpered Ferriby, "we're all of us un'inged."

Sibyl went to her father's door, and found it locked as it had been earlier in the evening. Sir Joseph had been in that room all day, so far as Sibyl knew. There had been no family meeting at dinner. Mr. Urquhart had sat at table alone under the searching eyes of butler and footmen, and, as reported by those attendants, had eaten about as much of each course as would lie on a shilling, and yet he looked cool enough, and hardly a bit cut up, said the butler.

Grief in the servants' hall was more demonstrative, but did not show itself in loss of appetite.

"Father, I want to speak to you. Pray let me in. It is about something urgent."

She heard her father cross the room, with a heavier tread than usual. He unlocked the door, and she went in, and father and daughter stood for a few moments looking at each other in the lamplight.

Sir Joseph's eyelids were red and swollen, his swarthy skin was livid, and his whole aspect bore the marks of a complete abandonment to grief. Sibyl put her arms round his neck, and kissed him with compassionate love.

"Dear father, I am so sorry for your grief. I know how dearly you loved her."

"Not so dearly as I ought to have loved her, Sibyl. I made her a dependent in my house—only a humble dependent. That is a bitter thought, Sibyl, now she is gone—gone from us by such a cruel fate. My God, my God!"

His hands clutched distractedly at his hair, he sank down into the chair where he had been sitting when Sibyl came to the door and the iron-grey head was bowed over the table, amongst the scattered papers which his trembling hands had tossed here and there in the vain pretence of attending to the day's business.

"Dear father, you denied her nothing; she was like my sister. You can have nothing to regret in your conduct to her. You were all goodness——"

"You don't know, child. Don't talk to me about her. It hurts me to hear you talk of her. The blow has fallen, and I must bear it."

"Father, I want you to answer one question. Do you believe that Brandon Mountford murdered her?"

"No, I do not—no, in spite of the damning evidence against him. No, for a man of his character and his lineage, my dear wife's race—such a deed must be impossible. I cannot believe him guilty, though every circumstance points to guilt. No, I believe she was sacrificed to the malignity of some ruffian who had a grudge against me."

"Against you, father? Why, all your men adore you."

"No, Sibyl. There are always black sheep. However popular an employer may be, he is never without enemies. If I have been a good master to good servants, I have been hard as iron in my dealings with bad subjects. I have made examples when they were needed. I should never have held my own with that rough lot if I had been afraid of letting 'em have it hot when they tried to get the upper hand. It's likely enough that some vindictive devil struck at me, through her, through my poor, innocent girl. Thank God for one thing, there were no signs of a struggle. The villain's knife took her by surprise. Three swift blows from the savage hand—no struggle, no time for terror and agony. Death, sudden death—only death."

The large, muscular hands were strained across his eyes, and the stooping shoulders were shaken by the violence of his sobs.

"My poor girl; caught like a lamb in the clutch of a tiger—but it was death, swift and sudden. It might have been worse."

Sibyl knelt by his chair, clinging to him, leaning her head against his arm, trying to comfort him by mute sympathy, a love that needed no words.

When the storm was over he looked down at her kindly but with a far-off look, as if he hardly knew her.

"You wanted something," he said. "What was it?"

"I want you to give me some money, father; a good deal—at least two hundred pounds, in cash. I can give you my cheque for the full amount. I have drawn very little of the five hundred pounds you paid into the bank for me on my birthday—but I must have two hundred to-night, in notes or gold."

Her father looked at her wonderingly, but with the look of a man whose troubled brain is only dimly impressed by any circumstance outside the point upon which all his thoughts are centred.

"I don't understand what you can want with so much money," he said. "Is it for someone in distress?"

"Yes, for some one in great distress."

"Surely to-morrow would be time enough?"

"No, no, it must be to-night."

"How impulsive you are—just like your poor mother. There is some money in that drawer—the drawer with the key in it—some notes that were brought me this morning. Nearly three hundred pounds; some of my March rents. Take what you want, and go. I am better alone. This muddled head of mine can't stand the strain of talking to anyone—not even to you."

He rose and walked up and down the room, while Sibyl knelt in front of his writing table and opened the money drawer. The notes were of various denominations, and it took her some minutes to make up the sum she required; and then she went to her father, kissed him silently, and left him with a murmured good night.

She met his faithful secretary creeping out of the billiard-room, where there was a solitary lamp burning.

"You will look after my poor father, won't you, Mr. Orlebar? He is in a sad state of mind."

"Yes, I am waiting for him. I hope I shall get him to bed presently. He was up all last night. It is killing work for a man of his age. I wish you could stay with him, Miss Higginson. You might help to persuade him to take some rest."

"No, no, he doesn't want me," Sibyl answered hurriedly, as she went towards the lobby that opened to the garden.

She had not taken off her hat or jacket. Andrew Orlebar looked after her wonderingly, as she vanished in the darkness of the corridor. That she should be leaving her father when her presence might have been useful to him was strange in so affectionate a daughter. That she should be dressed for walking at that hour of the night was even more surprising. While he stood thinking over her conduct he heard the lobby door shut, blown to by the wind which was just beginning to rise.

The door had slipped out of Sibyl's hand while she was trying to shut it noiselessly. The sky was moonless and starless, and there was a fine, drizzling rain falling, scarcely more perceptible than dew, and it was not till she was near the end of her journey that Sibyl knew the penetrating capacity of that fine rain, but by that time her thin cloth jacket was wet through.

There was a light burning in a lower window at the Fisherman's Rest, but the door was shut, and Sibyl stood for a few moments wondering whether she ought to knock, when she saw a bright red spot travelling towards her along the dark road, which proved to be the lighted end of Urquhart's cigar.

"You have been very quick," he said as he came to her. "Have you got the money?"

"Yes, two hundred pounds in notes—twenties, tens, fives," answered Sibyl, handing him the packet.

"Capital. You are a brave girl, and you may congratulate yourself in the days to come upon having saved Mountford's life. I have made my bargain with three of the best men in the village. They have a good boat, and they will be able to land him wherever he likes between here and Bowness. They will be ready to start before daybreak. One of them will be waiting on the beach with a dinghy. I have made everything square with Coxon. It wasn't an easy business, and he is to have fifty pounds—an exorbitant price for giving the key of the door and being deaf and dumb till to-morrow morning. He has lent me the axe with which he chops his wood, and when Mountford is off I am to slip the key under the door of his cottage, where I can find it in the morning, and I am to knock the door of the lock-up about, smash the lock, and so on, so as to give the idea of an escape by violence; and now I'll take you to Mountford, and it will be your business to get him off quietly, and without any Quixotic nonsense on his part, while I look after the men. Stay, you had better take him a couple of ten-pound notes. He may be without money, and you'll have to arrange with him where his goods and chattels are to be sent. You can do anything with him, you see. You will succeed where I might fail. Remember, it is a question of life or death——"

"Yes, yes, I know, and yet I may be doing him the cruelest wrong in urging him to escape. All the world will say he is guilty."

"All the world will think very little about him when once he has dropped through. In a case of this kind interest and curiosity soon die if they are not fed with daily scraps in the newspapers. When Mountford has vanished, and the funeral is over, this tragedy will be as if it had never been. Here we are at his door. Now, Sibyl, I leave you to manage him. When the men are ready I'll come and fetch him."

He unlocked the door and left Sibyl to go in alone.

Brandon was sitting at the table, in the dim light of the smoky candles, his watch lying in front of him, as if he had been counting the minutes in the weariness of waiting. He started up as she entered, and clasped her hand, and lifted it to his lips.

"My darling, why are you about at such an hour? To think that you should care for me so much—that you should be here in this wretched hole; you—in the dead of the night—caring and thinking for me—robbed of sleep and rest and comfort for me."

"I shall be better able to rest when I know you are safe, Brandon. I offered you my love yesterday. Do you think I offered myself lightly to a man I cared about so little that I could stop at home idle and content while he was in sorrow and danger? No, you could not think so badly of me. You know that whatever a woman can do I will do—bar the door with my right arm, like Kate Barlass,¹ to keep out your enemies, if need were."

She smiled at him through her tears—smiled with love so irresistible that he caught her in his arms and their lips met in a despairing kiss.

"My God," he cried, "a man might live and die for one such moment as this! I am content, Sibyl. No matter where I go, or what becomes of me—however I may be tossed about in the tempest of life—cast on whatever strand—I must still remember—still take comfort from the memory that you have loved me."

"And shall always love you, whatever may become of me. But now be reasonable, cool, clear-headed. And first, take this money," giving him the two notes.

"What for?"

"Because you may be wandering about for some time before you can get at your own money. And you may not have much about you."

"The change of a ten-pound cheque, of which I have given a sovereign to my gaoler."

"Mr. Urquhart was right, then, as to your wanting money?"

"Mr. Urquhart is very thoughtful. I don't understand why he should take so much trouble about me."

"It is surely common humanity in him. You and he have been companions and friends since you came to Ellerslie."

"Companions, yes. I don't know much about friendship. Mr. Urquhart has always impressed me with the idea that he has only one friend in the world—the friend who goes under his own hat."

"You have been unjust to him. Trouble brings out a man's better nature. He has been intensely in earnest about you—most energetic in helping you."

"Yes; but why, Sibyl, why?"

"Brandon, are you a cynic? I know he is, but I did not think you were an unbeliever in other people's goodness."

"An unbeliever, when Providence has sent an angel across my pathway? No, no, no, Sibyl. I believe there are stray spirits from Heaven who are allowed to visit this dull earth now and then, in the shape of women like you. But I don't believe in the friendship of Hubert Urquhart. Is it his money you have given me?"

"No, no, it is mine."

"I am glad of that."

She told him about the boat, and that all he had to do was to wait quietly till Urquhart summoned him. The interval was not likely to be long.

They waited longer than Sibyl had anticipated, waited with the rude wooden shutters open to the night sky, which was covered with ragged black clouds that foretold windy weather. The wind had been rising since midnight, and it had blown away the soft imperceptible rain, and seemed to be blowing the stars about—only a few stars scattered wide apart in the dark canopy.

"I'm afraid you'll have rough weather," Sibyl said, as she listened to the sobbing swell of the waves on the beach below, and the shrill note of the wind.

"No, no, it won't be much, or if it were I have not far to go. I can be landed at the first sheltered spot; the boat I am to sail in can hug the shore. No doubt the men know every inch of the coast between here and Bowness. They can land me where they like, and as soon as they like."

"Not too near here; remember everyone will know you are gone to-morrow morning. You will be hunted for."

"Yes, like a hunted animal. A position of that kind does not enhance a man's sense of personal dignity. I am to wear another man's clothes, to sneak about pretending to be something that I am not. I must try to talk like a Cumberland fisherman, and must inevitably be found out. My speech will betray me."

He was walking up and down excitedly, with suppressed impatience. He had promised to do this thing, but he hated himself for doing it. He had, as it were, given his life into Sibyl's keeping, but he could but feel he was something less than a true man in allowing a woman to dispose of his fate. He could but feel that the manlier course would have been to abide the issue of things, to wait for the worst that the world's injustice could do to him.

Or if he were in very truth a murderer, were it not better to let the law deal with him? What joy or peace could he ever know upon earth while he was unconvinced upon that point, while in his own mind it was an open question whether he had killed the girl?

There was but briefest speech during that long hour of waiting. Brandon paced up and down in moody silence. All had been said that words could say between those two. The story of hopeless love had been told.

Sibyl stood by the open window watching those rainy clouds, amidst which the rare stars glimmered. A sky of evil omen it seemed to her sad eyes. The dark, ragged clouds grouped themselves into a funeral train, and she shuddered as she thought of the dismal procession which was to leave Ellerslie early in the coming week. The first funeral which would leave those doors since her mother's death had taught her the inevitable end of all things human. Inevitable, yes, but not like this—not as it had come to her adopted sister.

"Poor Marie," she thought. "I am so selfish in my sorrow for the man I love that I have no time to grieve for her. Grief will come by-and-by when he is safe—safe, but far away—and when I shall have nothing to think of but the friends that are lost."

Brandon looked at his watch many times during that interval of waiting. Half-past two—the first hour gone—three, an hour and a half.

"Your friend is slow in making his plans," he said presently. "I fear you may be missed at home. The whole household would run distracted if that were so."

"No, there will be no one to miss me. I sent my maid to bed, and came out by the garden door, for which I have my own key. No one ever locks that door. We are not a nervous household at Ellerslie."

Quick footsteps sounded outside, a key was turned in the door, and Urquhart looked in.

"Now," he said, "all is ready. Look sharp. It will be light in less than an hour. Come, Mountford."

Brandon paused on the threshold. Sibyl went to him and put her hand in his, simply, confidingly.

"God keep you and comfort you," she said, "wherever you may go."

The words were low and fervent, and had all the earnestness of a prayer.

"My beloved, if I get clear out of the trap that Fate has set for me, I shall owe you my life; but it will be only a broken life without you."

"Come along," said Urquhart, angrily. "Don't stand there exchanging pretty speeches when every minute adds to the danger."

He took hold of Brandon's arm and drew him across the threshold.

"I'll come back for you, Sibyl, when I've seen him safe on board."

"No, no, I shall go home alone. I want no one. You had better lock the door."

"No; stay where you are till I come back."

He shut the door quickly as he spoke, locked it, and put the key in his pocket.

"For God's sake, don't leave her there!" said Brandon. "She'll be frightened in that dismal den."

"Not she. You don't know what a spirit that girl has. I shall be back in ten minutes. Come along; follow me down the path to the beach, and look out for squalls. The track is narrow and ragged, and a slip means death."

Sibyl was not frightened, but she was angry at being treated like a child, locked in that miserable room, with the burnt-down candles smoking and flickering on the dirty deal table, and the rusty grating between her and the outside world. Why should Urquhart have prevented her going back to Ellerslie alone, as she had come? She hated the idea of his company for the homeward walk. He would talk to her of Brandon, would discuss what had been done, speculate upon his future, and to hear Hubert Urquhart talk of the man she loved would be hateful. He had been useful; he had done things that she could not have done, with all her ardent desire to rescue her lover. He had acted while she had talked. He had the strongest claim upon her gratitude, but she did not want his company to-night.

She walked across the room, and, looking towards the grating, she was startled by the apparition of a face—two faces—peering in at her.

"Who's there?" she cried.

There was no answer, but she heard footsteps scuttling off in the loose shingle, and she felt assured that someone had been watching.

The thought was not a pleasant one. She knew not how long or how often those unknown faces had been there. Strange unfriendly eyes might have been peering in at her and Brandon, even in that one moment of abandonment, that kiss, which meant parting and despair.

She welcomed the turning of the key in the lock, and even Urquhart's company was better than her own vexed thoughts.

"Is he safe?" she asked.

"He is dancing gaily over the water, in the *Mary Jane*, with every thread of canvas straining in a favourable wind. He will be in Scotland before breakfast-time at Ellerslie, and it will be his own fault if he doesn't take the first steamer that will carry him across the sea, and so make a clean disappearance."

"There has been someone looking in at that grating," said Sibyl, pointing to the window, and then she described that brief vision of two inquisitive faces.

"I'm sorry for that!" Urquhart said, with a vexed air. "I'm sorry anyone in the village should know you were here."

Sibyl was outside the door by this time, and Urquhart was examining the lock, before beginning operations with the hatchet which he had brought with him.

"I don't like the idea of being watched," she said, "but as to their knowing I am here—I don't think that matters."

"Perhaps not, but your villager has an infernal long tongue, and you don't want the whole neighbourhood magging about Miss Higginson and her interest in a possible murderer."

"I will never admit that possibility; and I don't care who knows I am interested in him."

"You're a plucky girl. Now, just take a look round before I smash this lock, and tell me if the coast is clear."

He had taken off his coat, ready to begin work. Sibyl made a rapid circuit of lock-up and cottage, and came back to the door.

"All right?"

"All right!"

"Then here goes!"

He took a screw-driver from his pocket, and tried to get the screws out of the lock, but the lock was solid enough to have locked a fortress, and the screws were embedded in rust. He could not move them.

"I thought as much," he said. "The door couldn't have opened without violence. Now for a few artistic touches."

He hacked and hewed the woodwork round the lock, sending the splinters flying, and smashing the worm-eaten panel, which sent out a cloud of dust and rottenness at every stroke. Five minutes' work made a ruin of door and jamb.

"That will clear Coxon's character," he said; "and now to get rid of my tools."

He ran to the little garden, behind Coxon's cottage, and disposed of the hatchet and screw-driver under a thicket of gooseberry bushes near the back door.

Sibyl had walked some little way along the cliff path by the time he overtook her.

"What a hurry you are in!" he said, as he rejoined her.

"There is nothing more to be done. You are sure he got off safely?"

"I saw him on board the smack. If the wind holds as it is now he'll be far away north-east before noon."

There were ragged streaks of a pale cold grey in the east, and the sea showed faintly livid under that first glimmer of dawn. It was not a sky of pleasant omen, and Sibyl, who had been reared on that coast and knew the signs of sea and sky, saw the menace of a storm. Her hope was that foul weather might be slow in coming, and that the man she loved might be safe on shore before the beginning of evil.

She had nothing to say to Urquhart in the walk back to Ellerslie, and she walked her fastest, partly because of that agitated state of mind in which it was impossible to walk slowly, partly in her desire to escape conversation; but at the door he stopped her, with his hand upon her arm.

"How you must love that man!" he said, as if the ejaculation were the result of his brooding thoughts during that silent walk.

"I do love him," she answered, turning to look at him. "I am not ashamed of loving him. His father loved my mother before ever she saw my father's face. Fate parted them. Fate is parting Brandon and me—but I love him, I love him as the best and truest man I have ever known—except my father—or am ever likely to know."

"That sounds as if you had a bad opinion of my sex in general," said Urquhart, with a sneering laugh.

"I don't think you are all of you perfect—but I am not going to quarrel with you this morning, Mr. Urquhart, for you have done a kind and generous thing, and I am grateful."

"You will have more reason to be when you find how general the belief in Mountford's guilt is, and how strong the net which you and I have cut through."

Sibyl went quietly up to her room, supposing that Urquhart would follow her example; but instead of going upstairs he waited till the sound of her light footsteps had died away in the distance, and then he reopened the door by which they had entered and went out again into the bleak morning, and away at a swinging pace towards the road that led to the railway station, distant a long three miles.

He looked at his watch as he went out of the shrubbery gate.

"Four o'clock. There is a train that will do for me at three minutes past five."

CHAPTER XIV

"WHAT LOVE WAS EVER AS DEEP AS A GRAVE?"[1]

THE fatigue that Sibyl had gone through since nightfall had made no impression upon her physical being, or no impression of which her mind was conscious. If her limbs ached with the tramping to and fro and up and down over the rough ground by the cliff, she had no consciousness of her pain. Her mental suffering, her keen anxieties, her grief and horror at the deed that had been done, left no room in her consciousness for the sensation of bodily pain. She walked up and down her bedroom, and in and out to her balcony, in the light of a gloomy dawn, or stood looking at the sea and the sky.

A wild sky, a rough sea, a livid dawn that heralded a tempestuous day! And she had driven him out into the storm; she had urged him to act against his own judgment, which would have bidden him face his danger. Was it wise, was it well? Now that the act was irrevocable—now that the shattered door told its story of prison breaking and ignominious flight, she asked herself that question with maddening iteration.

Ignominious flight. Yes, that was the word. The man who flies from the face of Justice must needs submit to the ignominy that attaches to all flight. Innocence should stand firm, and wait the worst that Fate can do.

No doubt that was the idealist's view of the situation. But then came the thought of stern reality—the possible conviction—the possible gallows—the inscrutable perversity of Fate which sometimes dooms an innocent man to a disgraceful death, all for want of some little clue to thread that labyrinth of circumstantial evidence, and get at the core of truth hidden somewhere in the midst of it. Guiltless men have been hanged, even in this enlightened age, and to the end of time there will always be that cruel possibility of innocence paying the penalty intended for guilt.

On the whole, therefore, Sibyl was thankful that she had helped to get Brandon Mountford out of the clutch of the law. For the time being he might suffer in honour and reputation by that escape, he might have to exist under a heavy cloud—an exile in some distant country, living under a false name, cut off from all the friends and associations of his youth. But in the years to come the clue to the mystery might be found, and the wrong might be righted.

"Who could have done it?" Sibyl asked herself, with her hands strained across her forehead, as if she wanted to wring some sudden inspiration out of her tired brain—"Who could have done it?" she asked, and then told herself, despairingly, "I feel as if all my thinking powers were gone. I can imagine no one who would do such a deed. Everybody liked her. She had no enemy. It could only have been some ruffian, with the wild beasts' thirst for blood—some madman.

"A madman, yes!" Sibyl turned sick with agony as she remembered what Brandon Mountford had told her about that inscrutable disease which can change sanity to madness, the sudden clouding of the brain, the maniac's impulse towards evil.

"Oh, if it were he, after all! If my conviction of his innocence should be a mere delusion, born of my love for him! Well———," after a pause, "if it is so, I am the more thankful that he is free. My poor, afflicted love, marked out by Fate to bear so cruel a burden. Who would not help you to escape the bitter consequences?"

And then came a still more appalling thought. If he had done this thing; if his unconscious hand had taken Marie Arnold's life, who could say whether this first crime might not be the beginning of a series of murders? The murderous impulse might recur, and this man—the man she admired and loved, the man of high birth and gentle breeding—might become a scourge and a horror to his fellow-men; a wretch whose death or whose lifelong imprisonment would be required for the safety of others.

She flung herself upon her bed, and hid her face from the daylight, awe-stricken at the horror her own thoughts had conjured up. The wind shrieked in the chimney, and there was something hideously human in the sound. One gust more violent than the rest seemed to shake even those solid walls.

There was a dreadful silence in the house next morning when Sibyl awoke from a sleep of sheer exhaustion. She was lying on the bed, still wearing the black gown in which she had walked to and fro, with all the dust and chalk of the road and the cliff upon it; but careful hands had spread a down coverlet over her, and the morning cup of tea which she generally took at seven o'clock was on the little table by her bed, showing that the faithful Ferriby had been watching her slumbers. The window she had left open was shut, and the closed Venetians darkened the room. Sibyl sprang up from the bed, and ran to look at the clock on the mantelpiece.

A quarter to eleven. How long, how heavily she had slept—a dreamless sleep, unshadowed by any consciousness of the sorrow that made waking so terrible. The wind had been raging when she last looked at sky and sea. The sky was calm enough now, when she opened the shutters and looked seaward; a dull grey sky; but the waves were rising and falling with a slow and sullen force, and the livid patches of foam showed here and there upon the leaden-coloured expanse.

She rang her bell, and Ferriby came bustling in.

"Oh, how tired you must have been, miss—regular dead beat, to fall asleep in your clothes, and sleep from twelve o'clock to close upon eleven—all but twelve hours. You, too, such a light sleeper. I've got your bath ready; but let me fetch you a fresh cup of tea first. You can't drink that stuff," pointing to the neglected cup. "It's stone cold."

"Never mind the tea. Yes, I was very tired; my bones are still aching."

"And I don't wonder at it, miss. Dear, dear, what times we're living in! Such a storm early this morning! We shall hear of ever so many boats lost before dark, Hampton says."

And then Ferriby related how Mr. Mountford had broken out of the lock-up in the midst of the storm, a proceeding to which she evidently attached an idea of Satanic intervention, as if he must have made his bargain with Zamiel or Mephistopheles; and how the hue and cry had been raised, and the country was being searched far and near, and the telegraph wires at Ardliston Post Office were working as they had never worked before.

"And all I can say is I hope they won't find him," concluded Ferriby. "He was the nicest gentleman that ever came into this house—and if he did murder that poor young lady in a fit of madness—as they say he did—why, it was his affliction, and not his fault."

"Who says that he murdered her?"

"Well, miss, everybody thinks he did it, and madness would be his only excuse. Not that there was anything like madness in his ways. Thomas, who always waited upon him, says there was never a politer, quieter gentleman. None of your swearing or flying out

at a servant for nothing. He had rather a nervous manner sometimes, Thomas says—a little absent-minded—but never no violence—nothing that looked like being out of his mind."

Poor Brandon! To be discussed and anatomised in the servants'
hall—to have fallen so low—the talk of the village inn—hunted by
policemen, his description telegraphed from place to place.

It was nearly one o'clock when Sibyl went downstairs, white
as a ghost, in her black gown, and wandered aimlessly about the
house, almost wondering not to see Marie's bright face in any of
the rooms. This dread mystery of death was so difficult to realise,
even now, after all she had suffered within the last day and a half.
The horror of the murder was ever present in her mind, but she
had not yet realised the actuality of death, the disappearance
of one familiar face, the silence of that voice that had so lately
been part of her home and of her life. Never more to see Marie
Arnold—the companion of all her girlish years, the happy years in
which there had been no shadow of care. Now life seemed all care,
and terror, and difficulty.

It needed all her stoicism to visit the room where the dead girl
was lying—that room now so quiet, and pure, and peaceful—yesterday defiled by the muddy boots of the coroner's jury, filled with
ghoulish mutterings and whisperings. Not a trace of those rough
visitors remained to-day. The white curtained bed rose pale in the
dim light that crept through closely fastened Venetians, and the coverlet was almost hidden under white flowers—azalias, lilies, all the
most precious blooms that the hothouses of Ellerslie could supply.

Sir Joseph's own trembling lips had given the order.

"Be sure there are plenty of flowers. She was so fond of
flowers."

"You'd like to see her, wouldn't you, miss?" asked Ferriby,
when her mistress was dressed.

Like! No, it could not be a question of liking. Every nerve contracted with pain at the thought. Like, no. But it was her duty,
perhaps—a duty she owed to the dead, to stand for a little while
by that placid form, which could never more rise up and hold
out loving arms towards the adopted sister. It might seem cold-
hearted, self-absorbed, to keep aloof from that awful room, where

the great mystery offered its solemn question to Christian and phi-
losopher alike.

After this, what? Or is this the end?

Ferriby's tone implied that her mistress ought to look upon
the dead, and Sibyl wanted to do what was right. She wanted all
the household to know how truly she had loved Marie Arnold.

She went to the door of the room—that room which she used
to enter so gaily a dozen times a day—to show Marie this or that—
books, flowers, finery—to ask questions, to tell little scraps of
girlish news, to discuss an idea, any sudden fancy that had flashed
into her brain.

Marie had been the only close companion of those impressionable years—the years which change the child into a woman.

An upper housemaid opened the door at Sibyl's light knock,
and the cool darkness of the room, the perfume of lilies suggested
a chapel in some southern land. Sibyl looked fearfully towards the
white bed. Yes, there was that rigid outline under the snowy sheet.
That which she had seen and shuddered at in painting and sculp-
ture, but which her eyes had never looked upon till now in its terrible reality, for the father's thoughtful care had excluded the child
from the room where her mother lay in that last sleep. Slowly, and
with noiseless footsteps, she approached the bed, but when the
housemaid put out her hand to raise the snowy lawn which lay so
lightly over that marble form, Sibyl stopped her with a faint cry.

"No, no, no! Let me remember her as I knew her—not like
this."

She sank on her knees at the foot of the bed, covered her face
with her hands, and thought a prayer—a prayer for the repose
of that passionate soul—such a prayer as the Anglican Church
forbids, but which instinct prompts whenever the living look upon
the dead. She prayed for the peace of the dead, and prayed still
more fervently for that unhappy fugitive whose life was dishon-
oured by this untimely death, who, guilty or innocent, had to bear
the shadow of crime. Her eyes were drowned in tears when she
rose from her knees, and took one of those fairy-like blooms from
the shower of lilies of the valley which had been scattered over
the sheet, and with this poor little flower in her hand she stole
softly from the room where the middle-aged housemaid sat by an

open window reading her Bible in the flickering light that filtered through the Venetian shutters. For the housemaid, pious, middle-aged, and a confirmed spinster, there was a dismal relish in this quiet guardianship of the dead. To sit in a cool, flower-scented room, and read the Prophet Jeremiah in the spirit of unquestioning faith that seeketh not to understand what it readeth, was better than to overlook housework, and pry into those dusty corners which the pert young pink-frocked housemaid is apt to neglect. The upper housemaid felt the importance of her charge, most of all when Sir Joseph sat sobbing beside the bed, as he had done in the dead of the night, when those passionate tears of his had startled the watcher from a profound slumber. She felt that she was being admitted to the family secrets, that her situation, always a good one, would be on a higher footing from this time forward.

The door closed upon the chamber of death, but scarcely had Sibyl crossed the threshold when she met Hubert Urquhart in the corridor, where, even in the dim light from shrouded windows, she could see how pale and worn he was.

"Are you going to look your last upon poor Marie?" she asked.

"No, no; I never look on the dead. I shouldn't like to confess as much to a sportsman, but even the sight of a dead stag harrows me. It suggests what I must come to, sooner or later. I was on my way to your boudoir."

"You have news—of him?"

"Yes, there is news—of a sort. I want a few minutes' quiet talk with you, Sibyl—I may call you by that name, may I not? All we went through together last night gives me a kind of claim, doesn't it?"

"What does it matter?" she exclaimed, impatiently. "If you have anything to tell me, don't keep it back. If it is bad news I would rather hear the worst at once."

She looked as if she were going to faint, and he thought she would drop at his feet. He put his arm round her to steady her, and drew her gently towards an old-fashioned settee, under a large picture by Snyders, which represented the crisis in the life of a hunted boar, whose ultimate fate nobody had ever troubled to inquire into. Boar, hounds, landscape, had all mellowed to a dead level of brown varnish and blue mould.[2]

"She thinks only of him; cares only about him," thought

Urquhart, as he seated himself by Sibyl's side, with his arm still supporting her.

It galled him to see that she took no more notice of his arm than if it had been her old nurse's.

"You have bad news?" she said, agitatedly. "He has been followed—arrested?"

"Alas, if the worst has happened, it is even worse than that."

"O God, O God, have mercy upon me! What could be worse—except his death?"

"Ah, Sibyl, that is the point. I am so sorry for you—so sorry that this man's fate should have such power to afflict you. This man—a stranger here a few weeks ago——"

"Don't talk like that," she cried, imperiously. "I love him. That is enough for you to know. I am not ashamed of my love. What has happened to him? For God's sake, speak."

She clutched the lapel of his coat, looking at him with wild, despairing eyes; startling him with the vehemence of her feelings.

"Can you bear to hear what I must say, if I have to tell you my worst fear?"

"I must bear it. Nothing can be worse than this torture."

"My poor Sibyl! There was a gale this morning, after the smack sailed—a gale from the south-west, blowing dead on our coast yonder. They were to put him ashore in the early morning, and to come back to Ardliston with the news that all was safe. I was down at the village an hour ago, and the men had not come back. There was no news of the *Mary Jane*."

"They may have gone farther along the coast."

"Hardly with such a wind in their teeth. The storm was short and sharp, but murderous while it lasted. There is a feeling of apprehension in the village. I saw the skipper's wife. She flew at me like a tigress—told me that if her husband and his boy were lost it was my doing; it was my cursed money which had tempted him to take his boat out on such a night."

"What!" cried Sibyl; "was there any danger? Did you know that there was the risk of the boat being lost? Oh, if you did know that, what a wretch you are! Luring him to his death, under the pretence of saving him—over-persuading him, against his own reason—and I—I helped you!"

"This is sheer madness," said Urquhart, rising indignantly, and moving away from her. "If you take the thing in this spirit I can say no more. You knew as much about the night as I could know. You heard the wind rising, as I heard it. But neither you nor I could know that there was to be a squall after daylight. You knew what I knew of Mountford's peril, and that to stay where he was might mean a disgraceful death."

"And to escape a possibility he has flung away his life," said Sibyl, despairingly. "Well, we have helped him to some purpose! If the boat is lost, and his life with it, you and I are his murderers!"

"It is folly to talk like this—absolute folly," Urquhart answered savagely. "If he is drowned—well, it is a better death for a gentleman than being put out of this world by the common hangman. And, after all, he was nothing to you—not even your affianced husband—yet you have hazarded your good name for him, and now you are endangering your reason."

She looked at him with a vacant expression, as if she hardly heard him, or heard without understanding.

"What is the woman's name?" she asked.

"What woman?"

"The woman whose husband owned the boat that is lost?"

"Or that may be lost. There is nothing certain yet. The woman's name is Kettering."

"Where does she live?"

"In the lane at the back of the Fisherman's Rest. What are you going to do?" as Sibyl went towards the staircase.

"I am going to Mrs. Kettering."

"What madness! You will make yourself the talk of the village."

"I am going to see Mrs. Kettering. The boat may have come back, perhaps. There may be good news for me at the village."

"What will your father think?"

"He will not mind. He believes in Brandon's innocence as firmly as I do."

"He will change his mind, perhaps, when he hears that Brandon has run away," muttered Urquhart, walking up and down the gallery after Sibyl had left him.

He did not pace that long gallery from end to end, but turned at about two-thirds of its length, giving a wide berth to the door at the east end, that door which closed Marie Arnold's room.

Marie's room! How soon it would cease to belong to her—how soon that strong personality would have passed out of the daily life of Ellerslie House, leaving—to Urquhart's mind at least—a blank which none could fill.

There was no good news in the little sea-coast village, not a whisper of hope to be heard in all the length and breadth of the long, straggling street. Sibyl found the lane behind the Fisherman's Rest—a lane of about a dozen stone cottages—full of sad faces and weeping women. The *Mary Jane,* with her crew of four, had gone to the bottom—all hands on board—and there was scarcely one of those rough stone cottages whose inmates were not weeping for kinsman or husband, sweetheart or friend. The intermarriages of the small seafaring community had interwoven the whole village in the ties of kindred. There could hardly be a death at Ardliston which would not justify all the inhabitants in putting on mourning, whence it arose that rusty black was the chief wear from one end of the village to the other. Three family names prevailed along the straggling street, and if people were not Ketterings, they must needs be Hessles or Garforths—while Garforths, Hessles, and Ketterings were all allied by cousinship. Thus it was that lamentations for the loss of the *Mary Jane* filled the air in the narrow lane behind the Fisherman's Rest, and dishevelled women sat crying on the rugged stone steps leading up to cottage doors, while little groups clustered at the corners talking of the catastrophe, the fact of which no one doubted. Alas, there seemed no room for doubt, since fragments of the *Mary Jane* had been washed ashore near one of the most dangerous rocks on that iron-bound coast, between Ardliston and Allan Bay, and it was clear the ill-fated boat had been blown on to that rugged point—which the fishermen's wives all knew and had heard of as a devouring monster—and had been split into matchwood. Some among those old time-honoured boats in the little fisher fleet that sailed out so gaily from Ardliston in fair weather, needed no gigantic forces of Nature to destroy them. The *Mary Jane* had been renowned as a swift sailer, and had come off with flying colours in many a fisherman's race at the annual regatta; but age will tell, and the *Mary Jane* was older than her owner had ever cared to remember.

Well, she had gone.

"She'd have lasted out our lives if my good man hadn't flown in the face of Providence to please them at the great house—them that should have known better," sobbed the widow, sitting distractedly in the midst of a sympathising group, while her little children played in a corner of the room, and the latest baby—latest in a family where there seemed at least three babies—slept peacefully in the closet bed, a bed built into the wall, and capable of being enclosed with a sliding shutter.

The widow started to her feet at sight of Sibyl, and pushed back the ragged hair from her eyes with angry hands, almost as if she would have plucked it out by the roots.

"Oh, it's you, Miss Higginson," she cried. "I wonder you've got the cheek to come and look at me and my childer—you that have made those babies orphans, and me a miserable woman—all along of trying to save your sweetheart's life. His life! What was his life worth agen my poor Jack's—Jack as had wife and childer to work for—Jack as never did wrong to man or beast in his life—drownded trying to save your sweetheart—a murderer—that ought to have been hung? Oh, it's wicked, that's what it is. God Almighty didn't ought to let such things be. He didn't ought—but there, the world's too full of people now for God Almighty to care as He did for the Israelites, when there was only His chosen to look after. It's a wicked world—and you're a wicked girl, Sibyl Higginson, to have tempted my Jack to risk his life for the sake of your cursed money."

"Come, come, Mrs. Kettering," urged a motherly voice, "you've no call to fly at Miss Higginson, who's always been your true friend."

"My true friend, yes, till last night; but my bitter enemy for ever and ever after last night."

"Now, Susan, you know you was all in favour of Jack's taking the job. He told you there'd be dirty weather, but you were all for making the best of it. You was, now; you must remember that."

Susan Kettering threw up her arms and beat her careworn forehead with her clenched fists.

"Remember, oh, God, as if I could ever forget. It was to earn bread for the bairns. It was to earn more than two years' rent. What mother wouldn't have been eager to earn five and twenty pound by one night's work! Oh, God! oh, God! what a black night's work for me and mine! And it was your doing, Miss Higginson; it was all your doing."

"Susan Kettering!" remonstrated the woman who had spoken before, "you mustn't go on like this. There ain't no justice in it."

"Oh, let her talk," said Sibyl, standing on the threshold leaning against the door post, with white face and dry, haggard eyes, "let her talk, poor soul. But is it quite certain that the boat has gone down?" she asked, appealing to the women generally. "Is there no hope?"

"No, miss, there ain't no hope—there's been enough rotten timber washed ashore to show that the *Mary Jane* was mashed up in that heavy sea. But it's no fault of yourn, Miss Higginson, and if Susan wasn't just crazed with grief she'd never say such things."

"No hope!" murmured Sibyl, with quivering lips.

No hope for the grief-stricken wife and these fatherless children—but what of him for whom that fated boat had put out to sea? He might have been landed safely before the evil hour in which the *Mary Jane* was blown upon the rocks. All was uncertain yet as to his fate; and her pity for this mourner with the bloodshot eyes and wild hair and distracted movements of clenched hands and writhing arms was made keener by the thought that Brandon Mountford might be safe on shore.

"Was it far from here that the boat was wrecked?" she asked the elderly woman who had spoken last.

"Yes, Miss, half a dozen miles or more, if she went ashore where they all think she did—on the Hurraby rocks. It's a bad place, that is. There's been many a wreck there within the memory of the old people hereabouts."

"Six miles further north," mused Sibyl, "that would be near Allan Bay."

"Yes, Miss, this side the bay, a mile nearer home."

"And Allan Bay would have been a safe place to land anyone out of the boat?"

"Safe enough if they could have run along shore in such a wind—but the Lord knows if they could. It was a wicked wind."

"What time was the gale at its worst?"

"Between six and seven, Miss."

Yes, she remembered looking at the clock on her mantelpiece while that howling and shrieking of the wind was loudest, when the Venetian shutters were rattling as if they would be torn from their fastenings, and the solid window frames were shaken, and the massive stone chimney seemed to vibrate and tremble above the roof.

Past six—and Brandon had gone on board the *Mary Jane* before three o'clock.

There would have been time to land him at Allan Bay, and more than time under any reasonable conditions of wind and sea—but who can reckon time when the frail boat has to fight every yard of progress—when all the forces of Nature are set against the frail cockleshell in which the low-born bread-winner tempts the sea.

Still there was hope—hope for her, though not two of the *Mary Jane's* rotten timbers still held together. She bent over the weeping widow, gently touched the coarse dishevelled hair with delicate fingers, and gently stroked the burning forehead, rugged with the premature wrinkles that come of toil and care, hard weather and a hard life.

"I am deeply sorry for you, my poor friend, and you may be sure I will take care of you and these poor children always—always."

"Sorry for me?" cried the widow, starting up, and pushing away the gentle hand. "Who wants your sorrow? Who wants your care? Do you think I'd take another sixpence of your money—the money that bought my good man's life. You and your father think money can buy anything. What are we but your slaves. And we go about saying how good you are—you that have got everything, while we have to toil for our daily bread, in the pit or on the sea—danger and darkness both—it don't much matter which, there's always Death waiting round the corner for us—while you sit at home and take your ease and think there's nothing on this earth that's too good for you. And now, to save your sweetheart—a madman and a murderer—my true-hearted husband has gone to the bottom of the sea——"

"Hush, now, Susan, you mustn't take on like this—it ain't fair," remonstrated the elder woman, and there was a murmured chorus of disapproval from the others.

"Don't mind her, Miss, she's right down daft," said one. "It's a shame to go on at you, that has always been so good to us. She'll be sorry enough for what she has said when she comes to her right senses."

"I shall be sorry for her all the days of my life," Sibyl answered, sadly. "Let me speak to you a minute outside, Mrs. Garforth," she added, in a lower voice, to the widow's elderly kinswoman.

Mrs. Garforth followed quickly to the door.

"Don't take any money from her," screamed Susan Kettering. "Not one penny of her cursed brass. It's cost me my husband. Not a dirty penny—not——"

Her voice rose to a scream, and then there came a burst of hysterical laughter, as she flung herself violently on the bed, where the baby woke, looked about for a moment or two with scared eyes, and set up a piteous wail.

Two other babies took up the note, and squalled in sympathy.

"Oh, Miss, it's too bad of her," said Mrs. Garforth, when she and Sibyl had walked a few paces along the lane and were out of hearing of the tempest inside the cottage, "but she ain't in her right mind. And you looking so ill, too," she added, noting the girl's ashen cheeks and hollow eyes, "and such trouble up at the great house."

"Yes, trouble has come upon us—terrible trouble. I never knew what it meant till now. I have never been half sorry enough for others."

"Don't say that, Miss. You've always been kind to us. None that was in trouble or sickness ever went to Ellerslie for help in vain. Poor Susan has no call to blame you for her loss. Jack was asked to undertake a risky job, and he was offered a good price for it—and he could say 'Yes,' or 'No.' She persuaded him to say 'Yes,' and that's what makes her heart so sore, poor creature."

"Did they think there was a risk—last night—before the boat went out?"

"Lor, yes dear lady; them as know the coast knowed as there was a gale coming."

"And he knew—Mr. Urquhart! He must have known."

"Well, Miss, he's a landsman, you see—though he's bound to know the coast, seeing Killander Castle ain't far off. But o' course

he wanted to get your sweetheart away—when a man's in danger
of bein' tried for his life, and there's only one road by which he can
get away, folks can't be partikler about the weather along that ere
road."

"You mustn't talk of Mr. Mountford as my sweetheart,
Mrs. Garforth. He was nothing to me but a friend—a very dear
friend."

"What, wasn't you and him keeping company, Miss?"

"No, no."

"Ah, people hereabouts is good 'uns to talk. They'd all have it
as you and him was sweethearts, and you was a'most out of your
mind about him last night—like poor Susan to-day about her Jack,
and that you was at the lock-up with him best part of the night.
Martha Hessle said she and Susan saw you there parting with him,
just afore he went off to the boat with Mr. Urquhart——"

"Let them talk," Sibyl interrupted haughtily. "This gentleman
is a relation—we are distant cousins. I know he is innocent—know
it by my own instinct, you understand—and my father believes
in him as firmly as I do. I should have been a cowardly wretch if I
had not helped Mr. Urquhart to get him out of prison before more
injustice was done. All I could do was to help with money—which
my father gave me for that purpose. You can't suppose I care what
these people think."

She was beginning to feel the sting of public ingratitude. She
had been very kind to these people—though Ardliston lay beyond
the immediate surroundings of her home. She had gone out of
her way to be kind to them, and had thought herself beloved by
them.

"I must go home," she said, drying the tears that stung her
burning eyeballs every now and then, in spite of that proud spirit
of hers, which made her strong to bear calamity. "I want to help
Mrs. Kettering and her children as much as I can. Will you look
after them for me, Mrs. Garforth, and see that they want for
nothing? If you can come to Ellerslie Park this afternoon I'll give
you some money to keep in hand for them, and I'll tell you what
I want done in the future. If the father risked his life—and lost
it—for my kinsman's sake, those children ought to be my care till
they are old enough to care for themselves."

"You're a noble-hearted young lady; and by-and-by, when she's calmed down a bit, Susan will be as grateful to you as I am now for her sake."

CHAPTER XV

"AH, BUT FORGETTING ALL THINGS, SHALL I THEE?"[1]

No trace of the fugitive had been discovered, though £50 reward had been offered for his arrest—only £50, offered by the Treasury. People in the neighbourhood of Ardliston thought it odd that Sir Joseph Higginson had offered no reward. Yet there would be naturally a restraining influence in the fact of family ties. If Marie Arnold was dear as an adopted daughter, her supposed murderer was allied to Sir Joseph by marriage, and he could hardly desire to see a kinsman of his late wife's in the criminal dock. The prevailing belief in Ardliston and at Ellerslie was that the sea had closed over a lunatic murderer, and that this swift end of a terrible story was about the best thing that could have happened. Nobody outside Ellerslie Park had any doubt that Brandon Mountford had killed Marie Arnold, in a paroxysm of epileptic fury. The word epilepsy once having been uttered, the solution of the mystery was taken as found. The people who knew the least about that terrible disease and its influence on mind and conduct were the most boldly assertive as to the probabilities of the case, and there was no one in the neighbourhood of Ellerslie to suggest that in a criminal mystery the obvious is always the unlikely. There was a general assurance that the last word of the story had been told. The murderer had been shuffled off the scene of this world, to his own and everybody else's advantage. Much suffering and disgrace had been spared to him, and much trouble and loss of time to other people. The sea and the wind had accounted for a man whose continued existence must have been an affliction to himself and a burden to others.

The few county people within the influence of Ellerslie looked into their peerages, and descanted upon the lucky escape of the Allandales and Braemars, and all their kindred. The poor young man was so highly connected that to have had him tried for murder would have brought annoyance and discredit into half the drawing-rooms in Mayfair, and made dinner-table conversation even more full of pitfalls than it usually is. Those Mountford girls—Sibyl Higginson's aunts—and their sons and daughters, had married all over the peerage. There was hardly a family of rank that hadn't a Mountford in it. And how terrible an ordeal for that aristocratic clan had Brandon Mountford's trial for murder been in all the papers; the question of his lunacy or non-lunacy discussed in leaders and letters, fought over by medical specialists, clamoured about by benevolent busybodies; until the mind of fashionable London became permeated with the idea that the Mountfords were every one of them mad; to support which thesis stories would be raked up about every Mountford who had ever worn a queer hat or thrashed a valet from the time of Queen Elizabeth.

Much of this hateful publicity Mr. Mountford's clan had escaped. There had been a great deal of talk about the Ellerslie murder in that part of Cumberland; but the respect felt for Sir Joseph Higginson had exercised a restraining influence over the editors of local newspapers, and the pen of the picturesque reporter had been employed under restrictions.

Upon the report of the inquest there had followed the startling news of Brandon Mountford's escape from gaol, and the chances of his having got away from England, or perished with the luckless crew of the *Mary Jane*, were duly discussed; but after a paragraph or two in subsequent issues, the matter had been allowed to drop, and the local Press had done nothing to annoy the good man to whom the proprietors of the two local weeklies had always looked for aid in times of financial strain.

But though the Press might renounce the privileges of the new journalism in the interests of an old friend, there were tongues in the neighbourhood, old womanish tongues, not always owned by old women, which would not forego so fair an opportunity to blacken a millionaire's character, and breathe their venom on his daughter's fair name. And these tongues were busy, and these small gentry, dwelling in secluded places, afar from the burning questions of public life, were not to be deprived of their prey. In the whist club, on the tennis ground, and at many tea-tables, Brandon Mountford and Sibyl Higginson, and the murdered girl were the subject of low-voiced conversations, where the shrug, and the nod, and the half-expressed thought went a great deal further than plain speech.

Sir Joseph Higginson let them talk, or knew not that they were talking. Marie Arnold was lying in her grave on the landward side of Ellerslie Church, screened from the bleak wind that blows up from Solway Firth, after one of those terrible funerals which are always awarded, Heaven knows why, to a murdered victim.

People had crowded to Ellerslie from busy towns and from far-off villages to follow the murdered girl to the churchyard, and to stare at her mourners, concentrating their attention upon Sir Joseph's haggard face and grey hair, and inclined to resent the absence of his fair young daughter, who should have been a feature in the show.

That hideous funeral, with the rabble to whom the horror of Marie's doom served as a zest to a pic-nic basket and an excuse for an outing, was over, had been over for nearly three months, during the greater part of which time Sir Joseph and his daughter had been in Germany. He had fled from the scene of the murder directly after the funeral, and Sibyl had gone with him. For her, too, Ellerslie had become a place of bad dreams. The gardens and the wood she had loved so well were now clouded with a vague horror. She dared not even think of the spot where the body had been found, and where Brandon had been arrested, with blood-stained hands. Her maid, Ferriby, had insisted on describing the exact spot, had wanted to take her mistress there, with the tactless-ness of her kind. It was an infinite relief to Sibyl to leave England, and she was grateful to her father for proposing to take her to Schwalbach as soon as Miss Minchin could be recalled from her holiday.

It was not so agreeable to her feelings to hear next morning that Hubert Urquhart was to be of the party. He had offered to go as a kind of gentleman courier, to take all trouble off Sir Joseph's hands.

"Your valet is English to the fortieth power, and will be very little use to you in any excursionising," he said.

Sir Joseph protested that he was not going to excursionise. He was going to the quietest place he could find, just to get himself

and Sibyl away from the house that was full of agonising associations. He wanted no one but his old servant, and good little
Minchin to take care of Sibyl. They would live retired from the
world, till the memory of that dreadful night had lost something
of its haunting power, and they could venture home again.

"To stick in one spot and brood over the past, is the way to
remember and not to forget," remonstrated Urquhart. "You and
Sibyl will come back to Ellerslie in lower spirits than when you
went away. Come, Sir Joseph, be reasonable. This shocking event
has pulled you down. You'll want a friend at your elbow."

Sir Joseph was not in a condition to argue about anything.
His brain felt dazed and dull. He let Urquhart think and act for
him, and Sibyl, seeing him so broken down, aged in appearance
by ten years, had not the heart to oppose his wishes, or even to
tell him that Urquhart's company would be a burden to her. So
they started for Schwalbach with Urquhart and Miss Minchin, and
two servants, Sir Joseph's faithful valet of many years' service, and
Sibyl's maid Ferriby, who was utterly incapable of looking after
her young mistress's luggage, and in constant peril of being left
behind at railway stations, or losing herself in strange cities. Fortu-
nately little Miss Minchin was equal to the occasion, and took care
of mistress and maid. Her period of service was nearly at an end.
This was perhaps the last journey she and her beloved pupil were
to take together, the last time they were to be together as pupil
and governess, and her affection was intensified by the prospect
of parting.

"Whatever shall I do with myself without my darling girl?"
she sighed.

"You'll have other darling girls, Mousey dear; better girls than
me, perhaps."

"No, dear, I shall have no more pupils. Your good, good father
is going to allow me fifty pounds a year for the rest of my days, and
I am going back to Beverley, to my dear old mother, to be a help
and a comfort to her in her declining years. There never was such
a man as Sir Joseph, I think, since this world began."

"He is all that is dear and good, but it isn't a bit too much to do
for you, dearest Minchin. Why, if it wasn't for all the care you took
of me, I should hardly be alive."

She checked herself with a deep sigh, thinking how much heartache an early death might have saved her.

They stayed at Schwalbach, in spite of Mr. Urquhart's remonstrances. Neither Sir Joseph nor his daughter were in spirits for touring. Neither mountain scenery nor mediæval architecture offered any attraction for them. The minds of both were brooding on the past, and the thoughts of each were alike gloomy.

Day followed day in a dull monotony, week followed week, and still there was no sign from Brandon Mountford to show that he lived.

"If he landed, and left England for some foreign port, it is very cruel of him not to relieve my mind of this horrible uncertainty," Sibyl said to Urquhart, on one of those rare occasions when she spoke to him confidentially.

"I have no belief in his escape. I believe he went down in the fishing boat with the rest of them; and be assured that if the sea closed over him Providence was kind to us all."

"I don't believe that he was drowned," said Sibyl, obstinately. "He may have sailed for the Cape—and I shall hear from him by-and-by. No, I will not believe that he is dead."

"My dear enthusiast! And to think that you had only known him three weeks."

There was a covert sneer in the words and the tone, which passed unnoticed by Sibyl. She attached no importance to this man's ideas or opinions. He had behaved well upon the whole during those long dull weeks at Schwalbach. He had been useful to Sir Joseph, useful and companionable, and for that Sibyl was grateful. She was still more grateful to him for not having forced his society upon herself. He had not waylaid her in her rambles with sturdy little Miss Minchin, or intruded on her quiet evenings of study in her own sitting-room. He had tried sometimes to lure her from her seclusion, and had been occasionally successful in organising a drive to some distant point of interest, but however picturesque the scenery, he could see that her thoughts were otherwhere. He had never succeeded in making her forget Brandon Mountford. Yet he did not despair of reaching that golden goal to which all his efforts, since Marie's death, had been tending.

"It's a waiting race," he said to himself on that last night at

Schwalbach, as he paced up and down the hotel terrace in the grey interval between sunset and moonrise, "but the prize is such a glorious one! A man may well be patient, buoyed up by such a hope. A lovely woman in the bloom of girlhood, and a dower of a million or two. Yes, it's a question of millions. Jabberwoch, who writes the money article in the *Outside Broker*, told me that Sir Joseph Higginson is one of the richest men in the North of England, and will leave a big pile behind him when he hands in his checks. And he has only this girl—only this one ewe lamb. The stakes are stupendous."

It was August when Sir Joseph and his party went back to Cumberland—just three months after Marie Arnold's death—long enough with most people for sorrow to have assumed that milder form which may last for a lifetime, or dwindle by gentle degrees into forgetfulness. In this instance, however, grief had lost little of its intensity, and the return to familiar scenes was full of pain. Both Sir Joseph and his daughter were heroic in repressing all outward signs of sorrow, and the only change in the father was the look of age which had come upon him with a strange suddenness at the time of Marie's tragic death, together with a marked lessening of that physical energy which a year ago had made the active supervision of his estate an amusement and a delight. He handed over the burden of his cares to Andrew Orlebar, and rarely looked at a business document; languidly assenting to everything his secretary proposed; and had Orlebar been of a less incorruptible honesty, the great Argosy of Sir Joseph Higginson's fortune might have sprung a leak.

The change which grief had wrought in the daughter was less marked, and the outer world might have supposed only that Sibyl Higginson was ripening from the light-hearted girl into the thoughtful woman; but Urquhart, who marked her closely, saw that all the gladness had gone out of her young life. She had a look of anxious thought which a wife of ten years' standing might have had in the absence of an adored husband—a look as of one whose heart is far away. All the amusements and occupations of her life had lost their savour, except only music, that divine art which of all others has the power to soothe, and even to console, to lift the mind from the actual to the unseen, to suggest, if it cannot reveal, the spiritual joys of a life beyond the grave.

Music had been, after religion, Sibyl's chief consoler during those dull days at Schwalbach, and now, on returning to Ellerslie, she flew to her piano in the octagon room where the frescoes on the walls seemed to smile a welcome after the longest interval in which the lovely living face had been absent since those fair ideal faces were painted. The thought of Marie flashed into her mind as she struck the first chord of a pensive voluntary, and she seemed to hear the rich, round notes of the mezzo soprano thrilling in the opening bars of the Agnus Dei they loved, in that 12th Mass, which, whether by Mozart or not by Mozart, will always be dear to music-lovers.

Yes, this was home—the familiar room where all that art could do had been done to surround everyday life with beauty. Sibyl was glad to be at home again, even although that home was haunted by bitter memories, and the shadow of a vanished form met her at every turn of the garden or the wood, on the moorland or by the river; the shadow of her companion of seven happy years—the shadow of the man who in a few short weeks had given a new colour to her life. Both were but shadows now; one lying in the village churchyard; the other vanished, his fate unknown.

As time wore on Sibyl began to believe with Urquhart that Brandon had gone down with the crew of the *Mary Jane*. If he were living he would surely have made some sign. He must have understood that she would be anxious about his fate—or even if he had been so dull of brain as not to sympathise with her feelings, common courtesy would have impelled him to write to the woman who had gone so far out of her way to aid his escape. Gradually, brooding over the work of that dark night, and recalling Urquhart's share in the work, she grew to suspect some hidden motive, and that an evil one, for the part which he had taken. Her suspicions were of the vaguest, for she could imagine no reason for double-dealing on his part; yet now that Brandon's flight had ended fatally, it seemed to her that no gentleman should have counselled so unmanly a course, and she hated herself for having urged Brandon to act against his own convictions.

Yes, it had been a mistake, and a fatal mistake—an error of judgment which had ended in ignominy and death. How much better to have faced the worst. The mystery of Marie Arnold's death might have been solved in the laborious investigation which a trial would have afforded. The keenest intelligence in the land, the quick intellect of the trained advocate, might have been brought to bear upon crime and motive. The clue might have been found, the labyrinth threaded, and the real murderer discovered. By his disappearance Brandon had left the mystery dark, and his name disgraced.

Urquhart ceased to be Sir Joseph's guest after the return from Schwalbach, but he was still a neighbour, as he had established himself for the autumn at Killander Castle, and rode or drove over to Ellerslie so frequently that it seemed to Sibyl as if he might as well have lived there.

She avoided him as much as possible, and spent the greater part of her life in the retirement of her morning-room, with no companion but the devoted Miss Minchin, and Muff, the old collie dog, which had been her faithful adorer from the days of puppyhood, when his youthful spirits had found vent in boisterous gambols and races on the lawns and in the pine wood. He was old and feeble now, and liked best to lie at his ease on the lion skin which Brandon Mountford had presented to her in the beginning of their acquaintance, a trophy from the shores of the Zambesi. The governess was to remain with her pupil as companion and friend till the following spring, when Sibyl's aunt, Lady Selina Mountford, was to assume all the cares of chaperon, and was to conduct the heiress safely through the fiery furnace of smart society, to a brilliant marriage. The migration to Arlington Street was to take place in February, and Miss Higginson was to be presented by Lady Braemar at the first drawing-room of the year.

The Braemars were established in the family house in Hertford Street, the shabby old house within whose panelled walls Sir Joseph Higginson had wooed and won his wife. Lord Allandale was now a confirmed invalid, and spent his life between Bath and various Bohemian health resorts, ministered to by a valet who was nearly as old as himself. Braemar, the heir-apparent, was to all intents and purposes head of the house of Mountford. He was a busy man, a sportsman, fond of racing, fond of all amusements that cost money, and having very little money to spend, a man always over-occupied, upon whose crowded brain even such an

awful episode in the family history as Brandon Mountford's arrest
on a charge of murder, had made no deep impression. He had
written to Sir Joseph, expressing horror at the tragedy, and sympathy with the friends of the murdered girl, together with his
opinion that Brandon could not have done the deed, or could only
have done it in a fit of lunacy. "Mother died mad—very sad history.
Nothing bad on the Mountford side. Foolish marriage. Know very
little of the young man."

This letter, in Braemar's jerky style, natural in a man who
conducted his private correspondence chiefly by electric wire,
had been the only notice of the Ellerslie tragedy by the house of
Mountford, which had a happy knack of dropping any member
who got into trouble.

"With such an immense family as ours, if we didn't cut the
black sheep, we should be always in the law courts," said the philosophical Braemar. "Our time would be taken up in watching Tom,
Dick, and Harry through their troubles."

CHAPTER XVI

"IN THE GREY DISTANCE, HALF A LIFE AWAY"[1]

SIR JOSEPH and his daughter had been at home nearly a month, and
the grouse were being slaughtered on the moors. Lord Penrith was
at the Castle with a small party of shooters, and had ridden over to
Ellerslie twice within a week, and on his second visit had lunched
alone with Sir Joseph, a visit that had lasted late into the afternoon,
the two men strolling up and down the terrace after luncheon
smoking their cigars—Sir Joseph's Infantas and Henry Clays were
famous among his friends—and talking confidentially. Urquhart
had been at Ellerslie on neither occasion. Indeed, Penrith had made
a point of his brother stopping to represent him with the shooters.

"I didn't know you cared about Sir J.," said Urquhart sulkily,
when he heard of the second visit to Ellerslie.

"I don't know what you mean by caring. Sir Joseph is a shocking old bounder, but as good as gold—and if one didn't consort

with bounders nowadays, one would have to take to a cavern in the desert."

"But you are so exclusive," sneered Urquhart, "and you care so little about society. You could afford to do without the bounders."

"No doubt I could in a general way, but I can't afford to do without Sir Joseph Higginson. I like the man, and I like his cigars, and I like—his daughter."

"Oh," exclaimed Urquhart, with a sudden drop of his lower jaw, "that's the way the land lies, is it?"

"Yes," answered Penrith, "that is the way. Have you any objection?"

"Objection! Of course not. The younger must give way to the elder. I am no Jacob."

Penrith laughed a dry, short laugh, as he stepped lightly into his high dog-cart. Poor Hubert! Well, he had had a long innings with the heiress; and it was Penrith's turn now. The fortress might be invincible; but putting a woman's fancy out of the question—and it was evident that Miss Higginson had no fancy for Urquhart—the suitor who could offer a coronet must have the better chance.

He found Sir Joseph a broken man. It was less than a year since they had met, and it seemed to him that ten years of an ordinary lifetime could have made no more marked alteration in the old man's appearance and physique.

Penrith knew that in dealing with so shrewd a man as Joseph Higginson any beating about the bush would be useless. He had not finished his first cigar on his second visit before he came to the point, and offered himself as a suitor for Miss Higginson.

"My title is one of the oldest in the North of England," he said. "I won't say anything about my estate—for as the bulk of my property is near your own, I daresay you know its value as well as I do. I have suffered, as most people have suffered, from the fall in rents—but not to such an extent as some landowners. I don't pretend, by any means, to be a rich man—but the Penrith property is a fine property, and only needs the outlay of a few thousands here and there in restoration and improvement. Houses, gardens, parks have gone to seed for want of ready cash. My house in Berkeley Square, for instance—a house in a walled garden—one of the few old-world houses left in London. My wife might make a very pretty figure in the world, if she had a fortune of her own—and still more if she were young and beautiful, as your daughter is. She might be a leading light among the very best."

Sir Joseph's wan face brightened. He did not love Lord Penrith—that hard Urquhart manner had always repelled him; but so far as he knew Penrith was a man of reputable character. Such dark things as had been said of Hubert Urquhart had never in Sir Joseph's hearing been said of the Earl. It was known that he had tried and failed to marry wealth on more than one occasion; but that failure could hardly be considered disgraceful.

Sir Joseph wanted a coronet for his daughter. Last year, perhaps, strong in the bold ambition of a self-made man, he might have considered this particular coronet hardly good enough. He might have aspired to ducal strawberry leaves—or at least to rank allied with more prosperous fortunes than those of Penrith. But since that calamity of last May a weariness of life had come upon him, and he wanted to see his daughter married as soon as possible. He was perfectly frank with his visitor.

"Only six months ago I was looking forward to Sibyl's first season with a good deal of pleasure," he said. "I loved to think of the splash she would make in society with her fresh young beauty, and her expectations. I wanted to see her admired and followed, and to pick the best man among her followers. But I'm not so keen upon next year as I was a little time ago. I'm breaking up, Penrith. I fancy my race is nearly run. I suppose I used to think myself immortal, for I was always castle-building about the future—my grandchildren—my great-grandchildren even. I thought I might live to see new generations. God knows what I thought—ridiculous in a man of seventy. Well, that's over, and now I am anxious to see my daughter settled—as people call it—before the curtain drops. That dark curtain comes down unexpectedly sometimes, especially where a man has worked his brain as I have worked mine. A fibre snaps, and the tale is told."

Penrith murmured some soothing remark about a fine constitution, a green old age.

"Men live well into the nineties nowadays," he said.

"Some men do. I shan't," answered Sir Joseph, briefly. "I've had the tap of Constable Death on my shoulder, and the notice to move

on. If Sibyl likes you well enough to be your wife, Lord Penrith—
likes you as well as her mother liked me when we married—why,
I will back your suit. And I will make such a settlement as will
secure her fortune against all contingencies, but which shall not
be illiberal towards you. There shall be margin enough of available capital to restore the family seat and the house in town, and
to improve every homestead, and cottage, and every acre on your
estate. If she can but like you? That's the question."

"I hope it may not be impossible for me to win something
even better than liking," said Penrith, with a stately air. "It ought
not to be a hopeless task if the young lady's affections are disen-
gaged; and I take it that in the retirement of Ellerslie she is hardly
likely to have met anyone worthy of her notice."

"No, no, she is heart-whole, I have no doubt," Sir Joseph
answered somewhat confusedly. "She was terribly upset at the
trouble we had here last May—our poor Marie's death—and
Mountford's arrest. Mountford is a kind of cousin of my daughter's. A dreadful business altogether. She misses her adopted sister.
She has not been the same girl since, any more than I have been
the same man. Neither of us can forget."

Penrith looked at him keenly at that mention of Mountford
and then, in cold, incisive tones, he said—

"A shocking business, indeed, Sir Joseph. I conclude that there
can be no doubt of Mountford's guilt, so far as an epileptic can be
held guilty of a crime committed in a paroxysm of his disease."

"I don't know about that. Indeed, I am very doubtful. I should
never have believed in his guilt if he had not broken out of gaol.
Till I heard of his getting away like that I could have staked my life
upon his innocence."

"But if not he, who could the murderer have been?"

"God knows. Some roaming devil, who may have murdered
her for the sake of her trinkets—a gold bangle—a diamond ring
that I gave her on her last birthday, and which she always wore.
The fact that the trinkets were not taken proves nothing, for the
murderer may have been surprised by Brandon's appearance on
the scene."

"They told me he was kneeling by the body, taken
red-handed."

"Any one who came accidentally upon the spot, and touched my poor girl's blood-soaked gown, as I believe Brandon did, would have been red-handed as he was. That proves nothing. The only suspicious circumstance to my mind is his running away."

"Mightily suspicious. A painful story altogether, Sir Joseph. I am sorry for Lord Allandale and the family. I need hardly say that I am still more sorry for you, and your loss of a dependent you were fond of in such a tragic manner."

"My loss of a dependent—yes—of whom I was fond. A dependent! I dare say you have heard people speculate upon the relations between Marie Arnold and me."

Penrith shrugged his shoulders in languid assent.

"People will talk," he said. "I am the last to trouble myself about what the world says, in print, or by word of mouth."

"People may have said that I should hardly have been so fond of a mere dependent, and that Marie Arnold must have been my daughter."

"That is the kind of thing people always say."

"Well, in this case they were right. She was my daughter."

Penrith bent his head gravely.

"I am flattered by your confidence, and your directness," he murmured.

"You are entitled to my confidence. There should be no secrets between us if you are to be my son-in-law. There must be no after-claps; no asking for explanations. You know pretty well what I am myself. You shall hear all that there is to be told about Marie Arnold's birth and parentage."

"Sir Joseph, if this revelation be in the least distressing to you I must beg you to let the matter rest. I do not seek to pry into your history, nor could a flaw of that kind in the record of your earlier life lessen the respect to which your character and position entitle you, and which you must always receive, unstintedly, from me. Men of the world do not look severely upon such indiscretions. Pray let it pass."

"No, no, it will be a relief to tell you. I have been a most miserable man since my poor girl's death. I am not superstitious—but sometimes I think that her cruel death was a judgment upon me. I ought to have acknowledged her as my daughter. It would have

THOU ART THE MAN

been easy enough, my dear wife being gone, to assert a previous marriage. Sibyl would never have disputed the fact; and Marie could have been told to hold her tongue as to the date of her mother's death. I ought to have given my girl her rightful position as my daughter—not my heiress—but my amply-dowered daughter. But I was a hypocrite and a coward. I allowed myself to be talked about as the benefactor of an orphan. I allowed my own flesh and blood to wear the livery of dependence. Well, the story is short and common enough."

There was a pause, and Sir Joseph walked the length of the terrace in silence, lighted a cigar, smoked a few whiffs, and tossed it away impatiently.

"Arnold was an Englishman who had worked in Northern France for a good many years, and had married a French wife. She was from the South—a lovely creature, and had been married only a year when her husband came to me as overseer of an iron works which I had taken over from a bankrupt company. There had been folly, ignorance, neglect, and dishonesty. Everything was in confusion, and Arnold, who knew the district and the men, and who was half a Frenchman by long habit, was very useful to me. He was a man of remarkable talent, had been able to hold his own in various employments, but was a drunkard, and before he had been in my service three months I was told that he beat his pretty young wife, and I was asked to interfere for her protection. Well, I called at their lodging, saw the wife, lectured the husband, held out hopes of promotion, and promised to do my very best for him if he would only keep away from the brandy shop. He, on his part, promised amendment, was very plausible, and praised the virtues of his wife."

"And naturally broke his promise, before long," put in Penrith, whose languid air suggested that he was listening rather out of politeness than from any warm interest in the story.

"Yes. He went from bad to worse. He was a valuable servant, knew the place, and the plant, and where all had been chaos his knowledge and experience were particularly useful, but he was not a fit man to be in a post of authority, and there were continual complaints. I threatened dismissal, but didn't dismiss him. I saw his wife, and tried to bring her influence to bear upon him, but she was not a clever, managing woman. She was pretty, and she flung

herself upon me for protection in her helplessness, complained of
his violence, regretted her happy home in the south. Her people
were poor, but they had always been kind. With her husband she
was often in fear of her life. I urged her, things being as bad as this,
to go back to her family. I offered to send her home, but she was
timid and irresolute. If she were to leave George Arnold he would
follow and bring her back, and her position would be worse than
ever. I could do nothing."

Another pause, another cigar lighted and flung away—and
then Sir Joseph went on hurriedly.

"The crisis came one summer evening just as it was growing
dark. Arnold had been drinking all day—drinking, and leaving his
work to be done by a subordinate. I was afterwards told that he
had not been sober for a week. There was a desperate scene; and
his wife fled from him, came to my lodgings, and asked me to
shelter and protect her.

"Well, Lord Penrith, you know what usually happens in such
a case as that. She stayed with me. It was rather for fear of him
than love of me that she stayed, I believe. It was only with me that
she felt herself safe. As owner of the works, and as a rich man, I
was looked up to, and she fancied herself safer with me than with
anybody else. George Arnold came to my lodgings on the following day—only half sober—threatening and violent, and I flung him
out-of-doors like a dog. What pity could I have for a man who had
taken a lovely young creature into his keeping, and had ill-used her
from the very beginning of their married life? I had no pity, no compunction where he was concerned; but it was an awful thing to
hear next morning that he had been killed on the railroad, and that
it was more than likely he had thrown himself in front of the train.
No one knew that his wife had been under my roof at the time of
his death. I provided a new home for her in a village three miles
from the works. I did all I could to save her character, and I believe
I succeeded. No one ever said that Louison Arnold was more to me
than an ill-used woman whom I had befriended; but she was fond
of me, poor girl, her heart turned to me in her loneliness, and for
half a year after her husband's death she and I were all the world to
each other, and all my leisure hours were spent with her.

"I made her the promise which, I suppose, most men would

have made in such circumstances. I promised to marry her, and I meant to keep my promise, later on, after the birth of her child; but she had an unhappy disposition, fretful, exacting, jealous, and the bond of love had worn very thin before my daughter was born. The child's coming might have strengthened the tie, and I might have kept my promise, like an honest man, but Louison's conduct at this time was trivial and foolish. I discovered a flirtation with one of my clerks. I was very angry, and took her back to her native town in Provence, at an hour's warning, and established her with her child in the house which she inhabited for the rest of her life. I allowed her a comfortable income, and I paid for her daughter's education at a convent near the mother's home, but I never saw her after my marriage. Love had long died out, and I could have approached her almost as a stranger, but I felt that to look upon the face of the woman who had been my mistress would be an offence against my wife.

CHAPTER XVII

WHAT PEOPLE SAID

SIR JOSEPH was pleased with Lord Penrith's quiet manner, both in advancing his own claims and in receiving that frank confession of past error. There was some touch of comfort for the sinner in Penrith's tranquil acceptance of the story, as a mere matter of course, an incident likely enough to happen in every man's life. He himself had been inclined to take a tragical view of that old story, and to recognise the scourge of the Furies in those sharp strokes which Fate had dealt him—first, George Arnold's suicide, for he had never doubted that the drunken husband had flung away his life in a fit of jealous rage—then Lady Lucy's death—by an accident so common, but a blow so crushing to the man who adored her—and last and most terrible the murder of his unacknowledged daughter. A remorseful conscience perceived in these calamities the judgment of an offended Heaven. It was a comfort, therefore, to talk to a man of Penrith's advanced school, who did not believe in angels, avenging or otherwise, and who looked upon man as the creature of circumstances and environment.[1] Sir Joseph wanted to see his daughter married, settlements made, his colossal fortune secured so far as legal defences can secure wealth against the weakness or the folly of a wife or the dishonesty of a husband. The thought that this splendid fortune could be scattered and wasted was madness—this fortune which had grown under his care, from the first earnings of the peasant lad to the wealth of the man who owned property of almost every shape and form, stretching from mines and smelting works close at hand to the furthest limits of mining enterprise in America and Australia. It would be a grand thing to see his daughter a countess, with an impregnable marriage settlement. The conviction that his working day was nearly done had been growing upon him ever since Marie's death. He felt the shadows darkening round him. He had worked his brain with relentless activity, and of late there had been moments of trouble and confusion—the vain effort to recall a familiar name— the sudden clouding of ideas—which indicated that the fibres were wearing thin, and that the final obscuration, the fall of the curtain, might come suddenly. He was inclined, therefore, to assist Penrith's suit with all his paternal influence.

Why should not Sibyl like this aristocratic suitor? He had all the markings of an ancient race in the refined features and slender yet athletic form, the small hand and tapering fingers, the narrow arched foot—a true Norman type, with its suggestions of more distant ancestors in the dim remoteness of the centuries before the conquest. The difference in their ages was considerable—the girl only eighteen—the man between thirty and forty, arrived at an age when a man begins to feel that the glory and the freshness of youth have departed, and that he is nearing the crest of the hill, the other side of which is all downward travelling. But this seniority should only lend dignity to his suit. It ought to be more gratifying to a girl's pride to be admired and esteemed by a man of Penrith's age and intellectual weight than to be worshipped by a stripling fresh from Christchurch or Sandhurst.

It was a bitter disappointment to Sir Joseph when, after confiding Penrith's hopes and his own views to Sibyl, he was met by a deliberate refusal.

"I don't think I shall ever marry," she said. "At any rate, there is nothing further from my thoughts at present. I want to stay with you, dear father—always."

"Always may not mean very long," Sir Joseph muttered moodily, and then he strongly urged the advantages of a marriage with Penrith—an old peerage—an estate adjoining that which she was to inherit, a castle that had stood like a rock against the assaults of Scottish freebooters in the days when it was a perilous thing to live on the Marches. For dignity, for historic interest, there could hardly be a finer match. Sir Joseph grew angry as he noted Sibyl's scornful lip and resolute eye.

"Do you want to marry a duke?" he exclaimed. "Is that why you turn up your nose at an offer most girls would snap at?"

"I don't want to marry at all, father."

"No, not this year; but next year you will be in London, sur-rounded by adventurers, and the first fortune-hunting scamp—rake-hell or gambler—who takes your fancy will have a better chance than Penrith, with his thirty thousand acres and ancient name."

"I am not afraid of fortune-hunters."

"Very likely not; but I am."

"Don't take me to London, then, next year, or any other year. I don't care for society, father. I am as happy as I ever can be, here with you."

"Sibyl, that's all very well, but it can't last. I am an old man, and our parting—our last parting, my dear—may come sooner than you expect. You think it nothing to give up society, and all the pleasures to which my daughter has a right, but that's only because you don't know what the great world is like. You've heard it abused—its pleasures called Dead Sea fruit. That's all nonsense. It's a very pleasant world for youth and wealth, whatever it may be for the worn-out and the needy. No doubt they taste the dust and ashes—but the fruit will be fresh and sweet to your lip. You must take your position in society next season, Sibyl, married or unmar-ried. Your aunt Selina would not hear of your presentation being delayed after your nineteenth birthday."

Sibyl did not dispute this point, but she was firm in her refusal of Lord Penrith.

He was to come to Ellerslie in a few days to hear her verdict.

He had begged that she might not be hurried in her decision. He wished that she should have ample time to consider the manifold advantages he had to offer. He would have been cut to the quick could he have known with what indifference Sibyl contemplated his offer, and that the only words of her father's that had touched her feelings had been his gloomy foreshadowing of his own death. Her thoughts were full of sadness as she walked up and down the terrace where only a few months ago she had been so light-hearted and happy. It was still early in September, and Autumn had scarcely touched the foliage in park or woods—only September, and she remembered herself as she had been last Spring, when the leaves on yonder plane tree were unfolding, while the beech buds were still purple. How happy, how thoughtless she had been in those lengthening April days, amused with the veriest trifles; and now it seemed to her as if life were one load of care. Look where she would, the horizon was dark.

She had lived almost in seclusion since her return from the Continent. The few cottagers—fisher families at Ardliston, pit-men's families nearer home—whom she had visited had received her, as she thought, somewhat ungraciously. There was a change of some kind, a want of cordiality. They had answered all her questionings as to their own welfare, and had accepted her gifts with a certain sullenness. She had avoided Susan Kettering, shuddering at the memory of the widow's frantic vehemence in the day of mourning; but two or three days after Penrith's second visit to Ellerslie she called on Mrs. Kettering's aunt, the widow Garforth, and again offered help for the orphan children. The aunt declined all help in the niece's name.

"It's poor Susan's whim to do without your help, Miss," she said, "and she must have her own way. She's just a heart-broken creature, and, right or wrong, she lays her grief at your door, and she says she'd rather see those children starve than touch a six-pence of your money. They needn't starve, anyhow, poor bairns, for Susan can earn a little with charing. She's been working up at the Arms four days a week, and there's others—uncles and aunts—to help a bit, so there's no call for you to take it to heart, Miss, whatever folks may say."

"I care nothing what people say," Sibyl answered, haughtily. "I only want to help those poor children. I cannot be in the slightest measure responsible for their father's death. He was asked to take out his boat, and offered a price for his night's work. He was free to refuse, if he saw any risk."

"Of course he was, Miss. Everybody can see that, except Susan. She raves about the money that tempted him—your money. I don't believe he had ever had the chance of earning so much in all his life till that night."

"He refused at first, then?"

"Yes, poor fellow. He saw there was dirty weather coming. He didn't mean to take his boat out that tide, but it was a heap of money to earn in a single night, and Mr. Urquhart put it to him—it would be the making of his fortune, and it might save Mr. Mountford from the gallows. And when Susan heard of the money, she begged him to go—that's what preys upon her mind, miss; but she has no call to lay the blame at your door and set people talking."

Those phrases of Mrs. Garforth's about what people said haunted Sibyl's memory with uncomfortable persistency. What should people say to her discredit? What reason had she to be ashamed, even if all that could be known about that dreadful night were known to the little world of Ellerslie and Ardliston? She could understand that the widow might be blindly resentful, but what right had other people to blame her? There was no act of hers upon that night of which she felt ashamed; for the violation of the law at which she had assisted did not trouble her conscience. She saw no more shame in that than lion-hearted Winifred Nithsdale could have seen in the trick that saved her husband's head from the block.[2]

What could people say?

The neighbours at Ellerslie were of the fewest, for, except Killander Castle there was no country seat within a radius of ten miles, the greater part of the land within that radius being owned by Lord Penrith and Sir Joseph Higginson. A retired colonel of a Highland regiment, with his wife and daughters, and an evangelical vicar and his wife, both middle-aged people, were Sibyl's only genteel neighbours within walking distance, and these two families provided enough gentility to keep a whole parish going. What could people say? Sibyl asked herself with troubled brow, as she paced the terrace, where so much of her life was spent in fine weather, while the horses were idle in the stable, and the boats lay unused in the boat-house by the river—that river which she had never willingly looked upon since Marie Arnold's death. What could people say? She remembered now a certain touch of patronage in the manner of Mrs. Denton, the vicar's wife, a sort of "poor dear" air; a soothing look and tone which seemed to say, "I shall always be your friend, however other people may treat you." She had thought nothing of that indefinite change at the time, too weary of mind and heart to be on the alert for shades of meaning in Mrs. Denton's local twaddle; but now, recalling that last tea-drinking she remembered that there had been a change. Those fulsome flatteries which had implied that Sir Joseph's daughter was only a little lower than the angels, had given place to a pitying tenderness of tone, insufferable to think of now that she took the trouble to recall it.

She remembered too that there had been a shade of coldness in Mrs. Macfarlane's manner when they met in a pitman's cottage, the elder lady distributing tracts and good advice, the younger orders for soup and wine. She remembered that the Macfarlanes, who had always been precise to pernickettyness in the interchange of afternoon calls, had not called at Ellerslie since her return from Schwalbach. Sibyl had not noticed the omission till now, thankful to be left in her melancholy solitude; but now it seemed to her that her neighbours had been purposely distant.

She went from the terrace to the drawing-room, where an open piano and a volume of Beethoven offered that form of consolation which always soothed her nerves and lifted her soul out of the abyss of gloom. But to-day even music seemed to have lost some of its power. She played the first movement of the Moonlight Sonata, and then rose, and moved slowly about the room, looking at the pictures on the walls, the marble Hebe, coldly white against a background of tall palms, the tables loaded with bric-à-brac, the valuable books piled carelessly on other tables—books that had been chosen mostly for her sake, Sir Joseph ordering any new book or new edition which he thought might please his daughter.

How splendid it all was; but how lonely! Sir Joseph lived chiefly in his own rooms, seeing no one but Andrew Orlebar, and only joining his daughter at dinner, and after dinner, when he would ask her to play to him, and sit in melancholy silence while she played.

Miss Minchin had gone home to her invalid mother. Lady Selina was in Scotland with the Braemars, but was to arrive at Ellerslie early in October and take up her position officially, as Miss Higginson's chaperon, till she should be released from that grave duty by Miss Higginson's marriage. Sir Joseph had contrived to convey to her mind that, as he could not presume to offer stipend or pecuniary consideration of any sort to a woman of Lady Selina's social standing, her kindness to her niece would be substantially remembered in his will, on which his sister-in-law had assured him, firstly, that she hoped he would outlive her; secondly, that she existed only to be useful to her people; thirdly, that any little legacy he might be generous enough to bequeath to her would be a most welcome addition to her wretched income.

"You know what a struggle it is for the unmarried daughters of a poor nobleman to live like ladies," said Lady Selina; "the wonder is that they manage to live at all."

Sir Joseph further conveyed to his sister-in-law that the frocks and millinery which she would require during Sibyl's first season were to be included in Sibyl's bills.

"You are too good, my dear Joseph. You won't find me extravagant. One or two walking gowns, my court gown, and a satin frock or so, with my own lace, for dances, will carry me through the season. I won't ruin you."

Everything had been settled, therefore, and in the mean time Sibyl, who dreaded her aunt's frivolous loquacity, had been thankful to be alone. Till to-day there had been no oppression in the sense of solitude, only an immense relief, but now, by this new light, suggested by Mrs. Garforth's tactless speech, the solitude galled.

Was she, Sibyl Higginson, who from her babyhood had been accustomed to the adulation of everybody about her, and had grown unconsciously—without any lessening of her generous impulses and sympathy with others—to regard herself in some sort as a personage—was she to be patronised by a vicar's wife, and cut by a half-pay Colonel and his family? The thought was intolerable. The impetuous blood of youth mounted to the fair temples, and when a servant threw open the drawing-room door and announced Mr. Urquhart, Sibyl hardly waited for the door to be shut before she turned to the visitor with indignant vehemence, and exclaimed—

"Did you know this, Mr. Urquhart? Have you known all along of the cruel things people have been saying about me—here, in this place, where they have known me since I was a little child?"

She burst into tears, the first she had shed since the interview with Mrs. Garforth. They were tears of anger rather than of sorrow.

Bewildered for the moment by this outburst, Urquhart gently questioned the indignant girl, and drew from her all the story of Susan Kettering's insolence, and Mrs. Garforth's hints of scandal—of Mrs. Denton's compassionate airs, and Mrs. Macfarlane's coldness. Hubert Urquhart was essentially an "Opportunist," quick to profit by a crisis that could be turned to his own advantage—and in Sibyl's wounded feelings he saw a golden opportunity for the ripening of his own schemes. Until Penrith's appearance on the scene he had meant to take things very quietly—to wait and watch with the patience of Bruce's proverbial spider.[3] His faith had been large in the opportunities that time always brings. But Penrith's rivalry altered the whole aspect of the case, and his only chance of success was a coup de main.[4]

"My dear Sibyl, I am sure you have too enlightened a mind to be distressed by village gossip," he began, deprecatingly.

"They have talked about me, then?"

"Of course they have talked—people talked about Joan of Arc—and there were slanders about Charlotte Corday.[5] Nothing romantic or heroic can escape being talked about. Your visit to the lock-up, and your help in Mountford's escape got known somehow—and naturally people have talked. There is not much to be said—no ground for scandal—but people in country places have a way of saying things. Miss Higginson must have been very much attached to Mr. Mountford before she could take such a step—and then they go on harping upon your attachment, and weaving a web of lies round a small nucleus of truth, until the thing grows into a scandal—and mothers shake their heads and say they would not like their daughters to behave as Miss Higginson behaved—and fathers say that Brandon Mountford was a scoundrel—and stories—so circumstantial as to seem true—are told of Sir Joseph's anger and your tears—and speeches that never were spoken are quoted and commented upon. There is nothing that grows so quickly as a scandal—there needs but a grain of seed to produce a mighty tree, and all the carrion crows of the neighbourhood flap their wings and croak and scream among its branches. But what need you care? You know the purity of your own motives."

"Yes, I know my own motives—and his noble character—but it is too cruel that he should be maligned. I can answer to my God for what I did. If I broke the law——"

"It is hardly so much the breach of the law these people talk about, as the departure from the conventional rules that hedge round a young lady in your position—forgive me if I wound you by repeating their malicious speeches—the running after your lover."

He tried to put as much unpleasant emphasis upon that last word as it would carry; but to Sibyl's innocence the word meant very little. She understood, however, that unkind things had been said—unkind to him whose fate she knew not, and whose memory she fondly cherished.

"Sibyl, there is one—and only one—way of cutting through the web that entangles you. The quickest, simplest way," he said, eagerly, drawing nearer to her, with a sudden fire in his cold hard face, taking her hand in both his own. "Give me the right to defend your reputation. I was with you all through that night. I can answer for the purity of your motives—the generous impulse that urged you to depart from the beaten track of conduct. No one will dare to speak ill of you when you have a husband to answer for you—a husband familiar with your life from your childhood, and who knows that it is spotless. Give me that right, Sibyl—give me the reward of my patient love."

"No, no, no, not for the world," she said passionately. "How can you dream of such a thing, knowing what you know? Do you think I am so fickle or so weak? You know I loved Brandon Mountford, and that it was only his sad affliction that forbade our being engaged lovers."

"The past is past. You can never marry Mountford—dead or living, he is lost to you. But marriage is your only escape from the scandal that has grown out of that fatal night. Sibyl, for your own sake, I must be plain with you. I know the world of which you know nothing—know it too well—and I know that the cloud which darkens your name in this place will follow you to London, and that your first appearance in the great world will be over-shadowed by that odious scandal—vague—from its very vague-ness impossible to confute. You cannot live down that scandal by yourself alone. It will be the signal for the basest adventurers to hunt you as their destined prey. No one but a husband—a man of position—can come between you and the venom of the world in which beauty and wealth are the chosen mark for malice."

"Is that so?" asked Sibyl suddenly, "would these people be sorry for their unkindness if I were to marry a man of position in their paltry world—a man of rank?"

"Assuredly they would," said Urquhart, his face lighting triumphantly.

She had wrenched her hand from his, and in this moment of fancied success he tried again to seize it—tried to draw her to his breast, fully believing that his cause was won—won much more easily than he had hoped, even when resolved on trying to take her by storm.

She repulsed him angrily. Her face was flushed; her eyes flamed. She ran to the bell and held the button down till a footman appeared.

"Was that Lord Penrith's phaeton which drove past the window half an hour ago?" she asked.

"Yes, ma'am. His Lordship is with Sir Joseph in the study."

"Ask him to come to me—here—directly."

"Sir Joseph, ma'am?"

"No, Lord Penrith."

"What do you want with my brother?" asked Urquhart, when the man was gone.

"You shall hear."

Sibyl was walking about the room, her heart beating violently, her breath quickened, her hands clasped tightly together in the agony of a desperate determination. She was at the age when the happiness of a lifetime is sometimes hazarded upon the impulse of a moment—the age of sudden resolve and reckless action. Wounded pride had mastered every other feeling.

Penrith appeared, pale, grave, prepared for a serious interview, but in no wise prepared for his brother's presence. He gave Urquhart a curt nod, as he approached Sibyl.

Their hands met, and he stood looking at her, surprised at the crimson flush on her cheeks and the angry light in her eyes.

"You sent for me, and I came with delight," he said gently. "I'm sure you must know how eager I am to see you. But you look distressed—I fear there is something the matter."

He turned from Sibyl to Hubert questioningly.

"Lord Penrith, my father told me a few days ago that you wished me to be your wife. Do you still wish it?"

"Still—always—with my whole heart."

"But perhaps you don't know that people in this neighbourhood have said unkind things about me because I helped Mr. Mountford to escape—convinced that he was innocent of poor Marie's death."

"I have heard nothing. If I did hear—well, I should let people know my opinion of them, for daring to speak unkindly of you."

"But you know that I broke the law in helping Mr. Mountford to escape—that I provided the money which tempted the owner of the *Mary Jane* to risk his life. The boat was lost—with all on board. They say at Ardliston that those lives lie at my door."

She clasped her hands before her face to hide the tears that rushed to her eyes at that thought.

"I know that you can have done nothing that was not noble and high-minded."

"I loved him," faltered Sibyl. "I am not ashamed of my love—even now. I can never care for any one on this earth as I cared for him—but if," she continued, dashing away her tears and confronting Penrith with a resolute look, "if, knowing this, which I have told you in the presence of your brother, who was with me—and acted for me—on that fatal night—if knowing this, Lord Penrith, you still wish to take me for your wife——"

"Still wish—earnestly, passionately!" cried Penrith, seizing her hands, and trying to draw her to his breast.

There was triumph, ecstasy almost, in his face and voice, if not the ring of real passion. To have won her—to have won beauty, youth, and fortune so easily—was more than he had hoped. He flashed an exultant glance at his brother, as he put his arm round Sibyl's waist.

"My love, my wife," he cried. "Life has nothing left to give me more than this."

Hubert Urquhart had been standing a little way off, with his back to a wide window—a window with plate-glass doors, opening on to the terrace, a window which gave light and brightness, and air, and egress and ingress, but which every æsthetically-minded visitor at Ellerslie condemned as an error in taste.

Standing with his back to that flood of light, Urquhart's face had been in dense shadow, and neither the diabolical scowl nor the livid hue of his countenance as he witnessed this impromptu betrothal had been noticed by his brother or Sibyl. Both were startled by the venom which hissed from his lips in a burst of ironical felicitation.

"I congratulate you, Miss Higginson, upon a coup de theatre that would have done honour to Rachel in her zenith[6]—a dramatic situation more daring than anything Sardou has ever attempted.[7] You wanted a husband to patch up your damaged reputation— that fact was clear to me just now when I offered you my unworthy self and a younger brother's modest status. But you are more ambitious than I thought you. I did not know that you wanted to repair your blemished character with the prestige that hangs about an Earl's coronet, that you counted upon buying a title with the million or so which your worthy coal-mining, iron-founding, money-grubbing father is ready to give as solatium to the husband who is willing to marry——"

Some word followed, only half pronounced between clenched teeth—only the beginning of some infamous word, no syllable of which ever reached Sibyl's ear, and which ended in a crash of plate-glass that rang through Ellerslie House and brought master and servants, indoor and out-of-door, hurrying to the scene.

Happily for Hubert Urquhart, and perhaps still more happily for Lord Penrith, the heavy glass doors were standing ajar when with one blow, impelled by passion too strong for speech, the elder brother hurled the younger backwards through the parting casements on to the terrace outside. It was the shock of the doors flying asunder as Urquhart fell between them which had shattered the two tall panels of glass and sent a shower of splinters flashing and sparkling in the sunlight. The flush of anger had faded from Penrith's forehead by the time Sir Joseph entered the room, and he met the baronet's eager questioning with perfect self-possession.

"I am sorry I lost my temper and broke your window," he said; "but if a scoundrel insults the woman one loves—or indeed any woman—what can one do but knock him down? and Mr. Urquhart happened to be standing in front of your window. Pray don't be distressed, Sibyl. You will never again be subjected to my brother's brutality, for he shall never enter any house of mine, and I am sure your father will have nothing more to do with him."

"What has he done—what has he said?" asked Sir Joseph, bewildered and alarmed.

"Nothing worth talking about—only an explosion of malevolence. He wanted to marry Miss Higginson, and behaved like a lunatic when he heard her promise to be my wife."

"What? Has she promised?"

"I am proud to say she has," answered Penrith, taking Sibyl's hand.

"Thank God!" said Sibyl's father.

While this brief conversation was proceeding Hubert Urquhart was lying on his back upon the gravel walk outside, unconscious of surrounding things.

Dr. Dewsnap, who looked to his injuries half an hour afterwards, was able to assure Sir Joseph that although his patient was suffering from slight concussion of the brain, and was somewhat shaken and bruised by the fall, he would most likely be quite well in a few days.

CHAPTER XVIII

LADY PENRITH'S IDEA

THE story of Sibyl Higginson's girlhood has been told. She now reappears on the scene in the maturity of her beauty, in the calm strength of a cultivated intellect, with all the power and influence that rank and wealth can give in a world where both are objects of fanatical worship, a woman much admired and courted, and sincerely loved by the numerous nephews and nieces to whom she is never weary of showing kindness. Yet for all that a lonely woman, childless, fatherless, living her own life, unsustained by the sympathy or affection of her husband.

Sir Joseph's anticipation of the end proved a true forecast. He died suddenly at his house in London, in the first year of his daughter's marriage, and after seeing her take her place in the great world with distinction; and the vast wealth which he had accumulated in half a century of laborious enterprise passed at once to Sibyl, Countess of Penrith, guarded and hedged round by those wise restrictions which Sir Joseph's lawyers had attached to her marriage settlement. Sibyl's fortune might make Lord Penrith a rich man, but Lord Penrith had no power to make his wife a pauper. Sometimes in an angry mood he spoke of himself contemptuously as her ladyship's pensioner.

The house in Arlington Street was sold soon after Sir Joseph's death, and according to the terms of his will; but all that was choicest in a remarkable collection of pictures and curios was transferred to Lady Penrith's rooms in Berkeley Square, or to the castle in the Marches. She was pleased to surround herself with the things her father's taste had selected. Nor was she unwise in the desire to keep the pictures which he had chosen, for the self-educated, humbly-born millionnaire had early learnt to discriminate between good and bad art, and his taste and judgment had ripened in the studios of famous painters, and in Christie's sale-rooms. Even the sweepings of his gallery sold well.

No ray of light had been cast on Brandon Mountford's fate in the ten years that had gone by since his escape from the lock-up at Ardliston, and Sibyl could hardly doubt that he had gone down to his death with the crew of the *Mary Jane*. Susan Kettering's children were growing up into sturdy lads and lasses, and it had been Lady Penrith's care that they should be well provided for, the boys apprenticed, the girls started in domestic service with all the belongings of respectability. Susan Kettering had long ago repented of her unjust anger against Sir Joseph's daughter, and had learnt to be grateful to the benefactress who had made the years of her widowhood smooth and prosperous. There was no one in that north country more beloved and respected than Lady Penrith.

She was a personage in Mayfair and Belgravia; but in that smaller world around Killander Castle and Ellerslie Park she was a queen.

Ellerslie House had never been occupied by strangers, though in the nine years since Sir Joseph's death Lady Penrith had only lived in it for a few days at a time once or twice a year. His Lordship spoke scornfully of the folly of maintaining a house and grounds which required the labour of about a dozen people, for such brief occupancy; but Sibyl reminded her husband that as the shooting and fishing were of use to himself and his friends he had no right to complain.

There was at least one inhabitant of Ellerslie House above the status of a servant, and that was Andrew Orlebar, who had occupied his old rooms and moved about house and gardens and home farm in his old quiet way ever since Sir Joseph's death. He was Lady Penrith's land steward and business manager. He held all the threads of that golden web of which she was the centre. He knew the value of every investment Sir Joseph had ever made, for he had watched them all from the beginning; and he might have been questioned at any moment as to yesterday's closing price of any stock held by Lady Penrith without being out in his reply by so much as an eighth.

Andrew Orlebar lived at Ellerslie all the year round, and never complained of wintry weather or want of society. He was much respected in the district, and looked up to as a man whose advice on money matters was worth a little extra courtesy. He was nearly seventy, but no less active and industrious than when he entered Joseph Higginson's service as timekeeper and clerk at thirty. Nothing at Ellerslie had been altered. The rooms in which Sibyl's childhood and youth had been spent were exactly as she had known them then; and it pleased her sometimes to turn her back upon a large house-party at the Castle to spend a quiet day in those silent rooms, with no companion but Andrew Orlebar, with whom she would take tea in Sir Joseph's study, and who delighted to make her look through his account of the half-year's payments to her banker.

"You have a surplus from last year's income that ought to be invested," he would say. "Your balance is needlessly large."

"Do what you like with it, my dear Andrew," was her usual reply; "your investments never go wrong; but first let us remember the poor."

And then she would tell him of some charity in which she was interested—some great work vouched for by good men, and she would allot to that scheme of beneficence perhaps the whole of her surplus. If Andrew Orlebar argued that she was giving away too much, that she was not allowing her fortune its natural development, she would answer with a sad smile that she had no motive for being richer, that she had enough and more than enough, having no children among whom to divide her fortune, no family to establish, spreading out into other families, carrying her riches into new channels.

"For a solitary woman to go on amassing wealth for the mere pleasure of piling up money would be horrible," she said.

Orlebar shook his head dubiously.

"Great fortunes must grow," he said; "it doesn't do for them to stand still. The value of the sovereign steadily dwindles, and a rich man who doesn't increase his capital will find himself a poor man some day, without knowing why. You must really allow me to invest half your surplus in one of our home railways. The stock is very high, but it will go higher."

The discussion generally ended in a compromise. Half the surplus income went to the charity, and half was invested at Orlebar's discretion. He was very careful in his administration of his principal's fortune. The days of neck-or-nothing enterprises which had helped to make Joseph Higginson a millionnaire were over.

"I go plodding on among investments that cannot bring more than four and a half per cent. at the outside," he said; "but the responsibility is too great for me to risk anything. I can't play pitch and toss with tens of thousands, as your dear father did. Ah, those were fine times in Arlington Street, when you were a little girl. He used to take my breath away; but whatever stock he touched always turned up trumps. He had the genius of finance. And it was all for your sake. 'I am building up a pile for my little girl,' he used to say; and he did build up a pile. Those old Egyptian Pharaohs were thought to have done a grand thing when they left a pyramid behind them, but what's the good of a pyramid? It's neither useful nor ornamental. The fortune your father left is both. Look at the Higginson Orphanage, the Higginson Almshouses for pitmen's widows, the Higginson Schools! Aren't those useful, and ornamental too? Your work, all your work, I know, my dear lady; but you couldn't have built 'em without his money."

"No, indeed. They are his work, and his only. It has been my greatest happiness to found institutions that will make his name remembered in the years to come, when there will be no one living who can remember him."

"Ah, that's a sad thought, ain't it? Fifty years, or so, and there's no one left whose memory can conjure up the figure of the man as he lived. There's a portrait or two, more or less like him. Herkomer's is about as like as paint can be to flesh and blood.[1] But the memory of him as he lived and moved—the quick turn of his head, all life and energy—the curious little twitch of his eyebrow when he was puzzled—that slow, thoughtful smile when he was going to do a kindness to any one—his deep, full voice, a little rough sometimes, but very gentle to those he loved! Fifty years, and no one on this earth will be able to recall those things that are so near and vivid now! It seems hard, don't it?"

Sibyl loved to hear the old man talk, were he never so prosy; and those afternoons at Ellerslie were always a restful change from the statelier life of Killander Castle.

Coralie having expressed herself very anxious to see a house of which she had heard a great deal, Lady Penrith took her over to Ellerslie one October afternoon—within a few days of that long afternoon wasted on futile inquiries and the vain endeavour to solve the mystery of the pencil scrawl.

Cora ran about the house looking at everything, and rapturous about everything, with that equality of praise which bespeaks the ignorant admirer; and while the younger lady was amusing herself by a tour of inspection the elder was closeted with Andrew Orlebar, from whom she had no secrets, and to whom she showed the scrap of paper which had stirred such hidden depths of feeling.

"It is so like his hand," she said.

And then she placed the poor scrawl side by side with a little note written in the early morning, before one of their river excursions—proposing a pic-nic luncheon at a particular spot, suggesting that Sibyl and her companion should take their books and sketching materials—or their latest craze in the way of needle-work—

and make a day of it; a note sportive and playful, which committed the writer to no expression of feeling, yet which seemed to breathe fondest admiration of her to whom it was written. It was his first letter. How she had treasured it, in that golden time; and in all the years since that brief dream of love!

Other letters had followed—letters about further excursions—about books—about music—playful little notes written in the morning about disputed points in the conversation overnight, a misquoted line by Tennyson or Browning—notes about anything, or about nothing. There is no surer sign of a man being deep in love than this inclination to scribble futilities to a lady while living under the same roof with her. The necessary separations of daily life are too long for him. He must needs bridge them over with nonsense-letters. He cannot stand under her window and serenade her, like a lover of old romance; so he writes, and writes, and writes.

"There is certainly a resemblance between the two hands," said Orlebar, after scrutinising both documents through a reading glass, which magnified every stroke, "but what of that? You may often find a resemblance as marked in the penmanship of men who are total strangers to each other, and cannot have grown to write alike by unconscious imitation; and how can you for a moment suppose that this scrap of paper given you by some crazy mendicant on the moor could emanate from Brandon Mountford, who disappeared ten years ago, and whom we have every reason to believe dead?"

"Every reason, but no positive proof," answered Sibyl, thoughtfully. "The man who gave me that paper may have been crazy, but he was certainly not a beggar. He thrust the paper into my hand, and ran away. He wanted nothing from me. His conduct was like that of a messenger—an ignorant man—who had been told to watch for my carriage and to give me that paper."

"And you think he was sent by Mountford?" asked Orlebar, with a pitying smile.

The delusions of romantic love know no limits. He knew—partly from his observation of her, partly by her own confession—how fondly this woman had loved Brandon Mountford—and he contemplated her hallucination of to-day with tenderest compassion.

Poor child, poor woman, whose life had, for the last ten years, been loveless! What wild possibilities an empty heart can conjure out of the thinnest cloud of suggestion!

"I don't know what to think."

"My dear lady, pray don't delude yourself by hopes that are as unreal as those mountain ranges and giant's caverns which you used to show me in the evening sky, years ago, on the terrace, when we walked up and down together after dinner. I don't think any rational person can doubt that poor Mountford went down in the *Mary Jane*, or that—under the influence of his terrible disease—he committed the crime which brought such misery on this house."

"That I will never believe," said Lady Penrith indignantly.

"No, no; you won't believe because you can't understand. You don't know what it is when a devil of madness—blind, desperate, raging against he knows not what—enters into a man, and cries 'Kill! Kill!' You can't understand that—nor can I, or any sane person. But we know that such things are. And if it was so, don't you think Providence dealt kindly with all of us—in sending that poor fellow to a death that had no shame in it—a moment's wild uncertainty, and then whirled out of this life in one deafening blast, one uplifting of the furious sea? Upon my word, Lady Penrith, since everyone of us must die somehow, I doubt if one could die easier than in a tempest."

"He was innocent—innocent!" said Sibyl, her eyes brimming with angry tears. "I know quite as much about it as you do. I have studied the books that describe his malady. A man does not reach that violent stage of the disease all at once. Brandon had only suffered from the milder form of attack. He may have had a worse seizure that day, perhaps. He had been agitated and unhappy—he had been anxious and worried for some time previously. The period of unconsciousness was much longer. No doubt it was a bad attack—but the impulse to kill never touched him. I would stake my life upon that. You must look somewhere else for the murderer of Marie Arnold—somewhere as near, perhaps——"

"What do you mean?"

"I can't tell you. There are some suspicions too dreadful to be uttered. I dare not tell you mine. But I can and do declare that Brandon Mountford was no murderer."

There was a silence. Orlebar was perplexed and troubled by those dark hints of hers. He was quick to catch at an idea—and the only idea that Sibyl's words suggested was terrible. He would not give it room in his mind.

"But if this unhappy man were alive, why should he have allowed all these years to pass without making any sign—without writing to you, to whom he owes so much?"

"He may have been unable—for some cause or other."

"It is difficult to imagine a cause, and if he were living and a free agent, such silence would imply base ingratitude."

"No, no, what I did was nothing—or it may have been the worst that could have been done—the worst for his good name, certainly—for it confirmed the people about here in the idea of his guilt. I may have fallen into a trap set for him and me. He had no cause for gratitude, and there might be reasons—his regard for my reputation among other reasons—why he should hold no communication with me."

"Granted. But in that case, why after a silence of many years approach you in such a lunatic fashion as this?" asked Orlebar, pointing to the scrap of paper with those few incoherent words scrawled in pencil.

"Must I tell you what I have thought of in the long sleepless nights since that message was given me? It is hateful to speak of it, but I can imagine no other solution. I believe he is somewhere in this neighbourhood, mad, and a prisoner."

"My dear lady, that is the wildest flight of imagination upon your part."

"Perhaps—but that is the only explanation I can find for this."

She laid her finger on the pencilled lines before Andrew Orlebar, and then took up the little scrap of paper and put it away in her purse as carefully as if it had been the most precious thing she possessed.

"I have begun to look for him," she said, quietly, "and I shall go on looking for him."

CHAPTER XIX

CORALIE'S JOURNAL—FOR PATERNAL INSPECTION

MY dear aunt has certainly become an altered woman within the last week. She who was lately calm as a statue, composed, dignified, moving with queenlike motion through a life that seemed to have lost all interest for her, now looks like a woman whose every nerve is strung to highest tension, whose delicate frame vibrates with suppressed energy.

This sudden change from snow to fire interests me more than I can say. I take as much delight in trying to thread the mystery of this wonderful woman's mind as an enthusiastic pianist can feel in unravelling the web of a Beethoven sonata, or a crabbed composition by Sebastian Bach. My whole mind is bent upon finding the secret springs of her action. Those inquiries among the cottagers at Cargill had assuredly something to do with the matter that so absorbs her. Not for nothing would she have been so keenly interested in a casual wayfarer—not for mere charity, were she as charitable as that St. Helena, about whom Mr. Coverdale told me some fairy tales yesterday evening, across the billiard table.

One of the symptoms of this transformation in Lady Penrith is her obvious desire to escape my companionship in her drives.

"I know you prefer going with the shooters, Cora," she has said, on three several mornings; and thus instigated I have gone with the shooters, for the honourable and Reverend John is game worth stalking, and as he is not so keen a sportsman as the other men—indeed, no sportsman at all—I contrive to enjoy a good deal of his society—and I am getting as familiar with the romance of mediæval saintliness in Rome and in the East—as I am with the characters in Balzac's novels.[1]

Pleasant as it is, however, to tramp over brown heather and bracken, and tear my pretty tweed frock among the furze bushes, in this enlightening society, yet the very fact of her ladyship not wanting me has determined me to force my company upon her, so yesterday I met her usual remark about the shooters with a flat refusal.

"I am not going with them ever again, aunt, or at any rate not for ages," I answered. "I dare say they are tired of me, and I know I am tired of them. All my sympathy is with the innocent birds they massacre; and why should I put myself in the way of having my feelings harrowed?"

"Why, indeed?" said my uncle, a remark I might have anticipated from him.

I spoke with some soreness of feeling, for in all that tramping over the lumpy moor, and in all those prosy legends of impossible saints, the Reverend John has not committed himself to the faintest expression of admiration for me, the sinner. I am as far from the hope of winning his saintly affections as when I played my first game of billiards with him.

"No, aunt, no more long days with the guns for me," said I. "If I don't bore you too much I should like to share your drive this afternoon."

"Of course you don't bore me, Cora, but——"

My aunt's reluctance expressed itself so strongly in that monosyllable as to attract my uncle's attention. He looked at the speaker suddenly, with keen, cold eyes.

"No doubt your aunt will be very glad to have you," he said, "she must want your society in those dreary drives of hers more than we do——"

"Except at luncheon," put in Reggie Mountford, a callow subaltern in the Grenadiers, one of Lady Penrith's innumerable nephews. "We shall miss you awfully with the lunch cart. You say such awfully good things, regular rowdy things. Oh, you needn't stare, Mr. Coverdale. The best things she says go over your head; but Villars and I are in the know, ain't we, Vill?"

Mr. Villars, who might be this flippant brat's grandfather assented with a nod. I felt that I had sunk fathoms deep in the estimation of the Churchman; and I had the pleasure of hearing my uncle's scornful laugh, as he rose from the breakfast table, with a muttered "My niece is her father's daughter."

After luncheon Lady Penrith informed me, rather coldly, that she was going to Ellerslie for a business interview with her land steward and general adviser, Mr. Orlebar, whom I have heard you speak of not too admiringly. She warned me that I would have a very dull afternoon, as she might be engaged for a long time. I assured her that my delight in seeing the house in which she was born and brought up would make dulness out of the question.

She was right, however. I endured an afternoon of inexorable dreariness, since the amusement to be found in prowling about a great empty house, and trying her Ladyship's piano was exhausted in about twenty minutes; and then I had nothing to do but roam in the autumnal garden, count the chrysanthemums, and think over that odious young Mountford's impertinence. My regular rowdy speeches, forsooth! What is the use of having a sharp wit, which seizes the ludicrous aspect of everything? I fear I have been a little weak in letting them talk of French novels and sensational cases in the divorce court before me, and putting in my pert little tongue occasionally. But what can one talk of in this end of the century, if not sensational cases, when every new case goes beyond the old ones in sensational elements?

There is a feeling in the air as if it were not the end of the century, but the end of the world.

I wandered about, solitary and disconsolate, thinking of only the unpleasantest things, and without so much as a cup of tea. Whatever the housekeeper was doing, she was too busy to think of poor me.

It was past six o'clock when Lady Penrith came to me in the drawing-room, where I was trying to hammer out the one mazurka of Chopin's which had been hammered into me at Madame Michon's and which I now only remember in shreds and patches. The Arts have not been propitious in my case. My musical education was a lamentable failure; and I was never able even to produce the stiff chalk drawing which every pupil at Madame M.'s was supposed to execute, with the aid of bread-crumbs and a patient master. Yet I think for mere brains I might pit myself against most of those underbred girls who used to sneer at my shabby frocks.

Lady Penrith looked ill and miserable when she rejoined me, after her two hours' conversation with her man of business. If their talk had been solely of money matters, one might suppose her on the brink of ruin, but I don't believe financial cares had anything to do with her low spirits.

She scarcely spoke to me in the drive home, and she did not

appear at dinner that evening. We were informed before dinner that her ladyship was suffering from a neuralgic headache, and keeping quiet in her own rooms. The maiden aunt, Lady Selina Mountford, a portentous person in a point-lace hood, like Juliet's nurse, had arrived while we were out, and I spent a dismal evening in the shadow of her respectability, not daring to propose an adjournment to the billiard-room, although that impertinent young guardsman asked me to join in a game of pool.

"You can play to me, Miss Urquhart, while I work," Lady Selina said curtly, with a glance at the open piano.

"Thank you, I don't play," replied I, as curtly as she.

"Indeed! I thought every young lady nowadays was a good pianist."

"There are quite enough of them to make the piano a nuisance, but I happen to be an exception," I retorted, feeling every nerve set on edge by this horrid old woman in a shabby red velvet gown, ensconced in the most comfortable chair—my own pet chair—by the great mediæval fireplace, where rampant brass lions guard a wrought-iron basket of blazing ship's timber, which casts an uncanny green and blue light on people's faces.

Surrounded as we are with coal-pits, I need hardly mention that it is the correct thing in a gentleman's house to burn nothing but logs.

Lady Selina settled down to a piece of the ugliest fancy-work I ever remember seeing—a coarse olive-green blanket into which she laboriously dug a huge carpet-needle laden with orange worsted. It was just such a piece of work as one of an African chief's hundred wives might have chosen for the amusement of her leisure hours: altogether hideous and savage.

Perhaps that idea sent my random thoughts in a particular direction.

"This detestable old woman is a Mountford," I said to myself. "She must know something about Brandon Mountford, who wrote the African book."

At any rate there would be some fun in questioning her.

"I think you had an African traveller among your relations some years ago, Lady Selina," said I, squatting on a stool at her feet, as if I loved her.

"Most young men travel in Africa nowadays," she answered. "It is part of a liberal education."

A troubled look had come into her face, and I could see that she was shuffling with me.

"Ah, but you must know all about this one—a Mr. Brandon Mountford, who wrote a book of travels. Do tell me something about him."

"There is nothing to tell, except that he was a distant relation of mine, and that he died many years ago."

"Did he die in Africa?"

"No."

"Oh."

Her manner was so forbidding that I dared not ask another question. She dug her skewer into the green serge—oh, such a bilious colour—as if she would like to dig it into me. She looked like a witch, with the blue and green flames reflected upon her red gown, a horrible lurid figure, a horrible blue-green face.

There is evidently some tragic story to be told about Brandon Mountford—some misfortune, or even disgrace, which involves Lady Penrith. I dare say you know all about it, and will grin when you read this diary; but when next we meet I shall insist upon your telling me all you know.

I might question the maid who dresses me, and who is most likely to be posted in all scandals affecting the family, but I make it a rule of my life never to be confidential with servants. It doesn't pay. The poorer one is the more uppish one ought to be.

This morning Lady Penrith reappeared, none the worse for yesterday's headache. After breakfast she informed Lady Selina that the barouche would be at her disposal for the morning or the afternoon as she might prefer, and that I would go with her.

"Cora is fond of driving," she said.

"But you'll come too, I hope, aunt," said I.

"Not to-day, Cora. My aunt will excuse me. I am going to see some people beyond Ardliston."

"But we could all drive that way," I suggested.

"It would not be worth while. I should keep you waiting too long. You can take Lady Selina round by Hanborough Point."

Lady Selina protested that she adored the scenery round Killander Castle, so wild, so deliciously bleak and barren, so unlike
Berkshire, where she had just been staying with Mrs. Tilbury St.
George, another niece. As the days were growing short she preferred driving in the morning, so behold me, told off to sit and
talk twaddle with this odious spinster, who entertained me with
an endless web of prosiness about her quarrel with Mrs. Tilbury
St. George's maid, who had waited on her, Lady Selina, during
her own maid's holiday, and had been guilty of various offences
against the ancient spinster's dignity, and had never brought her
morning tea before eight o'clock.

"My niece is a fine horsewoman, and hunts four days a week,"
concluded Lady Selina, "so one can't be surprised that there is
laxity in her household. She notices the slightest shortcoming in
the stables, but permits chaos in her house."

At luncheon Lady Penrith looked pre-occupied and excited.

She left the table with an apology, before her aunt had finished
nibbling a bannock with her cheese, and five minutes afterwards I
heard her light pony-cart drive away.

More inquiries, I suppose, and further afield.

I was not to be beaten as easily as her ladyship thought. I determined on a skirmishing round in the direction Lady Penrith had
talked of—beyond Ardliston. There are two or three poor little villages within a mile or so of that wretched place. I might gain upon
the carriage by a short cut across the moor, and contrive to meet
her ladyship, in a guileless, unpremeditated way.

Those long tramps with the shooters, if they have been no
other gain to me, have at least made me a good walker. I am in
training for twenty miles a day, and six or seven miles across the
moor are as nothing to me. And then what a blessing to escape
from Lady Selina, who had established herself again in my favourite chair, by the drawing-room fire, olive green tapestry, and all *en
règle*.[2]

Not a word said I to this Medusa, lest she should offer to accompany me, for these active busybodyish old women can sometimes
walk as well as the youngest. I slipped out of the drawing-room,
found hat and jacket in the hall, and started off at a good four miles
an hour, across the hills to Ardliston, where I arrived just in time

to see her ladyship's pony-carriage disappear over the crest of a further hill in the direction of Allan Bay.

On one side of the bay there is a miserable concatenation of fishermen's huts, and a churchyard with two old wind-blown firs, gaunt and distorted, their great bent arms curving inward as if beckoning the dead from the depths of the sea. "Come here and rest in the calm, quiet earth," they seem to say.

Don't laugh at this dropping into poetry on my part. I am only quoting the Reverend John, who showed me a water-colour drawing he had made of the churchyard and fir-trees, and confided his sentimental notion about these wind-warped branches. He has all the accomplishments—paints charmingly, fiddles a little, knows Beethoven and Mozart as well as I know Balzac and Dumas—and hangs enraptured over Lady Penrith's piano whenever she condescends to play to us poor creatures in the drawing-room, which is not often. She prefers communing with the spirit of melody in the seclusion of her morning room.

That village over the hill—St. Jude's is the wretched hole's name—is a good seven miles from Ardliston. It was useless for me to attempt to follow Lady Penrith's carriage. So I crossed the moor again, and walked slowly back, not altogether baffled, for I had at least discovered the direction of her ladyship's drive.

CHAPTER XX

THE CARPEWS HAVE A BOARDER

THAT village with the old Norman church and the bleak, wind-blown churchyard, where the graves were sometimes washed by the salt white spray from a stormy sea, consisted only of about half a dozen stone cottages, and the congregation which sparsely occupied the old oaken pews on a Sunday morning and afternoon was mostly made up of smock-frock farmers from the neighbourhood, or an occasional pitman's family, which had come over the hill to afternoon service for the sake of the walk. Poor as the parish was, and few the dwellings it contained, there were a Vicarage and a Vicar—the Vicarage a low, rambling house, with stone walls and slated roof, over which lichens and stone-crop had spread a friendly covering; the Vicar an elderly, careworn man, whose shoulders seemed to have bent under the burden of a large family.

This gentleman, with his wife and children, were the only people with any pretence to gentility within a longish walk from the Norman church, and although Mrs. Carpew, the Vicar's wife, had grown worn and wan with domestic cares, and rarely enjoyed ten minutes leisure between breakfast and bedtime, she had not yet left off lamenting the want of society in the neighbourhood. What leisure or entertainment she could have given to society, or what gowns she could have worn in society, had society been there, was a problem which she had never tried to solve. She went on lamenting the barrenness of the neighbourhood with a certain ladylike forlornness which secured her the sympathy of friendly farmers' wives, with whom she occasionally condescended to partake of a substantial north-country tea.

If this poor lady could afford herself one reputable gown and one smart bonnet in which to appear at such homely tea-drinkings she thought herself happy, for there were three growing girls to be clad and shod, and there was an eldest son at Durham, and a second son at Marlborough, and two small boys running wild at home whom the Vicar was supposed to teach, so that in the long vacation—very long seemed that vacation to the house-mother—there were seven hungry mouths round the Vicarage table, to say nothing of the father and mother, who almost lost all appetite in horror at the amount of food those seven hungry maws consumed.

"A little more beef, please, ma," "A little more pudding please, ma." What a chorus it was! Mrs. Carpew had much need to comfort herself with the vulgar aphorism that it is better to pay butcher and baker than doctor and chemist—but that consolatory reflection did not tend to make the bills lower.

"If it wasn't for their boarder the Carpews would never be able to make both ends meet," said the farmers' wives, who knew how poor a living this parish of St. Jude's provided for its pastor.

There was a boarder at the Vicarage, a mysterious gentleman boarder, whose face but few of the neighbours had ever beheld, but whose existence in the house was not made an absolute secret, though it was talked about as little as possible.

"It is beneath your father's position as Vicar for us to have
a boarder; so the less you say about him the better, dears," Mrs.
Carpew told her brood. "He is a poor, afflicted creature, and it is a
charity to take care of him."

The young Carpews were so far of the world worldly as to be
able to act upon this maternal counsel. The words "boarder" and
"afflicted" were equally hateful to them, and never passed their
lips. "Affliction" in that sense meant to their young minds something revolting and horrible to look upon; and they would have
walked miles to avoid meeting the boarder who lived under the
same roof with them.

All that these younger members of the family knew of the
unseen occupant was that he lived in a portion of the house that
had been added by a former vicar, a man of sporting tastes and of
larger means than the present incumbent, a squire's son from the
Lake District, whose father owned a good deal of property near
Keswick, and who could afford to indulge himself with a kennel of
shooting dogs, a well-filled gun room, and as many jovial bachelor
friends as he cared to entertain in the shooting season; altogether a
very different type of man from Ebenezer Carpew, who had struggled out of the dismal swamp of Nonconformity into the loftier
atmosphere of the Church of England, viâ Durham, and who had
never recovered from the effects of the struggle.

The wing added to the Vicarage early in the century by the
bachelor parson, consisted of four good-sized rooms affording
ample accommodation for an afflicted gentleman, even if he were,
as the neighbours insisted, a sprig of nobility. Four rooms, locked
off from the rest of the house, were reserved for the unknown;
and it was the popular idea that the unknown was not right in
his mind, and had been confided to Mr. Carpew's care by his relatives; not right, but not so wrong as to render his residence in Mr.
Carpew's house illegal.

St. Jude's Vicarage was so remote from civilisation—such a
lonely and isolated nook along that bleak Cumbrian coast, that
questions which might have been asked in any other neighbourhood were not asked here. The village of St. Jude was less than a
mile from Allan Bay, and while prosecuting her inquiries among
the little group of fishermen's cottages clustered on one side of

the bay, Lady Penrith heard of the mysterious inmate of St. Jude's Vicarage, but beyond the mere fact of his existence, her informant could tell her nothing.

"Nobody ever sees him," said a fisherman's wife, who was aunt to the servant girl at the Vicarage. "Mr. and Mrs. Carpew wait upon him theirselves, the girl told me; take him his food, and clean his rooms, and look after him. They're too poor to keep a servant on purpose; and the girl—it was my own niece, Mary Martin—she was over two years at the Vicarage, and never see him in all the time—said Mrs. Carpew told her she was to hold her tongue, and say nothing about him to nobody, and she didn't, except to me, and two or three others she'd known from a baby."

"What kind of man is Mr. Carpew?" Lady Penrith asked, thoughtfully.

"Well, your ladyship, he's what I should call a poor creature. There's no grit in him—he's regular broke down with trouble and care—all those hungry boys and girls to feed, and always in debt to the butcher or baker. They say the living ain't worth more than a hundred and seventy pounds a year, all told—and there's nine in the family—the youngsters all growing up and hearty—and a servant girl makes ten. Poor Mrs. Carpew works her fingers to the bone sewing, and helping with the housework. If ever there was a white slave, she's one, poor lady—but I think she's got more spirit than the Vicar and bears up better."

"Does nobody help them?"

"The farmers' wives, they helps a bit, with a couple o' chicken now and then, or a pound or two of butter and a score of eggs; but that don't go far. There's no gentry near enough to take any interest; and they're not like regular poor folks, you see, my lady. They can't ask for help, or else I daresay they would have asked up at the Castle, for it was the old lord who gave Mr. Carpew the living, such as it is."

"His lordship's father? That must have been a long time ago."

"Yes, my lady, it must be nigh upon five-and-twenty years. Mr. Carpew was tutor at the Castle before Lord Ardliston and his brother went to college. Ah, he used to have fine times then, poor gentleman! His back was straight enough in those days, and he was quite smart in his dress, and held himself ever so high. Life was a'most all pleasure for him then. He used to racket about at all the race-meetings in the neighbourhood with the young lord and his brother. He's not as old a man as you'd think, looking at him now, and I don't believe that he's more than six or seven years older than Lord Penrith."

"And they were great friends, no doubt, he and his pupils?"

"Oh yes, they was very good friends; him and Mr. Urquhart in particular. His lordship was always high, my lady, even when he was Lord Ardliston; but Mr. Urquhart, he allus made more free with folks, and he and Mr. Carpew was a good deal about together. They say the Vicar was a great scholar in those days. He'd been helped on at college because of his talents, and people said the Earl was lucky to find such a man in the neighbourhood, ready to his hand. Mr. Carpew's father was a Dissenting minister at Workington—a small tradesman that had taken to preaching in a little chapel up a back lane—so you may suppose it wasn't no easy matter for him to send his son to Durham College."

"How long has the person your niece spoke about been at the Vicarage?" asked Lady Penrith, after a thoughtful silence.

"Ah, that's more than I can say, my lady. I don't suppose anyone knows when he came there, or that any one see him come, but he's been there a long while."

"Twenty years?"

"I can't say, my lady. It's four years or more since Mary told me about him, and she was at the Vicarage going on for three years, and he was there all the time, though she never laid eyes on him; and that's all I know."

"Do you think there is any one here or at St. Jude's who knows more about him?"

"No, I don't, my lady, for we've talked it over among ourselves, here and up at St. Jude's, and if there'd been anything more to hear I should have heard it. They've kept it all very close, the Carpews have; but we all know that if the Vicar didn't get a little money beyond his wage as parson him and hisen must have been famished."

When Coralie saw the pony-carriage disappear over the crest of the hill Lady Penrith was on her way to St. Jude's, to make a formal call at the Vicarage. That seemed the simplest manner of approaching the Carpew mystery in the first place, and she put a strain upon herself to suppress all signs of agitation, and to appear with the manner of a person interested only in a case of possible distress. The mysterious message delivered to her on the moor was a sufficient excuse for pushing her inquiries to the furthest limits, and as the wife of the patron of the living she was at least entitled to respect from the Vicar and his family. Indeed, her conscience smote her at the thought that she had been living within a dozen miles of genteel poverty such as this, and had done nothing to brighten these poor people's lives.

Her first attempt was baffled by Mrs. Carpew's abject terror of being discovered in her untidy parlour and her worse than shabby gown. The Iceland ponies, neat little cart, and smart groom had been visible to the Vicar's wife from the windows of her bedroom, where she had been engaged the whole afternoon, in a favourite species of occupation which she called a good turn out, and which involved the emptying of drawers and closets, old trunks and old bandboxes, and the piling up of shabby raiment on the bed, a proceeding lengthened by the minutest investigation of said raiment, and much discussion with her eldest daughter—now old enough to be admitted to the strictly feminine rites of the turn out—as to the possible rehabilitation of certain garments which had been put by as hopeless, or the conversion of last year's finery to this year's fashion—the fashion as known at St. Jude's, which was two years behind London, and fifteen months behind Edinburgh.

From an open window mother and daughter saw the Penrith pony-carriage approaching.

"It's Lady Penrith," cried Miss Carpew. "I saw her driving those ponies the last time I was at Ardliston. To think of her coming to call on us after all these years, and we not fit to be seen. Do be quick, ma, and wash your face, and smooth your hair. You look dreadful, and so do I," glancing at her own heated countenance in the cloudy glass on the littered dressing-table.

"Gertrude, we can't see her!" exclaimed Mrs. Carpew. "It's out of the question. The boys are in the drawing-room. I looked in just before I came upstairs. Luke and Jack were playing double dummy, and Joe was washing Snapper in a tub by the fire. He will wash that dog in the drawing-room. Run down to Sarah and say not at home."

"It seems a pity," faltered Gertrude, lingering on the threshold. "If we say not at home to-day she may never come again. And she may have come to ask us to a party."

"Not she. What, after her being at the Castle off and on nearly ten years? She's only come to bother about some of the poor people, I daresay. Perhaps to complain of something—to find fault with your father for not going to see them when they're ill—miles and miles on a winter night. Run, Gerty, this instant," cried the Vicar's wife, almost hysterically, as the grinding of the wheels drew near upon the hard chalk road;—"as if he could go out on cold nights, with his asthma," concluded Mrs. Carpew grumblingly, to the empty air.

Gertrude rushed downstairs, three steps at a time, after her manner, and reached the kitchen passage just as the groom rang the bell.

"Not at home—nobody at home," she gasped to the maid-of-all-work. "Wipe your face as you go along the passage, do, for goodness' sake. It's all over blacks."

Gerty dropped into a chair by the fire as the girl hurried out—scrubbing her dirty face with an apron as dirty—and burst into tears.

"How horrid it all is!" she moaned. "To be obliged to hide from well-dressed people, as if one was a murderer. I wish I was in one of the colonies where there are no fine ladies—no pony-carriages—nothing to belittle one and make one feel wretched. I wish I was dead—or married to Steve Maltby."

Stephen Maltby was the son of a small tenant farmer, whose comfortable homestead Mrs. Carpew visited condescendingly, and whose honourable advances to Miss Carpew had been flouted by her parents.

"If you want to sink into the class out of which I raised myself by the most strenuous toil, you had better marry Stephen Maltby," said the Vicar severely.

Gertrude felt in her heart of hearts that she had better marry Stephen, without any retrospective considerations; but she submitted as a dutiful daughter. Stephen was tall and good-looking, but his hair was decidedly sandy; and she was not so much in love with him as to defy father and mother for his sake. So she told herself that wretched as life was at the Vicarage she did not want to lose caste, and to sink to the level of a tenant-farmer's wife.

She heard the hall door shut, and the slow, slipshod feet of Sarah returning along the passage. The Vicarage spread itself over a good deal of ground, and the drawing-room where the Vicar's sons were playing whist was at some distance from those rooms which the sporting Vicar of fifty years before had built on the east side of the house, abutting on a walled garden of about an acre. This garden, with its fir trees and shrubberied walk on one side, and its old apple trees, rose bushes, and asparagus beds, on the other, had been the pleasure and the pride of the previous Vicar and his wife; but Mrs. Carpew was too harassed and hard driven by the stress of daily care to take pride in anything, and Mr. Carpew seemed to have lost all interest in life except a feeble concern as to what horse was likely to win any great race, a subject he would discuss with his sons or his neighbours, with a faint revival of human feeling. For the rest he was like a man whose spirit had gone out of him years before, and who only moved about automatically, a mindless, nerveless body.

"What did she say?" asked Gerty, meeting Sarah at the kitchen door.

"She seemed regular put out when I told her there wasn't nobody at home. She asked first for the Vicar, and then for Missus, and then was there any member of the family as she could see, and I says no—you was everyone of you out. And then she asked when Master and Missus was likely to be at home, and I says to-morrow afternoon, for, thinks I, if Missus knows beforehand she can redd up things a bit."

"Yes, yes, of course. That was very sensible of you, Sarah."

"And then she says she will come to-morrow, at about three o'clock; so now you know what you've got to do, Miss Gertrude, and there mustn't be no washing dogs in the drawing-room."

"No, nor yet those horrid cards—as if the evening wasn't long enough for whist, when they can have me and Lilian instead of double dummy."

"Lady Penrith must have made up her mind to know us," mused the Vicar's daughter, as she ran up to her garret bedroom to take a last look at her ladyship's pony-cart. "Perhaps she has heard how hard it is for us to live here, without society, and means to be our friend."

She opened her lattice and put her head out into the autumn wind. There was no sign of the pony-cart, not even a cloud of dust in the direction where she first looked, and then, sweeping the landscape, her eyes descried groom and ponies stationed a little way off, in the opposite direction, eastward, towards the Scottish border, and, behold, the pony-cart was empty.

Gerty ran to another dormer at the east end of the house, which commanded garden and common land beyond, and from this look-out she beheld Lady Penrith standing far off, on the steep heather-clad slope which rose outside the garden wall, evidently looking at the house and its surroundings. Gerty watched her for ten minutes or so, and saw her walking slowly about the hillside, and looking from time to time at the Vicarage, while Gerty, fearful of being seen at her post of observation, screened herself behind the faded chintz curtain.

CHAPTER XXI

CORALIE'S PRIVATE JOURNAL

IT is three days since I sent my father the latest chapter in my critical and exhaustive study of Lady Penrith, and I really thought I had done my work so carefully and so well as to deserve praise even from him. But not one word of acknowledgment have I yet received, and if I had not taken the trouble to register my little packet I might think that my manuscript had gone astray. I have guarded against even this contingency, for in the copy I made for paternal perusal I used ciphers instead of proper names, enclosing a key to those ciphers in a separate letter. My original journal I keep for my own amusement in days to come, when my life at Killander Castle will be but a memory—a memory to prose about perhaps to girls who will be as tired of me as I am of Lady Selina and her rambling stories of her innumerable nieces and their splendours.

"My sisters all married well, and I might have married as well as any of them," she explained to me yesterday. "The newspaper people used to write about us as the beautiful Mountfords, and at my age I needn't mind saying that though I was the eldest I was by no means the plainest of the sisters."

Indeed she needn't mind, for there isn't a trace of that youthful beauty left in her wrinkled old countenance; so she may prate of the conquests of the Lady Selina of those days without being accused of egotism.

I was home an hour earlier than Lady Penrith the day before yesterday, and had the felicity of pouring out Lady Selina's tea, a burden which was somewhat relieved by the Reverend John's appearance in the drawing-room. He had left the shooters on the moors.

"You were tired of killing innocent little birds, I suppose," said I.

"No more tired than you are of eating them, Miss Urquhart," he answered.

This was rather crushing, as he had seen me demolish the best part of a cold grouse at breakfast that morning.

"Oh, I am strictly utilitarian there," answered I; "when once they are killed they may as well be eaten."

He looked round the room with a disappointed air, I thought.

"What has become of Lady Penrith—not another headache I hope?" he said.

"There was not nearly so much talk of headache when I was a young woman," said Lady Selina.

I explained that my aunt had gone for a long solitary drive, and then, with my own hands, I carried that starched parson his cup of tea, after I had put a sweet little Vernis-Martin table[1] by the side of his chair. I pampered him with cream and muffin until the primly pious creature looked up with a chilly smile and said, "If I were a Mussulman this would be my idea of Paradise, Miss Urquhart. A low, easy chair, and a nice young lady to give me my tea."

"Yet, when you missed Lady Penrith just now you looked round the room as if it were a blank," said I.

Would you believe it, my dear Letts, the creature blushed to the roots of his nice wavy hair—like an iceberg crimsoned by the setting sun?

"Lady Penrith's absence must leave a blank wherever people

are accustomed to see her," he answered, as the blush faded, leaving him in his usual iced-cucumber condition.

Trying to please a man of his temperament is like punishment labour—the hardest form of human toil—with the conviction that it is all wasted effort. Yes, I think I would sooner turn the crank than try to fascinate the reverend and honourable John. Yet plain women have achieved even greater successes. I know of plain Peeresses—who had no money-bags to counterbalance blunt features and dull complexions—plain millionairesses, who have married millionaires on the strength of being plump and comfortable looking. Let me remember this, and go on trying. After all I have nothing else to do in this fortress on the Marches except to watch Lady Penrith, and it is in a woman's nature—especially a plain woman's—to try hard for any great catch in the matrimonial line that circumstances may throw in her way.

Circumstances have thrown Mr. Coverdale in my way, and I should be a fool not to do my uttermost to improve the occasion.

No more rowdy talk in the billiard-room. I feel angry with my father for having told me so much of the club smoke-room slang. He never told me anything really bad, but just those touch-and-go stories that give zest to conversation among men and women of the world, yet which are of a kind to disgust this High Church puritan. I shall devote to-morrow morning to fishing out the biographies of saints in the "Encyclopedia," and in the evening I'll read Newman's "Apologia"[2] or Montalembert's "Monks of the West."[3]

The mystery thickens. To you only, dear Letts, could I confide my adventures of this afternoon. It has been a day of surprises.

The first occurred at the breakfast-table, when Lady Penrith who is generally reticence itself about her own doings, thoughts, and fancies, and who rarely initiates any conversation with my uncle, began to talk to him about her drive of yesterday.

"I took the Icelanders further than usual," she said, "but they did their work capitally. They are dear little things, and I am very much obliged to you for them, Penrith."

The Iceland ponies are a recent present from my lord to my lady—a kind of set-off against the thousand or so of her money which he paid for the hire of a grouse moor in Argyleshire.

"I'm glad you like them," answered that human iceberg. Curious to find two such men as my uncle Penrith and Mr. Coverdale under one roof. Yet they wear their ice with a difference. I suspect the parson of hidden fires, but I believe his Lordship frozen to the core.

"I went as far as St. Jude's. I wanted very much to see the Vicar's wife. I have heard a saddening account of their poverty. However, there was no one at home, so I had my drive for nothing."

Her manner of watching her husband's face as she said this convinced me that there was some serious motive for her speech and that she was trying the effect of certain allusions upon his Lordship.

"It was a pity you gave yourself the trouble," he answered carelessly. "The Vicar of St. Jude's is no poorer than a hundred other parish priests scattered about the country in villages as solitary and wretched."

"The living is yours, I am told."

"Yes, the living is mine, but I can't make it any better than it is. Carpew was very glad to get it when my father gave it to him."

"He hoped it was only the beginning, I suppose. He could hardly think it would be the end."

"I believe it's his own fault that he's still at St. Jude's. He's a lazy vagabond, who would rather vegetate than work. He shirked all trouble, I remember, when he was my tutor; though he came to us with a great reputation for mathematics. He was always glad to do as little work as possible, and Hubert and I would have preferred doing none, so we were good friends. He and Hubert were tremendous chums, indeed—for Hubert always liked low company."

"Low company! A famous mathematician!" exclaimed my aunt.

"Mathematics won't turn a cad into a gentleman," answered my uncle, lifting his eyebrows. "His people were small shopkeepers, Primitive Methodists, or something of that kind. The poor wretch had struggled out of the mire—and now I suppose he has slipped back into it. I have not seen him—to my knowledge—for the last ten years."

"Do you know anything about his wife?" asked my aunt, still watchful of her husband's face.

"I remember hearing that she was the daughter of an adjutant of a line regiment, and by way of being immensely genteel. Poor creature. Her gentility must have rusted and mildewed in twenty years at St. Jude's."

"Have the Carpews been twenty years at St. Jude's?"

"More than twenty. My father gave him the living before Cora was born. I remember my brother begging the berth for him, and it was before Hubert's marriage."

Now this was one of the longest conversations I ever heard between this lady and gentleman. They are always civil to each other before company; courteous even; but it is the rarest thing for them to talk to each other as if they had an interest in common.

After luncheon, Lady Penrith again informed me that she was going for a long drive alone, and suggested the barouche for her aunt and me. I was spared that infliction, as Lady Selina had acquired a fine cold in the head, one of those colds which inflict keener suffering upon the spectator than upon the patient, and which I believe to be distinctly infectious, whatever doctors may say to the contrary. As she insisted upon nursing this loathsome complaint by the drawing-room fire I deserted that room for the afternoon, and started for a long walk, first with the idea of getting a glimpse of her ladyship's Icelanders going or returning, and secondly because fresh air and exercise will help me to maintain at least a clear complexion, if not a beautiful one.

Now, my good Letts, comes surprise number two. I walked across the moor to Ardliston, and in the long, straggling street of that bleak wind-blown village, whom should I meet but my very own father!

Yes, my father, who has always expressed his hatred of this part of the world, and has congratulated himself that while his brother was born at the Castle, Berkeley Square had been thought good enough for him, the younger son; so that he was not called upon to feel any affection for Cumberland as his native soil. There in front of the Higginson Arms whom should I see but that very father of mine!

He did not seem particularly pleased to see me. Indeed, I may say that his manner was strictly paternal.

"Come inside, Coralie; I want a few minutes' talk with you," said he, after his first curt greeting; and then he led the way into the inn—hotel, forsooth, on the signboard—and into a wretched parlour, where the decorations comprised a magenta table-cover that hurt my eyes after the cool, harmonious tints of the autumnal sea and sky, a pair of cut-glass lustres on the mantel-piece, and a fearful and wonderful composition in gaudily coloured shells under a glass shade on the side-board.

"There isn't a chair in the room fit to sit in," said my father with a vindictive shove to an American-cloth-covered monstrosity, into which he flung himself, leaving me to perch where I liked.

"Are you here for long?" I asked.

"No. Possibly not more than twenty-four hours."

"Oh! You received my manuscript, I suppose?"

"Oh yes, that came to hand. You have the pen of a ready writer, Cora. You ought to do something in literature, by-and-by."

"And my manuscript brought you here, I suppose?" said I, ignoring the paternal praise.

He did not condescend to answer.

"Lady Penrith drove through the place half an hour ago. Do you know where she is going?" he asked presently.

"I have a shrewd suspicion," said I; and then I told him of the conversation at the breakfast-table, watching his face meanwhile as keenly as Lady Penrith watched her husband.

Whether my father is less master of himself than the Earl, or whether he had more reason to be concerned, I know not, but his countenance betrayed intense anxiety. He started out of the odious, sticky chair, and walked to the window, where he stood looking into the street for some minutes.

"Curious, this sudden interest in the Carpews," said he, after a long silence, and with a very poor attempt at careless speech.

I should have given my father credit for being a better actor, but I fear that pegs and late hours are beginning to tell upon him. He has aged considerably since I left school, and looks older than my uncle Penrith.

"Yes, it is rather curious, ain't it?" I answered. "I believe it all springs from her insane anxiety to trace that wretched lunatic who accosted her on the moor. Can you conceive any reason for this interest in a half-witted peasant?"

"Yes; the strongest of all reasons," he answered bitterly; "she is a woman, and women love to make molehills into mountains. Now, listen to me, Cora. I am here on business—business of importance. You can understand that, as you know I loathe the place, and am ill friends with my brother. Not a word about your having seen me here to any living creature, gentle or simple. I shall vanish as suddenly as I came. Last night's mail brought me; to-night's mail may probably take me back to London. Go on with your journal. It is capital practice for your pen. You are cultivating exactly that pert pessimism which readers like nowadays. The task is so good for you as a literary exercise that I won't even thank you for doing it. Indeed, you ought to thank me for putting it upon you to do."

"Bravo!" cried I; "that's an easy way of escaping the sense of obligation."

"Go on with your journal. Keep a strict watch upon her ladyship. Don't be afraid of being diffuse. Note the smallest details, and send me your report every day, or twice a day if there is anything serious to report."

"There can be no further doubt as to my position," said I. "This is secret police work."

"It is work that may save your father from a great danger, and you from the risk of the disadvantages that his disgrace must entail upon you," answered my father, sternly. "I won't trifle with you any longer, Coralie. This is a matter of life and death—life or death to reputation, I mean."

He was almost livid, and his lower lip worked in an agitated way when he left off speaking.

There must be something very serious behind this anxiety. I saw him wipe the beads of perspiration from his forehead, though the room, with its wretched turf fire, felt damp and chilly. There must be something very serious in my father's past history—something which nearly touches Lady Penrith. I am devoured with curiosity, yet dare not ask any questions of any one about the past, lest I should excite suspicion and injure him. He is my father, after all; and, as he tells me, any discredit to him must reflect discredit upon me.

I must be loyal to him, however disloyal I may be to my uncle's wife.

"And now, good-bye to you, Cora," said my father, after looking out of the window again for some minutes. "You'd better get on with your walk. There's not a mortal in sight, and you can slip out of the house without anyone knowing that you've been in it."

The parlour was close to the inn door. He just touched my forehead with his hot, dry lips, and put me across the threshold.

One o'clock. This habit of diary-writing grows upon me, and I am shortening my hours of rest; but what is the use of beauty-sleep when one has no beauty?

CHAPTER XXII

"SO WE BUT MEET NOT PART AGAIN"

MRS. CARPEW and her daughter toiled all the morning in the expectation of their aristocratic visitor. They could have very little help from Sarah, the maid-of-all-work, who had her hands full with the every-day work of the family—scrubbing floors, peeling potatoes, making beds, carrying water, cooking the poor little bit of meat that had to be eked out with much plain pudding and home-grown vegetables. All Sarah could do in the cleaning of the drawing-room was to come with her worn-out carpet-broom and sweep, raising such a mighty dust in the process that it might have seemed almost wiser not to sweep.

When Sarah had swept, Mrs. Carpew and her daughter began to tidy; and tidying the Vicarage drawing-room was a work that ought to have ranked almost as high as the labours of Hercules. The mother went about the business in a desultory way, murmuring complaints against fate and her own children as she worked. Were there ever such untidy boys—cards here, dominoes there, pipes everywhere—and such pipes! It made her sick to touch them. What would her mother, whose drawing-room, under the difficulties of barrack life, was always refined and artistic, think if she could see such a room as this?

"But then my mother had only me," sighed Mrs. Carpew.

"Well, mother, I suppose you'd hardly like to see all of us reduced to one girl," said Gertrude, who was working briskly and steadily, cleaning corners, polishing the shabby old Chippendale chairs that the Vicar had bought cheap at a farmhouse auction, going for a mere song because of their old-fashioned shape, before anybody in that remote world knew that such chairs were things of beauty—shaking the dust out of the window curtains, bringing the blacklead brush, and giving an extra polish to the old iron grate. Gertrude stopped at nothing that could improve the aspect of that shabby old room.

"But it really don't seem much good doing anything unless one could whitewash the ceiling and re-paper the walls," she said, looking round despondingly, after nearly two hours' hard work. "That odious paper was a triumph of ugliness to begin with, and dirt hasn't improved it."

Mother and daughter dined sketchily at one o'clock with the depressed father and the hungry lads and lasses, who reduced the shoulder of mutton to so bare a bone that it promised badly for a grill for the Vicar's breakfast—"especially if Sarah is to dine off it," he remarked discontentedly.

Mrs. Carpew reassured him. Sarah was dining on a dumpling. Any scraps of meat served to make Sarah a dumpling.

The younger girls were excited at the idea of Lady Penrith's visit.

"Shall we see her?" asked Lilian, who came next to Gertrude, but was not considered "out."

"Certainly not," replied Gerty. "Look at your frock— positively disgraceful."

"Shall we see her, ma?" repeated Lilian, scorning the sisterly reply.

"Of course not. You and Ethel have treated those nice alpacas shamefully."

"They never were nice," grumbled Ethel. "They are the most hideous frocks you could have chosen."

"What is all this about Lady Penrith?" asked the Vicar, looking up from his plate to join in the family talk, which he usually ignored. "Is she coming here?"

"Yes; at three o'clock this afternoon."

"What for?"

"Why, to pay us a visit, of course. I daresay she has heard

that Gertrude is growing up, and sympathises with our want of society."

"Gertrude has society enough when she is marching about the place with Stephen Maltby," grumbled the Vicar. "Society, forsooth. I'd swop the best society in Cumberland for a five-pound note."

The sons laughed; the daughters sat in dumb disgust. They had inherited all their mother's longings and regrets; had heard thrilling stories of the gaiety of garrison towns, regimental dances, archery meetings, a brilliant world in which their mother's girlhood had been spent, a dazzling sphere inaccessible for them. Gertrude would have sacrificed five years of her life for one garrison ball, if Mephistopheles had offered her the opportunity.

"I can't understand Lady Penrith coming to this house," said the Vicar, with a troubled look. "She can want nothing here but to pry and spy."

"I suppose you can't conceive the possibility of her wanting to see ma and me," retorted his eldest daughter haughtily.

"No, I can't," answered the Vicar, with paternal candour. Dinner concluded under a cloud, not a much heavier cloud than usually enveloped the family meal—for there was seldom a dinner that went from start to finish without trouble of some kind, trouble about underdone meat or overdone meat, watery vegetables, cold gravy; trouble about insolent rejoinders from the boys, possibly not meant to be insolent—Mrs. Carpew insisted that in meaning they were as doves—which provoked the father's wrath. Trouble, trouble, boiled and bubbled every day in the cauldron of life at St. Jude's Vicarage.

To-day Gertrude sacrificed her share in the sloppy rice pudding in order to make her toilette in good time for the expected visit; and at a quarter to three Mrs. Carpew and daughter were seated in the drawing-room, employed in some genteelly useless needlework, and trying to look as if they sat there every afternoon. The odour of dogs and tobacco had been subjugated by widely opened windows, and the room was really tidy. Sarah had been instructed as to the bringing of afternoon tea, and urged to serve it with more style than she had ever done for the farmers' wives.

"Suppose she doesn't come after all our trouble," speculated Gerty, watching the road from the bow window.

"I couldn't suppose her guilty of anything so unladylike."

"Oh, well, I don't know. It would be just like our luck if she didn't turn up, after all. Oh, there she comes. I can see those heavenly ponies. Dear little things. I wonder if Sarah has come downstairs?"

Gertrude ran to the kitchen to assure herself. Yes, Sarah was there, dressed as she was rarely dressed at that hour, in her Sunday stuff gown, clean apron, and cap. And the tea-tray was ready on the kitchen table, and there were tea-cakes baking.

"She's coming! Look sharp, Sarah," said Gerty, and then flew back to the drawing-room, and took up her crewel work once more.

"Lady Penrith," announced the maid-of-all-work.

How handsome, how graceful in form and movement; how simply dressed. Gerty wondered at the plain cloth gown, whose only merit was the perfection with which the severely-cut bodice fitted the finely-proportioned figure. Only a rough brown cloth. This mistress of many thousands a year was more plainly attired than a farmer's wife in her Sunday gown. But Gerty felt instinctively that the cloth gown and neat little felt hat were just the right things for a country drive on a dull autumn day, and she had the felicity later of seeing and even handling the long sealskin coat which her ladyship had left in the hall.

"This is quite too kind of you, dear Lady Penrith," exclaimed Mrs. Carpew, with a reminiscence of garrison manners. "It is such a pleasure to my daughter and me to become acquainted with you personally, after hearing your praises so perpetually."

"You are very good, and I am very glad to know you and Miss Carpew," Sibyl replied graciously, and then, with an earnest look and grave voice, she continued, "I must not sail under false colours. I had a very serious purpose in coming here to-day."

"A bazaar," thought the Vicar's wife, "and she wants us to work for it. Just like these fine ladies. They never take anyone up without a motive."

Mrs. Carpew was quite willing to be "taken up," if the price to be paid were not too high.

"I want to enlist your sympathy for myself, and for one who

is very dear to me, and who is, I have reason to believe, a dweller under this roof."

Mrs. Carpew started, flushed, and then slowly paled.

"I don't understand."

"You don't understand the link between me and the unfortunate gentleman who lives under your charge," said Sibyl, looking intently into the weak, commonplace countenance. "Pray be frank with me. How long has he been with you?"

Mrs. Carpew hesitated, stammered an inaudible word or two, in evident distress.

"I really don't know," she faltered, after that embarrassed pause. "I can't tell you anything about him. He is in my husband's care. I never interfere. The Vicar took him—from benevolent motives, I believe—to oblige an old friend. Of course we are paid something for his maintenance—we are too poor to dispense with payment—but not nearly so much as would have to be paid anywhere else."

"To oblige an old friend," repeated Sibyl; "yes, that is just as I thought. But, think, now, Mrs. Carpew—you must remember how long he has been here?"

"Indeed, Lady Penrith, I do not. One year is so like another in this dull place."

"But you can surely fix the date of an important event like that—a stranger coming under your roof. And then you have a living calendar in your children—their ages would tell you."

"I remember, ma," interjected Gertrude, who had listened with keenest curiosity, and who rushed into the conversation, unconscious of her mother's frowns. "It was the year Bobby was born. You hadn't left your room—he was a tiny, tiny baby—and one day old nurse Bond told me there'd been a fine to-do, and two gentlemen had arrived early in the morning—they must have come by sea, she thought—for one of them was wet through, and his coat dripped sea water. He wasn't right in his mind, and he was to stay."

"It was a stormy morning?" suggested Sibyl.

"Yes, it was a stormy morning. Nurse Bond had to light a fire and get dry clothes for the gentleman who stayed—she told me all about it when she came to the nursery at breakfast time," added

Gertrude eagerly, and then for the first time became aware of her mother's warning scowl.

What had she done? Mischief, perhaps. She had been expressly forbidden to talk of the mysterious boarder. Her mother's white face and distracted look smote her with sudden terror.

"Mrs. Carpew, I appeal to you as woman to woman," said Sibyl, with clasped hands, and a voice that thrilled both listeners, such depth of earnestness was in its tone. "Let me see this person. He may not be the person I think, but if he is I would sacrifice half my fortune to look upon his face again, and to give him help and comfort in his affliction. You shall be no losers, you and your husband, for doing me that kindness. You shall, indeed, be greatly the gainers. You know that I am rich, and you may suppose I would not count the cost where—where my affection was concerned. I firmly believe that the person in your care is a kinsman of mine, one whom I loved years ago, before Lord Penrith asked me to be his wife. I am quite frank with you. I keep nothing back from you or from your daughter, for I can see that she sympathises with me."

"Indeed I do," interjected Gertrude.

"And I don't think you can refuse me your sympathy. Let me see him, if only for five minutes, and then, among us all, the Vicar, and you, and I, we may arrange some plan for making his life happier. Only let me see him; let me be sure he is the man I am looking for."

"What could possibly make you suppose that he is your relation, Lady Penrith?" Mrs. Carpew asked, her countenance expressing a conflict of ideas in a brain that afforded very little room for the struggle.

"A letter in his own hand."

"A letter. How could he send a letter? He has not written to anybody for years. He has no messenger."

"He has written to me; he has found a messenger," answered Sibyl, "out of the depths—out of the depths," she repeated to herself. "Woman, for God's sake, show that you have a woman's heart," she cried passionately, losing all patience with the flabby creature before her.

"Yes, ma, do. If you've any more feeling in you than a bran pincushion," put in Gerty, indignantly.

"It is such a small thing that I am asking. Only to see him for a few minutes."

The tears were streaming down Sibyl's pale cheeks. Gertrude with difficulty refrained from hitting her mother.

"It is not a small thing. It is a very big thing. No one is allowed to see him—not even my own children. I appeal to Gertrude."

"Don't appeal to me. I hate you," cried her rebellious daughter.

"If I wished ever so—and indeed, dear Lady Penrith, I do sympathise with you—I couldn't let you see him. That part of the house—he has quite the best rooms in the Vicarage—is locked off, and the Vicar keeps the key. It would be impossible, if I wished ever so—and I do wish——"

"For gracious sake don't go on rambling like that," cried Gerty. "You can ask pa, I suppose. If he does keep the door locked he can give you the key. He's not a Bluebeard."

"Yes, yes, I can ask him," faltered Mrs. Carpew, as if catching at an escape from present perplexity. "I will ask him, Lady Penrith. You may be sure I will do all in my power to accomplish what you wish. But, indeed, I believe you are labouring under a delusion. In the first place our poor friend could not possibly have communicated with you."

"I tell you he has communicated with me. Mrs. Carpew, for pity's sake don't beat about the bush. You say you will ask your husband. Go and ask him—or bring him here and let me plead my own cause. I feel assured he will hear reason."

"He is out," answered Mrs. Carpew.

"Are you sure of that?"

"Quite sure. I saw him go out—half an hour ago."

The latter part of the speech was a falsehood. Mrs. Carpew had seen her husband creeping past the bow window, with furtive glances at the occupants of the drawing-room, only five minutes before, and she knew that the Vicar had been, in her domestic language, "on the listen."

The Vicar might be "on the listen" still, perhaps, outside the drawing-room door. In any case it would not do for his wife to compromise him. There must be time for consideration. She hoped that he would see his way to serving Lady Penrith rather than that other person who rewarded them so scantily for watchful care and service. She hoped, but she felt that extreme caution was necessary upon her part.

"How long will he be out?" asked Sibyl, impatiently. "I can wait."

"He is so very uncertain," answered Mrs. Carpew, with a warning look at her daughter. "He may be away for hours. This is such an immense parish—so poor and so few people, but stretching over such a lot of ground. He may have gone to one of the furthest farmhouses; and he is a slow walker."

At this point the tea-tray bumped against the door, which was opened rather awkwardly by the bearer of the tray. Sarah sailed in, and began to spread a very smart tea-cloth—an unsold item in a sale of work for parochial purposes, which had lapsed as a perquisite to the Vicar's wife.

"I will wait," said Lady Penrith. "Perhaps you would kindly put up my ponies for an hour or so."

"I am so sorry," apologised Mrs. Carpew. "We have only a two-stall stable, and as we keep no conveyance, the boys have filled both stalls with their rabbit hutches——"

"And the stable smells—too dreadful," ejaculated Gerty.

"Never mind, I see the groom has put their rugs on," said Lady Penrith, who had been looking out of the window; "and they are very hardy. I should like to wait for the Vicar's return, Mrs. Carpew, if I am not in your way?"

"In my way, dear Lady Penrith? How can you suggest such a thing?" exclaimed the Vicar's wife, her garrison manner struggling with mental agonies.

Gertrude, who had heard that it was the right thing for the daughter of the house to pour out the tea, had seated herself at the tray, a position she was wont to seize on state occasions, in defiance of her mother.

"I'll slip out and inquire if the Vicar has left word where he has gone," said Mrs. Carpew, making for the door. "Perhaps he may not have gone to any of his distant parishioners after all."

She had disappeared from the drawing-room before anyone could reply. She hurried along a passage—looked into the Vicar's den. It was empty. She crossed a lobby, went up three steps, and knocked at the door which divided the new wing from the original building. It was an additional door, which had been put there within the last ten years—a heavy door, covered with green baize, shutting with a steel spring.

She knocked twice before the door was opened by the Vicar himself.

"Well, has she gone?"

"No. She is waiting for you. Oh, there has been such a scene. I feel so sorry for her."

And then, standing just within the green baize door, Mrs. Carpew related her conversation with Lady Penrith.

"Cream—and sugar?" inquired Gertrude, smiling across the table at her guest, as she poured out the tea.

Sibyl was too agitated to answer the trivial question.

"Now we are alone let me thank you for your sympathy," she said. "I know you are a kind, warm-hearted girl, and if you will help me—as I feel sure you can—you shall find that I am not ungrateful. You—well, you shall have something better than rabbits in your stable."

"Oh, please, please don't think me mercenary; don't think that I am influenced by the idea of your money or your rank. Indeed, I am not so paltry-minded as that, Lady Penrith. I should be just as sorry for you if you were as poor as ma and pa. But I'm afraid there's nothing I can do to help you—nor ma either. Ma is the most helpless person I know. She's just under pa's thumb. If he were to tell her to shut us all up in an attic and feed us on bread and water, she'd do it. She'd be very sorry for us, and she'd go about the house crying all day, but she'd give way to pa. She hasn't any backbone. That's what Stephen says of her, 'No backbone.'"

"Stephen is your sweetheart perhaps," speculated Sibyl.

"He wants to be, but he's not allowed. His people are only small tenant farmers, like the Martins in Miss Austen's 'Emma'— and pa and ma say I should lose caste. Of course, I don't want to lose caste, but the Maltbys are ever so much better off than we are, and live in a sweet old house, and keep a gardener, and a boy to look after the stable, and a Whitechapel cart, and have everything about them as neat as a new pin, and here everything is wretched, and pa is trying enough to break the spirit of the whole family."

Sad and agitated as she was, Lady Penrith could not refrain from a faint smile at the idea of Mrs. Carpew's daughter losing caste by marrying a farmer.

"I don't want to suggest disobedience, Miss Carpew, but if this Mr. Maltby is a good young man, I think your father should reconsider his decision."

"He is good—as good as gold; but please don't think I care much about him."

"Well, you will give me your confidence another day, perhaps, when I am happier; and now tell me, have you never seen the gentleman who lives in those shut-off rooms?"

"Never."

"That's very strange. Surely he goes out into the air sometimes, if not every day."

"I believe he sometimes walks in the garden at the east end of the house—a walled garden, with a row of fir trees inside the wall. We can't see into it from any of our windows. No, strange as it may seem, I have never seen him. He might be the man in the iron mask for anything I know about him."

Mrs. Carpew reappeared at this moment, and informed Lady Penrith, with polite regrets, that the Vicar had gone out an hour ago, and that he had left word that he might not be home till late in the evening. He had gone to one of the furthest cottages in his parish.

"Then you think there would be no use in my waiting for him?" said Sibyl.

"No use—delightful as it is to Gertrude and me to see you here. But I hope you'll at least stop for a second cup of tea."

"Thank you, no. I have a long drive home. I am very glad to have made your acquaintance, and your daughter's. But I must see the Vicar without an hour's avoidable delay. Will you ask him to be kind enough to stop at home to-morrow morning? I will drive here directly after breakfast."

"I am sure he'll be charmed to see you."

"And willing to grant my request, I hope. I shall think it very strange if he refuses," said Lady Penrith, with a touch of sternness.

"I think you rather overdid it, ma," said Gerty, when the visitor had been escorted to her carriage, and had driven away.

"What do you mean, Miss, by overdoing?"

"About pa and the furthest cottage. It's very odd if Lady Penrith didn't see him walk past the window while she was talking."

CHAPTER XXIII

"FANCIES THAT MIGHT BE, FACTS THAT ARE"

LADY PENRITH was again missing at afternoon tea, and again John Coverdale looked round the drawing-room with a countenance expressive of blank disappointment. He had not been with the shooters, who had just returned, and who were having a sub-stantial egg and toast tea in the breakfast-room. He came to the drawing-room from a long afternoon's reading in the almost unused library—a spacious apartment, which had once been an armoury, and in which three great carved oak bookcases, filled with eighteenth-century literature—books which nobody ever looked at—represented culture at Killander Castle. He came for rest and relaxation in society which was always delightful to him, and missing that one gracious figure in his survey of the drawing-room, his disappointment was no less obvious than it had been yesterday.

Coralie looked at him sharply with her bright grey eyes. She was beginning to entertain very unpleasant suspicions about Mr. Coverdale.

"No, she hasn't come home from her solitary drive," she said, answering his look. "My aunt is getting quite dissipated, ain't she? Those ponies are spoiling her orderly habits."

"She ought not to be out after five o'clock on such an after-noon as this," remarked Lady Selina. "I don't understand this passion for long drives."

"I have no doubt Lady Penrith has gone upon some kindly errand," protested Mr. Coverdale, seating himself near the great Tudor window, from which he could watch the drive.

The landscape was darkening without, and the room was darkening within. In a few minutes the servants would be coming with lamps, and curtains would be drawn, to shut out land and sky.

Coralie poured out the tea, and waited upon Lady Selina and Mr. Coverdale. The lady gave her plenty of work, took two cups and a half of tea, and played havoc with a dish of hot currant cake; but the gentleman let his tea grow cold while he sat silently musing by the window.

"Ain't you cold over there, Mr. Coverdale so far from the fire?" asked Cora.

"Thank you, no," he answered with a start.

"And you haven't touched your tea. Let me give you a fresh cup."

"You are very kind. It really doesn't matter."

The lamps were brought in. The curtains shut out sky and moor. It was night now—or it seemed night. Mr. Coverdale rose with a sigh—

"I'll take a turn on the terrace," he said. "You keep this room rather too warm for me, ladies, with your splendid wood fires."

"Yes, it's rather too like the tropical house at Kew,"[1] agreed Coralie. "I'll go with you."

He smiled resignedly, and made way for her to pass out of the door before him. However much a man may wish to be alone with his own thoughts, he can't say so when a lady—charming or otherwise—volunteers her society.

They went to the gravel walk in front of the Castle, a walk which commanded the carriage sweep. They walked up and down briskly under the grey autumn sky; but Mr. Coverdale was no more conversational here than he had been in the drawing-room. In vain did Coralie start subjects which usually interested him. He answered absently, or did not answer at all.

"What a dreamer you are," she exclaimed at last.

"A man must dream, however futile some of his dreams may be," he answered quietly. "Ah, there is her ladyship's carriage."

"What a quick ear you have."

"Don't you hear it?"

"Yes, I can hear it now; but I didn't when you spoke. I had not been listening so intently as you," added Cora, significantly.

He did not notice the insinuation, but walked quickly towards the carriage sweep, and was standing at the foot of the stone steps ready to help Lady Penrith out of her carriage when it stopped.

"I am very late," she said, apologetically, "but I have been a long way."

"And you must be expiring for want of your tea," exclaimed Cora. "Do come into the warm drawing-room and let me minister to you."

"No, thank you, Cora. I have had tea, and am very warm in this fur coat. Mr. Coverdale, would you mind taking a turn on the terrace with me before we go indoors? I want a little serious talk with you."

Coralie stared aghast. With her growing suspicions about John Coverdale, this seemed extraordinary conduct on her aunt's part.

"And I should be in the way if I stayed," she said pertly.

"For this one occasion, yes, Cora."

"Then I retire, as gracefully as I can. But I hope you'll change your mind, aunt, and let me order some fresh tea to be ready when you come indoors."

"Please no. Don't trouble about me. I shall go straight to my room."

Lady Penrith and Mr. Coverdale walked nearly to the end of the terrace before the silence was broken. And then Sibyl opened her heart to this Anglican priest, fearlessly, and told him the story of those eventful months before Lord Penrith appeared upon the scene as her suitor. "I know you are the soul of honour," she said, "and you are a priest. I can confide in you. I can ask you to help me, as I dare not ask my husband—although all that I am telling you to-night is known to him—all except the events of the last month, of which he knows nothing. You will help me, won't you, Mr. Coverdale?"

"With all my heart and mind," he answered, with an earnestness which she could not mistake.

She told him every detail of that night in the village gaol; how she had allowed Urquhart to act upon her fears, and how she had urged Brandon Mountford to escape.

"Was I wrong?" she said. "Was I his enemy rather than his friend?"

"In my view of the case he should have stayed to face his accusers. He should not have allowed himself to be persuaded."

"Oh, it was my fault. I was made to believe that I was saving him from death, or, at the least, from life-long misery and shame. And I sent him to his death, or—or to wretchedness worse than death."

And then she told him of that pencil scrawl, and her interpretation of it, and of the scene with the Vicar's wife and daughter that afternoon.

That this unknown inmate of the Vicarage was Brandon Mountford seemed to Mr. Coverdale the wildest and most romantic of fancies. On the other hand, that pencilled appeal in a handwriting which Lady Penrith recognised as Mountford's had to be accounted for; and then place and time agreed. The stormy sea, the coming of the unknown lodger in the early morning, the hidden life, with its studied seclusion, these facts pointed to some guilty secret, and any man to whom these facts became known was bound in honour to investigate them.

Had John Coverdale lighted upon such a mystery in his own parish he would not have rested till he had unearthed the evil doers. His mission was to carry light into dark places.

"You may be mistaken as to the identity of this person," he said, after a thoughtful pause, "but there can be no doubt it is a case for investigation. I have heard something of Mr. Carpew's character and antecedents which makes me inclined to think he might lend himself to a villainous scheme, if it were made worth his while."

"I am going to St. Jude's to-morrow, directly after breakfast. Will you go with me, Mr. Coverdale?"

"Certainly. It is the very thing I was going to propose. Let me be with you, and it shall go hard if we don't succeed in seeing this poor gentleman."

"Yes, yes, with your help I must succeed. How good you are."

"Good, when it is such happiness to serve you."

She did not notice the earnestness of his tone in that one instant of self-betrayal, did not notice how the cold, grave manner changed suddenly to warmest feeling, only to lapse again into that thoughtful calm which was his distinguishing characteristic.

"With you at my side I shall be strong," she said. "I felt so weak and helpless to-day, so easily baffled by that shifty woman. I did not know what I ought to do—whether I ought to insist upon waiting for her husband's return. It seemed so feeble in me to leave that house, convinced as I was that Brandon was there, so near me, and in such bitter need of me. But you can help him. You can release him from bondage. They won't be able to trick you."

"There is one thing to be remembered, Lady Penrith. A terrible accusation hangs over this man's head—if he is the man you think—and for him to reappear in the neighbourhood will be to re-open that old story."

"Let it be re-opened. I would risk that. Let him face the accusation, as he would have done in the beginning, but for me. I know that he was innocent—that it was another hand that killed my adopted sister."

"Whom do you suspect?"

"I cannot tell you yet. I may trust you even with that suspicion by-and-by. No, I would not fear for Brandon to face his accusers. New evidence would come to light perhaps—if the history of that night were gone into coldly, quietly, the facts sifted and weighed as they could not be a few hours after the tragedy, when every one was bewildered with the horror of that poor girl's death. I know that he was innocent."

"And if he is living hidden in St. Jude's Vicarage you would risk the consequences of removing him—the almost inevitable reopening of the enquiry?"

"Yes, I could risk that."

"So be it, Lady Penrith. Then you and I will tackle the Vicar to-morrow morning, or if he be out of the way when we call, we will make things so unpleasant for him that he won't be able to evade us very long."

"You think he may not see us to-morrow?"

"I think—if he is the scoundrel you believe him to be—he may find some excuse for not receiving us."

Sibyl breathed a despairing sigh.

"Oh, how difficult it is to right a wrong," she exclaimed.

Lady Penrith and Mr. Coverdale drove away from the Castle before ten o'clock next morning in the lady's barouche, with a pair of horses that made light work of distance or of hilly roads. The shooters had set out before the barouche drove up to the front of the Castle; and there were only Lady Selina and Miss Urquhart at home to wonder at this strange proceeding.

Coralie ran out to the steps to watch the departure.

"Oh, what a delicious morning," she cried. "How fresh and crisp the air feels," and then, as with a sudden impulse, "Do let me go with you, Aunt."

"Not to-day, Cora. I am taking Mr. Coverdale to see some poor people. You would only be bored."

"No, no, I wouldn't. I am positively longing for a drive."

"Then gratify your longing. You have not driven your own particular pony for ever so long."

"I hate driving myself. I like to enjoy the air, and the landscape."

"Then get a groom to drive you," said Sibyl curtly, and the barouche drove off, leaving Cora standing at the top of the steps discomfited.

"Now, what in the name of all that's ridiculous, does this mean?" she asked herself. "Can it be that the sage, the calm, the ineffable Lady Penrith is carrying on a flirtation with this pious parson, under all our noses? I know that he is in love with her. The creature has not even the art to conceal his emotions."

She ran upstairs to her own cosy den, and wrote her account of Lady Penrith's strange conduct of this morning, for transmission to Jermyn Street. All compunction that she had felt in the beginning, when the office of spy was first proposed to her, had died out of her crooked little mind. And now that Lady Penrith's influence was spoiling her chances of a great match, gratitude to the benefactress who had redeemed her from bondage was a thing of the past.

"What frauds these icily-beautiful women are," she said to herself, as she folded the closely-written sheet which had occupied her for nearly an hour. And then, opening her secret volume, she relieved her mind by scribbling ideas and feelings which she would have imparted to no living confidante.

Life at the Castle was growing lonelier and duller. The smart soldier who frankly admired her sharp sayings and gave her a nightly lesson in billiards was to leave that afternoon, and a Keswick squire had left the day before. The house party after to-day's luncheon would be reduced to Lady Selina and Mr. Coverdale, whose holiday from parish cares was lasting longer than he had intended.

His parish was at the East End of London, where he lived a life which would have been self-sacrifice for the son of the poorest commoner, and where he was generally known to all the over-worked mothers and all the dirty little children as Father Coverdale.

CHAPTER XXIV

THE VICAR OF ST. JUDE'S

Yes, the Vicar was at home. Sarah ushered Lady Penrith and Mr. Coverdale into the drawing-room, and went to fetch her master, who kept them waiting some minutes before he came.

A pallid, miserable-looking creature when he did appear; a man with careworn face and bent shoulders, and those furtive glances which the parish priest had seen in many faces, whose meaning he knew only too well. He knew when he saw those shifty, down-looking eyes that he had to deal with a difficult subject. He had never been able to do much good with any man who had that kind of look.

He went straight to the object of their visit, after briefly introducing himself.

"Lady Penrith is very anxious to see the invalid gentleman in your care," he said. "I hope you will make no difficulty about the matter."

"I regret that it is out of my power to gratify her ladyship's wish. The gentleman left me, in the custody of a friend, early this morning."

"Left you—left this house after ten years of imprisonment," cried Sibyl. "I don't believe it."

"That remark is hardly civil on your ladyship's part. You have no right to use the word imprisonment in relation to a sufferer who was entrusted, for his own comfort and safety, to my care—nor have you any right to doubt my assertion."

The words were firm, but the voice was tremulous, and the manner was as bad as it could be.

"How and why was this inmate of the Vicarage removed, Mr. Carpew?" asked Coverdale.

"I really cannot gratify your curiosity so far as to say why he was removed. That is the business of the friend who removed him. I can tell you how he left this house—in a fly, ordered from Ardliston. My responsibility ceased from the moment he crossed my threshold."

"Your responsibility before God will never cease," exclaimed Sibyl passionately. "You have played a sordid and wicked part—you have lent yourself to the scheme of a villain. The friend you talk of—the friend—oh, what a friend—is Hubert Urquhart, who wove a web of treachery round Brandon Mountford's life."

"Lady Penrith, pray, pray be calm," pleaded Coverdale.

"I cannot—I cannot be calm when I see to what a cruel plot this man has lent himself. But I don't believe his victim has been removed—he is still under this roof, and we are not to be put off with lies."

"Lady Penrith, you seem to take pleasure in insulting me. Perhaps you would like to see the empty rooms—they are very untidy—but their emptiness may remove your doubts."

"Yes, let me see the rooms—his prison of all these years."

The Vicar took no further notice of the obnoxious word but quietly led the way from the drawing-room to the long dark passage which went between the dining-room and kitchen to the east end of the Vicarage, and there ended in an ascent of three steps and a baize-covered door. The Vicar opened this door and ushered his visitors into an empty room—a sitting-room, sparsely furnished, like the rest of the house, but by no means a bad room, light enough and airy enough, with a French window opening into that walled garden, of which Gertrude Carpew had spoken. A door opened into an adjoining bedroom, where the iron bedstead and shabby furniture were about on a level with the accommodation of third-rate lodgings at a popular watering-place.

A charwoman was busy clearing up litter and sweeping out corners. There were a few books on a chiffonier, and a pile of old newspapers on a side table.

Sibyl took up the books one after another and examined them.

They all belonged to the Vicar, and most of them had his name written in them. Shakespeare, Macaulay, Byron, Thackeray, Pope, Milton. The Milton, the Pope, and the Macaulay were college prizes; but the calf bindings were shabby with much usage.

"There are two more rooms above, if you would like to see them?" said the Vicar.

"Yes, I should like to see them," answered Sibyl curtly.

"They are quite empty—they have never been furnished—but if it gratifies you——"

A shrug of the bent shoulders finished the sentence, and Mr. Carpew led the way by a narrow essentially modern staircase to the floor above, which was as blank and bare as he had asserted.

"He is gone, you see," he said.

"How do we know that you have not hidden him in some other part of the house?"

"You are at liberty to examine my house from cellar to garret."

"No, no," interposed Coverdale, "we have no wish to doubt your word, Vicar. I have not, nor I am sure has Lady Penrith, though she spoke hastily just now in her disappointment. You must admit that it is a strange and perplexing fact that after inhabiting this house for ten years——"

"Who says that he was here so long as that?" exclaimed Mr. Carpew.

"I say so," answered Sibyl, resolutely. "I say that he was brought to this house during the storm that wrecked the *Mary Jane* fishing smack, the morning after my foster sister's murder. He was brought here by your old pupil, Hubert Urquhart, and he has been spirited away by the same man, to prevent my seeing him. He has been robbed of liberty—perhaps of reason—by that man, for his own ends."

"My dear Lady Penrith, consider how wild and improbable these charges are."

"Answer me one question. Did Mr. Urquhart bring you your lodger, or did he not?"

"I cannot answer any such question. Your ladyship must understand that there are many cases in which the friends of an afflicted person desire the utmost secrecy."

"Mr. Carpew, are you a clergyman of the Church of England or the keeper of a lunatic asylum?" demanded John Coverdale, with a severity which shook the Vicar's shattered nerves. "If the gentleman whom you kept shut up in these rooms was out of his mind you were guilty of a breach of the law in keeping him here, and the fact ought to be brought before your Bishop."

"You are in a great hurry to misjudge one of your own cloth, Mr. Coverdale. A man may be helpless and afflicted without being a lunatic. The person who occupied these rooms was not a lunatic; but he was in more need of care and privacy than many lunatics."

"He was an epileptic patient," said Sibyl, white to the lips with anger; "a patient for whom open air and movement, change of climate and scene, were essential—a man who should have been roaming the sea in a yacht, or wandering amidst wild, beautiful scenes, free and unharassed. To keep him in this squalid hole," looking at the square, shabby parlour with eyes accustomed to the lofty spaciousness of Killander Castle and Ellerslie House, "to keep him in such rooms as these—in that dreary, sunless garden—was to murder body and soul. And you, sir, are guilty of murder—you who call yourself a clergyman of the Church of England. But your Bishop shall know of your infamous conduct—you shall be punished——"

"Dear Lady Penrith, for God's sake be calm," remonstrated Coverdale, strongly moved by her passionate outburst.

She flung herself sobbing upon his shoulder, instinctively clinging to him, to save herself from falling to the ground. He could feel the stormy beating of her heart as his arm supported her—an arm held as King Arthur might have held his in a similar crisis. Never before had this woman—his ideal among all women—been so near his heart. So near, and yet worlds away! Alas, how fondly she must have loved that unhappy man! How much that old story meant in her life!

"Pray be calm," he repeated; "we have no right to jump at conclusions. After all, you may be mistaken as to the person who occupied these rooms. I have no doubt," with a propitiatory glance at the Vicar, "Mr. Carpew will be good enough to tell us the name of his charge, and where he has gone, and with whom. And then you will be satisfied and at ease again."

"I decline to tell anything, or to answer any question put to me by you, Mr. Coverdale. I have been attacked in a most outrageous manner in my own house. This is a free country, and I have done nothing in violation of the law. This wretched living was given to me by the late Earl, so I suppose I must endure any amount of contumely from Lady Penrith, but I will not submit to insult from you."

"I understand, then, that you positively decline to satisfy Lady Penrith's doubt by giving her the fullest information in your power about the person so lately under your care?" asked Coverdale.

"I most distinctly refuse to be interrogated about my private and domestic life—even by Lady Penrith," replied the Vicar, doggedly.

"In that case, we must take stronger measures. Come, Lady Penrith, we are only wasting time here. I wish you good-day, Vicar."

The Vicar's sullen reply was only half-audible. He led the way back to the hall, and Lady Penrith returned to her carriage, attended by John Coverdale.

"There can be no doubt," she said, as they drove off. "If I had doubted before, I am certain of the fact now. They have smuggled him away between them, to some still more wretched hiding-place. Hubert Urquhart and that man——"

"Stop!" cried Mr. Coverdale to the coachman. "There is someone running after the carriage—a young lady. She came out of that field."

The horses were pulled up about a hundred yards beyond the field gate, and Gertrude Carpew ran to the carriage door.

"I have been watching for you ever so long, Lady Penrith," she said. "I suppose it's awfully wicked for a girl to hate her father, but I can't help hating mine for the cruel trick he has played upon you—after what happened yesterday afternoon. He swore it was all arranged before you came to the Vicarage—that it was settled for the poor gentleman to leave us. But, if it was, Ma knew nothing about it."

"My dear Miss Carpew, pray tell me exactly, as clearly as you can, all that happened since I saw you," Lady Penrith said eagerly; and then turning to Coverdale she added, "This young lady is the Vicar's daughter, and she sympathises with me in the kindest way."

"Who could help sympathising with you? Poor Ma was crying all the evening. She and Pa had a long talk, and I know they had high words, for Pa was horribly cross to all of us at supper; and directly after supper he walked out of the house."

"Does he often go out so late as that?" asked Mr. Coverdale.

"Not once in a blue moon. It was past ten, and dark as pitch; and it was midnight before he came home. I heard him let himself in with his latchkey, for I was too miserable to go to sleep easily; and I was awake very early in the morning, and I heard a good deal of bustle and moving about downstairs. I lay listening, half awake and half asleep, and then not long after the clock on the stairs struck seven I heard a carriage drive to the door. And I got up and looked out of the window, and could just see father and another man huddling someone wrapped in a cloak into a fly."

"Could you see what the other man was like?"

"Tall and slight, that was all I could make out. They were very quick. Father and the stranger both got into the fly, and it drove off directly they were in. When I came down to breakfast mother was looking awfully miserable, but she wouldn't tell me anything. She's too completely under father's thumb to trust any of us. We'd finished breakfast before father came home in the fly—alone."

"Did he say nothing as to where he had been?"

"Not a word. He was crustier than usual, and sent us all out of the room before he began breakfast. As a rule he takes very little breakfast, and wonders at us for being able to eat so early in the day. I am so sorry you should be disappointed, Lady Penrith; but perhaps after all, the gentleman who left us this morning isn't the person you think."

"I am more than ever convinced he is that person," answered Sibyl. "You are a kind, true-hearted girl, Miss Carpew, and I rely on you to help me with any further information you may be able to obtain—any circumstance that may give a clue to the place where my poor friend has been taken. I promise that your kindness to me shall do no injury to your father. Whatever may happen, he shall be protected for your sake, so far as I can protect him. The chief mover in this cruel business is another person. I shall not rest till he is punished."

"Ah, but I'm afraid if father has done wrong in the matter it must all come out sooner or later, and we shall be disgraced," said Gertrude, despondently. "But whatever is going to happen to us, I'll do all I can to find out where they have taken that poor gentleman."

"I thank you with all my heart. Be assured you shall be compensated for any trouble your kindness may cause."

Sibyl and the parson's daughter clasped hands as they said good-bye.

"Ardliston Road station," ordered Mr. Coverdale, and the barouche continued its way, while Gertrude started on a circuitous journey through a field and across a common, so as to arrive at the Vicarage from an opposite direction to that in which Lady Penrith's carriage had gone.

"I may as well make some inquiries at the station before we go back to the Castle, if you've no objection," said Mr. Coverdale, explaining the order he had just given to the coachman. "It may make us a little later in returning."

"What does it matter? Let us stay out all day if there is anything to be done," answered Sibyl, and then lapsed into silence, exhausted by the scene at the Vicarage, and absorbed in gloomy thought.

She did not speak till they were at the station, which was nearer St. Jude's than it was at Ardliston. Here Mr. Coverdale left the carriage for nearly a quarter of an hour.

"I have seen the station-master and the two porters," he told Sibyl, when he came back. "There seems no doubt that the two men went to Keswick. The one who appeared to be an invalid was so wrapped up in an Inverness cloak and large white muffler that it was not easy to distinguish his features. The men only saw that he looked white and haggard. The other man wore a shooting cap, pulled down upon his forehead—a cap with a peak—and he, too, had the lower part of his face muffled in a scarf, but this circumstance attracted no attention, as the morning was raw and cold. I asked the station-master to describe the man in charge of the invalid—his figure and carriage, if not his face—and he said he was about the height and figure of Lord Penrith, and reminded him of his lordship."

"Hubert Urquhart!" exclaimed Sibyl. "That is conclusive. Now,

Mr. Coverdale, what are we to do? Go on to Keswick, I say, by the first train that will take us."

"My dear Lady Penrith, that would be a wild proceeding. Keswick is a large place—and for you to be seen there, going from pillar to post—and then, to absent yourself from home without explanation to Lord Penrith——"

"I can send a message by the coachman. I can explain afterwards."

"No, no. It would be waste of time and trouble for you to attempt to trace these men. I will follow up the clue and see what can be done, and if I make any discovery before the evening I can telegraph to you, and you can come to Keswick with your maid, and put up at an hotel for a day or two."

"Yes, that would do; I should be near."

"But even that would be rather a wild thing to do—and if you could make up your mind to trust this business entirely to me——"

"I do trust you. I know how much better able you are to help me in this matter than I am to help myself. But when you find him, if he should be very ill and broken, I should like to be near at hand. I might be of some use then."

"In that case I promise to summon you without an hour's delay."

"And you will go to Keswick, and give yourself up to this search?"

"With all my might. Have I not promised to devote myself to your service? I shall think of nothing else till this is done. If Penrith should inquire about me you need only say that I had business at Keswick, and that my return to the Castle is uncertain. If you'll allow me, I'll ask your footman to see about sending me a portmanteau. I may be absent for some days."

"How good you are!"

"Please, don't say that! Only trust me, and keep up your courage. Bear in mind that my East End experiences have made me acquainted with strange people and strange things.[1] I am not so unequal to this task as you might suppose."

"I know how clever, how resolute you are."

"My train will not leave for half an hour, so I had better tell your coachman to drive you home."

"Mayn't I wait till you leave?"

"Please, don't. You have had a trying morning, and you will be better at home."

He gave his instructions briefly to the footman, and then the carriage drove away, he watching till the pale, anxious face looking back at him vanished altogether from his sight.

"How she must have loved him!" John Coverdale repeated to himself, with a sigh.

CHAPTER XXV

CORALIE'S PRIVATE DIARY CONTINUED

HER ladyship's conduct becomes hourly more extraordinary. After leaving the Castle early this morning with the parson—coolly declining my company, which I offered in my gushing little way, on the spur of the moment, determined at any rate to embarrass her by forcing a refusal—she returns at three o'clock this afternoon without that saintly man. When I ask her in a casual way what she has done with him she replies that he has gone to Keswick, and that he has business there which may detain him for some days.

"Business in Keswick," say I, not concealing my surprise. "I thought the only business in Keswick was making lead pencils and showing Southey's house.[1] That is all I've ever heard of in connection with Keswick."

"You can't be expected to know everything in the world, Cora," answered she, "least of all to know Mr. Coverdale's business."

"Oh, if it is a kind of secret service of course I needn't be ashamed of my ignorance," retorted I.

Lady Penrith is my benefactress—my easy life here, my purse filled with pocket-money, all the frocks in my wardrobe, testify to the fact—but I am afraid I am beginning to hate her; and I am afraid she is beginning to hate me. Our relations are at best an armed neutrality. Who knows when war may be declared?

After all I need not exaggerate her beneficence or my obligation. The benefits she has bestowed upon me—the frocks, the lodging, the pocket-money—are bagatelles for a woman of her means. If she really wanted to befriend me how easy for her to settle the six thousand pounds, which my father tells me has always been the portion of Lord Penrith's daughters, upon me—sole daughter of the house of Urquhart. Six thousand pounds. With her fortune she would have but to sign a cheque for the amount, and might forget the next hour that her coffers were diminished by that paltry sum. But instead of playing a really generous part, and making me independent for life, she lets her dressmaker clothe me, just as my uncle's tailor clothes his liveried servants, and she tolerates my presence in her house. Whatever chance I might have had with Mr. Coverdale—that pattern of starched propriety—Lady Penrith has contrived to spoil. She must see that he admires her far too much for his peace; and if she were really that model of all the domestic graces for which she poses, she would have chilled him by quiet avoidance, instead of leading him on by making him the confidant of her sorrows, whatever those mysterious sorrows may be.

In my delight at escaping from the dusty horrors of a second-rate lodging-house, I have been over-enthusiastic about my uncle's beautiful countess. These quiet women are never to be trusted.

Another surprise, and a very painful one, awaited me this evening.

It was just on the edge of dark. Lady Penrith had not honoured the drawing-room with her presence after coming in from her long drive, minus Coverdale. Lady Selina, after having usurped my favourite chair all the afternoon, clamoured for an early tea, and for one solid hour I was administering to her gormandising propensities.

Released from this genteel slavery, I made my escape from the drawing-room, lest I should be called upon to hold a huge skein of that teeth-on-edge-setting worsted which she calls Pre-Raphaelite wool. I thought that in the almost deserted state of the house I should at least have the billiard-room to myself, and might enjoy knocking about the balls, and deliverance from Lady Selina's society.

Oh, how sick I am of her married nieces, their houses, their diamonds, their babies, their servants—with the latter of whom she is always quarrelling.

She tells me the same prosy stories over and over again, and the possibility that she may be boring me to death never for one moment flashes across the great dismal swamp which she calls her mind.

The lamps in the hall had not been lighted, and its stony spaciousness looked cold and grey in the gathering dusk. All the principal rooms open into this sepulchral hall, and I am often reminded of that hall in Macbeth's castle, where the murderer prowled up and down seeing imaginary daggers, while he waited for the bell that was to tell him his pre-historic toddy was ready.

I had opened the billiard-room door, and was just going to shut it again when I heard my father's voice. My father's voice in a house which he had not entered since the Earl's marriage!

What could it mean?

Certainly not reconciliation. Those rasping tones came from a heart full of bitterness.

Nor was there much of brotherly love in my uncle's reply.

"You had better hold your tongue," he said. "You have been drinking, or you would not have dared to enter this house."

Lord Penrith was standing in the open doorway of his own sitting-room, a smallish room next the library, while my father stood in the hall.

"Dare!" he echoed with an angry laugh. "Dare! Dare enter the house that was my father's a few years ago."

"If it had been your own a few years ago it would make no difference to me. It is my house now, and I mean to keep you outside it."

"You treat me like a dog."

"Oh, no, I don't," answered that cold-blooded monster, my uncle. "I am fond of my dogs. I treat you like what you are, Hubert Urquhart. If there's any animal as vile I have never met with the species."

"It's a treat to hear you talk like this, after I played your game, made the running for you, helped you to a rich wife."

"You tried to win her for yourself by the very basest means the human mind could invent."

"Oh, come, now, this is only tall talk."

"You know how you imposed upon her ignorance of life, tried to persuade her that her good name was forfeited, that she had fallen so low in the world's esteem that her best chance of redemption was to become your wife."

"And with the devil's own luck you struck in, caught her in a fit of hysterics, and won the stakes. There was never such a fluke. Come, Penrith, you can't frighten me away with big words. All that high-falutin of yours has about the same effect upon me as water on the proverbial duck. Hard words don't kill, and hard words won't send me off these premises without hard cash. I have asked you, my brother, and a rich man, to help me out of a difficulty. I asked you just now for a monkey. It was not much for you to give if you had a spark of generosity."

"I have not one scintillation, where you are concerned. I have only one feeling—abhorrence—the kind of abhorrence which includes contempt."

"Nonsense; we both angled for a big fish, but you were able to bait your hook with a coronet. I wasn't, and I had to diplomatise. Come, Penrith, if you won't stand a monkey, give me your cheque for two hundred and fifty pounds, and I'll wish you a civil good-night. Remember, after all, I am heir presumptive to your title, and all that goes with it. There is only your life between me and all the good things of this world. Hard lines for a man of my temper to remember that. You ought to consider the circumstances, and if I can bring myself to ask you for money—after what happened at Ellerslie ten years ago—you shouldn't be such a churl as to refuse."

"I wonder you care to show yourself in this part of the world—after what happened at Ellerslie," said my uncle.

The last words were spoken slowly, as if they had a hidden meaning. My father was silent, and then Penrith went on in his heartless voice.

"As for your privileges as heir-presumptive I have no doubt you have had the market price for them."

"The market price was a very bad one. Unhappily the Jews consider your life as good as mine—or better. The difference in our ages is not worth considering, and you are supposed to take more care of your superior carcass than I take of this poor bundle of vices. Once for all, Penrith, will you help me or will you not?"

"Once for all I will not; and if you don't make yourself scarce immediately you will oblige me to ring for the servants, and get you turned out neck and crop, which will cause a scandal, and make things uncomfortable for your daughter."

"For my daughter. Yes, I suppose you would rather like to revenge yourself on her. Well, good night, my brotherly brother. I won't make a rumpus in this abode of peace and pleasantness, this temple of conjugal love. I'll find my own way out."

My father crossed the hall, opened the big oak-door, and closed it quietly behind him. Penrith waited on the threshold of his room till the hall door shut, and then shut himself in his den. I don't know if he felt relieved in mind when my father was outside the castle. I know I did. There was no light in the billiard-room, and I had been standing just inside the door, which I held a little way open, and was thus able to hear every word that was said on the other side of the hall.

Oh, what a life! To grovel like a hound, and to be driven out of his brother's house, like a hound. Surely Providence can't expect much good out of any woman who starts in the race of life handicapped with such a father as mine.

"After what happened at Ellerslie ten years ago."

I must get to know all about Sibyl Higginson's engagement to my uncle. There are evidently tragic circumstances—something that comes nearer Lord Penrith and his wife than the murder of her ladyship's foster sister. I must make Lady Selina give me the history of her niece's marriage. She is so fond of talking that I have only to get her in the right vein and she will tell me everything she knows.

The dinner this evening was the most melancholy meal I have sat through since I came to the castle. There were only my uncle and his wife, Lady Selina and myself. His lordship was silent and gloomy, evidently brooding over that fraternal conversation I had overheard. Her ladyship seemed lost in thought. Lady Selina prosed and twaddled for the whole party.

"I am very tired, aunt, so I shall go straight to my room, and leave you and Cora to amuse each other," said Lady Penrith, as we three women left the dining-room.

"I can't think what you are about all to-day," Lady Selina

answered pettishly. "If your cottage visiting keeps you engaged as you have been lately I'm sure it must be too fatiguing for you. You should make Cora help you."

This last remark was accentuated by a malevolent look in my direction, as if I had deliberately refused to help.

"Her ladyship knows that I am always at her service," said I.

Lady Penrith noticed neither her aunt's speech nor mine. She just nodded good-night to us both, and went upstairs, leaving me to the unspeakable dreariness of a night with Lady Selina, and no possibility of escape to the billiard-room, where my uncle would be sitting alone—not a pleasant person to intrude upon in his meditative moments.

There was one compensation. I had a whole evening before me in which to make Lady Selina talk about what I wanted to hear.

Needless to record the insidious means by which I approached the subject. I doubt if she liked me any better than on the first night of her visit; but custom had made her familiar and confidential, and as it was natural for her to talk, she soon began to expatiate upon the folly of her niece's marriage.

"Sibyl might have married ever so much better," she said. "A beautiful girl, who was sole heiress to I am afraid to say how many thousands a year, would have had magnificent offers as soon as she appeared in the great world. Her connections on our side of the house would have admitted her at once to the most exclusive circles—if there are any exclusive circles left,"—interjected Lady Selina with a sigh. "She might have married a Duke. But through my brother-in-law's folly—his mind was utterly unhinged, I believe, by the fate of that mysterious waif—she was hustled into a marriage with a man for whom she never cared a straw, and who was a very poor match for her."

"My uncle's family is one of the oldest in the North of England," said I.

"My dear young woman, old families are cheap nowadays. Sixty thousand a year is too much to pay for an old family, and a neglected estate, encumbered as this was when my niece married. She could have married the bluest blood in England on much easier terms, if I had been allowed to chaperon her, as was intended, before that awful business at Ellerslie."

"Pray tell me about the murder, Lady Selina."

"Have I never told you?" she exclaimed, quite oblivious of her curt replies on the first evening we spent together. "It is a most painful story—peculiarly painful to me, since a connexion of our family was involved in it, was actually accused of the murder, and locked up in the wretched hovel that used to accommodate smugglers and such people. They have pulled the place down, I am happy to say, and built a respectable police station."

And then she told me how Marie Arnold, a handsome young woman of foreign birth, had been brought up at Ellerslie, almost as a daughter of the house, and how she and Sibyl Higginson had lived together like sisters, and how people had naturally supposed—

At this point the spinster deemed it necessary to sink her voice to a ghastly whisper, like Lady Macbeth in the sleep-walking scene, although she and I were alone in the spacious drawing-room.

"At any rate, my dear, Sir Joseph was greatly attached to this girl, who, I am glad to say, for the credit of humanity, was five or six years older than Sibyl, and was therefore born some time before my sister's marriage. He never recovered from the shock of her death."

"But do you really believe that Mr. Mountford—your relation—was guilty of this crime?" I asked.

"My dear Miss Urquhart, I don't know what to believe. Brandon Mountford was subject to epileptic attacks when he was at the University; not in any violent degree, but enough to make him shun society. He had wandered about in Africa—where that kind of thing wouldn't matter—for some years before he appeared at Ellerslie. Everyone spoke well of him——"

"And your niece liked him?"

"Yes, Sibyl liked him. I never saw them together, but I believe she entertained a romantic regard for him. She has always shunned any allusion to him; so I have never fathomed the hidden depths of her mind upon this subject. There is a great deal of reserve about Lady Penrith. As to the young man's guilt or innocence, that I fear must for ever remain a mystery. So much has been written of late years about the horrors of epilepsy—and how it can change an amiable being into a wild beast—that one may believe anything of an epileptic sufferer. This poor creature was found kneeling by the murdered girl, his hands dyed with her blood. He did not even deny his guilt, Mrs. Morison told me."

Mrs. Morison is the housekeeper at Ellerslie, with whom doubtless the spinster aunt has held lengthy confabulations. There is no one like an old and trusted servant for telling family secrets.

"Since he was taken red-handed, I suppose there can be no doubt of his guilt," said I. "But if he were not the murderer, who else would be likely to have committed the crime? Was anyone else ever suspected?"

"No. Poor Brandon's guilt seemed only too obvious. And the murder was too motiveless to be the act of a sane person. The young woman had no enemies. There was no one at Ellerslie besides Brandon and your father."

"Then my father was there at the time of the murder?"

"Yes, your father used to come and go like a member of the family, before Sibyl's marriage. I don't know what the quarrel was about, but there was a quarrel at the period of her engagement to Penrith. Mrs. Morison hinted at an ugly scuffle between the brothers—blows, broken glass—but the particulars were never clearly known. Your father was certainly hurt, and the doctor had to be called in; but the servants were told he had had a fall. Whatever the actual circumstances may have been, there was bad blood, for Mr. Urquhart never entered Ellerslie House again—after that fall."

> "'And when he falls, he falls like Lucifer,
> Never to hope again.'"[2]

muttered I. "My father told me that he and his brother had quarrelled; but he never explained the rights and wrongs of the story."

And then she told me how Brandon Mountford had broken out of the lock-up at Ardliston, and was supposed to have perished in a storm at sea.

"Only supposed to have perished?" said I. "Then there is really no evidence of his death. He may be alive at this hour."

"That's not likely. His family must have heard of him if he were living."

"Why should anyone hear of him?" asked I. "It would be the business of his life to avoid being heard of. A man accused of murder—a man conscious of his own guilt! In all probability he would go back to Africa. I have heard that men who have once been there always want to go back—must go back. The Dark Continent draws them like a loadstone. Rely upon it, Lady Selina, this poor Mr. Mountford is in Africa."

"I have no doubt you know a great deal more about him than I do," said Lady Selina, with an offended air. "Young women nowadays are nothing if not positive."

In my own mind I had no doubt that the man was, or had been, in Africa. Those books of African travel in Lady Penrith's room testified to so profound an interest in that uncivilised world. He had made his escape from England, and had sailed to a land where there are no detectives or magistrates' warrants, or extradition treaties.

But if my aunt knows Mr. Mountford to be in Africa, how account for her intense anxiety about this wandering lunatic, for whom she inquired at all the cottages, and the fuss and driving to and fro, and the suppressed emotion of the last ten days?

All these indications point to Brandon Mountford's presence in the immediate neighbourhood, or at any rate to her conviction that he is near.

CHAPTER XXVI

HOME QUESTIONS

CORALIE sat late over her private diary. The clocks had struck one before she closed the book and put it away in the box where she kept her money and her few trinkets, under lock and key. She slept little that night, and the sleep she had was disturbed by troubled dreams. That interview between her father and her uncle had left a sense of bitter degradation in her mind. She had never really loved her father; there had been nothing between them but the bond of relationship—a bond which he had shown himself very glad to loosen. Yet he was her father, a part of her existence, the only being upon whom she had any strong claim; and it tortured her to think of degradation that reflected upon herself. To be the daughter of such a father! There was the sting! To hear him ask for money, and to hear him so heartlessly refused by his own and only brother! Little as she liked Penrith, there had been that in his tone which told her he had some justification for his brutality. And she was to go on living under the roof of this man—she, Hubert Urquhart's daughter—or go back to the dreary existence from which Lady Penrith had rescued her.

"Oh, if Coverdale had only cared for me!" she sighed, again and again, in her restless turnings and tossings, while the inexorable clock ticked and the night lamp flickered.

And then she thought, as many a woman thinks when the future lies dark before her—lit by not one gleam of hope—thought of what her life might have been if this man had chosen her for his wife. It was all very well to write of him scoffingly as a prim pattern of the uninteresting virtues. In her heart of hearts she revered him for those qualities at which she scoffed. The gulf that lay between them was bridged over by her growing interest in his personality. She had begun by thinking of him only as a good match, heir to title and fortune, a man who, with a word, could change the whole tenor of her existence. She knew now by the blank his absence made in that house, by her jealous despair at his too evident regard for Lady Penrith—a regard of which he himself might be hardly conscious—she knew now that she loved him, and that if he had been an impecunious curate she would have been content to share his life and let fortune go.

"But who would marry Hubert Urquhart's daughter?" she asked herself. "Even if I were ever so handsome there would be that against me. And a plain daughter! I must have been mad ever to hope."

She was in the breakfast-room early, neat and fresh looking in her smart tailor gown, and with no indication, save a heavy look in her eyelids, of her miserable night. Her uncle had gone out before breakfast. Lady Penrith talked a little more than she had done at dinner on the previous evening, but was evidently anxious and expectant.

A telegram was brought to her in the middle of breakfast, and Coralie could see that her aunt's hand trembled as she tore open the envelope.

"Let the messenger wait," her ladyship told the servant, after she had read the message twice over with profound attention.

"No bad news, I hope, my dear," said Lady Selina.

"Oh, no; a telegram nowadays does not imply bad news."

"Of course not; but in this remote place you can't have many trivial telegrams—invitations, acceptances, excuses—the sort of thing one gets in London."

"No; not that kind of thing," Lady Penrith answered absently, as she put the message in her pocket.

On her aunt asking her if she was going for a drive in the morning or afternoon, Lady Penrith answered "No." She had a good many letters to write, and was not going out all day.

"You and Cora can have the barouche or the pony cart, whichever you prefer," she added.

"Thank you, neither. I have not quite got over my influenza cold, and the only inducement to drive would have been your company."

"Complimentary to me, after my patient endurance of the old creature," thought Coralie, and then she said in her clear young voice—

"In that case, I shall go for a long walk directly after breakfast. You won't be angry with me if I should be late for luncheon, will you, aunt?"

"Your aunt has been so irregular herself lately, that she can hardly find fault with you for unpunctuality," Lady Selina remarked, somewhat snappishly.

Any deviation from the clockwork round of daily life was an offence to this lady.

"Angry, Cora, certainly not," said Lady Penrith. "But on what tremendous pilgrimage are you going? It is not ten, and you think you won't be home at two."

"Oh, I am going for a long tramp—towards the sea."

"You can get that in this garden—too much of it for the poor flowers."

"Ah, but not like the wind one gets on the very edge of the sea—along Allan Bay or at St. Jude's, for instance."

Lady Penrith gave a little start at the mention of St. Jude's, a movement which did not escape Coralie.

"I may go to Ardliston," she continued. "It is just the grey, breezy morning I adore."

"Do as you like, Cora, only don't fatigue yourself," Lady Penrith said carelessly, as she left the room.

"Now, if I were a pretty girl," mused Cora, "she would hardly let me ramble for three or four hours alone. There would be suspicions of a lover—I might be going to meet someone. But in my case, there can be no such danger. An ugly woman is what Cæsar's wife ought to have been—above suspicion."

Miss Urquhart had told the truth for once in the way, albeit she was a young person who preferred falsehood. She was going to Ardliston—in quest of her father. After that conversation of yesterday evening she felt that she must see him, must question him, at any hazard of hard words. She could exist no longer in this cloud of ignorance.

She stopped on the crest of a wind-blown ridge, hugged her neat little cloth jacket tighter round her, and looked back at the grey towers of Killander Castle.

What a noble old place it was—originally a rude border fortress, enlarged and improved by successive generations. Sibyl Higginson's money had set the final touches on the picture. Whatever was wanting of convenience or dignity had been supplied within the last ten years. The gardens and terraces had been extended, a spacious palm-house had been built in the one angle where it would not be a blot upon the rugged grandeur of the exterior; and within doors there had been improvements in every detail. Money had been spent like water.

"And she is not even tenant for life," mused Coralie. "If my uncle were to die to-morrow she would be houseless—so far as yonder great grey pile is concerned—or the house in Berkeley Square. Hard lines, to spend one's money upon somebody else's property. But then she can afford to waste a few thousands. And she has Ellerslie House standing ready to receive her, if she were to leave the Castle. Ellerslie House! What a difference between the spick and span modern house, built by a self-made millionaire, and that grey fortress over there, which seems still to echo with the tramp of armed feet, and the blare of trumpets."

Coralie turned her back upon the grey towers, after that contemplative pause, and tramped steadily on, with her face to the sea. It was a long walk from the Castle to Ardliston, but Miss Urquhart was a good walker, well broken in by the weary promenades of Madame Michon's pupils in the Bois, or along chalky roads in the white suburbs that skirt the Bois, and later by lonely wanderings in West End London, rambles which were her sole respite from the dullness of the lodging house at the back of Piccadilly.

She met only one shepherd boy between the Castle and the beginning of the long straggling street of Ardliston; and Ardliston itself might have been asleep for any signs of life or movement, except at the schools, where she heard the sing-song voices of the children chanting the multiplication table, a sound that told her it was not yet noon, and saved her the trouble of looking at her watch.

Her father might have gone back to London by the night mail, or by an early morning train, she thought, in which case she would be much disappointed. She wanted to see him—wanted to question him about the past, though she knew not how she would venture to shape her questions. But she had helped him, had watched for him—she had sacrificed her own instincts of loyalty and honour at his bidding—and she had a right to his confidence.

"I will do no more for him unless he trusts me fully," she said to herself.

No, he had not left the Higginson Arms. The landlady, who was busy in the little bar on one side of the entrance, recognised Coralie.

"Come to see your pa, miss? He is very late this morning. You'll find him at breakfast."

She came out of her snug little nest among the bottles and glasses, and ushered Coralie into a sitting-room where she found her father reading a newspaper at the breakfast table. He rose, startled at seeing her.

"What brings you here so early? Anything new?"

"Nothing very important. Ten minutes to twelve. Do you call that early?"

"Early enough for a man who is such a beastly bad sleeper that he seldom gets a wink of sleep till daylight. Sit down, Cora. Would you like some tea? It was made a few minutes ago."

He poured out a cup and handed it to her, with some show of attentiveness, while she sat looking at him dumbly, full of thought.

He looked haggard and careworn, older than his elder brother, and it seemed to her that all the indications of a debased character were stamped upon his countenance—the furtive eye, the tightened lips, the curious twitch of the nostril now and then before he began to speak.

"Well?" he asked, when he had mixed a brandy and soda for himself, "what's your news?"

She told him briefly how Mr. Coverdale had left the Castle with Lady Penrith yesterday morning, and had not returned with her in the afternoon.

"What kind of a man is this Coverdale?"

"A good man."

"Good? I don't quite follow your meaning."

That seemed likely enough, Coralie thought.

"Conscientious and God-fearing. He is devoted to Lady Penrith, but even for her sake he would do nothing that was not strictly honourable."

"And you think he has gone upon some kind of mission for her."

"I think so. She had a telegram this morning at breakfast—a long message—which I fancy may have been from him."

"What's the use of fancies? It may have been from her dressmaker. Had you the sense to find out where it came from?"

"No, I was not near enough to see that. I could only see that she was agitated at receiving it."

"Humph, that tells me nothing. Well, keep your eyes open, Cora, and let no detail of her daily life escape your observation. Straws show which way the wind blows. Try to find out where the parson has gone."

"Are you going to stay here much longer?"

"That depends upon circumstances. I have no particular inducement to go anywhere else just now. I may go further north, perhaps, for a little shooting—but I have made no plans yet."

There was a silence of some minutes. Urquhart took up the newspaper again, and read, or pretended to read.

Cora felt it easier to begin upon a painful subject now that his face was hidden.

"Father, I was crossing the hall—from the drawing-room to the billiard-room—yesterday afternoon, when you and my uncle were talking, and I could not help hearing a good deal——"

"You mean you couldn't help listening. Your curiosity got the better of your good breeding," retorted Urquhart, throwing down the paper, and turning to his daughter with an angry scowl. "And you heard all that passed between my affectionate brother and me. Well, who cares?"

"I care very much. I have been heart-broken ever since."

"You need not waste your emotions upon me. I have a pretty tough hide. It has toughened in a long experience of hard knocks."

"Father, what odious things he said of you—and you did not deny them."

"Why should I trouble myself? He is not judge or jury. I wanted help, and he didn't want to help me. The easiest way of refusing was to be abusive. You are woman of the world enough to comprehend that, I hope, Cora."

"No, I am not. I can't comprehend that you should let him say such things."

"If I had knocked him down there would have been a scene and a scandal; and you would have found yourself homeless. I know of no other way of dealing with him."

"But that you should ask him for money—importune him—swallow all his insults. Father, what degradation there is in that."

"Degradation, yes, perhaps. And you wonder that I should put myself in the way of being insulted. You wonder that I should beg of my brother who married the heiress I was trying to marry—the woman who cared not one straw for either of us. You wonder that I should ask him to open his wife's coffers for me. You are a fool, Cora. A man hemmed round with debt—distracted for want of money as I am—isn't likely to be scrupulous as to the mode and manner of getting it. Don't whine about what you heard yesterday. You may think yourself lucky if I don't turn forger or highwayman, sign her ladyship's name to a stolen cheque, or hold up a train carrying bullion. What might not a man do, at his wits' ends as I am? And my elder brother has the command of eighty thousand a year, for his wife denies him nothing, and won't give me eight hundred, or eighty, or eight pounds. That's what brotherly love means nowadays, Cora. Very much like the ointment upon Aaron's head, ain't it?"

"Why does he hate you? What did you do to offend him?"

"Nothing. We both courted the same woman—he won her by a fluke. Unintentionally—by sheer ill-luck—I helped him to win her. He ought to be grateful to me, but he ain't. He finds it cheaper to ride the high horse and blackguard me."

"But there must have been something, father, on your part—some cruel wrong—some act of treachery that gives my uncle and his wife the right to hold themselves aloof from you."

"She chooses to fancy herself wronged; and he takes advantage of the position. Come, Cora, I am not going to be questioned about my past life by my own daughter."

"And I am not going to act as your spy any more unless you give me your confidence," Cora answered resolutely, looking her father full in the face.

There was no filial love in that look. If she felt his degradation strongly it was because the degradation was reflected upon her. To be the daughter of such a man, to live on sufferance in a house whose threshold he was not allowed to cross! That was the sting! It was her own pride that was hurt. She had borne the brunt of poverty, and suffered from shabby frocks, and school-bills in arrear, but never till yesterday evening had her father's fallen state been brought home to her.

"Spy. That's a most unpleasant word, Cora, and you seem to repeat it with gusto simply because it is unpleasant. I asked you to keep your ears and eyes open in Penrith's house——"

"In her ladyship's interest—because of your friendship for her. That was the fable you imposed upon me."

"Fable and imposed!"

He shrugged his shoulders with a light scornfulness, as if such words hurt him very little, even from a daughter's lips; and then he rose, and walked to the window.

"But I am to be hoodwinked no longer," pursued Cora impetuously. "I know now that you hate her."

"Do I?" asked Mr. Urquhart, drumming on the pane, with his back turned upon his daughter. "If I do it is only the hate that every strong-natured man feels for the woman he loved in vain. She had but to marry me, and I would have been the most docile and devoted of husbands—her head servant out of livery. But you see she preferred my brother, and so I can't be expected to go on loving her for ever. He has treated me like a pariah dog, and she has treated me no better, which is shortsighted on her part, for she should at least remember that I am heir presumptive, and that if anything happened to Penrith all her grandeurs would pass to me. It doesn't matter to him, for his rights and interests in this life must be over and done with before mine could begin; but it would matter to her to the extent of two fine houses, and a large domain, and all the money she has sunk upon them."

"Must they go with the title—both houses?" asked Cora, her indignation lapsing suddenly into interest.

"The Castle, and Penrith House, Mayfair, both go with the title. He was born in one—the heir—at the Castle, of course—an occasion for bonfires on all the hills, and roasted oxen, and kilderkins of strong beer, which my father could very ill afford. I was born in the other, and I doubt if the household had so much as an extra bottle of wine to celebrate my nativity. Yes, the house in London must go—whenever Penrith goes—and all her ladyship has spent upon it—something like thirty thousand pounds, I believe—will go to the heir, whoever he may be."

"Heir presumptive has a grand look against your name in the peerage," said Cora, waxing bitter again, "but I don't think you have much chance of outliving my uncle."

"Bar accidents, none—but the bursting of a gun, the running down of a yacht, a smash on the railway, a fall from his horse—anything of that sort would be as big a fluke for me as his marriage was for him—but I don't expect it," drumming louder with finger-tips whose sharp touch denoted nervous irritability—"expect it, did I say? I know that it will never happen. I am one of those men who come into the world with bad luck branded on their foreheads."

"There's no such thing as bad luck, father. It's the idlest nonsense to talk in that strain. You inherited a younger brother's portion—and you squandered it. You married foolishly, before you were of age—offended your father, and spoilt your chance of a fortune with a wife. You lived recklessly, and loaded your shoulders with debts. You have never struggled or worked as other men of good race and small means have done. You should have gone to the Bar—or into politics—or to the Colonies. There must have been some career open to you—something better than the miserable life you are leading now—a beggar to the brother who hates you—a beggar, and refused with contumely."

She brushed away her tears—so rare in those cold grey eyes—tears of shame and mortification.

"Have you nothing more to say?" sneered her father. "This moral lecture might be continued ad infinitum—the daughter's rebuke of the reprobate father. A very pretty subject, and offering fine scope for the prosy and the trite."

"Well, I will say no more. I know that all lamentations over the irrevocable are worse than useless. Let the past be past—only if you want my help in the future you must let me into your secrets. Why are you keeping this watch upon your brother's wife?"

"Why? For my own satisfaction. She is my enemy, and would injure me if she could."

"But how could she injure you—what could she do?"

"Never mind that, Cora. Knowledge is power, and it suits me to be informed of all that happens at the Castle."

"Trust me, then. Be frank, if you can. What was your quarrel with Lady Penrith? Why does she hate you?"

"Pooh! It was a girl's silly hatred, to begin with. She was madly in love with her cousin, who murdered Sir Joseph's adopted daughter in a fit of epileptic rage!"

"Is it certain that he was the murderer——"

"Certain? Yes. He was found almost in the act of murder—his hands, and clothes stained with her blood. There is no room for doubt. Miss Higginson visited him in the lock-up yonder—a wretched hole that was done away with soon after. I found her there, and helped in his escape—was indeed the chief means of getting him away, and when the boat, on board which I put him, was wrecked in a gale that was only beginning, when the boat started, she laid his death at my door."

"But was that the only cause of her dislike? Penrith accused you of trying to win her by the basest means—trading on her ignorance of life."

"Rot. People in the neighbourhood looked coldly at her after that escapade at the lock-up. Her conduct was too unconventional to escape slander. I may have somewhat magnified the village scandal when I urged her to marry me. I wanted her to feel the need of a husband to defend her good name."

"A shabby trick—and it failed?"

"Yes, it failed—the turtle dove—for Brandon Mountford she had been a very dove—turned upon me like a tigress. She flung herself into my brother's arms—partly from sheer malignity to me, and partly because she knew that whatever scandal there had been would be best covered by a coronet."

"Well, it was a shabby business. However, I am glad I know the past. But I can't understand the situation in the present. Why should you fear her? Why should you watch her?"

"That's my affair. I shan't answer any more questions."

He turned and faced her again, frowningly.

"I won't trouble you any more, except to ask how long you are going to stay here."

"I don't know. Perhaps for a few days—perhaps only a few hours. Look here, Cora. If anything out of the common should happen at the Castle you had better come here, as you have done this morning, on the chance of finding me. On reflection I am inclined to wait till the parson's return from his mysterious mission."

"You think his mission may have something to do with you?"

"I don't say that, but I should like to know the meaning of it. I rely upon your shrewdness for that. Come, Cora, there's no use in your riding the high horse. Remember that your interests are interwoven with mine. Anything that hurts me must hurt you."

"Yes, I know that," she answered, with a sigh. "Your disgrace is my disgrace. It wraps me round like a dark cloud. I live and move in it."

This was no idle complaint on her part. The burden of her father's evil reputation had seemed to her a much heavier load since she had known John Coverdale, who, without self-assertion of any kind, had impressed her with the idea of what an honourable man's life and mind ought to be—how fair a record the one, how high a standard the other. And in that pure atmosphere of noble thought and lofty aspiration how foul and grim her father's character looked.

CHAPTER XXVII

CORA EXPATIATES

HEIR presumptive! How the phrase rang in my ears last night when I lay down to sleep, after another long, dull evening, for the most part alone with Lady Selina, Lady Penrith having retired soon after we left the dining-room, leaving the spinster and me to amuse each other. The spinster is a late bird, and complains of the dull evenings here, and talks of the superior attractions of other houses owned by other nieces—the large house parties, with a constant succession of guests, the theatricals, the charades, and dumb crambo, and music, and cards. Yes; this dissipated old person actually sighs for a riotous game at roulette.

Heir presumptive! Of the two lives my uncle's, so far as I can judge, is the better. His two years of seniority count for nothing against my father's habits—late hours and, I fear, deep drinking. Yet an accident might alter the situation in a breath; an accident, and my father might be Earl of Penrith and master of this house— master here, where he has been treated with contumely; sole owner of the house whose door has been shut against him for the last ten years. Life hangs by so thin a thread.

No, I won't suffer my thoughts to dwell upon such possibilities. I am not particularly fond of my uncle, and I owe him nothing, since anything I enjoy in this house is given me by his wife; but I won't indulge in castle-building upon such a ghastly foundation.

Notwithstanding which resolve I could not resist the temptation of drawing Lady Selina on the subject of the Penrith property when she and I were left alone, and I had to perform my nightly task of sorting her worsteds and admiring her hideous blanket. She is one of the people who think that high art begins and ends with muddy greens and dingy yellows; when if they had eyes to see they would know that the leading note of high art is brilliant colour.

"I have been rambling about his lordship's estate," said I. "What pretty old homesteads and farm-buildings! And all so neat and substantial."

"Those homesteads and barns are monuments of my niece's folly. She has squandered her money upon Penrith's property; and her own flesh and blood will never be one penny richer for all she has spent."

"What a pity she has no son to inherit the estate!"

"Ah! that would have made all the difference," sighed Lady Selina. "Here is my niece, Lady Hilborough, with an enormous family, and my sister, Lady Ranthorpe, with three great, hulking boys at Eton and Cooper's Hill, and two more in the nursery: and here is poor Sibyl childless. That is her misfortune, poor girl! But it does not excuse her folly for lavishing tens of thousands upon her husband's estate."

"Why should she not spend her money upon improvements?"

"She might spend it upon Ellerslie, which she can leave to her own family."

"Ellerslie is perfection. There is very little room for spending money."

"She could buy more land. There is always land to be bought nowadays, and ridiculously cheap. She ought to have quadrupled her own estate rather than sunk a fortune upon her husband's property. Penrith was almost a pauper when he married—but she has paid off every mortgage—and doubled the value of his farms by her improvements."

"No doubt it has amused her to improve. I can fancy nothing more delightful than messing about a large estate, picking old buildings to pieces and putting them together again; seeing order and beauty where all was squalor and ugliness."

"All very well, if there had been an heir, but in the existing state of things sheer lunacy," said Lady Selina decisively.

And if Penrith were to die, my father, whom Lady Penrith detests, would be enriched by the wealth she has lavished. He would spring at once from poverty to riches, and his riches would be derived from her—an unencumbered estate, land in the perfection of high farming, tenants who know they are better off than any other tenants in Cumberland. He would owe all to her, and could turn her out of doors if he liked—as Penrith turned him out two days ago.

Well, I won't dwell upon the thought. This journal of mine is not a starched composition, but it shall not be ghastly. I won't let my mind brood upon the chances that hang by the fine-spun thread of one life.

But if I dismiss one hideous subject—shake off the gloom of one idea—other fancies crowd in upon me as dark or darker. I cannot get the thought of that murdered girl out of my mind. Curious as I have been about that tragic story, I had resolved not to ask any questions of the servants, but I have broken down in that commendable resolution. A lady never talks to servants except in a purely business-like manner. "Put out my blue gown. Put away my red. Where are my satin shoes?" and so on. Nothing more interesting than an Ollendorff dialogue ought ever to pass between mistress and maid.[1] Well, I am as much a lady as I can be, but I am first a woman; and I am devoured by a morbid curiosity that must be satisfied.

The horror of that murder haunts me—a young woman, young, and beautiful, full of the pride of life, caught like a hunted fawn in a wood, caught and slaughtered by a raging maniac—for the epilepsy that hungers for blood must be lunacy under its most revolting aspect.

No one saw her struggles. If she had time to cry for help no ear heard her cry. In the loneliness and darkness the murderer's knife did its work.

I know all about it, now. The picture presented by Lady Selina was vague and shadowy, but last night I let her ladyship's maid come into my room after her mistress had gone to bed, and while she was brushing my hair I led up to the story of Marie Arnold's death.

The woman has all the ghoulish relish for horrors which seems natural to persons in that sphere, and she was charmed to dilate upon every detail. She took immense credit to herself for having been at Ellerslie at the time. One of her male relatives could have been no more proud had he ridden along that avenue of guns we all know so well in the Balaclava charge.[2] She was at Ellerslie.

She followed in the murdered girl's funeral procession. She never hopes to see such a funeral again.

She distinctly used the word hope.

She was really very interesting. She conjured up the image of the young woman in all her showy foreign beauty. She suggested the unrevealed link between her and Sir Joseph. Everybody in the steward's room had suspected that she was something nearer and dearer than an adopted daughter, though she had been put somewhat in the background; and when they saw the poor old gentleman's grief after her death they were sure they had guessed right.

And then she described Brandon Mountford as a man from whom no evil could have been anticipated—so handsome, such a gentleman, always polite to the servants, though he kept himself very much to himself. He had no valet, and on the morning before the murder he had been in his own room packing for some hours. The servants noticed a change in him at luncheon that day. He was in the garden with Miss Higginson after luncheon; and later in the afternoon my informant saw him going into his own room again, and he looked pale and agitated—"Very much upset" was her expression. She was sitting at her needlework by a window in the corridor, and she could hear him walking up and down his room, and throwing things about; and when she looked into the room after he had gone downstairs she found his portmanteau still open, and his books and things scattered about, as if he had been too upset to get on with his packing. He was seen by one of the men going out into the garden again; but at dinner there was no sign of him, nor of Miss Arnold.

And then she told me how Miss Arnold also had seemed very much upset at luncheon, and had left the room before the meal was finished; and she told me there was no doubt in her mind that poor Miss Arnold was deeply in love with Mr. Mountford.

"And he with her?" I asked.

"Oh no, miss," says the woman. "It was a regular game of cross purposes. Mr. Mountford was in love with my young mistress. One could see that with half an eye; but there was someone else in love with Miss Arnold, and had been for a long time."

"Who was that?" asked I.

"You might be offended, miss, if I was to say."

Her meaning flashed upon me in a moment.

"Do you mean my father?"

"Yes, miss. Mr. Urquhart was very much attached to Miss Arnold. He wanted to marry her, but she wouldn't have him. One of the gardeners overheard their talk in the conservatory one afternoon. He was at work behind the tree-ferns, and they didn't know he was there, and they talked quite free, and the young man didn't like to show himself after they began to talk, so he stopped quietly there till they left the conservatory. Mr. Urquhart was quite violent—carried away by his feelings, the young man said—but Miss Arnold was very haughty and determined; she couldn't have been prouder had she been a duchess."

This revelation throws a new light upon my father's character.

I did not think passionate love was in his line, even when he was ten years younger. And that he could be in love with the poor dependent while the millionaire heiress was in the house, to be wooed and won. That was strange. And then, when this poor girl was dead, he had set himself to win the heiress—and had failed dismally.

I asked Ferriby if she and her fellow-servants believed in Mr. Mountford's guilt.

"I'm afraid there's no doubt about it, miss," she answered, shaking her head. "He was the nicest of gentlemen—but he was not a bit like himself that day—several of us saw the change in him—and he must have killed her in a fit of madness. They say his poor mother was mad for many years, and died in a madhouse. If he wasn't guilty why should he run away?"

Yes, that flight of his was the strongest evidence against him.

"Was no one else ever suspected?" I asked.

"No one, miss, not by any of us—but Sir Joseph, he would never believe that Mr. Mountford was the murderer. He told the steward so. He believed that the poor young lady was killed by a tramp, for the sake of the jewellery she was wearing."

"Was her jewellery taken?"

"No, miss—not a thing—but then, Sir Joseph said the murderer must have been surprised by Mr. Mountford's approach before he had time to rob his victim, and had slipped off through the wood without being seen by the two stablemen who were searching for the poor young lady. If Mr. Mountford was innocent he'd no call to run away—even if those who were interested in him over-persuaded him."

"You mean your mistress," said I.

"Yes, miss, my mistress and Mr. Urquhart were both mixed up in it. They acted for the best, no doubt—but if the poor gentleman was innocent they made him look guilty."

They made him look guilty. I have thought of those words a good deal since her ladyship's maid uttered them.

May not one of those concerned in the wretched man's flight have meant to damage him rather than to aid? There can be no doubt of Miss Higginson's good faith—but my father's motive is not so obvious.

I'm afraid I am as much of a ghoul as Ferriby, for ever since that young woman brushed my hair last night I have been haunted by the image of the handsome, amiable young man tormented by one of the direst diseases that afflict humanity—a disease which can change the man who would not hurt a worm into a blood-thirsty murderer.

So haunted have I been all day by that ghastly suggestion of a kindly and courteous gentleman suddenly transformed into a human wild beast, that I have been absolutely unable to stay quietly indoors, least of all to endure solitary confinement with Lady Selina, which I should have had to endure if I had not taken the key of the fields.[3]

Lady Penrith retired to her own room after breakfast, with the meagre excuse of having letters to write. I believe she does really cover reams of note-paper in the course of her correspondence with innumerable aunts and cousins, among the latter of whom there is always one who is just engaged or just going to be married, and who requires extra sympathy and something magnificent in the way of a wedding present. But I doubt if aunts or cousins are profiting much by her ladyship's present seclusion, as I shrewdly suspect that her only correspondent is Mr. Coverdale, and that she sits in her morning-room waiting for "wires" from that clerical knight-errant.

I left the Castle soon after her disappearance, and in my purposeless wanderings on the moor whom should I meet but Mr.

Dewsnap, the family doctor, the dapper bachelor who attends her ladyship and my uncle for any small ailment, and who generally has a patient or two among the Castle household. He has been allowed to look at my tongue and feel my pulse on one or two occasions, and has been disappointed to discover me a wiry little person, never good for more than three visits.

He was riding an elderly white pony, but at the sight of my trim tailor gown and toque jumped off and put the bridle over his arm. He looks about forty, an elderly young man, very neat in his dress; with, I fancy, some pretension to lady-killing: and, above all, he is an inveterate gossip. He seemed delighted at the opportunity of talking to me. For Mr. Coverdale I may be only a plain young woman; but for the family practitioner I am the young lady of Killander Castle, an earl's niece, and worthy of attention. Under ordinary circumstances, I should certainly have kept him very much in his place, and he would have remounted his ancient steed in five minutes; but in my present mood I was delighted to get a talk with a man who could tell me all about that horrible malady which I had been brooding upon in connection with Brandon Mountford.

We talked of the weather, and then I said, casually—

"No doubt you are able to read all the local meteorological signs, for I am told you have lived in this neighbourhood for a good many years."

"Except when I was walking the hospital in London, I have hardly ever lived anywhere else," answered he. "My father had the only good practice between here and Workington. I began my professional career as his assistant, and I have continued it as his successor. I doubt if I shall ever extend my travels beyond these hills and moors. A country practice gives a vast variety of experience."

"No doubt. You must have seen many curious cases in all these years," said I, walking slowly along the footpath, while the medico sauntered at my side, and the medico's horse crept along, cropping the russet sward as he went. "I wonder if you remember that terrible event at Ellerslie Park, ten years ago——"

"If you mean the murder of Marie Arnold it would not be easy for me to forget it," replied the doctor. "I was acquainted with that unfortunate young lady. She was the most beautiful woman I ever saw."

"Was she handsomer than my aunt, Lady Penrith?"

"Quite another style of beauty—a more brilliant style—distinctly southern—a richer colouring"—he looked at my drab complexion, hesitated, and added, "though where there is an intellectual expression, where mind lights the face, colouring is of secondary importance."

Oh, with what weariness of spirit have I heard that specious lie about my intellectual expression—heard it from the lips of men who have shown in every look that I was of no more account in their sights than if my face had been cut out of wood.

"I see you greatly admired that poor girl," said I.

Mr. Dewsnap's only answer was a profound sigh.

"Can you believe that Mr. Mountford was her murderer?" I asked.

"My dear Miss Urquhart," cried the creature, growing disgustingly familiar, "I can believe anything of a madman. From the moment I knew Mountford was epileptic, and heard of his low spirits and discomposure on the day of the murder, I had little doubt of his guilt. That gloomy agitation presaged an attack, and there is no doubt that alone in the wood the devil of epilepsy seized upon him, and as the fit passed it left him like the demoniac of old, panting with fierce impulses, thirsting for blood. And with that savage rage upon him he met that poor girl, seized her as the tiger seizes its prey, and killed her more swiftly than the tiger kills. I have thought it all out—the image of the victim has haunted me."

He stifled a sob, and I began to feel more kindly towards him.

"Yes," he continued, after a pause, "the man whom I had only seen as a calm and well-mannered gentleman was the fiend who killed Marie Arnold—the same but not the same. And when the deed was done he fell down beside his victim, exhausted, in a comatose sleep, on awakening from which memory was a blank. He might remember nothing of that savage crime—he might feel nothing but a confused sense of trouble."

"Have you heard what became of him after his escape from the lock-up?" I asked.

"No one in this neighbourhood has any actual knowledge of his fate. He may have been landed somewhere along the coast, within a few miles of Ardliston, before the fishing boat in which he left came to grief; but the general idea is that he went down with the skipper and his crew. Nothing has ever been heard of him since that night by anyone about here."

"Then it would seem likely that he was drowned. Or might he not have left the country—gone back to Africa, for instance?"

"Yes, that would be probable enough, if they were able to land him before the worst of the storm."

We had come to the junction between the footpath and the Ardliston road, and here the doctor bade me good-day, remounted his pony, and trotted homewards, while I turned my face towards the Castle, where I arrived only a few minutes before luncheon.

I was surprised to find the station brougham waiting at the door, with a portmanteau, a small black trunk, and a travelling bag on the roof.

"Who is going away?" I asked the groom, though the S. P. painted in bold red letters upon the portmanteau left no room for doubt.

"Her ladyship is leaving by the 2.40 train, ma'am."

"For London?"

The groom did not know. I ran into the house, and to the dining-room, where I found Lady Selina and her niece, the elder lady evidently out of temper, the younger grave and composed, but very pale, and with that eager look in her eyes which has distinguished her of late.

"What wonders are happening?" I exclaimed. "To think of you deserting us like this, aunt! Are you going to London?"

"Not nearly so far."

"Where then—if one may venture to ask?"

"One may ask anything, Cora, but my movements are so uncertain that it is hardly worth while entering into particulars. I hope to be home again in a day or two. If there should be any need to write to me my aunt has an address that will find me."

"What shall we do without you?"

"I dare say you will contrive to exist."

A servant appeared at the dining-room door.

"Are my things in the carriage—is Ferriby there?"

"Yes, my lady. Kingdon says it is time for you to start."

Kingdon is her ladyship's particular coachman. His office is to drive her, and no one else, and to be waited upon and worked for by three or four underlings.

"You had better let me go with you, Sibyl," said Lady Selina, as if following up a previous request.

"Impossible. Take care of yourself, auntie, and of Cora."

"How shall I explain your absence to Penrith?"

"I have explained it—in a letter. Good-bye."

She kissed her aunt, gave me a friendly nod, and hurried away. We both followed to the hall, and stood disconsolately watching as the brougham drove away, with Lady Penrith inside, and Lady Penrith's confidential maid with her.

Most women in her position would have a highly trained Parisian, with fairy fingers for the adjustment of ribbons and lace, and with fine taste in hair-dressing. Lady Penrith has kept the woman who came to her from a village school, and who has been in her service for over ten years. If one were inclined to think evil one might suspect her ladyship of some secret reason for keeping this woman about her. Old servants are not to be lightly dismissed. They know too much.

But I must add that Ferriby spoke of her mistress with a frankness and freedom which one would not expect if there were any secrets in Lady Penrith's life.

Lady Selina ate her luncheon in silence, evidently out of temper with her niece and things in general. She sent away some roast pheasant because it was too high; she objected to the fricasseed fowl because the mushrooms in the sauce were underdone.

"I think Lady Penrith has about as bad a chef as money could buy for her," said Lady Selina; "and I have observed that the higher wages people give the worse cooks they get. We had a cordon bleu at Basingstoke House for forty pounds a year. My father couldn't afford a man cook; but we had better dinners than people who were giving three hundred a year to a chef—better everyday food I mean, my dear."

And then the spinster thawed, and read me a long lecture upon the management of a great house, which I fear can never be of the slightest use to me. A shabby London lodging or a tiny villa in a dusty suburb is the only home I can see waiting for me in the dismal desert of my future. Lady Selina ate an enormous luncheon in spite of her abuse of the cook, and talked for nearly an hour about the folly of masters and mistresses and the iniquity of servants: of her nieces who managed well, and her nieces who managed ill; till I found myself upon the point of dropping asleep.

I proposed a drive before tea. Lady Selina has scarcely finished her lunch when she begins to look forward to her tea.

No, she didn't care about driving. There were only two tolerable drives, and she knew them both by heart. She would sit by the fire and get on with her work. So by the fire I left her—promising to go back to her at tea-time—and went to the billiard-room. My uncle had gone out shooting by himself directly after breakfast, and was not likely to return till dusk, so I had the room and the table to myself, and I gave myself an hour's practice, making the most brilliant flukes and some really clever cannons, and accomplishing the spot stroke six or seven times in succession. It is wonderful how good a game I can play when I have no opponent and no gallery.

An hour of this work tired me, so I put on my hat and set out on another ramble. My mind has been so thoroughly unhinged of late that nothing but a long walk seems to do me any good—a long, lonely walk in a wild, bleak landscape.

No doubt Lady Penrith has gone to Keswick. The 2.40 train stops at Keswick. I looked at Bradshaw[4] in the hall on my way to the billiard-room. She has gone to join Coverdale. There is something mysterious going on in which he is her agent and preux chevalier.[5] Were she a different woman, were he another man, I might suspect a guilty intrigue; but if I could suspect her of evil I could not believe evil of him. If ever there were truth and candour to be found in mankind they are to be found in John Coverdale. He is a King Arthur among priests.

Oh, if I had but been handsome! Oh, if he had but cared for me! How I would have cast off this slough of wickedness which has gradually grown over my mind and heart, and would have emerged from the dismal swamp of past experience a good woman, purified by his love, ennobled by sympathy with his noble nature!

I cannot imagine evil where he is concerned; so I can only think that secret business which engages Lady Penrith and her friend has some relation to her past life—to the romance of her girlhood—to the tragic story of Brandon Mountford.

My idea is that the man has come back from Africa, and that Lady Penrith and Mr. Coverdale are engaged in finding some safe retreat for him, some secluded spot where he may be out of reach of the law.

The afternoon has been dull and bitingly cold, and I am sitting as close as I can to the cosy fire in my comfortable room—half dressing-room, half boudoir—whose thick walls keep out wind and weather, a very comfortable room: indeed there are no comforts or luxuries lacking in my life at Killander Castle, and if it were not for the uncertain tenure by which I hold these things, the dependence upon her ladyship's liking, I might be happy. Happy, quotha, with such a father at my door! Happy, with the gnawing knowledge that my plain face cuts me off from the golden chances that lie all along the pathway of a pretty woman's life—like the enchanted apples that distracted Atalanta.[6]

When I came in at half-past five I found to my great relief that Lady Selina had a headache, and was lying down, so I came straight to my own snug room, threw some logs on the fire, and had my tea-tray, with a pile of those delicious little pastry cakes which the still-room maid makes to perfection, brought to me here, and here I am at a quarter to seven still scribbling the record of the day, for my own amusement only. I find an undiminishing interest in this volume, and the facility with which my pen runs along the page makes me think that I shall some day blossom into a novelist.

I see myself ten years hence a spinster novelist, in a snug little house—in Mayfair. The merest doll's house would do provided it were in a smart street. That would not be half so bad. My father might be dead by that time. I am not calculating on his death in a cold-blooded manner; but we are all mortal, and it is only natural that I should look forward to the years when I may stand alone in the world, free from a tie that galls me, but perhaps without a friend.

I must be a fool if I quarrel with the one friend who has made life pleasant for me—a fool if I let envy and all uncharitableness set me against Sibyl Penrith—yet when I see her absorbing John

Coverdale's attentions, see her spoiling what might have been my chance of winning his affection it is very difficult for me not to hate her. To see her so handsome, so richly provided with all the good things of this world, so scornful of the wealth for which most of us are ready to sell our souls to Satan! I can't help remembering that she has done nothing to deserve this good fortune except take the trouble to be born, as somebody said of a French patrician. Well, at any rate, let me think twice before I do anything to forfeit her friendship. I won't be in any hurry to tell my father of this sudden journey of hers. It is clear to me now that he means mischief.

I am worried and perplexed by his hanging about this neighbourhood—living almost in hiding at the inn at Ardliston—and I shall feel it a profound relief when he is gone. Why should he linger here? He can hardly mean to make a further appeal to my uncle, to be again insulted and repulsed.

What a hard-hearted wretch Penrith must be! Granted that my father behaved badly in his courtship of the heiress. What superior merit can the Earl boast of on his own part? He too wanted the fortune much more than the lady, and I daresay would have stooped to any meanness to win her.

I saw my father this afternoon—saw him amusing himself in his solitary way, just like his brother, who I believe is happier now the house party has gradually melted away, and he can prowl over the hills alone with his gun and dogs than he was when he had his friends about him, and when the great stone hall used to echo their talk and laughter as they set out in the morning.

I was walking along the topmost ridge of the hill in the keen frosty air when I caught sight of my father in the valley below, crossing a stubble field with his gun under his arm—a gun, but no dog.

Could he be poaching, I wondered? I know so little of the game laws that I don't know whether it would be poaching on his part to shoot any bird that he chanced upon in those fields; but as I believe all the land round here belongs to my uncle, and as they are ill friends, I concluded that the Honourable Hubert Urquhart, heir presumptive to the title and estates, can be no better than a common poacher when he knocks down a pheasant on his brother's land. Heir presumptive, quotha! In reading the description of some sprig of nobility's marriage the other day, I read that, as heir presumptive to the Duke of Dash, he had been handsomely provided for by that nobleman. As heir presumptive! All that my father has received as heir presumptive is what Lady Penrith's nephew would call "the dirty kick out." Hideous slang, no doubt, but it best expresses the treatment the younger brother received from the elder—as heir presumptive.

The sky was darkening, and the hard ground was hardening under the frosty wind. I saw my father creeping along by the low stone wall, with his gun, stopping to look about him every now and then, intent on pheasants, no doubt. There was nothing left of the sun but a low yellow light behind the dark shoulder of the moor, and eastward the shadows of evening were stealing over the leaden-coloured sea; but there was light enough for me to watch my father's movements. He was queerly dressed, and looked like a keeper or even a keeper's underling. It amused me to watch his movements, with a touch of contempt for the sporting instinct which could gratify itself at the sacrifice of self-respect. To steal the birds upon the land of a man who had heaped insult upon him—and that man his brother!

He passed through a gap in the stone wall into a second field—a field I know well, for it skirts the footpath by which the shooters often come down the hill on their way home, and along which I have tramped with them many a time. How merry we have been sometimes along that path; what trifles have set us in a roar! That little sub is an amusing little beast, and I'm afraid I used to laugh at his jokes with a frankness that disgusted the Reverend John if he happened to be with us—not that there was anything really wrong in the jokes—only a touch of vulgarity, a flavour of the messroom and the stables. But men like John Coverdale are so easily scared; and then there is all the difference between a pretty woman and a plain one. From Beauty's lips even the slang of the saddle-room has a charm. Human nature has such strange "sports" and varieties. There are men—starched prigs like John Coverdale—who are fascinated by their opposites, and who make themselves the world's wonder by choosing a wife out of the gutter; but such men are poor invertebrate creatures, in spite of the starch. Their prim propriety is only outside wear. Not so with John Coverdale. With him it is the whiteness of a lofty spirit. He is firm as a rock, knows his ideal, and will accept nothing less pure and perfect; and he has found his ideal in Lady Penrith, whom he can't marry, but whom he can worship.

The thought of those homeward walks in the twilight with him, in those hours when he condescended to talk with me as a friend and intellectual equal, and when I felt myself another crea-ture—the very thought of that past, so recent, yet so far away, made me melancholy. I am not prone to the melting mood, but there were tears in my eyes as I watched my father stealing along by the stone wall towards the high tangled hedge which divides the field from the footpath—one of the few real rustic English hedges about here, where the fields are so large, and for the most part bounded by ugly stone walls.

What a stealthy air a solitary sportsman has! How much more like a poacher my father looked, creeping along under the shadow of the hedge, waiting for his chance, no dog to point, or to put up his bird for him; only the chance of some belated pheasant lum-bering heavily home to its cover, or rising scared at the sound of those stealthy footsteps.

It seemed very poor sport to my mind; but I can imagine that my father may feel a malicious pleasure in shooting a brace or two of Penrith's pampered birds—which are said to cost him half a guinea apiece—almost within earshot of the Castle.

He was not very lucky while I watched him, for he only fired once, just as I was turning my footsteps homeward across the open moor.

Only one shot! How it echoed along the silent valley, with a sharp, rattling sound, which set a regiment of rooks screaming and chattering high above my head in the grey evening gloom. The cold grew sharper with the sinking of the sun, so I hurried home as fast as I could to my snug room and rousing fire and plenteous tea-table. Assuredly in choosing between my father and Lady Penrith, I should be a fool if I were to hesitate as to where my loyalty should be given.

Eight o'clock, and I am only half dressed. No matter, for there will be nobody sitting down to dinner in the Castle to-night.

I was in the midst of my dressing when I was startled by a tremendous ringing of bells and opening and shutting of doors below. Could Lady Penrith have returned unexpectedly? No, it must be something more than that. The sudden arrival of a whole family could hardly cause such a noise of hurrying footsteps and ringing of bells as I heard reverberating through the stone hall and corridors. I flew out to the gallery to listen, wrapped in my dressing-gown, with my hair streaming—and stood there trying to make out the meaning of those sounds—but they gradually died away into silence, and I was none the wiser.

An inexplicable terror was upon me. My hands were shaking then, when I knew nothing, my teeth chattering, almost as badly as my hand shakes now, as I write this, now that I know the worst.

Agonised with that dreadful uncertainty, I went along the gallery to the great open space at the top of the staircase, hearing low murmurs of several voices and the heavy tread of feet upon the stairs, as I hurried on. I knew what that tread meant—they were carrying something upstairs.

The something was Lord Penrith. Four men were carrying him—slowly—very slowly—up the broad staircase to his bedroom, and he lay in their arms without sound or movement of so much as one finger of the hand that swung loosely from the sleeve of his dark grey shooting jacket.

I drew back into the shadow, and saw that awful group pass by almost in silence, while a servant who had gone in advance opened the door of the bedroom, and lighted the lamps inside. They passed in with their burden, and the door was shut.

I ran downstairs, and found plenty of people standing about, eager to tell me what had happened.

He was dead. It was an accident, a common kind of accident, which might have been avoided by the most ordinary precaution on his lordship's part. He had been found shot through the heart and lungs, lying across a gap in a hedge, his gun by his side, one charge exploded. It was the old story of a sportsman scrambling through a hedge with his loaded gun in his hand.

His lordship had dismissed the keeper late in the afternoon, and had walked homewards alone. The keeper thought he would have gone the shortest way, by the footpath—but instead of that he must have taken a somewhat wider round, and skirted the big turnip field to get into the footpath by the gap at the lower end—a gap which the shooters had used very often that season.

They were all eager to give me the details. His favourite Clumber spaniel had been with him, and had come back to the Castle in a cowed and frightened condition, which had given the first alarm at the kennels, the men seeing that something was wrong with the dog, and apprehending an accident to his master.

And then the stablemen started in a body to search the home-ward track, and found their master in the hedge at the bottom of the hill. A stone wall divides the turnip field from its neighbours on three sides. There is only the hedge by the footpath—almost the only hedge upon his lordship's estate, moaned the house-steward.

Why do I place these things on record? God knows. My hand shakes so that it is difficult to write. My fire is nearly out—I sit shivering beside the smouldering logs, and my room which looked so bright and cheery an hour ago is now the picture of desolation. The north-east wind is shrieking outside my window.

I shall write no more in this journal. I close the book for ever this miserable night. My heart is frozen.

CHAPTER XXVIII

DEATH IN LIFE

THE telegram that had summoned Lady Penrith upon her mysterious journey early on that fatal November afternoon was of the briefest.

"Found. Come as soon as you like. I wait here for your reply.—Coverdale, Lodore Hotel, Keswick."

The reply was decisive—

"I start for Keswick by the 2.40 train to-day."

Mr. Coverdale was waiting on the platform when the train arrived. The grave kindly face seemed like a welcome, and Lady Penrith felt cheered and sustained by his greeting. He had a carriage waiting for her, looked after her maid and her luggage, and then took his seat beside her, and spared her all agitating questions by telling his story at once, and fully.

"In the first place, I have found him," he said—"plain facts

first, and details afterwards. I have found him—he is desperately
ill—a changed man from the man you remember at Ellerslie. You
must bear that in mind, Lady Penrith. You have to prepare yourself
for a terrible shock in seeing him after ten years which have done
more to alter him, poor fellow, than twice the number would in
happy life."

"Desperately ill—so ill, so changed," she faltered, trying to
keep back her tears. "Tell me the worst—don't be afraid to tell me.
Will he know me again? Is his mind affected?"

"Seriously affected, I fear. I would not say that reason is altogether gone, but it is no longer a sane mind. There are hallucinations, alternating with a dull apathy. The treatment may not
have been cruel—has not been actively cruel—for there have been
intervals since yesterday in which he has talked rationally, and
answered all my questions about his life at St. Jude's with perfect
clearness—but it has been the worst possible treatment for such a
case as his."

"It has been murder—deliberate murder, and those people at
St. Jude's have acted as hired murderers."

"Mr. Carpew has been your brother-in-law's paid agent. I
think there is no doubt of his guilt in that degree. Mr. Urquhart
has an extraordinary influence over him—some stronger hold than
money. But it is not worth while to enter upon that question. The
wrong has been done, and cannot be undone. It is possible that
this poor fellow might have degenerated—in bodily and mental
health—under the happiest circumstances."[1]

"What does the doctor say—no doubt you have called in a
doctor?"

"The man of highest repute in the neighbourhood. He considers the case one of epilepsy; pure and simple—epilepsy in that
severe form in which the frequent attacks tend towards lunacy, and
too often result in lunacy. He does not think the patient likely to
be long lived."

"Long lived, a life of misery! Oh, God! to think of what he was
when I knew him! Oh, if you could have seen him then, Mr. Coverdale—young, handsome, a king among men—his mind so highly
cultivated—knowing and loving all the books I loved. So full of
enthusiasm—telling us of adventures that showed such courage

and ready wit—unconsciously, for he was the last of men to boast of what he had done. And now you tell me that he is a wreck—a wreck in mind and body—a creature to be pitied. To hear you speak of him just now as 'this poor fellow—'"

She burst into tears, crushed and humiliated, as if Brandon Mountford's humiliation bowed her proud head to the dust.

"Pray, bear with me," she said, as Coverdale murmured some consoling commonplace, hardly knowing what he said, his heart aching for her as it had never ached before for a woman in sorrow. "Think what it is for me to have loved him—as I did love him—these lips told him so—only a few hours before Marie Arnold's death—and to find him—thus. Bear with me, Mr. Coverdale. You are a good man, my true, kind friend—the only friend I can look to now."

Coverdale was silent, not daring to trust himself to speech in answer to that declaration of friendship.

"How did you find him?" she asked, after a pause.

They were driving along the road by the lake, through the drizzling rain. An expanse of dark grey water stretched in front of them, with mountains on either side, and wintry gloom brooding over mountain and lake.

"It was not easy—but still it only required patience and the following up of every clue. I have had to hunt for people in the East End, and I have found out that there is only one way of doing it. I had the Keswick police to help me—two men who know the neighbourhood for a good many miles round, and with their help I soon discovered traces of him. The arrival of an invalid gentleman and his friend at a lonely farmhouse on the further side of Butter-mere had been heard of at an inn in the neighbourhood—an inn used by excursionists in summer, but almost deserted at this time of the year. We found the man who drove them there. Not one of the flymen who ordinarily meet the trains, but a man from a livery yard, engaged by telegram overnight. Had one of the station flies been employed, we should have made our discovery much sooner, for naturally my first inquiries were among those men."

"What kind of a place—what kind of people?" asked Sibyl.

"A decent farmhouse; very lonely, a place to hide in—decent kindly people, anxious to do their best for their charge, I believe.

He had been sent to them by Mr. Carpew, whom they had known years ago, when they had a farm near St. Jude's—a farm on your father's estate. They knew nothing of the man who brought him, had never seen him before to their knowledge, but they knew Mr. Carpew, and were willing to oblige him. They were to be paid for the gentleman's board and lodging, and for a man to look after him, and all that was wanted was seclusion and secrecy. The poor gentleman had relatives who wanted to put him in a lunatic asylum, and who would perhaps make out a case of lunacy against him if they could get hold of him, though he was by no means a lunatic. Mrs. Holloway, the farmer's wife, seems a kindly soul, and her sympathies were aroused by this story."

"Thank God, he has not fallen among thieves—so far as these people are concerned. Are you taking me to him—now?"

"I am taking you to the hotel, where I have engaged rooms for you. I hope you will rest quietly for to-night—and to-morrow morning we will start for the farm as early as you like."

"Why should I wait till to-morrow? I am longing to see him—to know the worst about him. You tell me he is ill—a broken man. Your manner implies that he is very ill. He may die before to-morrow morning; and then I shall go down to my grave without having seen the man my foolish unreasoning love helped to ruin."

"Lady Penrith, you must not look at this story in that light. No one can tell what influence surrounding circumstances may have had upon him. It is possible that he was doomed to suffer as he has done—that in the brightest lot his fate would have been the same. And if he committed the crime for which he was arrested——"

"No, no, no! He did not commit that crime. Don't speak of it. I am angry at the thought of my own folly—the web of lies in which I was caught. Let us go to the farm at once. We can stop at the hotel, just to get rid of Ferriby and the luggage, and then drive on."

"Not on a dark night like this. The distance is too long. The drive would not be without danger, and you would see the patient at his worst, startled by such a late arrival."

"I want to see him at his worst. I want to know all he has suffered in those long, dreary years."

"But think what the shock might be for him. He must be prepared for seeing you."

"Is he not prepared already? Have you told him nothing of my anxiety about his fate—my bitter grief for his sufferings?"

"Yes, I have spoken of you; but perhaps not enough. Be assured it will be better for you and for him that you should defer the meeting till to-morrow."

"You have been so good to me that I cannot disobey you," Sibyl answered, with a sigh. "What is the name of the hotel where I am to stop?" she asked.

"The Lodore. I thought you would like to be by the lake, and away from the town."

"Yes. I gave them no address when I was leaving. I was afraid Penrith might follow me, and interfere in some manner. I must go back to-morrow afternoon, when we have decided what is to be done."

"Has Mr. Mountford no near relations? Is he quite alone in the world?"

"Quite alone. He has no relation nearer than my uncle, Lord Braemar, and they are only second cousins, a relationship which does not count for much in a large family like my grandfather's. I was interested in him for another reason over and above relationship. His father loved my mother—hopelessly—loved her after he was bound to another. His son told me the story of that sad, hopeless love. Oh, Mr. Coverdale, forgive me," she said, startled by a stifled sob from the man sitting by her side; "pray forgive me if I have touched upon some sad story of your own——"

"No, no; it was nothing," he said, hastily. "That kind of story—the idea of a hopeless love, a hopeless grief, manfully battled with—is always pathetic. You remember Warrington's story—a mere episode in 'Pendennis.'² It moves one more than all the rest of the book, doesn't it? Ah, here we are at the Lodore; and now I shall leave you to get as much rest as you can till to-morrow morning."

The carriage stopped in front of the hotel; Lady Penrith's maid alighted; the porter took the luggage; lights shone brightly in the hall within, with all the stir and bustle of an important arrival. Head waiter and head chamber-maid were in eager attendance to show the way to her ladyship's rooms.

A titled visitor in that dead season of the year was worthy of exceptional respect.

"I am staying at the Keswick Hotel," Coverdale said, as he bade good night; "but I will be with you as early as you like to-morrow, with a carriage and a good pair of horses. You had better bring your maid. The journey will be long and tiring; and if we should have a hopelessly wet day——"

"I am not afraid of bad weather. Would eight o'clock be too early for you to be here?"

"Not too early for me. If I can get the livery people to be astir early, I will be with you at eight. Only I beg that you will try to rest to-night. They have given you rooms looking towards the lake, and I hope the sound of the waterfall will be only loud enough to serve as a slumber-song."

"Do not think of me. You have taken worlds of trouble. I don't know how I shall ever thank you."

"Don't thank me. I have to take much more trouble at the East End for duty's sake. It will be my most cherished memory that you looked to me for help in your anxieties. Good night."

He did not even stop to shake hands with her, but left her with a stiff bow which seemed curiously at variance with the sup- pressed emotion in his voice. He went back to the carriage through the rain, and she heard him drive away, leaving her with the long evening before her in a strange hotel.

A two hours' drive through the morning mists brought Lady Penrith and her companion to a solitary farmhouse hidden amongst the hills, a spot more lonely than even St. Jude's Vicarage; but this rustic homestead, with its group of barns and stable-yard in the background, and its little garden, where autumn flowers still lingered, had a more cheerful aspect than the straggling stone house at St. Jude's, with its walled garden and gloomy firs.

Brandon Mountford! Yes, this was Brandon Mountford; this tall wasted figure; this hollow-eyed countenance, with the down- ward melancholy lines about the mouth, and the nervous contrac- tion of the brow, and the wasted hands that lay in helpless inaction on the arms of the chair. Sibyl stood gazing at him in awe-stricken silence, almost as she might have looked at a ghost. She could find no words to say to him—no words of pity or affection. Speech seemed frozen. Vainly had Coverdale sought to prepare her for the shock. The anguish of the spectacle was not lessened by anything that he had told her.

The silence lasted for minutes. Coverdale heard the old clock in the passage ticking solemnly on, as if it were measuring out a long day, or a long lifetime, so hopeless seemed the duration of that agony; the woman standing statue-like, white as marble; the man sitting with eyes that gazed idly out beyond the open window, across the little garden, where the asters and marigolds made a bank of gaudy colour, to the grey dimness of great rugged hills.

The mists had cleared from the lower landscape, and the air in the shelter of the hills had a summer-like softness.

At last, over the blank melancholy of that altered face there crept a slow vague smile, and Brandon Mountford lifted his eyes towards Sibyl.

"I knew that you would come," he said slowly. "I knew that you would understand my message—though I have almost lost the trick of writing."

"Brandon, you know me, you know me," she cried, sinking on her knees by his chair, clasping one of his wasted hands, deadly cold to her touch.

"Know you—yes, of course."

"You have been cruelly treated: but that is all over now. All that this world can give of happiness shall be yours. It shall be my care—the object of my life to atone for your sufferings."

"No, no, there has been no cruelty. It was my doom—the curse laid upon me. What could they do but hide me—hide me from my fellow-men—a wretch—a murderer? I have suffered, but I have had my dreams—dreams of that wild country where I was so happy—centuries ago—centuries of dreams—the river—the forest. And I have dreamt that you and I were happy there—you and I sitting together by the camp fire. I have seen your face in the red light! And then the fire has changed to the fire of hell, and I have suffered like a soul in everlasting agony. I have suffered for my crime."

In broken sentences, with piteous entreaty, she protested against his self-denunciation.

"It is a dream," she said; "a horrible dream. You had nothing to do with poor Marie's death—except the misfortune to be the first to find her. You have been the victim of a diabolical conspiracy—a plot to hide away an innocent man in order to prevent suspicion falling on the real murderer."

He looked at her curiously, as if lapsing into a reverie in which her words hardly reached him—looked at her wonderingly, as if her face were strange to him. And then his eyes wandered away from that earnest, eager face to the gaudy autumn flowers and the great grave hills veiled in thin white mist. Alas! it was but too evident that the shadows which clouded his reason only cleared away now and again for a brief space, as the autumn haze parted and patches of the hillside showed clear and bright through a rift in the veil.

"It is not wise to talk to him of that dreadful event," said Coverdale. "What we have to consider is what is best to be done for him. The doctor will be here at twelve o'clock. You may be glad to hear his opinion from his own lips."

"Yes. I should like to hear what he thinks. But ought we not to have a specialist? We might telegraph to Edinburgh."

"There will be time for that by-and-by. Will you come into the garden with me——"

"What, leave him alone?"

"He has been accustomed to sitting alone. The woman of the house is within call. I should like to have a quiet talk with you out yonder."

Sibyl did not answer him, scarcely heard him, perhaps. She was looking at Brandon Mountford in agonised contemplation. Whatever there had been of intellect or of power in his face a few minutes ago had vanished. Weakness, physical and mental, was all that could be read in that face now, a countenance of sickly pallor, every muscle relaxed, dull misery expressed in every languid line.

This was what solitude and silence, the slow decay of monotonous years had done for Brandon Mountford.

If Sibyl could have looked back along that dark line of years— if some magic mirror could have shown her pictures of the past, what would she have seen?

First a strong man caught in a trap, fighting with his captors for release into the free air of heaven, then suddenly subjugated and rendered powerless, not by their violence or their persuasion, but by the fell disease which the horrors and agitations of his life had intensified, which set its grip upon body and brain with a force never felt till then.

She would have seen one seizure following upon another, with brief intervals of languor and exhaustion, till strength was sapped and intellect weakened—weakened, but not destroyed. She would have seen a brave man submissive as a child to a bondage from which he could have broken had he so willed—submissive because despairing. He was told that he was a murderer, that a warrant was out against him, that to escape from that dull prison house, that life of hopeless monotony, might be to doom himself to the gallows, or at best to the imprisonment of a State mad-house, a felon among felons, a lunatic among lunatics. She would have seen him—as his brain weakened, and the power of consecutive thought gradually diminished—fooled by the hope of release. He should be got away, later, when the coast was clear—should be got on board a steamer and drafted away to that dark continent of which he dreamt so often, where liberty and life were waiting for him, among the dark faces, under the tropical sun. Cozened from day to day, and month to month, and year to year, with that reiterated "by-and-by," she would have seen him turning the pages of books that he had once loved—reading and forgetting what he had read; she would have seen him gradually losing count of days and months and years, till time was one long blank, and his life knew no change save the change from heat to cold, and back to heat again—from sunshine pouring in at his open windows to the early darkness of endless winter nights—from the dark, iron blank where the firelight had leapt and sparkled so merrily, to the welcome fireglow coming back again to fill the dull black void. No changes save the rain whipping the widow panes—the wind roaring over the distant sea, or shrieking in the chimney. There was thunder sometimes—a thunder peal that shook the house, and made him wish that the roof would crack and the walls crumble, and bury him among dust and ruin, and so make an end of this dull blank space and time which seemed to be endless—infinite space—infinite time. He repeated the words sometimes as if they had been a formula—"Who disputes that either is infinite? I have proved them both," he said; for not only did time seem endless, immeasurable, but in his frequent periods of hallucination space also seemed without limit, and his weary spirit wandered in worlds that knew neither change nor boundary, neither night nor day—

dim greyness, peopled by silent ghosts—an endless labyrinth, or a wide stretch of barren sand leading to a horizon that was always the same, and yet for ever receding. The commonest dreamer in a dream of a minute can invent and people a place unknown to his waking intelligence—but in the diseased brain that dreaming power, increased by a hundred-fold, becomes a source of unspeakable suffering, a well-spring of horror.

And what of his more rational hours; those longer intervals between one attack and another, when there was time for the brain to regain some touch of reasoning power? Alas! those hours of reason and remembrance were the worst of all, for in those he believed himself Marie Arnold's murderer, recalled the image of the corpse in the wood, brooded over the cruelty of such an end to that bright young life, and the shame and disgrace of the crime— disgrace reflecting upon all who were of his name and blood.

"Better that I should rot in this seclusion," he told himself in those waking hours, "than that I should go out into the world to set men talking of my crime. Yet if it were possible—if I could get clear of England without scandal—could get back to Zambesi and my faithful Kaffir boys, they would hardly think worse of me for that story of bloodshed. They would only pity me as the victim of witchcraft."

And in such an interval, when his custodian came to him with the meal which only Mr. Carpew or his wife ever served to the mysterious "boarder," Brandon Mountford would urge the fulfilment of that reiterated promise. Surely the time had come when he might go away. Whatever watch had been kept upon the house must have ceased long ago. He had lost all count of time, but he knew that it must be long—and he looked down at his clothes, which had been replaced by ready-made garments more than once since he came there, and which yet were threadbare and worn at the edges. He looked at his wasted hands, where the muscles had been so firm and the flesh so hard and brown, in those old days by the salmon river. Yes, it was long, very long. Suspicion, watchfulness, must have been worn out long ago. Why could he not get away?

The Vicar had various excuses. The danger was not over. His lodger was a marked man. Any movements in that lonely spot would excite curiosity. And then there was the question of money.

It would cost a good deal of money to get him out of England—to pay his passage to the Cape.

"And you wouldn't like to land there penniless," said the Vicar.

Penniless, yes—penniless under those stars. He would not fear. Besides, he had friends in London—friends who would gladly help him—men to whom money was of no account—if he could remember their names, or where to find them.

Ah, there was the agony! He could not remember. Names, localities, even the faces of the past were lost in the thick mists of forgetfulness. Faces haunted him—faces appeared to him—rooms in which he seemed to have lived—gardens whose every tree and shrub seemed familiar—but he could not distinguish memories from dreams—the things which had been, and were real even to-day, from the things that his fancy invented.

If Sibyl could have known how, through the clouds that darkened mind and memory, one image had shone like a star, unchanged and unforgotten, and that image hers; if she could have heard his appeal to his gaoler, repeated day after day, "Let me see her. Has she had my letter? Have you sent a messenger to Ellerslie, as you said you would?" and how, day after day, he was put off with excuses and postponements. He was told that she had married Lord Penrith, and was a leading light in the London world. It was implied that she had forgotten her unhappy kinsman, and was indifferent to his fate. She was abroad—in the South of France—an assertion that had been justified by her actual absence in several winters—but the same story had been told him when she was at Killander Castle. To-morrow and to-morrow. There had always been the same promise that his desire should be realised by-and-by—and as the brain weakened he had grown to believe in that by-and-by, and to wait and watch for her coming.

He had written many such scrawls as the one which reached her hands—but on that last occasion he had been fortunate in his messenger, a starveling Jack of all trades who lived in a hovel at St. Jude's, and did odd jobs for the farmers. The key had been left in the lock of the garden door for once in a way, and Brandon, who was allowed to walk alone in this joyless enclosure, had opened the door unobserved and gone out. He had no idea of escape now, having been told that escape was hopeless—he was too weak and helpless even to contemplate any act requiring prompt decision or sustained exertion. He only wanted to see Sibyl—to find some messenger who would carry his appeal.

The garden door opened on the heath, but he could hear the sound of a pick in the road a little way off, and could see a bent figure breaking stones. It was the Jack of all trades doing a spell of parish work—and to him Brandon Mountford entrusted his message—hastily written upon a fly leaf torn out of the book he had been reading, as he stood on the windy road.

He entreated the man to find Lady Penrith—to put that bit of paper into her hand—her hand, and no other. He offered his watch as payment in advance for this service, but the man would not take it. The rough peasant was touched with awe and pity at sight of that spectral face, and was too honest to accept so valuable a gift. Half-witted himself, he may have had some instinctive sympathy with Brandon's clouded mind. He promised that the letter should reach Lady Penrith, whatever trouble it might cost him to find her, and he kept his word with a dogged faithfulness that would have done honour to the strongest intellect.

And thus, by the accident of a key left in a lock—but one act of forgetfulness on Mr. Carpew's part—Brandon Mountford had been released from a living grave.

"Have you made any plan for his future?" Coverdale asked, as he and Sibyl walked up and down beside the privet hedge which divided the garden from the road.

"I thought if we could take him to Ellerslie he might be happy there. He could have good servants. I could rely upon Mrs. Morison's care of him——"

"Not to be thought of for a moment!" said Coverdale, decisively. "In the first place, Ellerslie would recall the tragedy which changed the current of his life; the effect upon his mind might be disastrous."

"True. I forgot that. I have lived down the horror of those associations myself, and I forgot. Yes; you are right."

"Ellerslie would never do. Remember the warrant against him. Wretched wreck as he is, he might be put through all the torture of a magistrate's inquiry—might be indicted for murder,

and have to stand his trial—the result, a State madhouse. Ellerslie
would not do."

"No, no; the risk would be too great. Then what do you
advise?"

"Leave him where he is for the present; perhaps till the spring.
I have made inquiries about these people, and they bear an excellent character in the neighbourhood—the man a hard-working
tenant farmer, whose father and grandfather worked on the land
before him; the woman honest and God-fearing. Their connection
with Mr. Carpew is simple enough. He was curate at the nearest
parish church for a year before Lord Penrith gave him the living of
St. Jude's, and during that year he became very friendly with the
farmer and his wife. They are kindly people. Mr. Mountford will
be perfectly safe under this roof till we can think of something
better."

"But what if the men who brought him here should remove
him somewhere else, and we should lose sight of him again?"

"I don't think that will be attempted. In the first place, we must
engage a trustworthy attendant, accustomed to such cases, who
must be responsible to us for his safety, with a man under him, to
relieve guard. I shall go straight from here to St. Jude's, and after I
have talked with Mr. Carpew I don't think there will be any further
attempt to interfere with this poor gentleman's liberty. The Vicar
of St. Jude's will see the peril of his conduct, when I put it before
him, as I mean to do."

"You may frighten him—but he is only the tool of a wickeder
man—a man who will not hesitate at a crime."

And then Sibyl urged the necessity of removing Brandon
Mountford out of the power and beyond the knowledge of the
man who had hidden him from his fellow-men in order to sustain
the suspicion—the almost certainty—that he was the murderer of
Marie Arnold.

"So long as everybody at Ardliston believed in Brandon's guilt
no one took the trouble to look anywhere else for the criminal,"
said Sibyl. "That must have been the motive of his imprisonment.
To leave him in the power of Hubert Urquhart would be madness;
and how can we be sure of his safety so long as that wretch knows
where to find him?"

"Mr. Urquhart is your husband's brother. It seems a hard thing to suppose him such an unmitigated scoundrel."

"Ask my husband for his brother's character, if you doubt my estimate of him."

"But surely he would not suspect his brother of murder?"

"Perhaps not; but he would tell you he is vile enough to make any suspicion justifiable where he is concerned. Dear Mr. Coverdale, there is only one thing to be done. We must get Brandon out of this man's custody and into our own. Let us run all risks as to that warrant of ten years ago, and take him to Ellerslie. He will be safe there with my housekeeper and my father's trusted secretary, Andrew Orlebar, a man who knows the whole story, and who would go through fire and water to help me."

"You cannot take him to Ellerslie, to the scene of the murder, without arousing curiosity among your neighbours. However few they are, there are enough of them to talk, and to revive the old story and the old suspicions. If a few days hence he were to be arrested, you would be sorry——"

"Yes, yes. You are right. It might be dangerous. Oh, Mr. Coverdale, what are we to do? We seem hemmed round with difficulties. Here is a life—a poor ruined life—which has been given back to me as if out of the grave. Am I to jeopardise it—lose it again? Think, think what can be done. Something must be done to save him from the villain who plotted against him, who made me his accomplice, in my blind folly."

There was a silence, a silence that seemed interminable to Sibyl's anxiety, as John Coverdale walked slowly up and down the shingly path by her side. She could see that he was deep in thought, and would not interrupt his cogitations by a word.

Her patience was rewarded presently. He had thought out a plan, which he submitted to her briefly.

"My father has a shooting-box in Argyllshire. He was there with some friends in August and September, but the place is deserted now, except for a keeper with his wife, and a few shooting dogs. I will telegraph to the hospital at Carlisle for an attendant, wait here till he comes, and when he comes start at once for Scotland with Mr. Mountford, if he will trust himself to me. I can instal him in my father's cottage, in the care of the keeper and his wife, who are old servants, and will implicitly obey my orders."

"There could be no better plan, if Lord Workington will lend you his cottage."

"No difficulty about that. A telegram will settle the business. I must wait here till the attendant comes from Carlisle. You can return to the Castle this afternoon, and you can send my telegrams from the nearest office on your way back."

"But to leave you here—to take so much of your time."

"Don't mind that. I was to have been in London to-morrow afternoon; but one of my messages will be to the friend who is taking my duty, asking him to give me one more Sunday. By Monday or Tuesday I hope to have established Mr. Mountford at the Hut, and from there I shall go straight to London. You may believe that I shall not abandon him till I am assured of his safety."

"I believe in your wisdom and goodness as I believe in Heaven. I can never thank you enough for what you are doing. He will thank you, perhaps, some day—better than I can—if the power to think ever comes back—thank you for life saved, reason restored."

And then she gave him a cheque for a hundred pounds, which she had written before leaving the hotel, for travelling and other expenses. She begged him to be lavish—to use the power of gold to the utmost. She would send further cheques as they were needed.

He smiled his grave sad smile at her eagerness.

"It would be an impertinence on my part to refuse to let you pay any charges I may incur on your kinsman's account," he said; "but there will not be much money wanted. And now may I send for your carriage and your maid? You must be anxious to be on your way home again. I can write the telegrams while the carriage is being brought round."

"Yes, there is no time to lose. You will tell the house-surgeon at Carlisle that the attendant is wanted for a friend of Lord Penrith. My husband is a supporter of the hospital, and the authorities will do their utmost to oblige him. But I am to see the doctor," she said, looking at her watch. "It is past twelve, and he was to be here at twelve. I must wait to hear what he says about the journey to Scotland. And I may see Mr. Mountford once more before I go, may I not?"

"Certainly, if you like."

Sibyl went alone to the parlour where Mountford was sitting by the fire, while the farmer's wife, a kindly-looking woman, was laying the table for a meal.

"The gentleman has a very poor appetite," she explained, as she cut strips of toast to accompany a basin of broth. "It's difficult to get him to take his nourishment. He's nothing but skin and bone, poor soul."

Poor soul! Pity, the pity for a wreck of humanity,—that was Brandon Mountford's portion now.

He looked up with a sudden flush, and a brightening of the haggard eyes.

"Ah!" he cried, as if seeing Sibyl for the first time, "my messenger found you. Oh, my beloved, how I have waited and watched for your coming."

He stretched out his wasted hands to her in passionate greeting. He had no memory of half an hour ago, when he had greeted her with almost the same words. The evidence of a decayed intellect cut her to the quick.

The doctor came into the room at this moment—a young man, but serious and intelligent.

He looked at his patient, sat by his side for about ten minutes, questioning and observing him; and then went out into the garden with Lady Penrith.

"Be frank with me," she entreated. "It is a very bad case, is it not?"

"Yes, it is a bad case."

"One hardly likes to call any disease incurable nowadays. Medical science has taken to working miracles. Surgeons are cutting epilepsy out of the brain as they cut cancer out of the body."

"And with as much, or as little, success."

"With the same possibility of success and the same hazard of failure, perhaps."

"He ought to be seen by a specialist—a man who has made epilepsy the study of his life."

"Yes, it would be well, by-and-by, for the satisfaction of his friends, that this poor gentleman should have the benefit of the highest opinion. But there will be time enough for that when his bodily strength is restored, if it can be restored, by care and good nursing."

"You find him seriously, dangerously ill?"

"Not dangerously ill, but in a very low and feeble condition; in a state which would make any illness dangerous—a chill, a fever, an attack of bronchitis. He would have no resisting power."

"He has been cruelly treated, kept in worse seclusion than if he had been in a madhouse—solitude, silence, dull rooms, no change of air and scene."

"All very bad, no doubt, in such a case as his."

"And now it is proposed to take him a long journey—to Argyllshire. Can he bear such a journey?"

"Certainly, as travelling is managed nowadays. He might be taken at night in a sleeping carriage, with the greatest care, and with some one in attendance to administer stimulants. There need be no risk in such a journey, weak as he is, if the drive from here to Keswick is not made too fatiguing."

"Care shall be taken—the utmost care. We are sending to Carlisle for a nurse, but if you could spare the time to go with him, to superintend the journey, your fee should be anything you like to name. In a case of this kind there can be no question as to expense."

"You are very good. If he were to travel at night I think I might spare the time from my other patients; and my fee should not be exorbitant. My practice is not a very remunerative one, and I have no pressing case just now which would make my absence hazardous. I need not be away more than eighteen hours, if we travel by the night mail."

"Everything shall be arranged to suit your convenience. Your presence will be a comfort to me and to Mr. Coverdale, who is taking my poor cousin to Scotland. And you will see the attendant, and give him full instructions as to treatment," continued Sibyl.

"I will do everything that thought or experience can suggest."

"Then my mind will be at ease about him. Please write to me immediately after your return, and I shall have the pleasure of sending you a cheque."

The doctor smiled, for he did not know even the name of this beautiful woman, whose earnestness and evident affection for that ruined life impressed him deeply. He asked no questions, for he knew enough about Lord Workington's son to know that he had to do with people of good position.

The carriage was waiting in the accommodation lane which made the only approach to the homestead. Her ladyship's maid was there, and there were wraps and rugs enough in the open carriage for a journey to St. Petersburg.

Once again Sibyl went back to the farmhouse parlour, and alone with Brandon Mountford this time, bent over his chair, and pressed her lips to his wan forehead.

Oh, God! the memory of that first kiss in the garden at Ellerslie, before the coming of sorrow. This might be her last memory of him. Who can tell? He was passing out of her sight once more. Who could tell if life would ever bring them face to face again?

"Life is so full of sad surprises," she thought, as she drove away from that quiet hollow in the hills, remembering the sudden trouble of ten years ago, and in no wise foreshadowing that terrible surprise which was waiting for her within the hour.

CHAPTER XXIX

THE FURIES ON THE HEARTH

"Fatal Accident to the Earl of Penrith." That was the sentence—in large capitals upon a newspaper board—which caught Sibyl's eye as she drove through Keswick on her way to the railway station. Absorbed in thought, her eyes looked at street, and shop windows, and people, seeing things, but not noticing them. Her husband's name startled her from that profound reverie; that sad comparison of past and present.

Fatal accident! What accident? And the word fatal! What did that mean? She called to the coachman to stop, but he had hardly pulled up his horses when she let herself out of the carriage and rushed into the shop. "The newspaper," she asked, holding out a trembling hand—"the paper with the account—of the accident——"

The somewhat sleepy shopkeeper, roused from a droning conversation with a fellow-townsman, wondered at this unknown lady's pallor and agitation. He stared at her as he handed her the newspaper, and made no remonstrance when she left the shop without paying for it.

"Queer," he remarked, as he went on serving stationery to the customer whose business and conversation had been interrupted. "That must be somebody connected with Lord Penrith. I shouldn't wonder if it was his wife."

The carriage had not moved on yet. Lady Penrith was sitting where the two men could watch her, as she tore open the paper, looking hurriedly up and down the columns till she came to what she wanted.

Fatal accident! What did the word fatal mean? A limb shattered—the loss of an eye—some irreparable injury, which would make life less fair to the sufferer? Or must that word signify something worse than lameness or blindness? Had the word but one significance? Must it mean the end of all things?

How long it seemed before she found the column she wanted in the eight pages of that flimsy local paper! At last, here it was, headed in large type, at the top of a column—

"We regret to report the death of the Earl of Penrith, who was shot yesterday evening while trying to pass through a gap in a hedge on his own estate, at a short distance from Killander Castle. It is supposed that the trigger of the gun was caught by a twig in the quick set hedge, and that his lordship's injuries were immediately fatal. He had been dead some time when he was found lying in the gap, with his gun near him.

"The earl was in the prime of life, having been born," etc., etc., etc.

"Drive on to the station, as fast as you can go—stop, the man must be paid for his paper," said Sibyl, handing her purse to Ferriby, who had alighted from the carriage, and was standing at the door, watching her mistress's agitated countenance. "There is no hurry; the train will not start any sooner because I am anxious to be at home. We shall have a long time to wait."

That delay seemed eternal to Lady Penrith, sitting in the waiting-room, at first in solitude and silence, then amidst the bustle of fidgety travellers coming in and going out.

Dead! The husband with whom she had sat at breakfast yesterday morning, in that formal intercourse which seemed to the outside world more like an armed neutrality than a happy marriage. They had always been polite to each other; they had never frustrated each other's wishes in large things or in small; each had enjoyed perfect liberty to take life as pleasantly as possible; but each had known, and had not even affected not to know, that love went for nothing in their union. Penrith had kept the promise of his courtship. He had been, according to his lights, a good husband.

Dead! Could it be true? Was not that paragraph written in error, on the first hasty report of the disaster, the extent of the calamity exaggerated by outsiders in the confusion of the household? Well, she would know all in a few hours. It had never occurred to her in her agitation that she might have telegraphed to the Castle, and received a reply to her questions half-way on her journey. But during the last five minutes of waiting Ferriby reminded her that it would be necessary to telegraph to the stables for her carriage to meet her at the station, and Ferriby ran to the office with a hastily-written message.

The inquest had been held at noon, and all was tranquil at the Castle when Sibyl arrived. Silence and gloom prevailed in the darkened house—a silence and a darkness as of the grave where Lord Penrith was to lie before many days and nights were over.

There had been very little trouble for coroner or jury, very little room for question or conjecture, nothing mysterious in the accident they were required to investigate, no room for difference of opinion. The gun lay on the table before them. It was passed from hand to hand by-and-by, and those who handled it were more impressed by the beauty of the weapon than by any need of considering how it had happened to be fatal to its possessor. The catastrophe was so commonplace, so common, a repetition of old experiences, and pointed only to the familiar moral that it is better for a man to lose a few seconds in reloading his gun, even if he miss a bird by that brief delay, than to risk carrying a loaded gun over rough ground in a long tramp homeward.

Lord Penrith had saved himself a little trouble, and had thrown away his life. That is how the coroner and the jury read the story of his death. A sad pity—a man still in the prime of life—"hard as nails"—a fine shot, a splendid horseman, and in the enjoyment of an estate which it had been the business of her ladyship's life to bring to perfection.

He had died childless—that was the worst of it; and his title and estate would pass to Hubert Urquhart, a man of the worst possible reputation—gambler, blackleg, profligate, a man who at the age when a son of a local magnate is generally liked and looked up to in the neighbourhood of his father's house, had been hated and despised—a youth who had always preferred bad company to good, who had taken his pleasures grossly at rustic race meetings and village fairs; a man who, while consorting with jockeys and small horse-dealers, had shown no more respect for his humbler neighbours than if he had been at Unyanyemby or Ujiji.[1] Never had a young patrician been more heartily disliked than Hubert Urquhart in Cumberland. He had not even the good qualities that should have gone with his defects. He had affected low company without ever achieving popularity, even in the saddle-room or at the village inn. There had been a hardness about him—the Urquhart hardness—which gave a sting to his jests, and made his familiarity with inferiors brutal instead of friendly. He had cultivated the company of grooms and horse-dealers because they amused him; but he had never disguised his absolute contempt for them as a lower order of creatures.

Mr. Urquhart appeared on the scene an hour after Lady Penrith's return. He had come post haste from Perth, where he had spent the previous night, on his way to the Highlands, and where he had seen the news of his brother's death in the morning papers. He sent his card to his sister-in-law, begging her to see him, to which request she replied in a letter of three lines.

"No; not to-day. Three or four days hence I will see you. I have something to say about the past, and your part in it."

The funeral was over. All the late earl's tenantry and all that there was of gentle blood within twenty miles of the castle had been represented in the long line of mourning carriages that followed the open hearse, where the earl's coronet, on the crimson velvet pall, was touched with gleams of wintry sunlight as the cortége moved slowly along the moorland road. Crimson and gold made a splendour in the cold grey nave of the church at Cargill, where for many generations the Urquharts had been buried in a vault underneath the chancel. That subterranean burial-place had been closed for the last forty years, and Sibyl's husband was to lie in his father's grave in the little cemetery on the hillside, at the end of the village street.

Hubert Urquhart was chief mourner, and returned to the Castle to hear the reading of the will, a business promptly despatched, for the will was of the briefest. The late earl had only his surplus income to dispose of, and his bequests were limited to a legacy of a thousand pounds to his niece, Coralie Urquhart, a hundred pounds each to his valet and coachman, and fifty pounds to every servant who had been five years in his service. His personal effects, books, pictures, plate, and jewellery, not heirlooms, he left without exception to his wife. To his brother and heir presumptive he bequeathed not so much as a snuff-box or a walking-stick.

Hubert Urquhart stood with his back to the fire, listening to these details in a gloomy silence. He made no remark when the lawyer finished, and looked at him doubtfully, waiting his lordship's instructions.

"Thank you, Grant," he said at last, as if waking from a reverie. "The will is eminently discreet. My brother had very little to leave, except such things as were bought with his wife's money. It is right those things should revert to her. Go to your luncheon, Grant. I shall smoke my cigar quietly here. I seldom eat at this time of day."

"But your lordship has had an exhausting morning. Wouldn't it be better——"

"To eat a heavy meal. No, my dear fellow. But you can tell a servant to bring me a brandy and soda. Good day to you, if we don't meet again."

This was a shrewd indication of his lordship's desire that they should not meet again. The solicitor put the will in his pocket, and left the room without another word. There was a new stateliness about his client, whose affairs had compelled occasional resort to him in the past, and who had been a good deal more familiar in those impecunious days.

"The new earl is putting on side," mused Mr. Grant; "but he'll soon be coming to me to settle with his creditors. They'll want twenty shillings in the pound now, and he won't want to give them as much. I wish I'd bought up a little of his lordship's paper. It might have been had dirt-cheap last week."

The new Lord Penrith smoked his cigar by the library fire, sitting in a low armchair, in a restful attitude, his long legs stretched straight before him, his hands thrust deep into his pockets, his head bent a little. Every now and then his eyes glanced upward, with a curious look at the spacious room, and the walls of books which nobody ever read. The late earl's writing-table stood in front of the great Tudor window, with the seals upon all the drawers, and all the scattered litter of life cleared away from the top, leaving the blank emptiness of death.

It was something to be master in such a house as this—and the house near Berkeley Square—the house whose doors had been shut against him for the last ten years, just as inexorably as the door of this Cumbrian fortress. No more shutting of doors against him, Hubert Urquhart; no more empty pockets and importunate Jews, threatening every hurtful process that was left in the law of debtor and creditor. His troubles were over. He could stretch his legs by his fireside, smoke the best cigars that tropical Spain could produce, take his ease. The days of difficulty were done.

"You hadn't done me a single kindness in your ten years of prosperity," he said, apostrophising his brother's portrait, which looked down at him from the panel above the mantelpiece. "You had a good innings, and an easy death. Do you expect me to be sorry for you, I wonder, if there be consciousness or knowledge in the place where you are?"

The door opened, and the butler ushered in Lady Penrith. Urquhart dropped his cigar in the fender, and started to his feet. He had courted this interview, but it was not the less a shock when the moment came.

He faltered something confusedly, and drew a chair to the hearth.

"I am not going to sit down," Sibyl said icily. "I told you I wanted to see you after the funeral. This is your house now. My carriage is at the door, and as soon as I have said what I have to say I shall leave the Castle for ever."

"My dear Lady Penrith, I hope you understand that this house, and any other house which I possess, is laid at your feet."

"Pray spare yourself the trouble of making fine speeches," she answered, with a look which should have blighted him. "You know very well that nothing would induce me to enter any house that sheltered you, unless I came there to denounce you, as I might denounce you—as I would, had I not some regard for the name you bear; as I would denounce you, even at the sacrifice of that name, if my faith in God's justice were not stronger than my faith in a British jury."

The ghastly change in the brazen audacity of his face told her that he was hard hit. He gnawed his nether lip for a few moments in silence, looking up at her from under bent brows, with eyes that would have killed her if hatred could kill.

"What do you mean?" he muttered huskily, after that pause.

"I mean that you are twice a murderer."

He sprang forward a step or two, with his arm lifted and fist clenched. It cost him no small effort of will and muscle not to bring that clenched fist down upon the fair pale face, like a sledge-hammer. He knew that one such blow would kill her and he would have liked to kill her. He longed to see her dead at his feet.

"I am not afraid of your violence. You could do me no more harm than you have done if you were to kill me. You spoilt my life. You took all the hope and love and gladness out of my happy girlhood, so happy till you blighted it. You murdered my adopted sister, and broke my father's heart."

"I—I—murdered her? Great God, hear what this woman says!"

"I believe there is a God who hears and will punish your crimes. It costs you nothing, nothing to call upon a God in whom you do not believe. I say that it was your hand which killed Marie Arnold—it was you who wanted to marry her—wanted money with her—had tried to make a bargain with my father, and had been refused—and, goaded by her contempt for you, that devil of rage and cruelty which has always looked out of your cold, cruel eyes, took possession of you, and you murdered her. And then, when Fate brought Brandon Mountford to the spot, and circumstantial evidence pointed to him as the murderer, it was your interest to confirm that suspicion by every means in your power—best of all by getting him out of the way—by making him a fugitive, a prison-breaker. And to do this you worked upon my feelings—you took advantage of my love for him, my ignorance of life and its responsibilities. You made me the instrument of his destruction. And then came your second murder—the merciless imprisonment of a man for whom, of all

men, a free existence under God's sky meant health and life—you
made his days and nights a dreary blank—his world a prison of four
walls and half an acre of gloomy garden. If there was ever murder
done on earth that was murder."

"Oh, you call that murder, do you, Lady Penrith?" said Urquhart, with a saturnine grin. "I saved a homicidal lunatic from the
gallows—or the criminal ward in a State asylum—I put him quietly
out of sight, where he was taken excellent care of by an educated
gentleman and his wife—and you call that murder?"

"I say that it was a viler crime than even your murder of Marie
Arnold. That may have been the work of a moment's fury, an
ungovernable impulse of man's wickedness—but the slow torture
of years—the living death which you, the murderer, inflicted upon
an innocent man——"

"A man who was taken red-handed by the side of his victim.
My dear Lady Penrith, raving such as this can admit of no reply.
No sane man would take the trouble to argue with you."

He turned his back upon her as he bent down to draw the
smouldering logs together. Beads of sweat had been standing on
his forehead a few minutes ago; but he was calm and self-possessed
now, and his hard, sharply-cut face wore its old look of effrontery.

"I am informed that your friend has been removed from the
quiet retreat in mountain air, and amidst fine scenery, where I placed
him when it was considered that a change might be useful."

"A change—after ten years of dismal monotony! A change—
after mind and memory had been blotted out in that dreary
solitude!"

"Lady Penrith, you are not a doctor, and I am not here to
discuss Mr. Mountford's case with you. If you want to let the light
in upon his history—mental or otherwise—you had better let the
warrant be executed which was issued against him ten years ago
as a suspected murderer. If you believe in his innocence, you have
taken a very inconsistent course in spiriting him away to some
hiding-place of your own selection. I concealed his existence—in
his own interests and yours. Moreover, the thing was done at your
husband's instigation, and with your husband's full approval."

Had she been looking at him she would have seen the conception of that lie flash across his face as he began the last sentence.

Penrith was dead, and might be made responsible for everything.

"God is very patient with you," she said, with a quivering lip, "but I can endure no more."

She turned from him and left the room, shutting the door behind her.

His hands shook a good deal as he took out his cigar-case—he failed to find it at first, though it was in the usual pocket—and lighted a consolatory cigar.

"That's what I call a very unpleasant quarter of an hour," he muttered, "and I thought it was going to be worse."

CHAPTER XXX

"AND THE DEVIL MAY PIPE HIS OWN"[1]

HER ladyship's carriage was at the door, with her ladyship's coachman on the box. The late earl had had his people, and the countess her people, and it was only the inferior portion of the domestic polity which owned allegiance to both. Her ladyship's personal possessions—piano, books, bibelots of all kinds—were packed in readiness for conveyance to Ellerslie in a waggon from the home-farm, and before nightfall every trace of Sibyl's existence would have vanished from the Castle on the Marches, and the new lord would reign in undisturbed possession. The doors were open, the footmen were waiting to assist in their mistress's departure, when Coralie came hastily out of the billiard-room and approached her aunt.

"Dear aunt, let me go with you. I did not know you were to leave to-day. I have only just heard about it. And you would have gone without even saying good-bye."

"I have been too unhappy to think of leave-takings," answered Sibyl, coldly. "And I am not going far away—only to Ellerslie."

"Let me go with you. I won't bore you. I'll try not to be in your way."

"Come to the drawing-room, Cora. I shall be ready in five minutes."

The first sentence was spoken as she moved towards the

drawing-room door: the second sentence was addressed to the footman who was carrying her wraps, and whose black silk hose were affording amusement to her ladyship's favourite collie whose chain James was holding.

"Now, Cora, let us be plain with each other," said Sibyl, turning to her husband's niece, with no touch of softness in voice or face. "What can you want of me? I can understand that I was useful to you when I took you from a lodging-house and an out-at-elbows father, but the whole aspect of your life has changed since last week. Your father is a rich man and master of both the houses in which you have lived lately."

"But he is still—my father," said Coralie, deadly pale against the dull blackness of her mourning gown.

That dull black was by no means becoming to Cora's sallow complexion and plain features. Never had her lack of beauty been more apparent than in this moment, when her lips were whitened by emotion, and her eyes haggard with weeping.

"Your place is here, Cora, not with me."

"My place is under no roof that shelters my father; I will never live in the same house with him—never live where I must see him day by day. I have made up my mind about that. Yes, you are justified in thinking meanly of me. I am a very Urquhart—a sordid, selfish creature. I like luxury. I revel in splendour and high living and fine clothes. I abhor poverty. I see no silver lining to the cloud that hangs over the shabby-genteel; but for all that I would rather slave from morning till night among common drudges in a dressmaker's stuffy work-room than I would live in this house with my father."

"Is this so, Coralie?"

"It is so."

"I have wronged you," said Sibyl, gravely. "I have thought lately that you were your father's spy, set to watch my movements, full of malevolent curiosity——"

"Oh, only think that I admire and love you," cried Coralie, her sallow face crimsoning. "Whatever I may have been—whatever evil there is in my nature—I am honest and true to-day. I do respect you. I do love you. There have been hours in this house—in spite of all your goodness to me—when I have been envious of your fortune, your beauty, jealous of the worship your beauty

won, but," struggling against sobs that almost choked her, "that is
over now. I am resigned to my fate, resigned to see love pass me by,
resigned to ugliness and spinsterhood; only I want to live a clean
life—to hold no companionship with a man I cannot respect as a
father should be respected. Let me live with you, Lady Penrith.
You shan't find me troublesome or boring. I will give you as much
or as little of my society day by day as you like. I will never pester
you with attentions you don't want. I am not without what people
call—resources. I can amuse myself, and walk by myself, and live
by myself, and under your roof I shall be happy and at ease."

"What will your father say?"

"Nothing that he can say will alter my determination never to
live in his house. If you won't harbour me I must earn my bread
somehow, and live by myself."

"Then you shall live with me. I will try to trust you and believe
in you as I did a month ago. But remember that my life is a broken
life. If you live with me you must live secluded from society—a
dreary existence for a girl of your age—no house-parties in the
country—no London season. In your father's present position he
can give you a life of pleasure and variety. As an only daughter and
mistress of Penrith House, you will be a personage in London. You
may marry well——"

"No, no, I have made up my mind upon that point. There
shall be no more self-delusions. Let me share your solitude. Even
if there were no other reason—it will be happier for me than to
drink that cup of humiliation which plain girls have to drink in the
gay world—happier than sitting through dance after dance at the
ball of the season—or hearing a crowd of young men whispering
and tittering in the beautiful Mrs. Somebody's box next my own,
while I sit alone, pretending to listen to the opera. All other considerations apart, rustic seclusion is the happiest fate for an unat-
tractive girl."

"You are fond of exaggerating your deficiencies, Cora, but I
won't dispute that point now," replied Sibyl, with a faint smile.
"You can follow me to Ellerslie if you like."

"If I like—I shall go there with rapture. May I go to-night, as
soon as my goods and chattels are packed?"

"To-night or to-morrow, as you please."

"To-night—to-night. It cannot be too soon. You won't change your mind, and wire to me not to go to you?"

"Cora, am I that kind of person?"

"No, no; you are as steadfast as a rock. You are all that is good and noble in womankind, and I will try to be worthy of your love. I mean you to love me—and trust me—and believe in me as if I were of your own stainless race."

They went out to the hall door together, and Cora stood on the steps with the wind blowing her hair off her large intelligent forehead, till Lady Penrith's carriage vanished in the distance.

It was half-past seven o'clock. Cora's packing was finished, her trunks and possessions were all carried downstairs, to be removed with a second waggon-load of Lady Penrith's property, and Cora was dressed in her sealskin coat and hat ready for departure in the dog-cart which had been ordered to drive her to Ellerslie. It would be a long dark drive, but Cora thought nothing of possible dangers or discomforts on the road. All she thought about just now was getting away from Killander Castle.

The billiard-room door was open as she crossed the hall, and she could not resist going in for a last look round a room in which she had spent many pleasant hours. The men had been very gracious to her, even if she were in no wise attractive. They had laughed at her little jokes and flippant criticisms. They had taught her to handle her cue, and applauded her poor little breaks of ten or twelve, as if she had been a feminine Roberts.[2] It had all been bright and gay in those October evenings with the shooters, when the logs had been piled on the hearth, and the little table for drinks set out in the deep recess yonder, and she had been encouraged to mix brandies and sodas, and to make herself daintily useful, like an etherealized barmaid.

That was all over now. There was no fire, and only a single oil lamp burnt dully over one end of the covered table. All was gloom and silence.

"Will men ever sit in this room and talk and laugh now my father is master here?" she wondered. "Are there any men on earth who can like him, and trust him?"

The man of whom she was thinking met her on the threshold as she turned to leave the room.

"Where are you going?" he asked sharply.

"To Ellerslie."

"You should have had enough manners to ask my leave. This is my house, and you are my daughter. You must pay no visits without consulting me beforehand. I forbid you to go to Ellerslie on any visit—long or short."

She drew herself to her fullest height and looked at him with all the scorn a pert interrogative nose and thin sensitive lips could express.

"This is not a question of visiting, Lord Penrith," she answered, emphasising the title, which sounded so strange a form of address from daughter to father. "I am leaving this house for ever, and Ellerslie is the only home I have."

"You will do nothing of the kind," he answered fiercely, with a savage grip of her wrist.

She winced with pain, but looked defiance at him, even while her lip quivered.

"There is no use in that kind of thing," she said. "Your doing me bodily harm won't make any difference in my plan of life—unless you choose to shoot me," she added, very slowly, looking him full in the face, "and so make sure of my obedience."

He dropped her wrist, and stood looking at her—changed in one instant from bully to craven.

"Go your ways for a blatant hussy," he said in his most brutal voice. "You are not worth making a fuss about. Such a plain-headed one as you would be no ornament to your father's dinner table."

He turned away and left her to take her departure without further interest. He had the Castle to himself now, and in its loneliness it seemed to him about as cheerful as the castle at Inverness on the morning after King Duncan's bloody death.[3]

CHAPTER XXXI

"LET A PASSIONLESS PEACE BE MY LOT"[1]

A very few days served to re-establish Sibyl in her old home; and, with the old housekeeper, and the old secretary, and some of the old servants still about her, it seemed to her almost as if the past ten years had been one dreary dream—endless and infinite after the manner of dreams. Already in that strange exaggeration of time common after the shock of a sudden bereavement, it seemed to her as if Lord Penrith had been long dead. Already she was accustomed to the thought of his quiet resting-place on the hillside, to the idea of herself as a widow, childless and alone in the world. There was unspeakable comfort in the return to Ellerslie, comfort which even the horror that brooded over one unvisited spot in the wood could not spoil. The old associations of childhood were so many and so dear. The image of her indulgent father, the fainter image of the fair young mother, looking at her out of the cloud-land of childish memories like a picture of the Madonna looking benignly downward upon the worshippers at her altar, through a cloud of incense. These, and with these, many a recollection of her happy girlhood, filled the rooms and gardens with tender peaceful thoughts.

There were sad thoughts too, and chief among them the memory of him who was now far away on the northward side of the Tweed, a wreck of the past, so changed, so broken, that it was difficult to believe that feeble invalid was actually the same man—the same frame animated by the same spirit—whom she had admired and loved at Ellerslie.

The shock of her husband's sudden death had fallen heavily upon her. She had done her duty as a loyal and obedient wife. She had spent her fortune upon his estate with a lavish hand, had never reminded him that all he enjoyed of worldly prosperity had its source in the Higginson coffers. She had indulged no whim that he disapproved, had consorted with no acquaintance whom he disliked, had indeed been much more conciliating and obedient than many a wife who marries for love, and who talks of her husband in the first year of marriage as if a god had descended from Olympus to be her mate. Yet, faithful as she had been in small things and in great, she looked back now with a touch of remorse. The atmosphere of her wedded life had been colder than it need have been, perhaps—a little affection on her side might have warmed that hard nature into love. And then the thought flashed upon her that the mutual lack of love had made a peaceful union.

"If he had loved me I should have hated him," she said to herself. "It was better for both of us that our marriage was only a bargain—a bargain entered upon deliberately, on both sides. We did not try to deceive each other."

In our dealings with those who are gone for ever there is always something to regret—some reason for that dull aching of the heart which means remorse—some bitter memory, something said which ought not to have been said—some kindly word or act omitted when the opportunity for kindness was so obvious. Sibyl Penrith was very humble in all her thoughts of that married life which had closed like a story that ends unexpectedly at the turn of a leaf, and leaves the reader wondering. In her thought of future possibilities she had never imagined herself released from the marriage bond. She had accepted her position for life. She had looked down the long vista of joyless years, seeing herself still Lady Penrith, going about the world by the side of a man who cared very little about her, and for whom she had never cared very much.

He was gone, and she mourned for him as a fellow-creature snatched away in the strength of his days—a man to whom life must have been much more precious than it was to that poor sufferer on whose changed aspect she had looked with unutterable grief, whose haggard face was a haunting presence in her life. Archibald Penrith was gone, and the man she abhorred reigned in his stead, and she thought with a shudder of that border fortress which had so lately been her home.

A letter from John Coverdale, written at his East End vicarage, gave Lady Penrith tidings of Brandon Mountford, after she had waited many anxious days for any news of him.

"St. Stephen's Vicarage, Honduras Square, E.
"DEAR LADY PENRITH,

"I have allowed some little time to pass before writing to you, not wishing to break in upon the sadness of your life while your sorrow was still a new thing. I will not presume to suggest the consolations that alone can help you in this terrible bereavement, or to write to you of that Divine Source of all comfort to which I feel very sure you have been led without the intervention of any human guide. God bless and comfort you, and help and sustain you in strong and fearless faith through this and every dark path you have to tread. So far as one who has been taught that the way to Heaven lies through thorny paths may make the earthly happiness of a friend the subject of his prayers, be sure my fervent supplications will rise day by day to the eternal Father for you.

"And now to tell you of your kinsman and my charge.

"The journey was managed easily, and without any signs of exhaustion in the invalid. He slept a good deal, and his sleep was peaceful, and I thought him brighter and more interested in surrounding objects during the early morning drive from the station to the shooting lodge than in my previous observation of him.

"The doctor accompanied us to the end of our journey, and gave the most precise instructions to the attendant from the hospital, who is a strongly-built man of about thirty, accustomed to difficult cases, and equal, I believe, to any emergency. The housekeeper at the lodge and her husband are both people I can rely upon for faithful service, and all their warmest feelings are aroused by the patient in their charge. I have therefore felt justified in leaving him in the care of these servants and his trained nurse, supervised by a daily visit from the nearest medical man, until I am able to return to Argyllshire, which I hope to do in about a fortnight.

"The plan which I would propose for the winter is to hire a small house at Rothsay, where the climate is much milder than that of the Argyllshire hills, and to place him there in charge of his present attendant and any servants you may be able to send from Ellerslie, people whom you can be sure of for absolute silence as to the past. I can think of no better plan than this. My Scotch doctor was of Mr. Sanderson's opinion that nothing more could be done for the patient than we are now doing. A quiet life, with as much open air as the season will allow, a plain and nourishing diet, and bromide of potassium are all the treatment he prescribes.[2] He will be happy to meet a physician from Glasgow or Edinburgh in consultation should you desire a second opinion, but he assures me that the consultation would result only in the approval of his treatment.

"It is my duty to add that he does not hope for much improvement under the happiest conditions. The long continuance of the disease has weakened the brain, and a kind of atrophy has wasted the frame. Any permanent revival of bodily strength or intellectual power would be a miracle in nature which he dares not hope to see. I tell you his opinion in all frankness, dear Lady Penrith, thinking it right that you should know the worst about your unhappy friend.

"Flashes of reviving memory, intervals of brightness in the dull torpor of his usual condition there may be; but these brief periods of improvement must not mislead or beguile us with a vain hope.

"For myself you may be surprised to hear that I am about to abandon my flock in this hard-working, Eastern London; but I leave them in the hands of a man who has worked with me as senior curate during the greater part of my residence here, who understands this parish thoroughly, and who is my superior in working power. My father, whose health has been gradually failing for the last two or three years, has persuaded me to accept the living at St. Stephen's, Workington. He now rarely comes to London, and his life is chiefly spent at his seat near Workington, so I can but feel that it is my duty, as it will be my happiness, to live within easy reach of him. I shall find plenty to do at St. Stephen's, for parish and church have both been neglected under the rule of an absentee rector, who died at Torquay the other day. The living is in my father's gift, and it has long been his desire that I should hold it.

"I hope to have wound up my affairs here in less than a fortnight, and to be established within an hour's journey of Ellerslie, where I will call upon you at any time you may appoint to discuss all arrangements for Mr. Mountford's residence at Rothesay or elsewhere. You might, if you pleased, remove him to Devonshire for the coming winter; but the journey would be long, and I doubt if you would find a better climate than that of Bute, even in the West of England.

> "Ever faithfully yours,
> "JOHN COVERDALE."

Cora was with Lady Penrith when she received this letter. The girl recognised the strong, clear penmanship, bold, yet with a certain precision which marked the man for whom order was an instinct. Cora gave a little sigh as she noted the length of the letter, and then discreetly moved to the other end of the room to leave her aunt free to read those closely written pages unobserved.

She had subjugated the jealous agonies which had made her almost hate Sibyl Penrith, and had resigned herself to the idea of John Coverdale's affection for the beautiful widow. There was no help for it now. What man with sense or discrimination could think of her, Coralie, now that Lady Penrith was free to reward a lover's devotion? It was her business in life to be a looker-on, she told herself, and she must accept the portion that Fate had allotted to her. All her thoughts and desires had taken a sombre cast. Her character had sobered curiously since her uncle's death, and a cloud of melancholy hung over her, which brought her in sympathy with Sibyl's sorrows. For the first time since they had been associated, Sibyl's heart had warmed to the lonely, motherless girl. Heretofore all her kindnesses had been prompted by the sense of duty. Now there was actual liking—a far more cordial feeling than of old.

Before Mr. Coverdale reappeared upon the scene, Sibyl had told Coralie the story of Brandon Mountford's affliction and her girlish attachment to him, touching very lightly, with a scrupulous reserve, upon Urquhart's part in the tragedy. But Cora's keen eyes had watched the speaker's face, and Cora had divined much that was unspoken.

"You had reason to detest my father; and yet you took me into your house, and loaded me with benefits. Would any other woman in the world have done as much?" mused Cora at the end of the story.

"Most women would have done as much, I hope, Cora, seeing your need of a friend. I tried to dissociate you from your father in all my thoughts. Why should you bear his burdens?"

"Ah, but I was tainted with his bad blood. It was the old story of the adder warmed back to life and stinging the hand that had succoured it. My father told me to watch you, and I obeyed. He pretended to be your friend, and I pretended to believe him. I don't think I ever really believed him. I was grateful to you. I loved you at first, and then your beauty, your wealth, all your perfections, began to gall. I made comparisons. I compared our faces as we stood side by side in front of the same glass. I compared our fortunes, and then the venom in my blood began to work. My nature could not escape the hereditary taint—if the modern craze about heredity has any foundation. I was my father's very daughter, and I accepted my office of spy. My whole mind changed towards you when I saw the utter hopelessness of any little liking I might feel for the saintly parson—saw him devote every thought and feeling to you——"

"Nonsense, Cora; you mustn't talk in that absurd strain. Mr. Coverdale has been my kind friend in a desperate crisis—that is all. I asked him to help me, and he responded with all kindness and chivalry. As for the past, let it be forgotten between us. I saw of late that you were very inquisitive about all my movements, and that you had some motive in your watchfulness. You were under your father's influence then; but I think you have escaped from that bad influence now."

"For ever and for ever. I hope never to look upon my father's face again."

"I am glad you have been frank with me, Cora, even when frankness told against yourself. It will be the beginning of confidence between us. I like you ever so much better—now that I know the worst of you—from your own lips."

Cora did not prove unworthy to be pardoned and trusted. All that there was of good in her nature developed and strengthened in daily association with a noble woman, and in that atmosphere of perfect peace which reigned at Ellerslie. As the winter wore on, that life was not all solitude and monotony, for the neighbouring gentry were assiduous in their attentions to the widowed Countess, and Coralie Urquhart shared their attentions. If the widow held herself aloof from society, there was no reason that her niece should live in perpetual seclusion, and a few months after her uncle's death Lady Coralie Urquhart's neat figure and thorough-bred air began to be known and even admired at various entertainments within fifteen miles of Ellerslie. There was always some friendly matron eager to chaperon her to any dances or private theatricals in the neighbourhood.

"There are some advantages in a plain face," said Cora. "The mother of a pretty daughter is never afraid that I shall make her swan a crow. I think Mrs. Simper rather likes taking me about with her, as a useful foil to Miss Simper's alabaster complexion."

"But I am told that you were more admired than Miss Simper at Lady Hardacre's dance," said Sibyl, smiling at her niece's self-scorn.

"It is no overwhelming honour to be preferred to an idiot with blue eyes that look as if they had been bought in the Lowther Arcade," said Cora. "And then I got all the advantage of the smaller gentry's snobbishness. The second-rate young men like to dance with an earl's daughter, and Lady Coralie sounds better than Miss Simper in the ear of Bayswater or South Kensington. Lady Coralie! The name suggests a character in one of Gilbert's librettos.[3] Even the courtesy title cannot give dignity to my absurd name. I can't imagine where my father and mother found it."

Could the owner of the name have looked backward through the mists of time, she might have seen the hoardings of West End London decorated with the portrait of a certain Mdlle. Coralie,[4] who was delighting the gilded youth of the period by song and dance in the last new burlesque at the favourite burlesque theatre. The lady was a Parisian, and spoke her lines with difficulty, but her broken English was an additional charm. Hubert Urquhart had been among her most ardent admirers, had been even allowed the inestimable privilege of giving a very expensive supper-party in her honour, at a period when his young country-bred wife was obliged to forego all gaieties.

Then came the usual shilly-shally as to the naming of the first-born. Urquhart, disappointed at the sex of the infant, was very casual in his share of the debate, but vetoed all the family names on his wife's side of the house as too fine or too ugly.

"Call her Coralie, if you like," he said, looking up from his newspaper, where a column was given to the new burlesque of "Antony and Cleopatra," in which Mdlle. Coralie had startled the town by a wild dance with the asp. "Coralie's a very pretty name."

Even his mother-in-law, who generally disagreed with him, conceded this point. Coralie was charming, novel, uncommon, and could be shortened to Cora, which was still prettier.

"Coralie, let it be then," said Urquhart, as he walked off to the florist's to order a congratulatory basket of hyacinths—white

waxen bells, just faintly touched with roseate shadows—for the
lady with the asp.

The Yorkshire parson's wife had arrived in London the previous evening, and it was not till some days after the christening
that this good lady heard how the town was ringing with the fame
of the burlesque actress from the Chatelet Theatre, and guessed
that her granddaughter, the Vicar's granddaughter, the potential
Archbishop's granddaughter—had been called after that unholy
person.

The winter passed peacefully for Lady Penrith. Cora kept
her promise, and never intruded her society upon the widow's
thoughtful hours. They walked and drove together; they met at
luncheon and dinner; they generally spent the after-dinner hour
in each other's society; Sibyl perhaps dreaming over her favourite
music at the piano at one end of the drawing-room, while Cora sat
curled up in the most luxurious chair she could find at the other
end of the room, absorbed in a novel. Cora had a cat-like love of
warmth, and was always as close to the fire as she could be without
being roasted alive. Lady Penrith preferred the cooler atmosphere
by the piano, where the white lilac and palms made an indoor
garden. Their tastes in books, and music, and pictures were utterly
dissimilar; but they got on very comfortably together, and Cora's
lighter nature, which gradually recovered from the shock that had
sobered and depressed her, was a useful influence in Sibyl's existence. She might have sunk into a deeper melancholy and brooded
more persistently over the shattered life of the man she loved if
Cora had not been at hand with her keen observation and her
never-failing perception of the humorous side of all earthly things.
Cora amused her with descriptions of county festivities, and her
comments on county people—their limited horizons, their exaggerated estimate of local importance, their indifference to all the
great movements of the age, social, scientific, and literary. Cora
accompanied her in all her cottage visiting—in the little seaport—in
the miners' villages—to the schools and the cottage hospital—and
Cora had grown a great deal more sympathetic since she left Killander Castle, and was ripening day by day in her power of understanding the working classes. They no longer seemed to her all

of one type and pattern—all a lower order of beings, with hands stretched automatically to receive gifts from the rich. She was beginning to find out strong individualities among the masses—to find that hardly one cottager resembled another in character or instincts—and that though very few of them might be faultless and all of them might be what they called "having," there was a strong substratum of goodness which never failed when one dug down to it, kindness and pity for their own class, unselfish readiness to help each other, and a willingness to make substantial sacrifices with a good deal less fuss and talk than would accompany the same amount of self-surrender in their betters. Wives bore with drunken husbands, and held their tongue when the week's wage was spent at the public-house—husbands nursed the children and waited upon their wives in sickness—grandfathers and grandmothers stinted themselves to feed children whose unauthorised entrance upon the scene had brought them trouble and disgrace. Everywhere under the roughest outer seeming Coralie found the deep heart of human love.

"I used to hate the poor when first you took me among them," she frankly avowed one day, after a long round with Sibyl, "but I begin to see that they are not a bad sort, and I wonder less at the interest you take in them."

They were not at Ellerslie all the winter. Andrew Orlebar had been despatched to Rothesay, immediately after a visit from the new Rector of Workington, with instructions to hire the most comfortable house, with the best aspect, that he could find in that much-praised watering-place; and to that house, a villa on the slope of a hill fronting the south, and commanding an extensive view of mountains and sea, Brandon Mountford had been removed. Here was provided every amelioration which thought or science could devise for a life obviously dwindling towards its close; and here Lady Penrith and Cora came from time to time on visits of a week or a fortnight, during which visits some hours of every day were spent with the invalid.

His condition was far happier than it had been in his captivity at St. Jude's. There were times when he seemed fully to realise all that affection had done for him; but nothing could mend the broken life, or arrest mental decay, and Sibyl had to submit to the sad realities of the case. The Brandon Mountford by whose side she sat in the pretty drawing-room at Rothesay, the man whose hand often lay cold and listless in her own, was not the Brandon Mountford she had known ten years ago. Nothing could bring back that lost personality. This patient sufferer, weak-brained, joyless, indifferent to all the loveliness of earth and sky and sea, had nothing in common with the Brandon of the past; and alas! this state of dull apathy was the happier condition of his present life—for from time to time there came periods of stormy agitation, the throes and convulsions, the purple face and glittering eyes of the epileptic; and it needed all Sibyl's faith to believe the doctors when they assured her that the patient himself had no consciousness of these convulsive struggles, nor any memory of them when reason returned—only a vague melancholy, a dim sense of shame, and the apathy of weariness.

Could she wish such a life prolonged? Yes, affection valued even this shattered existence. All that she saw of weakness and decay could not extinguish the hope of cure. The ill-treatment of ten years was not to be undone by a few months of careful nursing, she argued. His cure must be a question of time. She would not accept adverse opinions; and when the doctors shook their heads or murmured some ambiguous phrase which implied a hopeless verdict, she argued against their experience, and refused to foresee the inevitable. A yacht was being built for her in one of the shipbuilders' yards on the Clyde, and she was planning a cruise to the Mediterranean as soon as the boat was ready to sail—a cruise during which Brandon might reawaken to a new life, transformed by sea air and frequent change of scene, the exhilarating sense of novelty in the movement from one spot of loveliness to another, as they coasted between Marseilles and Naples, or beneath Algeria's romantic hills.

The end came suddenly before the yacht was finished—suddenly and peacefully. The life so racked and worn failed all at once; and Sibyl felt as if her life must be objectless henceforth. She was at Ellerslie when Brandon died, having left him only a few days before, and it was John Coverdale who came as the messenger of death; John Coverdale, whose sympathy and help had sustained her through every difficulty, from the hour she entered St. Jude's Vicarage with him at her side. It was over. Her grief expressed itself in no vehement form. There was only the crushing sense of loss and of disappointment, the feeling that the business of her life was finished, and that all she had ever known of the poetry of existence lay buried in Brandon Mountford's grave.

CHAPTER XXXII

"FOR IS NOT GOD ALL MIGHTY?"

BRANDON MOUNTFORD had been lying in his quiet grave at Rothesay for some weeks when the yacht which should have carried him to a summer sea was ready to leave the ship-builder's yard; and it seemed to Sibyl that there could be no more useless toy than the boat which she had built for his sake, and which his eyes had never looked upon. All Coverdale's powers of persuasion were needed to awaken her from the apathy of grief into which she had sunk, and to induce her to start on a cruise for her own benefit—but, warmly seconded by Cora, his arguments finally prevailed, and before the spring was over the *Esperance* was sailing southward, with Lady Penrith, Cora, and Lady Selina, and two young cousins, naval and military, by way of escort.

The spinster aunt had swooped down from a great house in the North Riding, where she had been making a very long visit to one of her wealthiest nieces, a lady with a large heart and a populous nursery, and with whom Aunt Selina was an esteemed authority upon all juvenile ailments.

Life on board the *Esperance* afforded a pleasant relief from the atmosphere of measles, whooping-cough, and humdrum at Waddingly Park, and Lady Selina resigned herself to the loss of a London season,—thereby putting money in her purse—while she enjoyed the *dolce far niente* in Sicilian waters, or in the Greek Archipelago.

And so the spring months passed away, and in June Lady Penrith and her party landed at Genoa, leaving the yacht to go round to Marseilles in charge of the naval cousin, to be berthed there till her next cruise, while the three ladies settled quietly at Bellaggio till the end of the month, when Lady Selina went back to England, and Sibyl and Cora moved northward to the Tyrol, for July, August, and September, only returning to Cumberland in October.

Then came the long quiet winter, with friends fit but few, and for their most frequent visitor Mr. Coverdale, from his cure of souls at Workington, where he was doing good service among a crowded mining population.

It was a comfort both to Sibyl and Cora, in those quiet days of autumn and early winter, to know that the new Lord Penrith was not living at Killander Castle. He had indeed been there very little since he came into his estate. He was not popular in the neighbourhood; and he had frankly expressed his hatred of place and people. He had spent the winter after his brother's death at Monte Carlo, where he had achieved all he desired of fame by his success in pigeon-shooting—and the society papers reported that he was at Monte Carlo this winter, also that he had been laid up in Paris during the whole of November, and had been operated upon by a famous French surgeon, the nature of the operation not being stated. A letter from Lady Selina, who had been dissipating in the brief gaieties of a November session, informed her niece that Lord Penrith had been suffering from a tumour on the face, which was likely to cause lifelong disfigurement, and that people at Monte Carlo found him very much altered from last season.

An inquiry at the Castle, made personally by Mr. Orlebar, confirmed this account. His lordship had been very ill, and was still an invalid. He was expected to spend the rest of the winter at Monte Carlo, where he had taken a small villa near the Casino.

"He is your father, Cora, and you may consider it your duty to go to him in his affliction," Sibyl said gravely, when she and Cora had heard Orlebar's report.

"He is my father; but I recognise no duty where he is concerned—except the duty of silence," Cora answered, with a look so grave and resolute that Lady Penrith felt that there was no more to be said.

She knew enough of Coralie by this time to know that the girl was not heartless, and that her repudiation of all filial duty must needs be based upon some sufficient reason. There was nothing flippant or reckless in the daughter's manner. She dismissed the subject sternly, with solemn decision of purpose, as a Roman daughter might have done.

Brooding over the girl's conduct, Sibyl arrived at the conclusion that Cora had investigated the story of Marie Arnold's death, and believed her father to be the murderer. Some cause as grave would alone justify her conduct.

It was a shock for the nerves of both women when they heard early in the year that Lord Penrith was at the Castle. He had been brought there marked for death, Mr. Dewsnap told Lady Penrith one afternoon early in March, when they met beside a cottager's sick-bed, about a week after the earl's return.

"Is the case really hopeless?" she asked.

"I fear so. All that surgery can do for him has been done in Paris and here. The last word has been said. I saw him this morning. I see him three or four times a day, but there is nothing for me to do except regulate the amount of morphia that is given to him. He has excellent nurses. Dr. Malcolm comes from Edinburgh every third day; but science can do no more for him, and the only hope of relief is the inevitable end of all things. Life can be nothing but a burden to him; yet he clings to life with almost frantic intensity."

"Has he ever spoken to you of his daughter?" Lady Penrith asked, when she and the doctor had left the cottage, and were walking along the village street together.

"No. The greater part of his days and nights are spent under the influence of narcotics, and the realities of life outside his own room affect him very little. He asks for no friend, doesn't care who waits upon him, values his nurses for their skill and nothing else. He told me this morning that there was a time when he wanted fresh young faces about him—pretty faces for choice—but that now he would have Gorgons if the Gorgons had more skill in nursing than the pretty young women. He is very often in a state of semi-delirium, and acts hideous tragedies in a kind of waking dream—a common symptom when the brain is steeped in morphia."

"Unhappy creature! Then there is no hope for him? He must die?"

"He must die. And in his case no one can regret the end, since it is the only possible release from suffering."

Sibyl wrote an account of this interview in a letter to John Coverdale.

"Pray go to him, and if you can turn his thoughts to God, and persuade him to confess his sins, it will be one more good work done," she wrote.

Her desire was obeyed, and it was not possible for a Christian priest to approach the bed of suffering with more kindliness and discretion than marked Mr. Coverdale's visit to Lord Penrith. The two men had met in the past, and Coverdale entered the sick-room as a friend; but here friendliness was of no avail. The sufferer treated him with savage insolence, and ordered him out of the room.

"I know your craft," he muttered. "You sneak to my bedside under the guise of friendship—a man with whom I never had one thought or feeling in common—and presently you will bring a little black book out of your pocket, and drop on your knees, and pray me into worse horrors than those I suffer now. I don't want you or your Mumbo-Jumbo, your Abracadabra. Go to your starving miners, and wash your worn-out jargon down their thirsty throats with soup and wine—they'll swallow one thing with the other—but don't come here. Johnstone, show that gentleman the door, and if that won't do, throw him downstairs. I've no use for him here."

He laughed a spasmodic laugh at the American slang which closed his speech. His eyes were deeply sunken. Forehead and cheek were livid, and all the lower part of the face was hidden by linen bandages. Lazarus coming out of the tomb was the image which flashed into Coverdale's mind as he looked in sorrowful reproach at that dreadful countenance, a wicked Lazarus, with malignity burning in those sunken eyes—a Lazarus summoned, not out of the grave's dreamless slumber, but out of hell-fire.

Mr. Coverdale told Lady Penrith that his visit had been ineffectual, but he told her nothing more. He would not sadden her by any description of that bed of doom.

"It needs something higher than human influence to touch that hardened heart," he said. "We can but leave the sinner to his God. The only death-bed repentance that is not an idle mockery is the repentance that comes from within—not from without. The sinner may find God in his own heart, even after he has mocked at Christ's message from the lips of the priest."

It was more than a week after this when a letter was brought to Lady Penrith, sitting alone in the March twilight. The note had been delivered by a groom from the Castle, who was to wait for her ladyship's answer before he rode back.

She told the servant to return in a few minutes, when her answer would be ready; and then she went to the window to read her letter by the fading daylight, while the footman lighted the lamp on her writing-table.

The envelope was addressed in a strange hand, the letter was written in pencil, and, except that it was on thick vellum paper headed with the Castle address, it was almost as uncanny a scrawl as that which the ragged messenger threw into her lap on the moor.

"The doctors tell me my end is near. You have suspected and hated me for the last twelve years. It may gratify you to know that you had reason. Come and hear my confession, and if you want to hear it come at once. My life is like a thin little flame in a spirit lamp—sustained by strong stimulants, and will soon vanish into darkness. Don't be afraid that you will hear a puling death-bed repentance. I believe in neither pardon nor pity. I die the victim of an inexorable scheme of Creation which includes the horrors of diseases that torture and kill, damnable maladies which no human skill can cure. Do you think that any man, doomed as I am doomed, is likely to go out of this life listening to twaddle about Divine Beneficence?"

"I shall be with you as soon as my carriage can bring me." Those words were written hastily, and thrust into an envelope as the servant re-entered the room to receive Lady Penrith's order for her coachman. The light phaeton, with a pair of horses, was to be got ready immediately.

"Lady Coralie has not come in yet, I suppose?"

"No, my lady."

"When she comes, be sure she is told that I have been sent for to the Castle. She is not to wait dinner."

Cora, who had taken very kindly to riding since she came to Ellerslie, and who had always been well mounted by her aunt's liberal care, was out with the hounds. Cora was a success in the hunting field, where light hands, a neat waist, and indomitable pluck, tempered with common sense, scored almost as high as a handsome face. Beauty blundering over a hound, or beauty getting in the way at a gate, is not altogether precious to the sportsman.

The deep shadow of night was round the gaunt, grey fortress, the darker shadow of death was in the room, when Sibyl approached the sick-bed, and seated herself silently in the place which the nurse indicated—a large armchair at the head of the bed, beside those heaped-up pillows from which the ghastly face looked out, white as the linen with which it was bandaged, pinched by the invisible hand which had set its mark upon every feature.

"Leave me alone with Lady Penrith."

The voice was low and muffled, utterly changed from the metallic hardness of Hubert Urquhart's enunciation.

The two nurses vanished through a curtained door that opened into a dressing-room—where all the paraphernalia of the sportsman's toilet had been swept away to give space for the apparatus of sickness—kettles, and saucepans, and spirit lamps, new inventions for comfort or relief, extravagant in price and infinitesimal in value to the sufferer—contrivances tried once, perhaps, and never tried again—the dreary details in the history of failure.

Hubert Urquhart looked at his brother's widow with a cynical smile—a smile on lips contracted by pain.

"I thought my letter would fetch you," he said. "You have come to see God's judgment upon a sinner. You remember how Herod the king was eaten of worms, and gave up the ghost—an example of God's judgment, swift and sharp—a ready-money vengeance. And you think that this cancer which is killing me is God's judgment upon murder. Bosh, Lady Penrith. Clerical spuffle! There are good men and women all over the world doomed just as I am doomed—with pain as lingering—with a fate as hopeless—Christians of purest water, shining lights in the darkness of this world— suffering just as I suffer. When you, and such as you, talk of them you give your God praise for the blessed example of their affliction, and recognise the ineffable wisdom that tortures and kills. You see me stricken down and you exalt God the Avenger. You see no inconsistency in the hand that strikes wolves and lambs with the same rod. Come, own that your heart burns with triumph at seeing this living wreck which I still call ME. A few hours hence the undertakers will be talking of IT."

"I am as sorry for you as I can be, remembering what Brandon Mountford suffered."

"He suffered? Why, his life was a life of ease and comfort—his ten dull years were no worse than one dull afternoon—measured against what I have suffered in the last six months. Don't waste your pity upon an epileptic, whose convulsions may be ugly to look at, but leave no memory, inflict no pain upon the patient. He suffer? Keep your pity for the man whose tortured consciousness no narcotic can annihilate—whose sleep has been peopled and spun out into seeming eternity by dreams of indescribable horror. And where do you think those dreams took me—Lady Penrith—what do you suppose was the almost invariable background of those hideous phantasies?"

"The wood where you killed Marie Arnold?" she answered, her eyes looking into his, as he sat up in the bed, grasping her hand with his clammy fingers, and bringing his bandaged face near hers, so that she might hear the feeble voice.

"You are good at guessing. Yes, that is the place where the morphia fiend leads me. He takes me by the hand—a little black devil with a mocking grin—his skinny hand clutches mine, and he drags me to the wood; and she is there—lovely, and cruel as she was that evening—in the golden sunset. Oh, God, how beautiful her eyes were with that golden light reflected on their velvet darkness! How cold! how cruel! Such bitter scathing words—hatred of me— love of your lover—hatred that turned to loathing when I drew her to my breast, and kissed her reluctant lips, and tried to make her understand that passionate love like mine was to be valued or to be feared; that if she would not have me for her husband, and take her chance of my doing well in life, and making a great lady of her, I would be revenged on her somehow. A love like mine was not to be trifled with any more than a raging fire. But she was so bold, and so proud. She flung me off with her strong young arms. She laughed at my passion and my threats. She accused me of only wanting Sir Joseph's money—not really caring for her. She was so strong, such a grand creature in her strength and beauty. And I had a knife in my breast pocket—Mountford's knife, which I happened to have borrowed a day or two before—and clutching at my breast, beside myself with passion, I felt the knife, and knew that it was there. You can guess the rest. You may remember that I was late for dinner, but that I sat down with you and your father, and was wanting in no observance of a gentleman. It was not till a long time afterwards that you began to suspect me."

Sibyl heard him in silence, and remained silent now when the bloodless fingers loosened from her hand, and he sank back among the pillows, exhausted by the most sustained effort that he had made for a long time.

His breath came and went in hoarse pantings, his wan hands moved restlessly upon the coverlet, and those haggard blood-shot eyes rolled wildly in their orbits as he looked at Sibyl's white face.

"Have you nothing to say?" he gasped at length.

"Nothing. God help you in this dark end of your wicked life!"

"You are not surprised at my confession?"

"No, no. I knew you were the murderer. I have been convinced of that for a long time. You broke my father's heart; shortened his life. You spoilt Brandon's life and mine. And your victim—that young bright life—there never was a crueller murder. What good can I do here? Pray to God for pardon. What I think or feel can matter nothing to you. You can restore nothing—undo nothing."

"No; the past is the past. I cannot bring Marie Arnold back to life. I would have given twenty years of my life to undo that— twenty years, did I say?—I would have given all that was left of my life for one day with her—to die, knowing that I had not killed her—that the murder in the wood was only a hideous dream. Call the nurse. It is time for my morphia. The pain—the racking pain—is beginning. I must have my dose. And then the morphia fiend will take me by the hand and lead me under the fir trees, treading the paths where our footsteps have no sound on the fir needles, and I shall see her again in her white gown, with the red gash across her throat."

The nurses came, quiet, prompt, with quick movements of skilful hands—one on each side of the bed, one supporting the patient while the other administered the narcotic.

Sibyl sank on her knees at the foot of the bed, and with bent brow and covered face breathed a prayer for God's mercy to a dying sinner; then she nodded a silent good-night to the nurses, and stole softly from the room.

Those trained hands had rearranged the disordered pillows, had placed the sufferer's head in an easier position, had smoothed the silken coverlet, laying it lightly over the wasted frame, and the morphia was already at work, tranquillising the limbs, creeping through the labyrinth of the brain, giving respite from bodily torture, but bringing with it dreams that racked the mind.

In Hubert Urquhart's confession of past guilt there had been no word of a still darker crime, a crime planned in cold blood, thought out, and slowly resolved upon, carried out with unwavering craft and purpose, and with as little compunction as the hunter feels for the agonies of a noble beast tracked across the wilderness, watched and waited for, and slain without mercy. Of that crime, which Coralie knew, not one word had escaped the murderer on his death-bed; and the daughter's knowledge of that dreadful secret remained unshared and unsuspected.

Lord Penrith lingered for more than a week after his interview with Sibyl; but those last days and nights were one long morphia-sleep, and an almost unbroken pilgrimage through the dark maze of hideous memories. The skill and the care of doctors and nurses were employed to keep him alive when Nature would have let him die, and to reduce life to unconsciousness throughout those extra hours wrested from death.

At last the end came—only a sinking deeper into that morphia-darkness—only the fall of Death's curtain on those distorted memories of past sin. A gentlemanlike vulture—in the shape of an undertaker—came post-haste from Carlisle, and took possession of that which had been Hubert, tenth Earl of Penrith. There was a stately funeral, an earl's coronet upon a velvet coffin, an open hearse like a triumphal car, with six black horses tossing their Flemish heads and curving their heavy Flemish necks; and all the neighbouring gentry sent their empty carriages to express respect for a man who had been universally disliked, and whose absenteeism had been regarded—except by the local tradespeople—as a merciful dispensation.

The distant cousin who succeeded to the title and entailed estates was an elderly gentleman of unblemished respectability with a large family of sons and daughters, the sons sporting, the daughters plain, pious, and hopelessly unfashionable; just the sort of people to spend ten months of the year at the Castle, and to furnish an eldest son who would stand for that division of the county, and protect local interests in the stress and storm of the Imperial Parliament. The new earl and his family were aware how much of their prosperity they owed to the Dowager Lady Penrith, and they took pains to cultivate her friendship, and to be civil to Coralie Urquhart, who had been so unaccountably estranged from her father.

POSTCRIPT

WHAT remains to be told of Sibyl's life-history? Another year of quiet widowhood, in spite of the pleading of a devoted lover; and then, on a grey morning at the beginning of the year, the plainest of weddings in the parish church at Ardliston. Husband and wife went straight from the church to the station, and thence to London, on the first stage of their journey to Rome—to that city of churches, where it was John Coverdale's delight to expound ecclesiastical history written in all that there is of architectural grandeur, from the grey antiquity of St. Clemente to the gleaming granite and modern mosaics of the mighty basilica which commemorates the martyrdom of St. Paul. An Italian honeymoon, which lasted from winter to spring, yet seemed only too brief, and early in April Sibyl and her husband left Florence regretfully, on their return to England, he to resume the burden of duty—not among the miners of Workington, but in a populous and wealthy centre in the East Riding, where the fine old church is only a little less than a cathedral in spaciousness and beauty; a cure which has been always held by a Churchman of mark, and has been always regarded as the prelude to higher dignities.

John Coverdale has made himself known as a fine preacher and an indefatigable worker—a preacher with the philosophical breadth of Liddon,[1] and the magnetic personality of Frederick

Robertson;[2] a preacher who has been able to beguile the rough
miners from their sabbath luxury of shirt-sleeves and laziness, dog-
fights and rat-catching, and to hold them spellbound by his impassioned appeals to that best side of human thought and feeling
which will always answer to him who knows how to call. The man
whom Coralie described as cold, precise, and priggish, has shown
himself gifted with the finest qualities of preacher and priest, and
he is warmly welcomed to the great Yorkshire city by all the best
and most cultivated amongst the community. Difficulties and dis-
sensions will arise doubtless in some quarters, for Coverdale has a
strong hand in the reform of old abuses, and is one of those men
of whom it is said that they will have their own way; but his way
is a good way, and his influence is a good influence for all in his
parish, most of all for the poor, and for those who most need the
awakening call, the stringent, yet tender hand leading them to the
fold.

In this busy centre Sibyl learns to understand new phases of
life. She finds herself no longer in a small community, where one
man's wealth can achieve wonders of order and prosperity, and one
man's influence can shape all things to his liking, but in the thick
of the bitter battle, among the revolts and conspiracies of labour
against capital, and the exactions and injustices of capital against
labour; the contest of strength with strength; the appeals to public
opinion; the power, sometimes reckless and fatal, sometimes wise
and beneficent, of a free Press; the heat and strife of politics. Here
she must live through seasons of fear and sadness, the terrors of
a fever-stricken town, the alternations of local prosperity, good
times, and bad times, the collapse of great enterprises, the ruin of
great commercial houses that have been ranked among the stern
reality; and here she has to discover how little her wealth can do
where needs are so constant and so manifold. That her fortune and
her life-labour are used for the help of the suffering, for the recla-
mation of the lost, none who ever knew her could doubt.

"My aunt is a saint," said Cora, perched daintily on her hunting
saddle, sitting in a sheltered corner waiting for the fox to break
cover, and chatting cheerily with a group of admirers. "My aunt
lives only to do good to other people, and she could not have done
better than marry Mr. Coverdale, who is a remarkable man, and

would have made an admirable Pope, in the days when Popes did a great deal more good or a great deal more harm in the world than they can do now."

Coralie has no lack of admirers in these latter days. She is no longer Coralie Urquhart, for Mr. Nicholas Hildrop, of Hildrop Grange, near Workington, has allowed himself to fall a victim to her sharp tongue, neat figure, light hands, and good seat, and meeting and conversing with her through a couple of seasons mounted on all that is handsomest in thorough-bred hunters, has come gradually to believe that Cora is as good-looking as her horses, and has made her mistress of himself and his estate.

Lady Coralie Hildrop gives hunting breakfasts, has a furnished house in Mayfair for the season, goes everywhere, is liked by a good many people, and feared by the rest; is mundane to the tips of her fingers, an affectionate wife, a good friend, a bitter enemy, and without mercy for any pretty woman who misbehaves herself.

THE END.

NOTES

CHAPTER I

1   *barouche* (p. 2): Nineteenth-century horse-drawn four-wheeled carriage with two double seats facing each other and a collapsible top. The driver sat on a box seat at the front.

2   *Out of the grave . . .* (p. 5): Mark 9:44. In the ninth chapter of the gospel of Mark in the New Testament, a man shows his son who has a "dumb spirit" (9:17) and who "foameth, and gnasheth with his teeth" (9:18) to Jesus. The possessed boy, who suffers in fact from epilepsy, is healed by Jesus. Jesus then explains to his disciples that they must work in his name and fight sin; evil is represented by the fire which is not quenched. Braddon's revision of the Gothic manuscript and buried writing instantly associates evil and sin with epilepsy—the disease forming a bridge between the supernatural and possession and modern clinical discourse.

3   *escritoire* (p. 7): Writing desk.

4   *Bramah locks* (p. 7): Pick-proof locks first manufactured by the engineer Joseph Bramah (1748-1814) in 1784. To prove the resistance of the locks, the company had a "challenge lock," offering 200 guineas to the person who would defeat the lock displayed in the window of their London shop from 1790. It was not until the Great Exhibition of 1851 that a mechanic, Alfred Charles Hobbs, managed to pick the lock and won the prize.

5   *beaux yeux* (p. 10): beautiful eyes (French).

6   *Mayfair suicides* (p. 10): This may be an allusion to Machen's *The Great God Pan* (1894). In Machen's novel, rich aristocrats mysteriously commit suicide after visiting the rich Mrs. Beaumont—in fact, the daughter of the Great God Pan—who lives in the West End. Revealingly, Machen's novel hinges upon brain surgery, merging the supernatural with the progress of medical science. Though published as a novel in 1894, the first chapter of *The Great God Pan* had already been published in 1890 in *The Whirlwind*; Machen completed the manuscript in 1891 but failed to find a publisher before 1894. The great god Pan is also referred to later on in *Thou Art the Man*.

7   *Louis Seize* (p. 13): Louis XVI (1754-1793), King of France from 1774 to 1792. Guillotined in Paris on 21 January 1793.

8   *entre cour et jardin* (p. 13): Architectural term; French noblemen had their houses built not directly on the street but a few yards back, generally behind a protecting wall.

9   *Pour Milady on fait l'impossible* (p. 14): "I do my utmost for my lady, but—good heavens!—four days to make a trousseau!" (French)

10   *Elle est franchement laide* (p. 14): "That girl is so plain!" (French).

11   *Mudie* (p. 14): Mudie's circulating library. Founded by Charles Edward Mudie (1818-1890) in 1842 in London.

CHAPTER II

1   *causerie* (p. 16): chat (French).

2   *Mrs. Grundy* (p. 17): A symbol of propriety and prudishness. Mrs. Grundy was originally a character in Thomas Morton's play, *Speed the Plough* (1798).

CHAPTER III

1   *Lotos Island* (p. 19): A reference to Alfred Lord Tennyson's poem "The Lotos-Eaters" (1832; revised in 1842). The poem draws upon *The Odyssey*; the sailors on their way back home land on a strange island where people only eat the fruit of the lotos plant. Some of the sailors try it and refuse to continue their journey.

2   *Broadwood* (p. 19): The company John Broadwood & Sons originally manufactured harpsicords. John Broadwood's first piano was designed around the late 1770s. By the middle of the nineteenth century, the company was making over 2,500 pianos a year.

3   *Guy de Maupassant* (p. 20): Guy de Maupassant (1850-1893), French realist and naturalist writer. He was also famous for his supernatural short stories and his hallucinations which may have inspired his "Horla" (1887).

4   *bergère* (p. 22): wing chair (French).

5   *Livingstone* (p. 22): The missionary David Livingstone (1813-1873) explored the natural resources of southeastern Africa. His journal, *Missionary Travels and Researches in South Africa*, was published in 1857. He returned to Zanzibar (which is now part of Tanzania) in 1866 to seek the source of the Nile.

6   *Burton or Cameron . . .* (p. 22): Henry Morton Stanley (1841-1904), famous for his *In Darkest Africa* (1890), joined Livingstone in the town of Ujiji in 1871, and they explored the north end of the Tanganyika together. His expedition was recorded in his bestseller, *How I Found Livingstone*. Verney Lovett Cameron (1844-1894), who was sent to Africa by the Royal Geographical Society to relieve Livingstone in 1873, also reached Ujiji. He recorded his explorations in *Across Africa* (1877) and *To the Gold Coast*

for Gold (1883), which he co-authored with Sir Richard Francis Burton after their exploration of the Gold Coast in 1882. The latter (1821-1890) searched for the source of the Nile as well, and explored the east coast of Africa. He recorded his explorations in Africa in *First Footsteps in East Africa, or, An Exploration of Harar* (1856), *The Lake Regions of Central Africa: A Picture of Exploration* (1860), and *Wanderings in West Africa, from Liverpool to Fernando Po* (1863). Burton has often been seen as an imperialist and a racist who viewed the natives of Africa as savages who needed to be "civilized." Samuel White Baker (1821-1893) was another English explorer who started exploring Central Africa in 1861 to find the source of the Nile. His *The Albert N'Yanza* (1866) was another bestseller. He commanded a military expedition in the equatorial regions of the Nile in order to suppress the slave-trade and open the country to commerce. He recorded his central African expedition in *Ismailïa* (1874).

7   *Falls of the Zambesi* (p. 22): Victoria Falls, one of the largest waterfalls in the world, on the Zambezi river. They were discovered by British explorer David Livingstone in 1855.

8   *Mountains of the Moon* (p. 22): Mountain range in central Africa which was believed to be the source of the Nile. The place is highly connected to colonial explorations of Africa.

9   *Lady Hester Stanhope* (p. 22): Lady Hester Stanhope (1776-1839), intrepid traveller who travelled to Constantinople, Cairo, and the Middle East. She finally settled in Lebanon and died in poverty.

10   *Nineteenth Century* (p. 25): Magazine founded in 1877 by Sir James Knowles.

11   *chien* (p. 27): French: "avoir du chien": to have a certain something.

CHAPTER IV

1   *gazabo* (p. 29): Or gazebo; a turret on the roof of a house.

2   *Midas* (p. 31): in Greek mythology, King Midas could turn everything he touched into gold.

3   *houris* (p. 33): beautiful virgins believed by Muslims to be waiting in Heaven as a reward for men who die as martyrs.

4   *Millais* (p. 37): John Everett Millais (1829-1896), British painter and illustrator. He founded the Pre-Raphaelite Brotherhood (PRB) with William Holman Hunt and Dante Gabriel Rossetti.

CHAPTER V

1   *devant* (p. 45): in front of.

2   *avant* (p. 45): before.

3   *sauf* (p. 45): except.

4   *excepte* (p. 45): apart from, but for.

5   *dot* (p. 46): dowry (French).

6   *Mougins . . . Africa* (p. 47): This comparison of Mougins with an African desert is one of the many hints which connect Marie Arnold to exotic and "primitive" African women.

7   *partis* (p. 51): match (French).

8   *pretendent* (p. 51): suitor (French).

9   *Thierry* (p. 53): Jacques Nicolas Augustin Thierry (1795-1856), French historian. His *Histoire de la Conquête de l'Angleterre* (1825) was a rewriting of the Norman Conquest.

10   *Green* (p. 53): Mary Anne Everett Green, *née* Wood (1818-1895), English historian. She was the author of *Lives of the Princesses of England, from the Norman Conquest* (1849-55).

11   *Freeman* (p. 53): Edward Augustus Freeman (1823-1892), English historian whose fame mainly rested on his *History of the Norman Conquest of England* (1867-76).

12   *Mouton* (p. 56): Château Mouton Rothschild, French wine from the Bordeaux region. Brandon later refuses to drink Mouton, highlighting how epilepsy and alcohol were deemed to be related.

13   *Mashonaland* (p. 57): A province of Zimbabwe.

14   *De Musset's "Ninon"* (p. 58): Alfred de Musset (1810-1857), French poet, playwright and novelist. "A Ninon" (1837) deals with a man's hopeless love.

CHAPTER VI

1   *abolition of purchase* (p. 59): The 1871 abolition of purchase of commission was a reform which aimed to put an end to the buying and selling of commissions. Officers in the British Army could no longer buy rank and could only be appointed by merit and ability.

2   *Whitaker's Almanack* (p. 67): Yearbook of contemporary matters and directory of various establishments in Britain. It was originally published by Joseph Whitaker in 1868.

3   *up to the dead* (p. 68): This strange phrase occurs in both the London and Leipzig editions and may be a printer's error. The phrase does not figure in the *Oxford English Dictionary*, and when contacted shortly before the publication of this edition, an *OED* editor responded that he could find no definition for it.

4   *Hottentot Venus* (p. 74): The Hottentot Venus was a young Khosian woman from Southern Africa named Saarjite Baartman who was brought from Cape Town at the beginning of the nineteenth century and exhibited in Europe. She became an object of popular fascination because of her steatopygic appendage—her enlarged buttocks. When she died, her body was dissected and her genitals cast in wax. Her oversized genitalia encapsulated the threatening "primitive sexuality" which male scientists attempted to police through dissection and investigation. Revealingly, her brain was analyzed by Gratiolet, as the famous alienist Henry Maudsley recalls, who noted "a striking simplicity and a regular arrangement of the convolution of the frontal lobes, which presented an almost perfect symmetry in the two hemispheres, involuntarily recalling the regularity and symmetry of the cerebral convolutions in the lower animals. The brain was palpably inferior to that of a normally developed white woman, and could only be compared with the brain of a white idiotic from arrest of cerebral development" (Henry Maudsley, *Body and Mind: An Inquiry Into Their Connection and Mutual Influence, Specially in Reference to Mental Disorders* [New York: D. Appleton and Co., 1871], 52).

CHAPTER VII

1   *Marah* (p. 75): Hebrew name meaning bitterness. Place the Israelites visited after their Exodus from Egypt as they were looking for water. As the water was bitter, Moses threw a piece of wood into the water to make it fit to drink.

2   *Arthur Wellesley's Indian campaign* (p. 75): General Arthur Wellesley (1769-1852), best known for his victory over Napoleon in the Battle of Waterloo, was a famous soldier who took part in military campaigns in India.

3   *Sir Robert Napier* (p. 75): Sir Robert Napier (1810-1890) fought in the major battles of the Sikh Wars.

4   *masked prisoner* (p. 77): A reference to the man in the iron mask, who was a state prisoner in the reign of Louis XIV. Alexandre Dumas (the elder) drew upon the prisoner's mysterious identity in *Le Vicomte de Braguelonne* (1847-50). The novel was published in English in 1858.

5   *le petit mal...le grand mal* (p. 78): The "petit mal" was a form of epilepsy involving a great confusion of ideas or a temporary suspension of consciousness but without interruption of the epileptic's activity when he was seized, like a somnambulist. When the epileptic came to himself, there was very little or no recollection of the events. On the other hand, the "grand mal" involved genuine epileptic convulsions and complete loss of memory of the attack after it had passed off.

6   *that young woman . . . a saint to the last* (p. 79): Probably a reference to Mary Browne; John Evelyn (1620-1706), English writer and famous diarist, contemporaneous with Samuel Pepys, married her in 1647.

CHAPTER VIII

1   *"She loved me . . ."* (p. 90): From Shakespeare's *Othello* (I, iii).

CHAPTER IX

1   *the cloud* (p. 92): The motif of the dark cloud coming over the patient's senses appears in many reports of epileptic seizures. See Joel Peter Eigen, *Unconscious Crime: Mental Absence and Criminal Responsibility in Victorian London* (Baltimore: Johns Hopkins University Press, 2003).

2   '*Steep me in poverty . . .*' (p. 98): Misquoted from Shakespeare's *Othello* (IV, ii): "Steep'd me in poverty to the very lips."

3   *exorcise Satan's Crew* (p. 100): See note 2, chapter 1; a reference to the epileptic boy believed to be possessed in Mark 9.

4   *ami de la maison* (p. 101): an old friend of the family.

5   *souffre-douleur* (p. 101): a whipping boy.

CHAPTER XII

1   *angel who liberated Peter* (p. 131): The archangel Michael.

2   *Bazaine . . . St. Marguerite* (p. 131): Bazaine escaped from the State Prison of St. Marguerite on 10 August 1874.

3   *sleep-walker . . . during his sleep* (p. 132): Epilepsy and somnambulism were frequently linked, as both involved unconscious behaviour and absence of memory. The French medical term "vertige épileptique" (epileptic vertigo, or the "petit mal"), which was used for cases in which epileptic seizures were nonconvulsive and the patient acted automatically, as though in a trance, strengthened the connection between epileptics and sleepwalkers. See Joel Peter Eigen, *Unconscious Crime: Mental Absence and Criminal Responsibility in Victorian London* (Baltimore: Johns Hopkins University Press, 2003). Braddon draws upon the parallel several times in the novel.

4   *lifelong imprisonment* (p. 132): As suggested in the introduction, this highlights the extent to which individualized and medicalized solutions to crime increased throughout the century, ranging from sterilisation, preventative detention and incarceration to shipping to the colonies. Significantly, the stress was more and more laid on the importance of

good living conditions to prevent criminal behaviour. This is why the "Department Committee on Prisons," set up in June 1894, asked for more humane administration, emphasizing education and more individualized treatment. See Neil Davie, *Tracing the Criminal: The Rise of Scientific Criminology in Britain, 1860-1918* (Oxford: Bardwell Press, 2005).

5 *Hanwell or Colney Hatch* (p. 132): Hanwell Asylum was the first Middlesex County lunatic asylum. It opened in 1831 and was superintended by the English physician John Conolly, who advocated non-restraint in the treatment of the insane, from 1839 to 1844. Colney Hatch Asylum was the second Middlesex County asylum; it opened in 1851.

<h3 style="text-align:center">CHAPTER XIII</h3>

1 *Barlass* (p. 142): Catherine Douglas, later Catherine (or Kate) Barlass; she was involved in the assassination of King James I of Scotland in 1437. As the King and Queen were staying in a chapterhouse in Perth, the bolt had been removed from the door of the room in which they were staying in preparation for the murder. Catherine Douglas barred the door with her arm, but the assassins forced the door open and broke her arm, hence her surname of "Barlass."

<h3 style="text-align:center">CHAPTER XIV</h3>

1 *"What love was ever as deep as a grave?"* (p. 148): From Algernon Charles Swinburne's "A Forsaken Garden."

2 *Snyders* (p. 154): Frans Snyders (1579-1657), baroque Flemish painter born in Antwerp who was famous for his hunting scenes and his animals in combat. Many of his paintings show hunted boars, such as *Wild Boar Hunt*, or *Greyhound Catching a Young Wild Boar*.

<h3 style="text-align:center">CHAPTER XV</h3>

1 *"Ah, but forgetting all things, shall I thee?"* (p. 163): Quotation from "The Complaint of Lisa" (1870) by Algernon Charles Swinburne (1837-1909).

<h3 style="text-align:center">CHAPTER XVI</h3>

1 *"In the grey distance, half a life away"* (p. 171): Quotation from Alfred Lord Tennyson's "The Last Tournament" (1871) (*The Idylls of the King*).

<h3 style="text-align:center">CHAPTER XVII</h3>

1 *circumstances and environment* (p. 179): This remark is highly significant

as Braddon's novel also pivots around the fear of heredity. The ambiguity lays emphasis on the English response to the criminal-type. As suggested in the introduction, towards the end of the century, British criminology emphasized the influence of both biology and environment, thereby portraying the criminal as the victim of socio-economic and hereditary factors. The potential effects of urbanization increasingly entered the degeneracy debate, as British criminologists were influenced by the French *Milieu Social* school.

2 *Winifred Nithsdale* (p. 182): Winifred Maxwell, Countess of Nithsdale (c.1680-1749). Lady Winifred Nithsdale heroically liberated her husband, who took part in the first Jacobite rebellion of 1715, on the eve of the day before his execution.

3 *Bruce's proverbial spider* (p. 185): According to legend, King Robert the Bruce I, who was crowned King of Scotland in 1306, freed Scotland from the English, after having watched a spider building a web. After being defeated he hid in a cave where he watched a spider building a web little by little and never losing hope. He then decided to fight again and inflicted a series of defeats on the English, which eventually won him victory.

4 *coup de main* (p. 185): a helping hand (French).

5 *Charlotte Corday* (p. 185): Charlotte Corday (1768-1793), a French revolutionary patriot who stabbed Jean-Paul Marat, a member of the Jacobin faction, in his bathtub on 13 July 1793. She was guillotined four days later.

6 *Rachel* (p. 189): Elisabeth-Rachel Felix, known as Rachel (1821-1858), French actress. She was very popular in London between 1841 and 1855 and probably inspired Charlotte Bronte's Vashti in *Villette*.

7 *Sardou* (p. 189): Victorien Sardou (1831-1908), French playwright. George Bernard Shaw coined the term "Sardoodledum" in a review of one of his plays (*The Saturday Review*, June 1, 1895) to criticize the French dramatist's lack of talent.

CHAPTER XVIII

1 *Herkomer* (p. 194): Sir Hubert von Herkomer (1849-1914), British painter who also worked as an illustrator, in particular for the weekly *Graphic* magazine. He was one of the most popular portraitists of the 1880s.

CHAPTER XIX

1 *Balzac's novels* (p. 198): Honoré de Balzac (1799-1850), French novelist and playwright. He is most famous for his *Comédie Humaine*, a collection of a hundred interconnected novels and stories describing French society.

2   *en règle* (p. 203): French: in order.

1   *Vernis-Martin table* (p. 213): The French brothers Guillaume and Etienne-Simon Martin devised a lacquer substitute which imitated Chinese lacquer in 1730 using copal. The term vernis-Martin was used to designate the pieces of furniture on which the lacquer was applied.

2   *Newman's "Apologia"* (p. 214): John Henry Cardinal Newman (1801-1890) was a member of the Oxford Movement. He was one of the most famous English converts, and relates his conversion to Roman Catholicism in his *Apologia Pro Vita Sua* (1864).

3   *Montalembert's "Monks of the West"* (p. 214): Charles-Forbes-René, Comte de Montalembert (1810-1870) was a liberal French historian who was interested in monasticism; his *Monks of the West*, which he started in 1860, was left unfinished when he died, and was completed later.

1   *Kew* (p. 230): Kew's Royal Botanical Gardens in southwest London.

1   *East End . . . strange things* (p. 242): Coverdale's experience of the East End hints at the criminalization of the poor; in so doing, it reinforces the link between the suspected murderer and degeneration, turning Coverdale into a highly modern detective.

1   *Southey's house* (p. 243): A reference to Robert Southey (1774-1843), a Romantic poet, who set up home with his wife at Greta Hall (Keswick).

2   *"And when he falls . . ."* (p. 250): From William Shakespeare, *Henry VIII*, III, 2.

1   *Ollendorff dialogues* (p. 264): Heinrich Gottfried Ollendorff (1803-1865), German grammarian and language educator.

2   *Balaclava charge* (p. 264): A reference to the charge of the Light Brigade in the Battle of Balaclava (Ukraine) in 1854 in the Crimean War (1854-56). It was memorialized by Tennyson's "The Charge of the Light Brigade" (1854).

3   *key of the fields* (p. 267): literal translation of the French "prendre la clé des champs" (to run away).

4   *Bradshaw* (p. 272): railway timetable.

5   *preux chevalier* (p. 272): valiant knight (French).

6   *Atalanta* (p. 273): in Greek mythology, Atalanta, an athlete and hunter, wanted to remain a virgin, but she had to marry Melanion (or Hippomenes in some versions) as she lost the contest set up by her father, enchanted by Aphrodite's three golden apples.

CHAPTER XXVIII

1   *poor fellow might have degenerated . . .* (p. 279): This is another reference to the ambiguity related to degeneration as biological and / or induced by the environment.

2   *Pendennis* (p. 282): Thackeray's *The History of Pendennis: His Fortunes and Misfortunes, His Friends and His Greatest Enemy* (1848-50).

CHAPTER XXIX

1   *Ujiji* (p. 298): town in Western Tanzania associated with British explorers.

CHAPTER XXX

1   *"And the devil may pipe his own"* (p. 303): from Alfred Lord Tennyson, "Maud; A Monodrama," I, xix (1855). The poem revealingly deals with passion, murder and male insanity.

2   *a feminine Roberts* (p. 306): John Roberts Senior and Junior were important snooker players.

3   *King Duncan's bloody deeds* (p. 307): a reference to William Shakespeare's *Macbeth*.

CHAPTER XXXI

1   *"Let a passionless peace be my lot"* (p. 307): from Alfred Lord Tennyson, "Maud; A Monodrama," I, ix (1855).

2   *bromide of potassium . . .* (p. 310): Various remedies were used to cure epilepsy. Esquirol subjected his patients at the Salpêtrière to bloodletting, cathartics and antispasmodic medicaments. Among the remedies, turpentine, indigo, belladonna, and inhalations of chloroform were frequently found. Silver nitrate was particularly contested as it not only discoloured the faces but also entailed perforated stomachs, as post-mortem dissec-

tions showed. Bromide of potassium, producing temporary impotency in men, was tried by Sir Charles Locock on young women suffering from hysteria, then in cases of "hysterical epilepsy," and by the mid-seventies, 2.5 tons of bromide were used every year at the National Hospital Queen Square. See Owsei Temkin, *The Falling Sickness: A History of Epilepsy from the Greeks to the Beginnings of Modern Neurology* (Baltimore and London: Johns Hopkins University Press, [1945] 1994).

3   *Gilbert's librettos* (p. 314): Sir William Schwenk Gilbert (1836-1911), English playwright, librettist, and humorist. He collaborated with the composer Sir Arthur Sullivan and produced fourteen comic operas. He was famous for his burlesques, pantomimes, and farces. He targeted women's education in *Princess Ida, or, Castle Adamant* (1884).

4   *Mdlle. Coralie* (p. 314): Mdlle. Coralie is also an actress in Balzac's *Comédie Humaine*. She appears in *Une fille d'Eve* (1839), *La Rabouilleuse* (1842), *Un Début dans la vie* (1844), *La Muse du département* (1843), *Illusions perdues* (1845), *Splendeurs et misères des courtisanes* (1847).

POSTSCRIPT

1   *Liddon* (p. 327): Henry Parry Liddon (1829-1890), English theologian.

2   *Frederick Robertson* (p. 328): Frederick William Robertson (1816-1853), English preacher.

LaVergne, TN USA
29 July 2010
191329LV00002B/100/P